VINCE FLYNN

RED WAR

A MITCH RAPP NOVEL
BY KYLE MILLS

POCKET BOOKS

New York   London   Toronto   Sydney   New Delhi

Pocket Books
An Imprint of Simon & Schuster, Inc.
1230 Avenue of the Americas
New York, NY 10020

First Pocket Books paperback edition September 2019

POCKET and colophon are registered trademarks of Simon & Schuster, Inc.

For information about special discounts for bulk purchases, please contact Simon & Schuster Special Sales at 1-866-506-1949 or business@simonandschuster.com.

The Simon & Schuster Speakers Bureau can bring authors to your live event. For more information, or to book an event, contact the Simon & Schuster Speakers Bureau at 1-866-248-3049 or visit our website at www.simonspeakers.com.

Manufactured in the United States of America

10 9 8 7 6 5 4 3 2 1

ISBN 978-1-5011-9059-9
ISBN 978-1-5011-9060-5 (pbk)
ISBN 978-1-5011-9061-2 (ebook)

ACKNOWLEDGMENTS

It takes a village to get a book from vague idea to finished product, and I'm lucky to be surrounded by people whose knowledge, enthusiasm, and work ethic take some of the sting out of the process.

I wouldn't be where I am today without my agent, Simon Lipskar. Emily Bestler and Sloan Harris are always there for me when I need them. David Brown and his amazing team get the word out like no one else in the industry. Ryan Steck is a double threat—a tireless champion of the series and an encyclopedia of all things Rapp. My mother and wife slogged through my rough draft and gave me critical first impressions. Rod Gregg returned to clear up any questions I had about firearms. And, finally, Steven Stoll lent me some much needed lacrosse knowledge.

Finally, I can never thank Vince's fans enough for the warm welcome. I'm still amazed at how many people take the time to reach out and offer their encouragement. Without your energy, I would have never made it through the first book.

Salekhard/Салехард

РОССИЯ
RUSSIA

Ob River
Река Обь

Yenisei River
Река Енисей

Olenyok River
Река Оленёк

Lena River
Река Лена

Zhigansk/
Жиганск

Lake Baikal
Озеро Байкал

KAZAKHSTAN

MONGOLIA

UZBEKISTAN

KYRGYZSTAN

CHINA

0 Miles 400 800
0 Kilometers 800
Appoximate scale in central Russia

© 2018 Jeffrey L. Ward

PRELUDE

THE streets were overrun.

Despite his idiot advisors' assurances, the president of Russia found himself watching protesters enter Red Square. Current estimates were that more than two hundred thousand people had joined together to shut down Moscow's commercial districts and now a reckless few were marching on its seat of power.

The gray column of humanity was probably ten meters across and of indeterminate length, snaking out of sight in the steady rain. At its head was Roman Pasternak, clad in the red jacket and baseball cap he wore like a target, daring Russia's security forces to move against him. Maxim Krupin squinted down at the scene but couldn't make out anything but the vague shape of the man. There had been a time not long ago that his eyes would have been capable of taking in every detail, but no longer. The episodes of blurred vision were coming with increasing frequency, lasting hours now instead of minutes.

At his age, perhaps it was time to reconsider his opinion that glasses were a sign of frailty. Or perhaps not. He'd learned to exploit weakness and illness in others, but had suffered from neither since he was a child. He only availed himself of the medical system for injuries sustained during sports or hunting, the scars from which he wore proudly.

Men like Pasternak would never understand that control over Russia didn't flow from economic growth or freedom or security. No, it flowed from the perception of power. Krupin's own was unshakable of course, but it had become that way by providing his people with the illusion that they were the source. That he was nothing more than an instrument to carry out their will. A weapon to be wielded against a long list of carefully fabricated threats. The Americans. The Europeans. Gays. But most of all, the democratic forces seething just beneath the surface of their society.

In contrast to the willowy man organizing his followers below, Krupin was a bear of a man. Two hundred pounds of bulk hung on a six-foot frame. Still solid, but becoming less so every day. His black hair was thick on not only his head but across his broad chest and back. He was the soot-covered coal miner that had provided the heat and electricity so critical to Soviet domination. The factory worker who had built its machines and weapons. The farmer who had fed its hungry people. And, finally, the soldier who had made the world tremble.

He watched the people milling below and the security forces scrambling to maintain control. Predictably, most of the protesters were young—pampered university students or people involved in what had come to be called the new economy. Work that economists believed would be the future of the country but that produced nothing tangible. No military equipment, grand buildings, or massive public works. Just lines of computer code and an endless array of services to provide comfort to this new generation.

The pampered children marching solemnly through Red Square existed not for love of country but for love of themselves. They never spoke of the glory of Mother Russia, instead droning incessantly about their individual rights and the Western luxuries denied to them. But now the nature of the conversation was changing. In increasingly bold terms, they were defining themselves as the future of Russia. And relegating him to its past.

Krupin noted a series of dull flashes in his peripheral vision and braced himself for the wave of nausea that always immediately followed. Other than that, he didn't react. There was still time before the disorientation and searing pain descended. That time would be shorter than it had been during the last episode, though. It always was.

In an act of defiance that would have been unthinkable a few years ago, the protesters spread out beneath the tower where he was ensconced. And in response, he did nothing but stare through the dripping window at them.

His underlings were increasingly hesitant to move against the country's fragmented, but growing, political opposition. Instead of crushing it, they relied on the state media's ability to either ridicule it or to simply deny its existence. Anything more overt, they warned, could lead to a backlash that might careen out of control. The tide that for so long had risen and fallen only by the force of his gravity, could overwhelm him as it had Hussein, Gaddafi, and others.

The subtle loss of balance came even more quickly than Krupin expected, forcing him to turn away from the disturbing images filtering through the wet glass. The blinding headache would be next, starting as a nearly imperceptible pulse and growing to a level that was at the edge of his ability to tolerate. Then, finally, the confusion. That was the worst of it. For a man in his position, even a momentary lapse could be deadly.

He carefully lowered himself into a utilitarian chair behind an even more utilitarian desk. The tiny office was located in an uninhabited corner of the Kremlin that hadn't been upgraded since the Soviet era. The clock on the wall had stopped functioning years ago, but the numbers reading out on his cell phone were unwavering. 11:59.

He pulled a folder from a stack at the desk's edge and removed the band holding the cover closed. Its contents were meaningless, but they helped him hide the cracks in the façade that he'd worked so long to build.

The knock on the door came less than a minute later. Punctuality in others had always been one of the benefits of his near omnipotence within the borders of Russia.

"Come."

The man who entered walked with a slight hunch that made him seem older than his sixty years. Soft eyes and white hair worn a bit too long normally would have suggested weakness to Krupin, but now hinted at a hidden wisdom that put him uncharacteristically ill at ease.

He looked up from the folder and examined his personal physician, being careful not to squint in an effort to focus. His visits were typically for the purpose of routine checkups or minor complaints. They were never reported to the media unless they involved an injury that could enhance his image, but neither were they kept secret.

Today was different.

Eduard Fedkin had never been called to that forgotten corner of the Kremlin and would be startled to find Russia's leader there. Perhaps it was this surprise that had left him shifting his weight nervously from foot to foot. Or perhaps it was more.

"What news do you bring, Doctor?"

"Our tests, sir . . ." The man hesitated, but was unable to remain silent under the weight of Krupin's stare. "They've uncovered an abnormality in your brain."

A surge of adrenaline flooded Krupin, magnifying the growing pain in his head. His face, though, betrayed nothing.

"What kind of abnormality?"

"A tumor."

"And?"

"It's likely that it's the cause of the symptoms you've been experiencing."

Krupin concentrated on keeping his voice even. "Is it cancer?"

"Our tests were only preliminary. They weren't designed to determine that."

At Krupin's insistence, the exam had been done at his home with only equipment that could be transported in and out with complete secrecy.

"You must have formed some opinion."

"Given that you're only experiencing blurred vision and moderate headaches, my hope is that it's benign and slow growing," Fedkin said, choosing his words carefully.

Krupin hadn't been entirely forthright about the intensity of his headaches, nor had he mentioned the mental confusion that always followed. Fedkin was one of the finest physicians in the country, but hardly a loyalist. As near as Russia's intelligence services could discern, the man was largely non-political—one of the many Russian intellectuals who considered themselves above such pettiness. Still, information had to be carefully controlled.

"Obviously, we'll need to perform a more thorough examination, sir. This needs to be done immediately."

"I don't think there's any reason for hysterics," Krupin said with calm he didn't feel. "I'll have my assistant find a convenient time in my schedule."

Fedkin didn't immediately move, instead staring down at Krupin as though he was trying to decide whether to try to argue his position. Instead, he turned and left the room, closing the door behind him.

When the latch clicked, Krupin sagged over the desk, supporting his head in his hands and fighting back the nausea gripping him. Cheers erupted outside, loud enough to vibrate the walls, reminding him of the protesters clogging Moscow's streets. Enemies to be sure but not his most dangerous. That distinction was held by the men closest to him. The men who knew his age and were quietly positioning themselves for what was to come next.

He fought to focus his mind, assessing the strength, vulnerabilities, and ambition of men who would be the most likely to move against him. This was his true gift. Not economics or geopolitics. Not even military strategy. No, he ruled the largest country in the world because he was as good as anyone in history at keeping enemies—both external and internal—off balance. He meted out information and disinformation, flattery and threats, rewards and punishments, all designed to create a web that trapped everyone who came in contact with it. Effective, but also extraordinarily difficult to maintain. Without constant tending, it would collapse almost overnight.

More cheers from outside, this time followed by the amplified voice of Roman Pasternak.

"Why are we here?"

Krupin lost his train of thought. Pasternak had not only marched his ragtag followers onto Red Square, but now he was going to make a speech? The very idea would have been laughable five years ago. Time, though, could be controlled by no man and neither could the changes it brought.

He started to stand, but then fell back in his seat. No. Pasternak was a threat, but not an immediate one. He would be dealt with in due course.

"Russia teeters in and out of recession year after year, dependent entirely on the value of things we can dig from the ground. Our teachers and other workers don't get paid. Our infrastructure is collapsing . . ."

Krupin used a pencil to begin a list that only a few months ago he would have had no use for. The first name he added was that of Boris Utkin, his prime minister.

He was relatively young and technologically savvy, capable of connecting with the generation that held

Krupin at arm's length. A skilled politician, he feigned loyalty but always positioned himself in the middle ground—a bridge between the iron-fisted control of Krupin's administration and the anarchy offered by the man outside shouting into his bullhorn.

"We have a motivated, educated populace, but what do we make? What do we invent? Innovation is the future and all we can do is strip our land of its wealth and sell it to more prosperous countries for table scraps."

Grisha Azarov. The killer who had once worked so effectively for him. He had walked away from the power and wealth that Krupin had given him and was now living an anonymous life in Central America. Not a threat on his own, but unimaginably dangerous if recruited by others.

"Maxim Krupin is the wealthiest man in the world, doling out patronage to his inner circle while the rest of us starve."

Tarben Chkalov. The most powerful of the oligarchs, a man too old and too well diversified internationally to fear Krupin anymore. He sought only stability and would back anyone who could provide it.

"Five percent of our economy is devoted to the military. For what? Expansion? Our adventures in Crimea and Ukraine have cost billions of rubles and left us bowed beneath the weight of international sanctions. Protection from invasion?" Pasternak's amplified laugh was partially obscured by electronic feedback. *"Who would want this country?"*

Krupin let his pencil drop from numb fingers. The sensation of rage rising in him was familiar, but there was more. Something lurking behind it. Something alien.

Fear.

"The president keeps our old people blinded with nationalism and memories of Soviet glory, but those days are over forever. And I say good riddance."

It occurred to Krupin that he had forgotten to write the name of his most potent adversary: time. What did this abnormality in his brain mean for him? A slow decline into dementia and insanity? Invasive medical treatments that would leave only a husk of the man he was now? Would he rot while the weaklings around him maneuvered to be the first to thrust a knife into his back?

He thought of the meaningless people in the square, of the youth and vitality they wore so effortlessly. Of the millions of people who would continue their obscure lives while his own faded. Of a world that would cease to fear him and would be emboldened by that newfound confidence.

"Russia has a proud history but we can't stand at odds with the rest of the world any longer . . ."

The pain in his head continued to grow, pushing beyond anything he'd experienced before.

"We need to take our place in the world order, not lose ourselves in an old man's fantasy of dominating it."

"Shut up!" Krupin screamed, terrified by how his voice was swallowed by the tiny office around him. He leapt to his feet, shouting again as he grabbed for the phone on the desk. "Shut up!"

CHAPTER 1

MITCH Rapp slowed, letting Scott Coleman's lead extend to ten feet.

They were running on a poorly defined dirt track that switchbacked up a mountain to the west of the one he'd built his house on. By design, it was late afternoon and they were in full sun. Temperatures were in the high eighties with humidity around the same level, covering Rapp in a film of perspiration that was beginning to soak through his shirt.

Coleman, on the other hand, looked like he'd just climbed out of a swimming pool. He was pouring so much sweat that the trail of mud he left behind him would be visible from space. His breathing was coming in random, wheezing gasps that made him sound like the soon-to-be victim in a slasher flick. On the brighter side, his pace was steady and he wasn't tripping over the roots and loose rocks beneath his feet.

So, three quarters of the way to the summit, he was moving about as well as anybody could expect under the circumstances. Rapp wasn't anybody, though. It was time to see what the former navy SEAL could do.

He crashed through some low branches to Coleman's left, pulling back onto the trail a few feet ahead. After about a minute of matching his old friend's pace, he started to slowly accelerate. Behind him, the rhythm of footfalls rose in defiance. Like they always did.

Coleman had just spent more than a year focused entirely on recovering from a run-in with Grisha Azarov, the nearly superhuman enforcer who worked for Russia's president. Azarov had finally walked away from his country and employer, but unfortunately not in time to save Coleman a wrecked shoulder, a knife blade broken off in his ribs, and multiple gunshot wounds. The blood loss alone would have killed a man half his age, but the former SEAL managed to beat the odds and stay above ground.

That had turned out to be the easy part. When he'd finally been hoisted out of bed, it had taken him almost a month just to relearn how to walk. And then there was the mental side. Going from being stronger, tougher, and faster than almost everyone around him to someone who needed a motorized cart to navigate the grocery store had been a tough blow. Even worse was coming to terms with the fact that Azarov had torn through him like he wasn't there. Coleman was still struggling to regain the confidence he'd always possessed in well-deserved abundance.

So it had been a surprise—of the rare good kind—when he'd showed up on Rapp's doorstep and invited him on a trail run. It was good to see a hint of the old swagger. He'd been Rapp's backup for a long time and the truth was that the year without him could have gone better. In this business, you were only as good as the people you surrounded yourself with.

Rapp glanced at the heart rate monitor strapped to his wrist. One sixty-five—a hard but comfortable pace that he could hold for around three hours before blowing up. Behind him, Coleman's breathing was becoming desperate and his footfalls were losing their steady tempo. Stumbles, followed by awkward saves, were increasingly frequent as his thigh muscles began to give up. But no falls. Not yet.

They broke out of the trees and Rapp pushed the pace a little harder as the summit came into sight. Coleman tripped and went down on one hand, but managed to get back to his feet without losing momentum. He was running purely on determination and pride now, but that was okay. He had serious reserves of both.

One hundred and seventy-one beats per minute read out on Rapp's monitor.

Coleman was starting to wheeze, a sick whistle from deep in his chest. Something caught in his throat and he started to choke, causing Rapp to hesitate for a moment. Then he started to sprint. If his old friend was going to drop dead, better now than in Afghanistan or Syria when people were counting on him.

Rapp slowed to a walk when he reached the top of the mountain, squinting as he scanned the rolling carpet of green below. He could see the gleaming dot that was his house to the east, surrounded by a few homes erected on similar widely spaced lots. His obscenely rich brother had bought the entire subdivision and sold the individual parcels for a dollar each to Rapp's colleagues, ensuring that his older sibling would always be surrounded by shooters loyal to him.

To the south of Rapp's gate, a contemporary house of wood and blast-resistant glass was nearly finished. Whether its owner would survive the last hundred yards of this run to take occupancy, though, was an open question.

Fortunately, it was a question that didn't take too long to answer. Coleman crested the hill, lurching toward Rapp and finally collapsing to the rocky ground. He managed to rise to all fours but didn't stand, instead keeping his head down and concentrating on not throwing up. After about a minute, he regained enough control of his breathing to get out a single word.

"Time?"

Rapp glanced at his watch. "One hour, sixteen minutes, thirty-three seconds. Pick it up a little bit and you might qualify for the senior Olympics."

In fact, the pace they'd sustained on the climb would have shaken off a third of active duty SEALs. Not too bad for an old sailor the doctors said would need a cane for the rest of his life.

Coleman managed to lift one hand off the ground and raise his middle finger. "What's your best?"

Rapp considered telling the truth but quickly discarded the idea. The amount of work Coleman had put into his recovery and the progress he'd made was incredible. No point in discouraging him.

"Hour eleven forty."

"What would Azarov have done?"

"How the hell would I know?"

"Don't bullshit me, Mitch. You worked with him."

Rapp had recruited Azarov to help him with an operation that he didn't want to involve Coleman's men in. The former SEAL understood Rapp's rationale for using the man who had nearly killed him—it had been a straight up illegal action that he didn't want to blow back on the men who had been so loyal to him over the years. But that didn't make Coleman any less competitive.

"All he does these days is drink beer by his pool and surf with his girlfriend."

Coleman pushed himself to his feet. "Okay, Mitch. If you won't tell me that, at least you can stop lying to me about your real personal best."

"Fine. Hour four flat."

"Shit," Coleman said, lowering himself onto a boulder and staring out over the landscape. "I'll never be as fast as I was before. Too many years and too much mileage."

"Fighting's not just about running up hills, Scott. You know that. I'm more concerned about your head."

Coleman nodded, not taking his eyes off the horizon. "Over the last year, I've had a lot of time to think. Maybe too much."

"And?"

"I'm not afraid, if that's what you're wondering. When your number's up, it's up. And I've made peace with what Azarov did to me. He was a young guy pumped full of performance-enhancing drugs. An Olympic-level athlete with surprise on his side."

A barely perceptible smile appeared at the edges of his mouth. "And he damn near took you out, too."

It was a true statement. Rapp won his battle with the Russian but that win had ended with him getting blown off an oil rig with his hair literally on fire. Too many more wins like that might kill him.

"It's gonna get dark, Scott. And I want to take it easy on the way down. My knee's bothering me."

Coleman's smile widened at the obvious lie.

And that was another thing that would be impossible to replace if he decided not to come back to active duty. They always knew what the other was thinking and could anticipate each other's moves. They'd grown up in this business together and had a connection that Rapp doubted he could ever replicate with someone else.

"I'm okay with where I stand now," Coleman said, looking up at him. "The question is, are you? You can't be out there worrying about me leaving you hanging."

Rapp's cell phone rang and he pulled it out of a pocket in the back of his shirt. Claudia.

"What's up?" he said, connecting the call.

"How's Scott? You didn't hurt him did you?"

Claudia Gould had recently gone from being the woman he was living with to being the woman he was living with who was also the logistics coordinator for Coleman's company. Her late husband had been one of the top private contractors in the world before Stan Hurley tore his throat out. Not an ideal start to a relationship but it seemed to be working for both him and Coleman. She'd helped Rapp start living something that could pass for a life and she'd held SEAL Demolition and Salvage together while Coleman spent his days with personal trainers and physical therapists.

"He's sitting right here."

"Upright and under his own power?"

"Tell her you're fine," Rapp said, holding out the phone.

"I almost took him at the top, Claudia! Don't let him tell you any different."

Rapp frowned and put the phone back to his ear. "See?"

"Is he ready to come back to ops?"

"I think he's ready to come back and run the whole thing. Ops and logistics."

She switched to French as she always did when she was irritated. "You can wish all you want, Mitch, but he's not firing me. I'm running that side of the business now. And it's a good thing for us, because it pays a lot better than the CIA."

There was no winning this fight, he knew. Claudia had taken a lot of pressure off Coleman and he had precisely zero desire to go back to coordinating details. Besides, she was better at it—something Coleman was fully willing to admit. The problem for Rapp was getting used to having the woman he was sleeping with on the comm when things went south. Boundaries between their personal and professional relationship were complicated and still in flux.

"Now's not the time to talk about this, Claudia. Scott and I are going to start down, but it might take a while. Go ahead and feed Anna if she's hungry. We can do dinner when I get back."

"Actually, you aren't coming down and we're not having dinner together. Look to the north."

He turned and squinted into the horizon. It took a few seconds but he finally made out a small dot over the mountains.

"There's a laptop on board with a full briefing. Be careful, okay?"

She disconnected the call and he put the phone away before pointing to the approaching chopper. "So what's the story, Scott? Are you back or not?"

CHAPTER 2

"Not sleeping again, Grisha?"

Cara Hansen was lying next to him on the damp bed, naked and glistening in the glow of his phone. Normally, she would have pressed up against him but with the air conditioner off she opted to nudge him with a finger instead.

"Quit playing with that thing. There's no signal and you're wasting electricity."

Azarov used the house's internal network to shut off the lights in the upstairs master bedroom. He left them on to give the illusion that they were still sleeping there, though they'd abandoned it three days ago when the power had gone out across the region. The temperature was a good ten degrees cooler downstairs, but it wasn't helping him sleep. The only thing that could do that was solid intelligence on why the grid was down and when it would be repaired.

"Sorry," he said, darkening the screen. "I didn't mean to wake you."

"I was barely dozing. Too hot to do anything else. I mean, who do I have to screw in this country to get a couple hours of A/C?"

Technically speaking, that would be him. He'd never mentioned to her that he had three massive Tesla batteries under the house that he was reluctant to tap for more than a trickle of current. It had been cloudy for days, making his solar roof all but useless and the supply of diesel for his generators was becoming unreliable.

The people in the little surf town he lived above had largely shrugged and moved on with their lives. They'd never come to rely on technology like he did. Despite his years living there, he'd never mastered locals' cheerful fatalism.

"If you were to go to the gas station in the morning, that might be a good way to convince them to part with a little diesel."

"Funny," she said, poking him a little harder this time.

He was already struggling to remember how long they'd been together. Technically, the time could be measured in months, but in truth he'd loved her for years.

Originally from California, she was a surf instructor who'd worked part time for the company that maintained the subdivision where he lived. In the beginning, a relationship between them had been impossible. He'd been working as a problem solver for the president of Russia, a man who had an unparalleled gift for discovering what people cared about and then using it against them. So, while Azarov had passed up no opportunity to hire Cara for work around the house, he'd been forced to feign indifference to her presence.

He reached out and ran a hand through her damp hair. "You didn't have air conditioning before you moved in with me. You're getting soft."

"Too much of the good life," she said, rolling away in an attempt to escape the heat coming off his body.

Without the glow of his phone, the world was swallowed by darkness. Azarov stared in the direction of the windows, watching the vague outline of the flowers that Cara had planted on the other side of the glass. Beyond that was nothing but kilometer after kilometer of jungle dense enough to hide just about anything.

He had left the employ of the Russian government but it was unlikely that he was forgotten. Krupin had never agreed to release him and he wasn't a man accustomed to being defied. Would he take notice of Costa Rica's power failure? Perhaps use it to take revenge on Azarov for abandoning him and for failing to deal with Mitch Rapp? An example for anyone else who might dare challenge him?

Or maybe it was even worse. Maybe Krupin had charged his cyber warriors with attacking Costa Rica, a country completely unprepared for such an aggression. Would he cripple the country's entire southwest to retaliate against a man who had spent years faithfully serving him?

No. That was just paranoia. While Krupin was a megalomaniac who required complete control over everyone and everything in his orbit, he was also eminently rational. Everything he did was in direct pursuit of his own survival and power. Krupin never lashed out in a way that didn't objectively benefit him or that could blow back. At his core, Russia's president was a man of calculation. A coward and a manipulator.

Besides, according to Azarov's sources, he'd already been replaced with a man named Nikita Pushkin. By all reports, the younger man was quite gifted and in possession of the loyalty and sense of duty that Azarov had lost so long ago. All in all it seemed to be an improvement for everyone involved. This boy would be showered with everything he desired, Krupin would have a protector who would gladly die for him, and Azarov was free to explore the concept of happiness and perhaps even pursue it.

Next to him, Cara's breathing evened out and deepened, but his mind was moving in too many directions to follow her into sleep. What if it was someone else? Someone who was associated with one of the many people he'd killed and had heard he was no longer under Krupin's protection?

Unlikely. Powerful men, once dead, tended to garner very little loyalty. Their inner circles were generally more interested in fighting to fill the power vacuum left behind.

And that left America. Not Rapp, though. Azarov had helped him move against the Saudis and the CIA man had made it clear that he considered himself indebted. He could be trusted and Irene Kennedy wouldn't act without his consent.

Scott Coleman and his team? It was his understanding that Coleman had largely healed and . . .

Azarov closed his eyes for a moment, trying to clear his mind. If he was intent on reviewing every enemy he'd made over the years, it was going to be a very long night.

When he opened his eyes again, he reactivated his phone's screen and relaunched his security app. The perimeter alarms were still active, as were all emergency systems. His batteries still had more than eighty percent of their capacity. Satellite Internet was still technically online but so overloaded that it was all but useless.

Cara slapped lazily at him, hitting him in the chest. Her face was half buried in a pillow and he had to strain to make out what she was saying.

"If you're going to play with that thing, do it somewhere else."

It was unlikely that he was going to fall asleep anytime soon, so he got up and pulled on a pair of shorts. Cara attributed his restlessness to the heat and what she referred to as GRM—general Russian moodiness—but that was because she believed him to be a semi-retired energy consultant. And that's the way it would stay. He couldn't bear the thought of her knowing the things he'd done. Or of her being afraid. A woman like her should never have to feel anything but joy and security.

He padded toward the door, but stopped when she spoke again.

"You're not sad again, are you, Grisha?"

"No."

"And you're not tired of your girlfriend?"

He smiled. "Not yet."

"Do you want me to take a swim with you? Would that make you feel better?"

"No. Just go back to sleep."

The overcast skies from that day had cleared and the moon was bright enough for him to navigate the stairs to the second level kitchen. He considered opening the refrigerator but it was a waste of electricity and he didn't want the interior light to go on. While he was probably paranoid, there was no reason to be careless.

Instead, he got a glass of water from the sink and walked to the bank of windows facing north. Through them, the mountains were just outlines against the stars. His distant neighbors were all in bed and the ones who still had power reserves weren't wasting them on things like exterior lights.

He saw a flash that his mind—still under the influence of years of training—immediately recognized as a gunshot. It came from near a rocky knoll that he himself had scouted when he'd been deciding where to place his house. The distance was significant at seven hundred and fifty meters, but it was somewhat elevated and had the clearest line of sight to the structure.

The glass was theoretically bulletproof, but anyone good enough to be sent for him and to identify that vantage point would use a round capable of penetrating. Azarov dove to the floor, knowing that he had less than a second before the impact. He hit the concrete hard but then there was nothing. Just the muffled hum of insects.

Could he have been wrong? Might it have been someone lighting a cigarette? Turning on a flashlight?

He didn't have time to consider either possibility before the deafening sound of automatic fire erupted from the base of his driveway. The glass in front of him spiderwebbed and then finally collapsed, raining down on him as he crawled toward the island in the middle of the kitchen.

CHAPTER 3

NIKITA Pushkin had secured the high ground, giving him a reasonably unobstructed view north to Azarov's house. The disused dirt road he was parked on had become overgrown, but was still navigable, unlike the dense jungle surrounding it. Distance was just over a kilometer, making direct involvement in the operation difficult. But that wasn't his role today.

Through his binoculars, Pushkin saw the master bedroom light finally go out. Two a.m. Early to bed was apparently yet another of the military habits Azarov had abandoned.

There was a special operations team climbing the steep slope to the front of the house, but their activation was a last resort. The hope had been that the sniper positioned half a kilometer to the west would be able to end this before it even began. Unfortunately, Azarov hadn't left the confines of his home since Maxim Krupin's bold attack on Costa Rica's power grid. Caution, it appeared, was *not* a habit Azarov had left behind.

During the day, the reflection off the windows

made them opaque and at night he had an uncanny ability to stay away from them while running only emergency lighting angled to create glare.

It was insanity to expose his team for so long in this Central American backwater, even with the confusion caused by the power outage. He could have simply driven up to the property and killed the man but Krupin had forbidden a face-to-face confrontation. The president had made it clear that those kinds of actions were no longer his responsibility. That he wasn't the soldier he'd once been. Now, he was a general.

But was it really true? Or did Krupin believe that he was the weaker man? Pushkin couldn't escape the feeling that his mentor's confidence in him was less unshakable than it had been in Azarov.

It was entirely unfair. Had he not carried out to the letter every order he'd been given? Had he not demonstrated unwavering loyalty? Had he not killed Krupin's enemies and defended his supporters without question or hesitation? Had word of his existence and exploits not struck fear in the hearts of Russia's oligarchs, politicians, and military commanders?

He spat on the ground in disgust.

The vaunted Grisha Azarov. A man who existed in the twilight between legend and reality. An avenging angel who could walk through walls and kill with a mere wave of his hand.

But what was he now? Nothing. Nobody. Another retired foreigner getting fat while wandering the local beaches.

Azarov had turned his back on the man who had given him everything. He'd failed to carry out his mission in Saudi Arabia and allowed himself to be shot by Mitch Rapp. Then he'd run in terror from the broken-down CIA man, abandoning one of the most critical operations in Mother Russia's history.

Yet despite his cowardice and betrayal, his shadow continued to extend darkness over everything. Pushkin's trainers constantly held up Azarov's natural athletic gifts, his icy personality, and his robot-like ability to analyze tactical situations. All while dismissing the things he lacked: Belief. Gratitude. Patriotism.

Like his infamous predecessor, Pushkin had come from nothing—the fourth son in a family that had spent generations toiling in a forgotten corner of Russia. He had joined the military as a way out, but also out of a desire to be part of bringing his great country back to its former glory. He'd been accepted to the special forces and worked harder than anyone else around him. He had the ability to ignore pain and fear, and had never experienced the paralyzing effect of doubt.

After three years of distinguished service, Pushkin had been separated from his unit and put into a far more rigorous program overseen by some of the top people in the world. Weapons, tactics, extreme physical training aided by performance enhancing drugs. Language and cultural lessons that allowed him to disappear into the countries he operated in. Even instruction in literature, art, and elocution to help him navigate the social strata he was now a member of.

Everything he'd ever wanted was his at the snap of his fingers. The money, women, and power that had once been Azarov's were now his.

"Report," he said into his throat mike.

"We're in position and setting up the spotlights."

They would project a wavelength that was invisible to the human eye but still capable of penetrating glass. His sniper would soon have a view of the interior through his specially equipped scope.

After a few minutes the voice came over his earpiece again. "Lights are active."

Pushkin wiped at the perspiration rolling down his forehead. He wanted desperately to go down there and do it himself. To throw open the door, look into Azarov's terrified eyes, and put a bullet between them. To show Krupin that his former enforcer was less than nothing.

"Sniper. Report. Is the interior of the structure visible?"

Silence.

"Sniper! Report."

The response had a slightly stunned quality, audible even over the heavily encrypted radio frequency. "The target is standing directly in front of the north windows."

It was Pushkin's turn to sink into shocked silence. This was the man that the great Maxim Krupin feared enough to disable a quarter of Costa Rica's power grid? The man whose name was spoken only in hushed tones and behind closed doors?

"Take the shot. Now!"

There was a flash in his peripheral vision, but no sound. He turned toward the dark knoll where his sniper was set up, confused. At the very least, the crack of the round breaking the sound barrier should have been audible.

"Sniper, report."

Nothing.

"Report!" he repeated, looking through his binoculars. They weren't capable of picking up the infrared floodlights and registered only the darkness enveloping the house.

Again, no answer.

"Ground team. What's your situation?"

"No impact on the glass, but Azarov is on the ground and out of our line of sight."

Pushkin hesitated, his mind unable to make sense of what had just happened. In the end, though, it didn't matter. Going back to Russia having failed to deal with Azarov wasn't an option.

He turned and ran toward the Jeep he had hidden in the jungle. "Move in and take out the target. You have permission to fire."

CHAPTER 4

THE all too familiar din of machine gun fire and shattering glass made everything else around Azarov seem to disappear. He flattened himself against the floor and slithered toward the kitchen island, focusing on staying as low as possible. The shooters had managed to climb the steep, tangled slope north of his house and were now coming across his purposely expansive yard. So far, their rounds were only pulverizing his appliances and cabinets, but that wouldn't last. Based on an assessment made during the design of the house, he knew that when they got within seven meters they'd be able hit the floor near the island that was his objective. Five and a half meters if they were willing to lift their rifles over their heads and fire blind.

He could feel the turbulence from the bullets passing a few centimeters over his head when he finally reached the island and slid behind it. The dull thud of rounds hitting metal plate was added to the cacophony as the approaching men adjusted their aim toward the armored-enhanced cabinets he'd taken refuge behind. Azarov shoved up against the granite overhang and began tipping the entire island.

It fell, slamming down against the concrete floor, and the thud of steel was replaced by the sound of rounds hitting stone. He grabbed the pistol set into the bottom but ignored the extra magazines. He was wearing nothing but a pair of cutoffs and flip-flops. He had nowhere to carry them.

His phone, though, was still with him. He used it to activate a bank of powerful LED spotlights aimed outward. The glare would blind anyone approaching.

As expected, the incoming fire faltered and he rose from behind cover, firing two rounds in quick succession. Both hit center mass, but to no effect. The men were wearing state-of-the-art body armor designed to protect them from far more hard-hitting weapons than the custom pistol Azarov had designed more for stealth than power.

The sound of shattering glass returned, but this time behind him. The sliding doors that led to the south deck collapsed and a similarly armored man lurched through the hole. A second held back, covering. Trapped, Azarov dropped to the floor again, staying between the overturned island and a line of cabinets that housed what was left of his sink and dishwasher. He managed to get off a round that hit the approaching man's helmet near the attachment for his face shield, but did little more than snap his head back into the Kevlar collar protecting his neck.

Azarov continued to fire as the shooter swung his assault rifle toward him, but there was little hope. He was inadequately armed and surrounded by a heavily armored, well-disciplined incursion team.

His magazine emptied and he was preparing for the impact that would end his life when a flash of color appeared in his peripheral vision. He tensed even further when he recognized the bright red T-shirt with the ironic letters CCCP across the front.

Cara slammed into the man at a full run, actually managing to do what the bullets hadn't and knock him over. She rolled awkwardly over top of him and for the first time in his life, Azarov panicked. He was about to break cover to draw the men's fire when he saw her body jerk with the impact of a round hitting her back. She skidded across the floor and came to a stop, utterly still with a blood streak smeared across the floor behind her.

His stomach revolted at the image, pushing its contents into his throat. He looked right, wild eyed and confused as he saw the two men to the north find their angles and calmly take aim at him. He wanted more than anything to cross that concrete floor and to take her in his arms. To know if she was dead or alive. But it was impossible. His neighbors, distant as they were, would come to investigate and these men had no reason to harm her further. They'd leave when he was dead and the people who lived around him would take her to the hospital. And then she'd be fine. Right? She had to be.

The men's fingers tightened on their triggers and he found he didn't even care enough to brace himself. The shot that came, though, wasn't from them. The chest of the man on the right suddenly exploded as a round passed through his armor and then hit the refrigerator hard enough to slam it back into the wall.

Azarov still couldn't think clearly, but he managed to wake from his stupor enough to let instinct take over. The man who had come through the back was still struggling to his feet and his aim was partially blocked by a tree growing from the living room floor. He could wait. Azarov went right, charging the surviving man to the north, taking advantage of the fact that he'd turned to fire into the darkness in hopes of hitting the sniper who had taken out his companion.

Azarov grabbed him by the side of his helmet and dragged him down, twisting his head a full one hundred and eighty degrees before sprinting toward the shattered north glass. If he could get to the jungle, they would have no choice but to follow. He'd draw them away from the house and Cara.

His plan was initially hindered by his lack of physical training over the last year and then completely derailed by the appearance of another man to his right. This one was different, though, wearing only jeans and a T-shirt and with hair that partially obscured his face as he swung an MP7 level with Azarov's chest.

The Russian was about to dive into the shattered glass at his feet, but instead of firing, the man released his weapon. It arced toward Azarov, turning in the air to reach him butt first. He had no idea what was happening but caught the gun and spun toward the man behind him. A controlled burst defeated his armor and he collapsed against the tree next to him.

The long-haired man let his momentum carry him toward Cara and he grabbed her by the shirt, dragging her behind the granite island as Azarov laid down suppressing fire at the remaining attacker now pulled back out of sight to the south. The Russian made it to the island, letting his back slam painfully into the shattered cabinets as the man who had come to his rescue used a dish towel to cover the wound in Cara's back. When his head turned, the hair fell away from his face, making it recognizable.

"I've got a sniper near that obvious knoll to the northwest," Rapp said in the sudden silence. "But your friends out there will know that by now and they'll figure out how to stay out of his line of sight."

As if punctuating his words, a window on the west side of the house imploded and a grenade sailed through.

"Inside!" Azarov shouted, helping Rapp drag Cara's limp body into the open bottom of the kitchen island. It was a tight fit with the remaining pots and pans but they managed to get in before the explosion.

The room went dark as the bulbs were blown out but then began to glow with the light of various small fires. Azarov felt the burn of shrapnel in one of his bare legs but it wasn't serious. Rapp seemed unharmed and the Russian could see that he had Cara's left wrist in his hand. It wasn't to comfort her, though. He was checking to see if she was coming with them or staying there.

Azarov found himself unable to breathe until Rapp dragged her out and threw her over his shoulder. "I hope you have an exit, because these sons of bitches don't look like they're in the mood to quit."

The Russian nodded. "Do you have men out there? Other than your sniper?"

A short volley hammered the countertop from the north, forcing Rapp to shout his answer. "Yeah, but I'm not bringing them in any closer. *I* owe you. They don't."

The CIA man adjusted the cloth keeping Cara's life from leaking out of her and Azarov's eyes locked on it, becoming trapped in the image. Rapp reached out with his free hand and grabbed him by the hair. "Grisha! Our exit!"

"Down . . ." Azarov stammered. "Downstairs. We have to get to the storage room."

Rapp activated his throat mike. "We're headed to the storage room on the lower floor."

"Copy that," came Scott Coleman's immediate response. "Do you want us to move in?"

"Have you been able to determine the strength of the Russians?"

"Somewhere between four and four thousand. You could lose New York City in this jungle."

"Then negative. Stay put."

"Mitch . . ." Claudia's voice broke in on the satellite link from Coleman's Baltimore headquarters. "Confirm you said the downstairs storage room."

"Affirmative."

"There are no doors leading outside from that room and the windows are heavy glass block. You'll get cornered in there."

The CIA had information on the house in case Azarov ever needed to be dealt with, but it had been compiled only from architectural drawings and a single drone flyover. Better than nothing, but not exactly authoritative.

"It's Grisha's house and he says we're going down."

"Are you sure? He could be leading you into a trap. Sacrificing you so he can escape."

"Maybe. Scott can you give us any cover from where you are?"

"The men on the perimeter are staying out of sight and going for position on you."

"Can you at least make some noise? Get them to think twice?"

"Oh hell yeah."

"Do it."

The sound of automatic fire erupted outside, hitting the concrete walls and the dirt surrounding the structure. Rapp ran for the stairs with Cara on his shoulder while Azarov stayed to his left, shielding her with his body. A few shots came their way, but none got close as the incursion team was forced to focus on the fact that multiple unidentified shooters had flanked them.

They made it down a dangerously open staircase and into a hallway that came to a T with a bedroom to the right and the storage room to the left. As usual, Claudia was right—glass block and thick stucco had replaced floor to ceiling windows in this part of the house. The jungle and steep slopes would have been difficult to secure and Azarov had forgone the spectacular views in favor of defense.

They broke left into a relatively small room stacked with surfboards, kayaks, and other athletic equipment. Azarov pushed an unusually thick door closed and then tapped something into his phone. The sound of mechanical deadbolts sliding home cut through eerie silence.

Rapp lay Cara down next to the wall and checked for a pulse again. Getting out of there would be a hell of a lot easier without the extra weight, but he couldn't help rooting for her. There weren't many young surf instructors who would charge a heavily armed man in body armor. Definitely a keeper.

"Is she . . ." Azarov started.

"She's alive. But not for much longer if we let our-

selves get pinned down here. I don't care how thick
you made these walls, those assholes are ready for it."

Azarov nodded and moved to a mattress leaned up
against the wall. "Help me."

It was heavy as hell, but they managed to pull the
bottom back a couple of feet, creating a space that the
three of them could just fit into. Automatic fire began
to thud against the door as they sandwiched themselves inside.

Azarov began tapping commands into his phone
again and Rapp grabbed his wrist, suspecting what
was coming next. He'd had a similar escape route
built into his new house.

"Do we have anyone near the southeast walls?" he
said into his throat mike.

"That's a negative, Mitch. Maslick is in the best position to get there, probably six minutes out. Do you
need him?"

"No. Stay clear."

He released the Russian's wrist and nodded. Azarov
finished entering his password and they pulled the
mattress closer, pressing their backs against the wall.

The charges had been expertly placed and the majority of the blast's energy went outward, sending
shattered concrete and glass block spraying into the
jungle. There was barely enough residual energy to
shove the mattress back against them. Rapp slipped
out immediately, making his way through the thick,
chemical-scented dust to the hole leading outside. His
eyes weren't dark adapted, but he was able to make out
a single man down at the edge of the jungle. As his
vision sharpened, he could see that his body armor
and the surrounding trees were full of nails and

deck screws that must have been packed around the charges. You had to hand it to Azarov. The shrapnel was a nice touch.

"This way," the Russian said, handing Rapp the MP7 as he moved past with Cara in his arms. Rapp followed, watching their flank as they penetrated into the foliage. Time was against them. Their path was clear for the moment, but blowing the side off your house wasn't exactly subtle. It wouldn't take a genius to figure out the route they were using to escape.

By the time Rapp caught up, Azarov was crouched in the vegetation next to a pickup truck toolbox dragged from a trapdoor in the ground. He'd already cut through Cara's shirt and was fully focused on bandaging the wound in her back.

"Are you still strong enough to carry her or should I?" Rapp said, dropping to his knees next to the box, digging through its contents.

"Strong enough. I'll take her."

It was the expected answer, but Rapp had wanted to give him the option. The light from the fire starting to consume the house penetrated the jungle with enough strength to allow him to sort through the gear— boots, camo, a full CamelBak, a Beretta ARX100 assault rifle, spare mags.

Rapp slipped the CamelBak and Beretta over his shoulders, leaving the MP7 and clothing for Azarov. Near the bottom he found a surprise. A Russian RPG-7 rocket propelled grenade launcher. The longer he knew Azarov, the more he liked where his head was at.

"Where, to?" Rapp said, hanging the launcher over the top of the CamelBak.

"Straight down the slope," the Russian responded.

"It funnels into a canyon of sorts between the mountains. Water runs through it during the rainy season, so the bottom isn't as densely vegetated. You can move quickly. Take the night-vision gear in the box. I won't be able to move as fast and we have nearly a full moon. I'm familiar enough with the trail to navigate by that."

"How far and where's it come out?"

"About four kilometers to a dirt road that runs parallel to the ocean. That road is about a kilometer northeast of the town."

Rapp activated his throat mike. "Our rendezvous point is the junction of the canyon behind Grisha's house and a dirt road that runs parallel to the ocean about one klick northeast of Dominical. You're going to have to find a place to set the chopper down."

"We don't know what the Russians' capabilities are," came Claudia's reply. "A local SUV might be safer."

"Negative. Cara's injured and we need to get her medical attention ASAP. Bring the chopper in low and fast. Hopefully, the skids won't even have to touch the ground."

"Copy. How long?"

Rapp looked over at Azarov, who was pulling on his fatigues next to Cara's still body. "Time?"

"I've never trained on this route with so much added weight," he said, falling silent as he did the calculations in his head. "Fifty-eight minutes."

"One hour," Rapp said into his radio.

"Copy that. Fred'll be there."

"Scott," Rapp said. "Get a couple of men on that chopper and send the rest of them ahead to the hospital in Quepos."

"On it."

Rapp tossed Azarov his radio and the Russian put it on before scooping Cara off the ground. Before he started out, though, he grabbed Rapp's forearm. "If they come after us, it's likely that one of the chasers will be Nikita Pushkin, the man who replaced me. Don't play with him, Mitch. Kill him."

CHAPTER 5

THE semitruck fishtailed as it climbed the muddy road, intensifying Maxim Krupin's nausea. His vision was clear, though. As was his mind. He hadn't had an episode in three days, which he'd come to see as a mixed blessing. A welcome respite, but also a harbinger of things to come.

All he needed was another forty-eight hours of lucidity. Then he could return to Moscow with an excuse that would allow him to disappear into one of his homes and endure the inevitable attack in privacy.

The predicted rain hadn't materialized but they had ascended into the low clouds hovering over this desolate part of Russia. Mist swirled around the vehicle, thick enough to force the driver to turn on his headlights. The reflection off the wet trees lining the road was sudden and surprisingly powerful. Krupin adjusted his gaze to the shadowed floorboard of the truck's cab, fearful that the glare might trigger another attack.

Soon, hints of their destination began to emerge

from the wilderness. Clearings scraped from the forest, concrete bunkers, and finally rows of rusting military vehicles and outdated artillery. Through the fog, military planes appeared and disappeared like a ghost fleet.

And in many ways, it was. This dump was one of a number of forgotten repositories to Soviet military—the war machine that had once struck terror in the hearts of the West. Some of the equipment would eventually be stripped of anything that still had value, but most would slowly disintegrate into the earth and be forgotten.

It was a sobering reminder of how Russia had fallen from grace, but also a perfect location for the task at hand. Thick cloud cover was the norm and the Americans were both aware of the site's existence and indifferent to it—as were his many enemies inside Russia. While nothing was certain in these kinds of situations, he felt confident that he and his small security detail could slip in and out without fear of discovery.

A series of concrete and steel warehouses appeared ahead, scattered throughout the site almost as randomly as the refuse piled around them. The land had been cleared decades ago when this had been a working Soviet installation, but now it was in the slow process of being reclaimed by the forest.

The truck in front of them turned right toward the center of the complex while his own driver continued straight toward a warehouse on its northeastern edge. Finally, he circled on a worn track and backed toward a set of massive doors.

Krupin jumped out wearing the clothes of a common workman, opening the bay doors and taking a moment to direct the trailer through them. When the brake lights went on, he walked beneath a corrugated metal awning and found an unassuming door with the promised keypad next to it. A seven-digit code allowed him to enter and a moment later he was standing alone in a cavernous building that still seemed completely unremarkable.

He was initially surprised that no one was there to meet him, but upon reflection he shouldn't have been. He'd limited the number of people involved to the bare minimum—perhaps even below that minimum. Convenience was irrelevant in this situation. All that mattered was secrecy.

This warehouse had been used as both barracks and offices at some point in the distant past, and there were still vestiges of those functions. Now, most of the walls had been at least partially knocked down in order to facilitate the movement of cargo and equipment. In some places, stacks of decaying wooden crates looked as though they hadn't been touched in decades while in other places construction equipment showed evidence of recent use.

Krupin took the obvious path through the refuse, moving with uncharacteristic slowness. As he neared the back, the debris-strewn ground gave way to recently painted concrete. A glow, the source of which was hidden by a recently erected wall, grew in intensity until it overpowered the filthy overhead bulbs he had been navigating by.

On the other side of the wall was a clear plastic tent that measured probably fifteen meters square and four in height. It was full of medical equipment and machinery quietly raided from hospitals throughout

Russia. The people tending that equipment had been similarly scavenged from different parts of the country, different specialties, and different experience levels. Everything had been designed to avoid creating a discernible pattern.

When Krupin saw the examination table and the gown folded neatly on top of it, he slowed further, finally stopping a few meters away. His entire life had been about control. His rise through the KGB, his entry into local politics after the fall of the Soviet Union. His move out of rural administration and into Moscow's power elite. Then, finally, his ascent to the presidency and his transformation of it into a de facto dictatorship. Russia was now, for all intents and purposes, his. He ruled alone over its land and wealth, its commerce and finance, as well as its military and nuclear arsenal.

But most important, he controlled its information. The government-controlled media fed the Russian people a steady diet of propaganda, enflaming their nationalism and building him into the father, savior, and symbol that they so needed. Within the Kremlin, he meted out truth and lies to his people with a dropper, making certain that no one could ever grasp the big picture, no one knew who to trust, and no one could anticipate or see further than him.

Now he had stepped outside that universe. He didn't know what functions the instruments or people in that tent performed. He was utterly ignorant as to what the vials lined up on the tray next to the table contained. He didn't know what he would be asked to submit to or what secrets could be learned from his consent.

His body was betraying him but he was utterly

powerless to remedy the situation or indeed to even understand it. The potentially deadly truth was that he was entirely at the mercy of the people inside that circle of sterile plastic.

Due to the bright interior of the tent, no one was able to see out. He watched them, savoring his last few moments of having the upper hand. All were filled with the nervous energy that he'd come to expect of people anticipating his arrival. They busied themselves checking and double-checking their equipment, while Dr. Eduard Fedkin sat working on a computer that had no connection to the outside world.

The cold finally prompted Krupin to move again. He wasn't noticed until he pushed aside the plastic flap that served as a door. Fedkin leapt from his chair and rushed toward him.

"Mr. President! I was brought here with no prior warning. Some of the people with me were pulled from their beds. Even their families—"

"Calm down, Doctor. There are security concerns that have to be acknowledged. We're suffering traitorous protests throughout the country, illegal economic sanctions, and NATO closing in on our borders. If there's even a hint that I might be in need of medical treatment, it could mean chaos."

"I understand, sir, but there's no way to communicate with our colleagues and relatives who—"

"Then we best confirm my good health quickly so that I can return all of you home. My understanding is that you've been provided with everything you requested and that all the tests and lab work can be carried out here. No samples are to be removed and no outside sources are to be consulted."

"For this round of testing, that's correct. But if we find—"

Krupin raised a hand, silencing the man. "You'll use no drugs or anesthesia that could incapacitate me or have any effect on my mental function. And time is of the essence. I've made arrangements to be absent from Moscow for two days and not a moment more. Am I understood?"

CHAPTER 6

NIKITA Pushkin slowed as he approached the southeast edge of Azarov's house. The wall was little more than a gaping hole that likely wouldn't support the remaining structure for long. Fire was taking hold of the building but the blazing debris strewn out in the jungle was proving inadequate to spread through the wet foliage.

One of his men was down, now little more than a piece of meat pierced by countless nails and screws. Flames from the house would soon consume him, making extraction more complicated. Normally, that would be an issue that demanded his attention, but now it rated no consideration at all.

Pushkin stepped into the flickering shadow of a palm and went completely still. There was little of importance to see from this position, but a great deal to think about. If Azarov's woman was alive, then he was gone—running through the jungle in an effort to get her to help. If she was dead, though, the situation changed significantly. He would be standing similarly motionless just beyond the firelight. Waiting. Watching. Making those famously precise calculations as to how he could inflict maximum damage on the men who had taken his American girl from him.

Azarov's location, though, was only one of a number of deadly mysteries. What had happened to Pushkin's sniper? Who was the man that had appeared in the house at just the critical moment? What was the strength of his team and what were their orders?

The first—and perhaps least critical—question was answered when his earpiece crackled to life.

"We've located sniper one, sir. He was killed by what appears to be a single shot to the head. We've also found the fifty-caliber rifle placement that was used to fire down on our team."

"And the man responsible?" Pushkin prompted.

"There's no sign of him. We can't even find tracks in or out."

"Do we have any information on Azarov's position or the position of the man who went into the jungle with him?"

"Negative. We have a drone in the air, but the jungle canopy's too thick in the general vicinity of the house."

Pushkin considered retreating to his vehicle, but the idea didn't last long. He'd enjoyed the advantages of an overwhelming force, the element of surprise, and a power outage that covered a full third of the country. There was no way he was going to stand in the middle of Krupin's office and make excuses as to why Azarov was still alive. To see the disappointment in his eyes and watch the knowing nods of the men who trained him. To hear how they'd never really expected him to be capable of defeating the infamous Grisha Azarov, even now that he had retired to a soft life in the tropics.

No. He'd rather die here and rot.

Pushkin began moving again, searching the perimeter of the jungle. If he found the woman's body, then the battle lines were drawn. If he didn't, then she was alive and Azarov would be on the run, hampered by her dead weight.

"Converge on the house," Pushkin said into his throat mike. "I'll need two men with me to pursue the target. The rest will remove our casualties before the authorities arrive."

"In order to collect our dead, we'll have to expose ourselves," came the hesitant reply over his earpiece.

Pushkin didn't bother to respond, instead slipping into the jungle and paralleling the intensifying fire. It was impossible to know how many men his team was up against, but he was less concerned than his subordinate.

It was clear that the opposition was highly professional and that would play to his advantage. Their mission, for whatever reason, was likely to protect Azarov and they'd focus entirely on that. Using resources to harass the retrieval of casualties would be a waste of resources.

He heard movement ahead and crouched, concentrating on the rhythm of the jungle and crackle of the flames behind him. A second rustle of leaves was followed by a gurgling moan.

Pushkin crept forward, finding one of his men dangling from the branches of a tree, nearly three meters from the ground. His arms and legs were grotesquely broken and his body armor glittered with partially penetrated metal. A rusty bolt was lodged in the side of his neck.

His head moved in Pushkin's direction, though the clear face shield attached to his helmet reflected only flames. The young Russian felt his anger flare—at the disaster that this simple operation had become, at the deference and respect that Azarov commanded but that always seemed just beyond his grasp. At the uselessness of the soldier suspended above him.

Pushkin raised his weapon and fired a silenced round that penetrated beneath the man's chin. Blood spattered the inside of his face shield, distorting the reflections on the glass as he went limp.

Keeping him alive would have been little more than a distraction for the extraction team. And what if he survived to return to Russia? What would he be capable of? Warming a cot in some forgotten military hospital, straining the military's already disastrously tight budget?

A voice came to life over his earpiece. "Our drone has picked up a single man approximately half a kilometer down the draw leading southeast, Major. He's moving fast, but stopping periodically."

Pushkin tapped his throat mike in acknowledgment and penetrated deeper into the jungle, scanning the slopes on either side of him as they rose and steepened. With only one man accounted for, he moved slowly, feeling the heat from the fire subside along with the illumination.

It was in that twilight that he came upon an empty

metal crate with a bloody rag and other first aid implements next to it. But no body. And while it was impossible to know the girl's current status, she appeared to have been alive as recently as a few minutes ago.

The fact that Azarov was carrying her physical and emotional weight was good news but not so much so as to overcome the existence of the crate. It was now certain that he was armed, wearing full camo and boots, and had access to food and water. His mysterious companion was likely similarly equipped.

"We've picked up the lead man," came a voice over Pushkin's earpiece. "Approximately three quarters of a kilometer down the same draw. He appears to be carrying the woman."

In light of that, Pushkin felt comfortable responding verbally. "And the second man?"

"He was keeping an interval of about two hundred meters when we lost him beneath the canopy."

"Understood. And my backup?"

"Currently approaching the southeast side of the house."

Pushkin lowered the night-vision monocular attached to his helmet and gazed down the loosely defined path in front of him. It was unlikely that there would be booby traps. Azarov would be reluctant to put anything on his property that his woman or staff could stumble upon and there were too many animals deeper into the wilderness. That meant Pushkin could move fast, catching and killing the trailing man before intercepting Azarov.

He activated his throat mike. "I'm in the jungle approximately fifteen meters down the draw, preparing to chase. Have the men follow me and protect my flank. We're not leaving this place until we have Azarov's head."

Rapp kept an easy pace, taking care to avoid the endless vines, roots, and rocks on the jungle floor. No reason to push—he didn't want to run up on Azarov until he was just about to break out onto the road where they were to rendezvous with the chopper.

He looked up at a steep slope to his right and examined the mudslide that had at some point collapsed it. The strip of empty dirt was open to anyone watching from the sky but was also the first practical path he'd seen leading to high ground. After a brief hesitation, he turned up it, dropping to all fours as he scaled the loose, damp earth. At the top, he flipped down Azarov's night-vision monocular and set it to maximum magnification.

He'd almost decided that he wasn't being followed when he spotted movement approximately two hundred yards to the northwest. Whoever he was, he was moving with improbable speed over the steep, unpredictable terrain. Could it be Nikita Pushkin? The man he'd been warned about?

Rapp scanned back and forth, finally picking up two more men behind him, both moving at a less superhuman pace. Another minute of scrutiny turned up nothing more. Whether that meant his entire opposition consisted of three men, or that he was just missing the other fifty spread out under the canopy, was impossible to determine.

What he *was* sure of, though, was that the lead man was going to overtake Azarov before he could make it to the chopper. The former Russian assassin had softened considerably since his retirement and while Cara probably only weighed a buck fifteen soaking wet, that wasn't trivial under the circumstances.

Coleman's voice suddenly came to life over his earpiece. "These assholes look like they're going to gather up their casualties and back off. You want us to make their lives miserable before we bug out?"

"Negative," Rapp responded. He still had no idea what the hell Russians were doing there, but if they were willing to leave, he saw no reason to get in their way.

"Copy that. See you at the LZ."

Rapp took a pull of plastic-tasting water from the CamelBak's hose as he scanned the narrow draw he'd come down. Irene Kennedy had discovered that Maxim Krupin's cyber warriors were responsible for collapsing Costa Rica's power grid. What she hadn't been able to figure out was why the president of Russia would put himself at risk in order to harass a tiny Central American country that threatened precisely no one. After her Russia experts had come up similarly empty, her mind had turned to Grisha Azarov—the only thing in Costa Rica that Krupin might be interested in.

With no way practical way to get in touch with the Russian, she'd sent Rapp and Coleman's team for an operation that should have been easy. Extract Azarov and stash him in a safe location until the Agency could figure out what the hell was going on. As always, they'd been prepared for anything, but showing up at the same time as the Russian armada was a serious bit of bad luck.

And that bad luck seemed to be holding. The lead

man burst back into view for a moment before disappearing beneath the canopy again. Rapp had hoped the men in pursuit would turn back to join their comrades, but it was obvious now that it wasn't going to happen.

He played absently with the CamelBak hose, mentally reeling through his options. He could catch up with Azarov and significantly increase their pace by carrying Cara himself. Even at full gas, though, it was hard to do the math in a way that ended with them keeping ahead of the man chasing them. Best-case, they'd make it to the chopper and have a few additional shooters on their side when the inevitable clash came. It wasn't like they were flying a gunship, though. One stray bullet could strand them.

Rapp let out a long breath and reluctantly started crawling sideways along the steep slope, staying ten yards above the trail. Moving through the dense foliage was a constant battle, particularly when his mind was consumed with estimating the approaching man's progress.

All he needed to do was to find a practical place for an ambush—something high enough to keep him out of sight but not so high that he had a chance at missing his one chance. If that asshole got by him, it would be a tall order to catch him before he overtook Azarov.

Rapp reached out to push back a thick branch and saw a flash of movement at its base. He tried to draw his hand back but was a fraction too slow. The snake hit the side of his palm and hung there, its fangs trapped in the glove's Kevlar but not fully penetrating. He'd been wondering if they were worth the added heat and loss of dexterity, but fortunately had trusted Azarov's gear choice.

Rapp dislodged what he assumed was one of the pit vipers Claudia had warned him about and was about to kill it, but instead, threw it over the foliage and into the trail. It had been a pretty shitty day so far, but if one of the local reptiles took out Nikita Pushkin for him, it might just be salvaged.

CHAPTER 7

"**M**AJOR Pushkin. Do you copy?"

Pushkin slowed and moved off what barely passed for a trail. His breath was still controlled when he responded—the terrain was too complex to achieve a speed that would tax his drug-enhanced cardiovascular system.

"Go ahead."

"The drone has made contact with your trailing target again. He's approximately one hundred and fifty meters to the southeast. A few moments ago he took a ninety-degree turn to the west and started up a steep, open slope."

"And now?"

"We've lost him again in the canopy."

Pushkin scanned the jungle through his night-vision monocular and then took a few steps back, penetrating deeper into the vegetation. Who was this man? He'd walked knowingly into an ambush carried out by highly trained operatives and was now diverting from the path Azarov had taken with the girl. Was he concerned that he wasn't fast enough and was now trying to escape? It was possible but Pushkin's gut said no. He wasn't trying to escape. He was going for high ground.

The muffled crunch of footsteps on the jungle floor became audible to the north, followed by the sound of labored breathing. Pushkin remained utterly still as his man passed and faded back into the night. After about a minute, he stepped back onto the trail and started out again. This time at three quarter speed.

Rapp took advantage of a rare patch of rocky terrain and managed to accelerate a bit. Still, the steepness of the slope and the fact that he had to stay beneath the canopy limited him to a slow jog. He was about to vault a massive downed tree but then stopped, sighting along it. The extensive root system had ripped up the ground around it, while its trunk had crushed the vegetation where it had landed. Combined with its elevated position, the view was surprisingly unobstructed.

Instead of moving downslope to find an ambush site, he climbed, swinging around the upended roots and scanning the shallow hole they had left. No obvious snakes and no evidence of the venomous spiders that Claudia had warned him about, so he dropped into what turned out to be a good six inches of muddy water.

Not particularly comfortable for a man accustomed to fighting in the desert, but the vantage point turned out to be even better than he'd hoped. It took less than thirty seconds to pick up the lead chaser through Azarov's night-vision gear. He was staying to the bottom of the draw where intermittent runoff had cleared the ground cover to some extent.

The man was moving slower now, something that wasn't surprising as the slopes on either side steepened and made an ambush more likely. As Rapp continued to watch, though, he started to rethink his assessment. The reduced pace was easy enough to explain away, but there was more. The man he'd seen earlier seemed to float over the obstacles in the jungle floor, covering ground with an effortlessness that was more professional athlete than soldier. By contrast, the man he was tracking now seemed bent on overpowering the terrain instead of using it.

Rapp adjusted his focus to a small, unavoidable clearing well behind the lead man. The second man in line appeared after about a minute, moving at a cautious pace but with the easy grace Rapp remembered from earlier.

"Clever boy," he muttered under his breath.

His knee jerk reaction was always to handle these kinds of situations as quietly as possible. A suppressed shot to the head. A knife under the chin or snapped neck. But in this case his bias was probably wrong. The locals probably hadn't overlooked the fact that Azarov's house was throwing flames a hundred feet in the air. Stealth wasn't the word that came to mind to describe this clusterfuck of an operation.

He unslung the RPG from his shoulder and hung it on a branch within easy reach. The next task was harder—finding a comfortable position in the rocky mud puddle. Once done, he found a stale energy bar in his CamelBak and waited.

The sound of running feet below didn't materialize and instead Rapp heard a barely perceptible rustle carried by the humid air. With the help of the monocular, he was able to pick out a man inching along the edge of the trail, ten meters below and twenty to the north. His sudden caution confirmed what Rapp had already suspected. The Russians had some kind of overhead surveillance—likely a drone similar to the one Coleman would be flying if this hadn't been such a last-minute operation.

It seemed likely that he'd been spotted when he'd crawled up that open mudslide and the Russians had correctly assumed that he was setting up an ambush. The man passed by and eventually started picking up speed again, assuming he was beyond the point of immediate danger. And for the moment he was right.

Instead of chasing, Rapp concentrated on preparing the unfamiliar Russian launcher to fire. Once he was sure he understood its operation, he turned his attention north again. It wasn't long before he saw a brief flash of the trailing man, still dancing over the jungle floor but even more slowly now—he'd let his interval almost double. Undoubtedly he was on the comm confirming that his lead was still alive and planning his next move.

Rapp was getting sick of these drugged-up, thirty-something terminators whom Krupin was churning out. Azarov was bad enough. The world didn't need another one.

Sitting in a puddle and aiming through a light amplification monocular didn't exactly make for precision targeting, but that was the beauty of these types of weapons. What was it they said about horseshoes and hand grenades? Close was usually good enough.

Pushkin's body reacted even before his mind fully registered the sudden flare to the southwest. He dove right, bouncing off a tree and going limp, letting gravity pull him into a vine-tangled creek bed. Earlier, he'd identified the feature as a potential threat. Now it would likely become his savior.

The blast struck some five meters away, creating a powerful shock wave full of hot, pulverized vegetation that sprayed him through the vines. The jungle had taken the brunt of the blast, but not all of it. Pushkin lay still in the deep gouge in the earth, closing the eye served by his night-vision scope and using his naked one to scan the shadows created by the flames. Finally, he sat up and aimed his assault rifle over the edge of the depression. As expected, there was no human activity. The rocket had been fired from the last reported position of the man working with Azarov. It had been an attempt to dissuade further pursuit, not the first volley in an ambush.

Pushkin fell back against the bank, examining his bleeding side and pulling out a three-centimeter splinter of wood that had wedged between his ribs. That and the ringing in his ears appeared to be the worst of the damage, but it was enough. His situation was simple to evaluate but excruciating to accept. He had failed. He was temporarily deaf, his radio appeared to be badly damaged, and the injury to his side wasn't life threatening but was severe enough to slow him down.

He pounded his fist into the dirt until it came back bloodied. The operation had begun with everything in his favor. Now he was bleeding uselessly into the mud while his men tried to evacuate their casualties. At great cost, all he had managed to accomplish was to wound Azarov's woman—an affront that his predecessor wouldn't take lightly.

The smoke thickened to the point that it was becoming hard to breathe and Pushkin returned to the trail, reluctantly heading back the way he'd come. He'd reconnect with the man protecting his flank and regain communications. From there he could determine whether his lead was still alive and coordinate a retreat.

Then it was simply a matter of crawling back to Russia and delivering his report to its president. Azarov was still alive. And he would be seeking revenge.

Rapp slid headfirst down the slope on his stomach, finally finding what he was looking for—a sturdy tree hanging about fifteen feet above the trail. He scaled it and slithered out onto a thick horizontal branch, hugging it with one arm while holding the Beretta in the other.

He was covered in sweat and mud, wearing a helmet tailored to someone else's head, and fairly certain that some unidentified tropical creature had attached itself to his ass. It seemed impossible that his mood could get any worse until it started to rain. Hard. The branch was getting increasingly slick but he hung on as the water soaked his beard and worked its way into his mouth. Waiting and swearing under his breath.

It seemed longer than it probably really was, but he finally spotted a hazy outline through the sheets of rain. The man who had passed by earlier had heard the RPG impact and was coming to the aid of his comrades. The cover of the rain had made him far less cautious than he'd been the first time. His focus seemed to be on keeping his footing in the deepening mud and not on potential threats in the trees.

Rapp had no choice but to aim the Beretta awkwardly under the branch, but at least a few of the rounds from his burst found their target. Without the body armor his teammates had been wrapped in, the man crumpled and slid on his face through the mud.

Rapp dropped to the ground, sinking a good six inches as the runoff from the storm gained depth and force. A quick glance at his watch confirmed what he already knew. If this weather kept up, catching Azarov before he reached the LZ was going to be tight.

CHAPTER 8

THE rain had lasted only about ten minutes and the jungle floor was already beginning to dry. Despite the improved footing and improved light, Azarov had to admit to himself that it was time to stop.

His chest had constricted in a way that he'd never felt before in his years of training, operations, and athletic competition. He'd developed an ability to push beyond what his mind wanted to allow but then again he'd always done it while in peak condition.

Was it possible that at thirty-five years of age his heart was giving out?

He shifted Cara's weight to a less agonizing position and supported himself against a tree. His legs were trembling badly but he refused to sit, unsure if he'd be able to get up again. Instead, he gripped the branches and tried to gain control of his breathing.

Was she dead?

He pushed the thought from his mind and focused on the mission as he had been so meticulously trained to do. The only thing that mattered was getting her to the evacuation point. All other considerations were either irrelevant or could be dealt with later.

A distant flash turned the grays and blacks around him to dull yellow and green. He turned only his head, unwilling to expend any energy that wasn't directly related to enhancing Cara's chance of survival. Flames erupted from the canopy to the northwest and then just as quickly disappeared again.

What did it mean? Had Rapp fired the RPG? Or had he been the target? He was certain that the team that had attacked his home was Spetsnaz, but there was no way to know their strength or capabilities. Did they have drones? Helicopters? A hundred men closing from every direction? Had the CIA man been hopelessly outnumbered and finally met his end?

Azarov began coughing uncontrollably and bent forward at the waist, feeling Cara's limp body shift as he did. If Rapp was dead, his debt was paid. His team would do nothing further to help. Claudia Gould was terrified of him because of a confrontation he'd had with her late husband and he'd nearly killed Scott Coleman. He would arrive at the rendezvous location to find only a dark, empty road.

A dim flicker became visible to the south, likely a single kerosene lamp lit by someone who had been woken by the explosion. He knew the house well, having run past it hundreds of times during training. It was enough to give him a sense of his position on the trail.

His hand rose hesitantly, activating the throat mike Rapp had given him. "I'm fifteen minutes from the LZ."

The silence that ensued dragged out long enough that his mouth started to go dry. Then, finally, Claudia Gould's voice cut through the static.

"Copy that. Our chopper's inbound. ETA twelve minutes. I'll slow it down a little."

It was enough to get him stumbling forward again.

The slope turned steeply downward as it plummeted to the roadbed below. Azarov used one hand to keep Cara on his sweat-soaked shoulder and the other to grab trees in an effort to slow his descent. He slipped on a loose rock and managed to avoid falling only by intentionally colliding with a low stone outcropping.

In the moment it took him to regain his balance, a dull hiss behind him began to rise over the pounding of blood in his ears. He froze, listening as the barely audible static transformed into the familiar slap of wet leaves and breaking branches.

Someone was coming up behind him. Fast.

He moved into a dense tangle of bushes, laying Cara on the ground and gripping the MP7. The speed that his pursuer was sustaining over the difficult terrain would have normally been telling, but now it meant nothing. Rapp was one of the few men alive who could maintain it in a combat situation—something Azarov had been unlucky enough to experience personally. Unfortunately, Nikita Pushkin was one of the others.

Azarov moved to a defensible position behind a tree and aimed through the branches. When he did, though, the footfalls slowed and then disappeared into the light rustle of the breeze. It seemed impossible, but he'd been heard.

He continued to aim through the foliage, but there was nothing to see in the filtered moonlight. It was a stalemate that he couldn't afford. If he wasn't there when the chopper arrived, they'd turn back. The risks of landing and waiting would be too great.

"Mitch!" Azarov said in a harsh whisper.

The answer came a few seconds later, but instead of emanating from where the footfalls had gone silent, they came from behind him.

"Yeah."

The CIA man emerged from the jungle a moment later, crouching to again take Cara's wrist in his hand—something Azarov hadn't found the strength to do. His stomach tightened but then Rapp lifted her onto his shoulder and tossed Azarov the night-vision-equipped helmet.

"Lead us out."

Azarov started down the slope again, maintaining a better pace without Cara's weight. Rapp, who hadn't been burdened by her during his run through the jungle had no problem keeping up.

"I've rejoined Mitch and we're five minutes out," the Russian said into his radio.

"Copy," Claudia said simply. A more elaborate response wasn't necessary. The beat of chopper blades was already becoming audible.

The small sightseeing helicopter was only a few meters from the ground when they burst from the jungle and onto the poorly maintained road. Scott Coleman jumped out before the skids had fully touched down and helped put Cara inside.

"Only one of you can come! We're getting too heavy!" he shouted before jumping inside and cutting her shirt off, leaving her naked except for the stained bandage on her back. There was a blood bag hanging from the bulkhead and the former SEAL was already working to get the IV catheter into her arm.

Rapp grabbed Azarov and shouted into his ear. "You go."

"What about you? Do you need a pickup?"

"No. We need everyone at the hospital. I doubt the Russians will move on it but I'd have bet against that shit they pulled at your house, too. I'll find my own way."

CHAPTER 9

"HEY, we're here, man!"

Rapp woke, lifting a hand to shade his eyes from the lights illuminating the hospital's modest grounds. He pushed back a surfboard that had tipped onto him and climbed out of the open bed of the pickup.

"You sure you're gonna be all right?" a young American said, leaning out the driver's side window.

Rapp grabbed some cash from his pocket and shoved it in the breast pocket of the kid's shirt. "For gas. Thanks for the lift."

"No worries, man. I hope your friend's okay."

Rapp stepped back and the vehicle pulled away, leaving him standing in front of the Max Terán Valls Hospital. They were only running about half the lights to keep pressure off their generators, but the glare was still a stark contrast to the darkness Costa Rica had been plunged into.

He saw a shadow move on the roof, but didn't worry about it. Undoubtedly Charlie Wicker clutching the

Galil he favored. Joe Maslick was partly visible behind a brick planter, his eyes sweeping back and forth. Bruno McGraw and Scott Coleman were nowhere to be seen but undoubtedly close.

Rapp started along the outdoor corridor leading to the doors, finally finding Coleman in a dimly lit corner of the waiting room. He had one hand pressed to his earpiece and was nodding perceptibly.

"What's our situation?" Rapp said, grabbing a paper cup and filling it from a cooler. There were three other people in the room, but all appeared to be locals and likely had limited English.

"She's still alive. This is actually a pretty good facility and they had a surgeon on call. Our medical team is on its way from Bethesda but they're still five hours out. Claudia's melting down that she didn't have people in country when we arrived. Says it'll be her fault if Cara dies."

"Bullshit," Rapp responded. "What were the chances of us showing up at the same time as the Russians? Ten thousand to one?"

"Exactly what I told her. You can't stack the local hospitals every time you get on a plane. But it wouldn't hurt for her to hear it from you, too."

Rapp let out a long breath and drained the cup in his hand. Dealing with the emotional well-being of the people who worked for him wasn't why he got into this business. Claudia had handled logistics for this op the way she always did—flawlessly. If every eventuality could be anticipated beforehand, the world wouldn't need people like him.

"Cops?"

"Irene's been onto the ambassador and asked her to

make sure everything gets swept under the rug," Coleman said. "But so far it hasn't been necessary. We told the staff that Grisha was cleaning his gun when it went off and hit her. Pretty lame story, but he's so freaked out they seem to be buying it. I'm guessing it's been reported, but with the power outage, I think a Russian accidentally shooting his American girlfriend is pretty far down their priority list."

"With a little luck, we'll be out of here before we get anywhere near the top of it. Where is he?"

"We put him in an empty room in the back."

Rapp tossed the paper cup and started down the hallway. He got a few curious looks from the staff, who undoubtedly wondered where all these muddy, humorless foreigners had come from, but nothing more.

He finally spotted Azarov through the glass panel in a door near the end of the corridor. The Russian was standing at the foot of an empty bed, staring up at the television bolted to the wall. The volume was turned up high enough for Rapp to hear the commentary, but his Spanish was virtually nonexistent. Not that it mattered. He'd seen the shaky cell phone footage before.

It depicted an attack on a peaceful protest in Moscow a week ago. For reasons no one could figure out, a woefully inadequate security force had suddenly attacked a crowd gathered in Red Square. Because they had been so badly outnumbered by the demonstrators, the tide had quickly turned, causing the police to use deadly force. Bloodbath was too strong a word, but it wasn't far off.

No one—not even Irene Kennedy—had any idea what had happened. Maxim Krupin was a vicious dictator, but he was a calculating one. These kinds of images just didn't play in the industrialized world. If anything, they'd weaken the one thing he cared about: his grip on power.

Rapp pushed through the door and let it close behind him. Azarov's eyes briefly shifted in his direction before returning to the screen.

"It's my fault, Mitch. I might as well have shot her myself."

"How do you figure?"

"Krupin's desperate. The volatility of energy prices, breakaway states looking Westward, his political opponents and the oligarchs constantly searching for weakness in him. I let you defeat me in the Middle East and now he's desperate."

Krupin had put Azarov in charge of a plan to turn Saudi Arabia's oil producing region into a radioactive wasteland. The ensuing chaos in the energy markets would have bailed out natural resource–dependent Russia while trashing the economies of the rest of the world. Rapp had managed to stop it, leaving the aging Krupin to lead his country toward an increasingly uncertain future.

"What's that have to do with you anymore, Grisha? As near as my people can tell, all you do is surf and float around in your pool."

The television screen shifted from brutalized protesters to Krupin speaking from an outdoor stage. It was in Russian with Spanish subtitles, but the gist was clear. He was appealing to his core supporters—the ultra nationalists, the fascists, and the people old enough to remember former Soviet glory. He was calling on them to help him in his desperate fight to defeat the massive conspiracies being carried out by

the West. The imaginary plots to impoverish and sur-
round Russia, to finance political opposition and protests, to relegate their great nation to irrelevance. And
the people in the crowd were eating it up.

Azarov's eyes had gone dead, locked on the man
who used to control every aspect of his life.

"How is she?" Rapp asked.

"Living only by the grace of the machines she's connected to. I'm told that she'll need a new liver but that
there's a long list of people ahead of her to get one." He
turned away from the television and locked his dead
eyes on Rapp. "Why didn't you warn me?"

"We knew a lot of Costa Rica's power had gone
down but just assumed it was a technical issue. When
Irene got wind it was a Russian hack, we tried to get
you by email and phone. It didn't work, so I got on a
plane."

"When you came to me earlier this year and asked
for my help, we made a deal." His voice was emotion-
less, almost robotic. "I would help you take care of
Prince Musaid and in return you'd help me if enemies
from my past resurfaced."

His eyes narrowed slightly and Rapp realized that
this was what rage looked like in Azarov. He'd never
seen it before. The Russian tended to do what he did
because he calculated that it was in his best interest.
Now—maybe for the first time in his life—something
had gone wrong that he actually cared about.

"A blackout is nothing for the CIA!" Azarov
shouted, suddenly letting go of the icy exterior he was
so famous for. "You knew and didn't want to send
local assets. You didn't want to expose their identities.
And now Cara's paying the price!"

It was obvious that the Russian didn't really believe what he was saying. The number of valuable clandestine assets the CIA had tanning themselves in Costa Rica was precisely zero. But at this point, facts didn't matter.

Azarov was fast as hell, but not like before. He was exhausted from carrying Cara and had cut his training regimen by about ninety percent since retiring. Still, the impact between them lifted Rapp into the air and slammed him into the wall next to the door.

Rapp slipped an ankle around the back of Azarov's leg, pulling him in close enough that he couldn't get much momentum behind his blows. The first was an elbow coming in hard from the right. Rapp managed to get a shoulder up, causing Azarov's forearm to glance off it and absorb most of the force. What was left, though, nearly took him down.

Seeing him buckling, Azarov swung a knee up, but Rapp managed to block it and ride it away from the wall. Azarov tried to sweep his foot but Rapp put all his weight onto it, compromising the Russian's balance when his move failed.

Azarov's decades of training and the perfection they'd instilled in him were both his strength and his weakness. He could always be counted on to flawlessly execute exactly the right technique at exactly the right moment. It made him predictable.

Rapp took advantage of the Russian's split second of instability and ducked under his arm, getting behind him. He rammed a fist into the back of his head and then another into Azarov's kidneys. Under the circumstances, he would normally pull the punches, but it wasn't necessary in this case.

Azarov remained upright and shoved against the wall in front of him, trying to throw his weight back onto his opponent. Again, though, it was exactly the right move at exactly the right moment. Rapp was countering before it even started.

He sidestepped and stuck a foot out. That, combined with a firm grip on Azarov's hair, sent the Russian rolling across the tile floor.

He came to stop on his back and Rapp moved right, leaving Azarov with the worst possible line of attack. He didn't move, though. He just lay there staring at the ceiling.

"I'm just a Russian murderer, Mitch. Without the light she casts on me, I disappear." He let his head fall to the side so he could look up at Rapp. "You're responsible for your wife's death. How did you come to terms with that?"

If it had been anyone else talking, those would have been their last words. But from Azarov, it wasn't an attack. It was a serious question.

In fact, he'd disappeared into Southeast Asia and tried to forget with the help of whatever needle or pill he could find. At first it had worked, but after a time the memories learned to fight back. There was no cheating the grief, rage, and guilt. It was going to have its day no matter what you did.

"You don't want to use me as a model," he said, sliding down the wall behind him and sitting on the floor.

"Then what? What happens to me now?"

Rapp rubbed the bleeding knot rising on the back of his head. "There's a difference between us, Grisha. My wife was dead. Cara's not."

CHAPTER 10

"**G**IVE me the short version," Rapp said to the Costa Rican doctor leaning against the wall. Claudia had checked him out and given him the thumbs-up. A gifted general surgeon who had been trained in Madrid before returning to settle a few miles from where he was born.

"Are you sure it wouldn't be better if I came back in a few minutes?" he said through a Spanish accent that was easier to understand than Joe Maslick's South Carolina one.

Rapp's impact with the wall had left a gash in the back of his head that refused to stop bleeding. A local nurse was standing behind him plunging a suture needle in and out of the wound with impressive gusto.

"I've got time between now and her finishing. Go."

"Okay. The first aid your people performed was excellent but her wound is extremely serious. I was able to remove the bullet and stabilize her but that's all I can do here."

"Can we transfer her? To San José or back to the States?"

He shook his head. "I'm not even sure she's going to make it through the night. If she does, it will be a few days before we can even think of moving her."

"I heard someone say something about her liver."

"Yes. It's not salvageable. If she survives, she's going to need a transplant."

Rapp let out a long breath as the nurse finished up. It hadn't been long ago that he'd been in a similar situation with Scott Coleman. People who got too close to Azarov didn't do so well. It was a problem Rapp understood better than most.

"If you have good news, go ahead and give it directly to Grisha. If you have bad news, go through me."

His expression turned a bit confused. "Who are you? And what's your relationship to the girl?"

"Have you ever heard the saying 'shoot the messenger'?" Rapp said by way of answer.

"Of course."

"I'm going to tell you once and you're going to listen to me. If the message is that Cara's dead or dying, your life may depend on me being the one who delivers it."

Rapp's satellite phone started to ring just as he stepped through the hospital's front gates. The humidity was still oppressive, but the heat was down. Coleman had taken Joe Maslick's place behind a massive planter and was scanning the empty road in front of him. Mas had disappeared somewhere into the landscape.

It still seemed improbable that the Russians would attack the hospital in search of Azarov, but not so improbable that security wasn't a concern. If Krupin wanted him dead badly enough to take down a third of Costa Rica's power grid, there was no reason to believe he'd draw the line at shooting up a rural medical facility.

He pulled the phone from his pocket and put it to his ear. "Hello, Irene."

"How is she?"

"Alive, but it sounds like she might not stay that way. If she does, she's going to need a liver."

"I'll make some calls. In the meantime, do you have any idea what happened there? Why Maxim Krupin would go to these lengths to see Grisha dead?"

"We haven't had that conversation."

"I know it's a bad time, Mitch, but you're going to need to broach the subject. We're in crisis mode here. This isn't a completely isolated incident. There's also the recent attacks on Russian protesters and now we're seeing increasing military activity in Ukraine as well as on the borders of the Baltic states."

"You must have *some* idea what's happening."

"That's the problem. I don't. It's impossible to see Krupin's current behavior as anything but erratic and counterproductive to his own interests."

"Doesn't sound like him."

"Our thoughts exactly. The fact that he's not a man prone to rash action or self-sabotage suggests that he's working toward something. Something we're blind to but that Grisha might have some sense of."

They'd debriefed Azarov when he'd walked away from Krupin but hadn't gotten anything actionable. They could have pushed harder of course, but what was the point? Krupin was a rational actor surrounded by a massive military and nuclear arsenal. Azarov undoubtedly had some interesting dirt locked up in his brain, but it wouldn't change anything.

Now, though, the chessboard had changed. Krupin seemed to be blowing a gasket, and any residual loyalty that Azarov might have felt for the man had disappeared along with his house and Cara's liver.

"I'll talk to him," Rapp said. "And if we end up putting Cara on a plane to Bethesda, you'll have a chance for a face-to-face."

"I'll look forward to that. But in the meantime, anything at all would be helpful. I have a meeting scheduled with the president and I'd like to tell him something more than we're working on it."

"Understood."

He disconnected the call and adjusted his trajectory toward Coleman. "Where's Grisha? I looked for him inside and he's not there."

"He left."

"What do you mean, he left?"

The former SEAL shrugged. "He came out, turned right, and walked away."

"Why didn't you stop him?"

"You told me to keep the Russians out of the hospital. Not to keep them in."

Rapp reached up to grab him by the throat and have a serious conversation about how his orders should be interpreted, but managed to stop himself. His old friend was the best in the business and knew damn well what was expected. The fact that he'd decided to do only the bare minimum on this op was understandable. He'd follow specific directives, but going out of his way to protect the man who had nearly crippled him was a bridge too far.

Rapp turned and walked toward the road, dialing Kennedy as he went.

"That was faster than I thought," she said by way of greeting.

"Grisha's gone."

"What do you mean? Gone where?"

He stopped and looked out into the darkness. "I can't say for sure, but I have a pretty good guess."

CHAPTER 11

I T'S on every news station across the country!" Prime Minister Boris Utkin's voice continued to rise in pitch. "It's virtually all that's being reported on."

Krupin reached for the volume knob on the console in front of him. Utkin could screech like an old woman when his comfortable existence was disrupted.

"Try not to get hysterical, Boris."

The fog of his breath was barely visible in the glow that filled the shipping container. It had been moved into the warehouse on his orders and set up as a secure communications center. Internet was now fully functional, as was encrypted satellite phone, and various news feeds were playing out on screens attached to the steel walls. Other than that, the claustrophobic space contained little more than a scavenged chair and a desk made from a plank of wood. Not the surroundings he'd become accustomed to, but adequate. Comfort was no longer a consideration. All that mattered was security.

"Hysterical? The press has videos of my homes and

their grounds. A detailed inventory of my car collection. Photos of my personal closet, Mr. President! How is it possible these things fell into their hands?"

Of course, this conversation was little more than a game. They were both perfectly aware of how the state-run media got that information—Krupin had ordered it gathered by Utkin's security detail. A more courageous man would have simply voiced that accusation. But courage was hardly a word that anyone would use to describe the prime minister. He was a flatterer and back room dealmaker. A man who could always be counted on to protect what he had in place and pursuing more.

"I don't know how they got it," Krupin said, not bothering to hide his boredom with this contrivance. "I have no access to television and can barely hear you on this link."

"Then perhaps you should consider returning from your wilderness trip."

As far as anyone in Russia knew, he was on one of his beloved hunting expeditions.

"I hardly think I should be forced to cut short one of my few vacations because the Russian people are discovering that you like the finer things in life."

"They're not just making a fool of me, Mr. President. They're making accusations of corruption."

"Perhaps you should have thought of that before you gilded your doghouse."

There was a short pause over the line. "And yet I'm a pauper compared to you."

Krupin leaned back in the old chair and smiled at the pathetic attempt at defiance. Utkin was barely fifty years old, a good-looking sophisticate who had an ability to connect with the younger and more liberal elements in Russia. This made him a convenient political partner, but one whom Krupin kept distanced from the reins of power.

Still, Utkin wasn't entirely without ambition, nor was he without powerful allies in the government. Despite his pampered upbringing and political cowardice, he wasn't to be underestimated. If he saw an opportunity—a weakness—he would exploit it.

"A pauper when compared to me," Krupin repeated. "Perhaps. But I don't wear ten thousand dollar Italian shoes. Nor do I fly in British pop stars to entertain the guests at my parties. My focus is on more substantive matters."

"Ah yes, the glory of Mother Russia," Utkin said. "But I don't see how a corruption investigation into your prime minister enhances your position. You speak with great skill to people nostalgic for Soviet domination, but those memories are fading. The country is in and out of recession and slowly being surrounded by Western forces. The potential that NATO will offer Ukraine membership is quite high, something that will nearly complete the encirclement of our country under your leadership. Is now the time for a scandal in your administration?"

Krupin felt his anger rise at the man's tone and with it he felt the first twinges of pain at the base of his skull. "I think you're right, Boris. It may benefit all of us if you were to leave the country for a time. A goodwill tour. You can use your magnificent political skills to allay the world's concerns over the protests that I've been forced to put down. And in your absence I will—reluctantly—return to Moscow and deal with the media's coverage of your lifestyle."

"Leave Russia?" he stammered. "It'll look like I'm trying to run from the issue. We—"

"I'll have my people set up an itinerary," Krupin interrupted. "You'll depart in three days."

"Three days? How long am I to be gone?"

The flashing in Krupin's peripheral vision obscured the rusted walls of the shipping container. He suddenly realized that he couldn't remember what Utkin had said.

"Repeat that, you cut out."

"When will I return?"

"When your presence is required."

Krupin disconnected the call and closed his eyes, blotting out everything but the empty white light at the edges of his eyelids. Azarov would be dead by now and Utkin would soon be making empty speeches in Europe. There were still internal and external threats that needed to be dealt with, but those had been two of the most pressing. His next actions would be dictated by the contents of the medical report waiting for him just outside the steel walls surrounding him.

He sat silently for a few minutes before stepping from the container and locking it behind him. The only guard he'd allowed inside the warehouse snapped to attention and Krupin indicated for him to stay where he was.

At this point, the risks posed by additional interior security outweighed the benefits. The man he was striding away from was one of his most trusted and understood that neither he nor the medical personnel would communicate with the outside world until all this was over. The more substantial security force outside knew Krupin was there, but had no idea for what reason. They would assume that this was some top secret military or intelligence site and would have no reason to speculate further.

He took a circuitous route through the ruined interior of the building, heading for a still intact row of offices against the building's east wall. Dr. Fedkin would be waiting for him there while his people remained confined in a makeshift dormitory on the other side of the structure.

The door was closed and Krupin stopped in front of it, smoothing his suit jacket. After the hours spent in a hospital gown, it had the comforting sensation of armor. For a similar reason, he'd set the location for this meeting as far from the medical tent as the structure would allow. Surrounded by his machines and needles, Fedkin was a godlike creature. Without them, he was nothing. Just another meaningless technician.

Krupin opened the door without knocking, causing Fedkin to leap from his chair. The physician had done what he could to clean the room, pushing years of debris to one side and righting the furniture in a way that suggested less a practical need for order than compulsion.

"Mr. President. How are you feeling?"

"Quite well, thank you, Doctor."

The lie that rolled so easily from Krupin's tongue was apparently less convincing than it should have been. Fedkin looked straight into his face, probing eyes that Krupin suspected were slightly glassy and unfocused. Not enough that most people would notice but, somewhat dangerously, Fedkin wasn't most people.

"Are you in pain?"

"A bit of a headache," Krupin admitted. "It's nothing."

"I have medications that might help."

"I said it's nothing," Krupin repeated, lowering himself onto the stool that Fedkin had abandoned. "I understand your tests are complete. What do they show?"

The physician didn't immediately answer, instead licking his lips and reaching for an iPad lying on the table. It was unlikely that he needed it to recall the results, but instead saw it as a piece of his own armor. Krupin intercepted the man's hand, denying him that shred of protection. "I have to be on a plane to Moscow in a matter of hours, Doctor."

The physician withdrew almost to the door. "We've confirmed the size and position of the abnormality in your brain. Based on that, it's now almost certain that it's the cause of the issues you've reported."

"Is it cancerous?" Krupin said with practiced calm.

"At your request, we performed only minimally invasive tests. In order to be *absolutely* certain we'd have to perform a biopsy which would involve drilling a small hole in your—"

"Out of the question!" Krupin shouted, and then waved a hand around the room. "All this and you still have no information? It makes me begin to wonder what use you are."

The threat was intentionally vague, but Fedkin was smart enough to pick up on it.

"Based on our tests, I would say that there is at least a ninety-five percent chance that it is cancer, sir."

Krupin froze. Despite all the pain and other symptoms, he'd been completely unprepared to hear those words. The air seemed stuck in his chest. When he could breathe again he opened his mouth to speak but then paused, waiting until he was sure his voice would be steady.

"What does this mean?"

"That we need to start aggressive treatment immediately. The tumor is in a delicate area to access so I need to consult a surgeon, but it's possible that removal of at least part of the growth will be indicated. Then we'll follow up with a number of therapies including chemotherapy and radiation. Either way, we need to transfer you to a hospital that is—"

"What would the side effects of those treatments be?"

"If we deem the surgery necessary, obviously, there would be recovery time. How long would depend on—"

"What about the drugs and radiation?"

"Again, it depends on exactly what protocols we decide will be most effective and, of course, on your specific physiology. I won't lie to you, Mr. President. Even if everything goes well, it's going to be a difficult time."

"Time . . ." Krupin said numbly. "How much? How much time?"

"The worst of it should be over in three to four months. Maybe less."

His mind filled with images of him lying helpless in a hospital bed, head shaven, naked and unconscious. Three to four months? He couldn't afford a single *hour* of weakness. Even an unsubstantiated rumor of it could provide his enemies the opening they needed to depose him.

"Prognosis?" he said numbly.

"Your condition is quite serious—"

"We've already established that, Doctor."

Again, he hesitated. "If we move quickly, I believe you have many high-quality years ahead of you."

"Quality years," Krupin mumbled, wanting to stand but lacking the strength to do so. He controlled the largest country in the world. A nuclear arsenal that could destroy the planet. The lives of a hundred and fifty million people. And yet he was being spoken to like an old woman wasting away in a nursing home.

"Sir, you—"

"And if I do nothing?" he interrupted.

The aging physician seemed confused. "The symptoms you're experiencing will worsen until you're debilitated. I doubt you'd last six months."

Krupin's mind turned from his many enemies to his allies. In light of what he was being told, could they be counted on? How long before they started seeing him as part of Russia's past instead of its future? In their desperation to position themselves for what came next, would they turn on him?

"Perhaps you could temporarily step down and allow the prime minister to handle your duties," Fedkin said, trying to fill the silence.

The sound of his voice returned Krupin to the present. He'd spent his entire life beset by enemies. He'd fought wars. Influenced foreign elections. Amassed the greatest personal fortune in modern history. Survival and victory were simple questions of strength, cunning, and will.

He finally stood, meeting Fedkin's eye. "I'll need a detailed report on your proposed treatment protocols, their success rates, and their side effects. After I've reviewed that, we'll discuss which procedures will be acceptable and which won't."

"Of course. I'll start on it as soon as I get back to Moscow. I need to consult—"

"You won't be going back to Moscow, Doctor. You'll write the report here and any consultations or outside communications will have to be approved beforehand by me. Further, all the procedures will be done here."

"Here? That's not possible, sir. I—"

"It *is* possible, Doctor. Along with your report, I'll expect a list of equipment and additional personnel that you'll need."

Fedkin didn't seem to fully grasp what he was being told. "I have other patients, Mr. President. A family. And your procedures will be periodic. I can't just stay in this place until the full course of your treatment is completed."

"Let me be clear, Doctor. You're not just staying here until my treatment is done. You're staying here until I'm cured. If I'm harmed or killed by your therapies or if I die of my illness, you and your people will *never* leave this place."

CHAPTER 12

"JUST us, sir?"

President Joshua Alexander flashed Kennedy the smile that had charmed millions and indicated toward one of the Oval Office's sofas. She sat and reached for a cup of tea as he settled into a chair opposite.

More and more, their meetings were private affairs. As the country divided itself along ideological lines, the White House became increasingly prone to leaks. With her, Alexander could speak his mind without fear of his words being replayed on the news that evening. And she could do the same, though generally less colorfully.

In this case, though, it would have been advantageous to have his national security advisor and the chairman of the Joint Chiefs in attendance. Unfortunately, both were in Europe taking part in a massive NATO exercise centered on Poland.

"You're on my list, Irene. You promised me Krupin would take it down a notch if I didn't crucify him for the shit he pulled in Saudi Arabia. That was a nuclear attack on a sovereign nation and we had enough to lay in sanctions like the world's never seen. But we didn't. And now here we are."

"I don't recall promising anything, Mr. President."

"Of course, not. You probably said something like 'forgoing immediate retaliation could have advantages that might slightly outweigh the drawbacks. Over time. Maybe.' You may be the master of the hedge, but I'm the president of the United States. So I get to hear whatever I want."

"One of the benefits of the office?"

"This office has benefits?"

She smiled and took a sip of her tea. "What he tried to do in Saudi Arabia was an act of desperation, Mr. President. Krupin bet a lot on the success of that operation, and when Mitch stopped him, it weakened his grip on power. I'm still convinced that it wasn't the time to press our advantage."

"Looking at it from the opposite perspective, I might say that pressing your advantage when your opponent's weak and desperate is how you win."

Alexander had been a talented quarterback in college, and while he normally held an admirably nuanced worldview, some of the hyper-competitive athlete remained.

"Unless your opponent is guarding the end zone with nuclear weapons."

"I'm impressed." His smile looked a bit forced this time. "I would have bet that you wouldn't know an end zone from a hole in the ground."

"I try to stay informed on a wide variety of subjects."

"Yeah? Then tell me what the hell's going on in Russia."

It was both the question that she was here to answer and the question she most dreaded.

"We don't know."

The silence between them stretched out for a few seconds before the president broke it. "That's it? You don't know?"

"Our analysts and our people on the ground are working around the clock but haven't been able find anything unusual happening in Russia. It's a country in a slow, but relatively steady, decline. Certainly, Krupin is losing some support as his older constituency dies off, but it's not really a threat to his position. Obviously, the Europeans are making noises about accepting Ukraine into NATO, but considering the Russian presence in that country and your opposition, it's more posturing than—"

"But this isn't business as usual, Irene. The crackdowns on protesters, the attack on Azarov, the sudden jailing of his main rival. And now I'm hearing that his prime minister is going on an impromptu goodwill tour with no known agenda. Chaos isn't how Krupin operates. He hates it."

She nodded in agreement. "You called this meeting, so I'm a little embarrassed to ask this but . . ." Her voice faded.

"What?"

"Well, sir, while your experience is different than Krupin's, you're a very good politician who's managed to maintain power in a large, complex country."

"Hold on now. You're telling me you came here to listen to what *I* think?"

"I did."

He sank back into his chair and looked through the windows at the softening evening sun. "As the number of his supporters declines, he needs to increase the intensity of support from the ones he has left. Because of that, there's no way he can let Ukraine go to NATO. His entire persona is as a tough guy who scares the shit out of the rest of the world. He's not capable of making Russia stronger, so he has to make everyone else weaker. I'm sorry to say that it's human nature. People don't want their lives improved. They want the lives of people they hate made worse."

"So that explains the troop movement we've been seeing," Kennedy said. "But what about the crackdown on the protest in Red Square?"

"I can't explain that. Sure, his hardcore supporters would get a thrill from seeing the police bust a bunch of young liberal heads, but the blowback—both internal and external—would hit hard. The Krupin I know is a calculator. His gift is his ability to keep his incredibly complicated corruption machine humming along smoothly. He doesn't care about Russia or his people or his family and friends. All he cares about is staying in power. And it's hard to blame him. My retirement's going to be about getting paid half a million dollars to make a speech and playing too much golf. He's made too many enemies for that. More likely he'll end up with a bullet in the head or in jail."

"What about Prime Minister Utkin? Odd to send him on a tour so abruptly. We're concerned it could be a distraction. Maybe he's reinforcing his position in Ukraine for more than show. It's possible he's building a force that could move north and take control of the country."

Alexander frowned. "My gut says no. This isn't about Russia. It's about Utkin. Krupin's allowed the press to go after him and now he's going to make it look like he's turning tail. The question is, why? Sure, Utkin is more popular with young people, but nowhere near powerful enough to challenge Krupin. The only real threat to Krupin is time, Irene. He's not going to be able to hold on to that country forever and he doesn't seem to have an exit strategy. Ideally, he'd pass the crown to a relative and they'd protect him. But he isn't a king. He's a dictator in a country that's hard to keep your arms around."

"So we end where we started," Kennedy said. "With erratic behavior from the least erratic man alive."

"I hate to even suggest this because it's so terrifying, but could he be losing his mind?"

"It's something we've considered but it seems too sudden and too . . ." Her voice trailed off for a moment. "Coordinated."

He nodded and focused on the windows again. "I despise the Russians. At least the Iranians and Chinese are pressing their countries' agendas. Russia's just a drunk loser sitting in a bar at two a.m. looking for a fight. What I've learned over my life is that you don't provoke people like that. You patronize them. Russia's economy is smaller than New York's. And sure they're spending themselves into the poorhouse to build a big scary military but it's still only a fraction of the size of ours. The Russians don't need land—they live in the largest country in the world. What they want is respect."

"But we've given Krupin that, sir. And for reasons we don't understand, it doesn't seem to be enough." She picked up her cup and warmed her hands with it. "Maybe we should have pushed back against him. Even if we got bloody doing it."

CHAPTER 13

MAXIM Krupin stared through the limousine's window, squinting against the sun despite dark sunglasses that Fedkin suggested might help stave off attacks. Yet another equivocation from a man who seemed unable—or unwilling—to make statements that carried any force.

The afternoon light bleached the rocky coastline and flared off the Black Sea, providing a setting of such serenity that it seemed to mock him. He'd been returning to Moscow in the back of a cargo plane when he'd ordered the pilot to divert. It was dangerous to delay his reappearance at the Kremlin but there was little choice now. Despite the overwhelming resources he'd been provided, Nikita Pushkin had failed in the most spectacular way possible.

Not only had Azarov escaped, but his woman was badly—perhaps terminally—wounded. Initial reports were that the unidentified Americans who had intervened were now standing watch over the hospital treating her. Azarov was likely there, too, but it was impossible to confirm. And irrelevant. Whether it was today, tomorrow, or next week, he would be coming. He would take his revenge or die trying.

For the first time in his life, Krupin had to acknowledge that instead of being the master of the events taking place around him, he was at their mercy. His diagnosis and upcoming treatment schedule. Azarov's survival. The inexplicable American meddling. NATO's continued overtures toward Ukraine. Any one of those issues would have been difficult, but combined they were beyond anyone's capacity to handle. Particularly if that capacity was diminished.

He needed an ally. A formidable one.

Unfortunately, those were hard to come by in his world. Men strong enough to protect him in a temporary situation like this one or indeed in a lengthy retirement were too dangerous. Conversely, controllable, less ambitious men would be too weak to hold the country together and shield him from his enemies.

There was one exception, though. General Andrei Sokolov.

Krupin had first met the young Soviet army officer during his KGB days and their friendship had endured as they'd risen through the ranks. When Krupin became president, one of his first acts had been to promote Sokolov to head the Russian armed forces.

He was an unusually brilliant man who, in another time and place, might have become a researcher or preeminent university professor. In what field, though, one could only speculate. His interests seemed to shift almost daily. Physics, technology, history, psychology. All were equally valuable pursuits in his eyes. He'd even become obsessed with chess for a time, finally challenging the top player in Russia to a match. He'd been soundly defeated, of course, but in three times the number of moves as had been predicted.

It was Sokolov who had initially developed the idea of applying Krupin's internal disinformation methods to the rest of the world. At the time, it had seemed unlikely that a fledging technology called the Internet would ever provide a sufficient platform. But Krupin had indulged him with money and resources as he always did. And now that ridiculous little program started in a shed outside of Omsk had been used to undermine the European Union, destabilize Ukraine and the Baltics, and influence the political tide in America.

The concept of power was shockingly nebulous in the modern world. There had been a time when it flowed from surging economies, political alliances, and military hardware. Now it sprang magically from the keyboards of children.

Krupin shifted in his seat at a sudden sharp pain in his side. So many times before he'd attributed this kind of discomfort to age, but now it was accompanied by a surge of adrenaline. Had the cancer spread? Was it invading his body, siphoning off the strength and cunning that made him who he was?

A modern structure built into a hill came into view and the vague sense of panic eased. It was the only home in sight, and the nearest town of any importance was more than fifteen kilometers away. While the world's intelligence agencies were fully aware who lived there, no one in the region was. Sokolov never left the grounds of his opulent prison. He had no desire to. His role in leading Mother Russia had ended long ago and he was content to live in the company of his books.

As the limousine turned up the winding drive, Krupin realized that he hadn't communicated with Sokolov in almost five years. He had the man watched, of course, but it was an afterthought—more to ensure that he didn't fall into enemy hands than anything else.

It was an incredible waste to have such a man languishing in banishment like this, but there were few alternatives When it had been discovered that he had ordered the torture and execution of civilians in Georgia, the world demanded that he be tried for war crimes. Krupin refused, but the outcry made it impossible to keep him as the head of the armed forces or even to shift him to a less prominent role in the government.

And so this had been the compromise that had been struck. The most gifted and loyal man he had ever known would be relegated to obscurity and eventually buried in this Black Sea wilderness.

The building was constructed entirely of white stone block, a sprawling structure that Sokolov had personally designed to hint tastefully at Russia's past. Krupin's limousine paralleled a narrow pool looking over the Black Sea, finally coming to a stop at the main entrance.

He stepped out, waving his men back and starting toward the door. No one knew he was coming and Sokolov had no security. His only human contact was with an old local woman who cooked and cleaned for him.

It was she who answered, eyes widening in shock at finding the president of Russia on her doorstep. It was doubtful that she had any idea whom she worked for. In all likelihood, she assumed that Sokolov was just another minor oligarch attempting to live out his retirement in peace.

"Is Andrei at home?" Krupin said, already knowing the answer. He was always at home.

"Yes . . ." she stammered. "Please. Come in. I'll . . . I'll tell him you're here."

He accepted the invitation, stepping into the towering dome of an entryway as she scurried off to find her master. Of course, Krupin had paid for all of it. He'd also offered to provide young, beautiful women whose skills went well beyond housekeeping. Sokolov always refused, maintaining that they would distract him from his study and contemplation.

The former general appeared at the end of the hallway, moving at a surprisingly effortless jog. His tan slacks and starched white shirt still had a noticeable military precision, as did his close-cropped hair. He was four years Krupin's junior, with a less bulky physique maintained in an elaborate gym at the back of the house.

"Mr. President, why didn't you call? I would have prepared something."

There was no fear evident, despite the possible ramifications of a surprise visit such as this one. If Krupin decided that the former general's continued existence was no longer in Mother Russia's best interest, Sokolov would accept that assessment without question.

"Andrei," Krupin said, embracing the man. "It's been too long."

"Not long enough," Sokolov disagreed as they pulled away. "You shouldn't be here, sir. The Americans watch everything."

"Of course. Is there somewhere we can talk?"

Sokolov led him to a modest office in the east wing of the house. It was almost identical to the one he'd insisted on at the Kremlin so many years ago— windowless and lined with books on every subject under the sun. The volumes on his desk suggested that his interests were currently centered on the Roman Empire under Trajan.

On the rear wall was a map of western Russia and the countries bordering it. Sokolov had inserted red pins representing the Russian military presence on the borders of Latvia, Lithuania, and Estonia, as well as troops stationed in Ukraine. Blue pins depicted NATO forces, including surprisingly accurate information on the ongoing exercises in Poland. Undoubtedly the intelligence had been gleaned from news reports in English, Russian, and German, the languages he'd spoken when forced into retirement. Perhaps there were more now.

"Tea, Mr. President? Coffee?"

"Something stronger, I think," Krupin said, rearranging a few of the pins to create a more accurate picture. Sokolov froze for a moment, calculating the strategic ramification of the changes before continuing to a disused bar.

Krupin tossed back the vodka he was given while Sokolov pretended to sip at his. He'd never been much of a drinker. Dulling that magnificent mind apparently made him uncomfortable.

"You think you can intimidate NATO into refusing to accept Ukraine as a member?" Sokolov asked, glancing at the modified map again.

"You don't?"

"It's hardly my place to comment."

"It's always your place, Andrei. I greatly regret that I had to remove you. Your absence has been keenly felt."

"I put you in that position," Sokolov said. "It was my failure alone and I'm grateful for the generous way in which you handled the situation. I deserved less."

Krupin laughed. "Always the dutiful soldier. In fact, you deserved more than I could give. Do you know that in some American polls, I'm more popular than their president? Me, the man dedicated to destroying the Western alliance! That and everything else began with your vision, Andrei."

"Human nature can't be denied, sir. The world is so complex that the average person is no longer able to understand it. In the face of that, they can be counted on to retreat into tribalism. Nationalism. People need something to hate to reinforce their own identities. And it's the internal threats—the people they interact with every day—whom they hate and fear most."

"An astute observation made at just the right moment in history," Krupin said, taking a seat behind Sokolov's desk. It was the only chair and his exhaustion was starting to drag at him.

"But you've taken it far beyond anything I ever

imagined, Maxim. And you fanned the flames of chaos in Syria quite effectively. The refugee crisis you created has widened the cracks in Europe."

"But is it enough?"

"NATO spending is significant," Sokolov said. "But largely wasted creating theatrical displays instead of pursuing real readiness. Britain has left the EU behind, Poland, Turkey, and Hungary are moving back toward authoritarianism. And America is pulling back from its leadership role in the world with its democracy in turmoil. In many ways, the West is as weak as it's been in modern history."

He fell silent and Krupin watched as the former general ran a finger absently around the rim of his still full glass.

"I know you too well, Andrei. You're flattering me before dropping the other shoe."

"No," the man said. "I'm long retired. Let's drink and talk about old times."

"You don't like to drink."

Sokolov stared at him through a silence that wouldn't last long. He was a respectful man but one who found it difficult to hide the force of his intellect. The wait was even shorter than Krupin anticipated.

"The meddling in U.S. politics has been successful in weakening them but it's made them more volatile than docile. Further, now that they're aware of our disinformation campaign, they'll learn to combat it. And while the Europeans are suffering from divisions, their nationalist politicians are struggling to win elections. The rise of Russia and the United States turning in on itself has given Europe a sense of interdependence and purpose. Their reliance on America's strength has always given them the luxury of being weak. They're now realizing that time has passed."

"And what will the Europeans do with their new-found resolve, Andrei?"

"I don't know. But I wouldn't dismiss the possibility that they'll accept Ukraine into NATO. And if that's the case, Georgia and perhaps even Finland won't be far behind. Our buffers will be lost and with them our strategic flexibility. With a resurgent European military alliance posted a few hundred kilometers from Moscow, the Russian bear will be declawed."

Krupin reached for the bottle on the desk and poured himself another drink. His head was clear and pain free, making his time with Doctor Fedkin seem like a fevered dream. At that moment, he could almost make himself believe that the tests were a lie and Fedkin was working for the Americans. That the attacks had been a temporary affliction that would never reappear.

"I spoke out of turn," Sokolov said, misinterpreting the lengthening silence between them. "It's still a weakness of mine. I hope—"

"No," Krupin said. "You said what needed to be said. And now I'll do the same."

"Sir?"

"I'm sick, Andrei. Cancer."

"What?" Sokolov said, looking genuinely stunned. "What kind of cancer?"

"It's in my brain. They're talking about surgery and then starting a course of chemotherapy, radiation . . ." His voice faded.

"Prognosis?"

Krupin forced a smile. "It will take more than cancer to kill me, Andrei. But I'll be weakened during the treatment. Significantly so."

"Are you suffering from symptoms now?"

"At this moment? No. But I have episodes. Debilitating headaches. Blurred vision . . ." He paused. It was against his every instinct, but he had to disclose everything. "As well as brief periods of confusion."

Sokolov began to pace across the office. There was no guile in the man's expression, no indication of ambition. He had been presented with a problem and was now calculating a solution.

"Who knows about this?" he said finally.

"A handful of medical personnel know I'm ill. I haven't told them about the mental confusion, though it's possible they can extrapolate it from their examinations. One loyal guard knows I'm having medical tests done, but not the type or results."

"Where are these people?"

"I'm holding them in a hidden facility outside of Zhigansk with no way to contact the outside world."

Sokolov nodded thoughtfully. "I assume that you need to start treatment immediately?"

"That's what I'm told."

"Have you looked into unconventional protocols? I've read a great deal about them. Stem cells, viral ther—"

"My doctor is considering all possibilities, but he discounts many as too experimental, ineffective, or dangerous."

"Doctors!" Sokolov said in disgust. "They're nothing more than technicians. What do they know of science?"

"Whatever course of treatment I decide on, I'll need

the help of someone capable of operating the political machine I've built. And more important, someone whose loyalty I don't question."

Sokolov stopped pacing, looking genuinely confused. "Me?"

"You're the only one, Andrei. The only one I've ever been able to trust."

CHAPTER 14

RAPP disconnected one of the Gulfstream G550's last remaining passenger seats and shoved it through the open door. The plush leather cushioned its fall, leaving it to bounce across the dimly lit tarmac. He jumped out after it and handled one end of the gurney containing Cara Hansen. She wasn't particularly heavy, but the IVs and ventilator equipment made three people necessary.

A military ambulance was already backing toward him, its taillights turning her pale skin a deep pink. She'd taken a turn for the worse a couple days ago, forcing him to transport her in a CIA jet he'd virtually gutted to make room for medical gear and personnel. Now they were in a race to get her to a waiting surgical team at Walter Reed.

The ambulance crew loaded her into their vehicle under the supervision of a navy doctor who had cared for her on the flight. A few moments later, they were speeding up the runway in the swirling blue and red glare of their light bar.

It was déjà vu all over again. Not long ago it had been Scott Coleman clinging to life on a similar gurney. For some reason, seeing this girl he barely knew fighting for her life hit him almost as hard. Maybe it was because she hadn't chosen a life in harm's way like Coleman had. Or maybe it was because when he looked into Cara's face, it wasn't just her he saw.

Rapp grabbed his duffel and started for an Audi Q5 parked about fifty yards away. Claudia Gould didn't get out to greet him as she normally would, so he tossed his bag through the open back window and into Anna's empty booster seat.

He climbed in and Claudia accelerated away without a word. The night air flowing through his open window wasn't as heavy as it had been in Costa Rica. The feel of it on his skin and the familiar scent of city was comforting in a way that took him a moment to identify.

It was good to be home.

"How is she?" Claudia said finally.

"I don't know. They say the next twenty-four hours will tell. But they've been saying that for days."

"I should have had a medical team there," she said. "It's my fault."

"I wouldn't have authorized it. You can't plan for luck this bad, Claudia."

"We could have—"

"We could have done *nothing*. You play the percentages in this game. If you try to plan for every lightning strike and shark attack you just end up paralyzed. I'm not telling you anything you don't know here."

When she didn't respond, he leaned the seat back and closed his eyes. There hadn't been much time for sleep over the last few days. Now, though, Cara was inside U.S. borders and would soon be tucked away in Bethesda under an alias. Krupin might have gone nuts, but not nuts enough to assault an American military hospital to try to finish off a girl who probably couldn't find Russia on a map. She was safe and, just as important, someone else's responsibility. For now at least.

"What's happening in Costa Rica?" he said, breaking the silence in the car. There wouldn't be even a hint of a relationship between them until they got home. In an effort to make this situation work, they'd decided to completely separate personal from business. Coleman put even money on it working. Rapp saw the odds as somewhat worse.

"The Russians cleaned up pretty well and the local authorities are stretched to the breaking point by the power outage," she said switching to the French she was more comfortable with. "For now, they're satisfied that the fire is out at Grisha's house and Cara's left the country." She glanced over at him. "Did you blow someone up in the jungle?"

"I hope so," Rapp said, though he was less than confident. As much as he'd like to believe that he'd rammed that RPG right down Nikita Pushkin's throat, he doubted he was that lucky. "Where do we stand on finding Grisha?"

"Irene and I agree with you that he's on his way to Russia, but we're not sure what he's planning on doing there when he arrives. I know he's good, but taking on Maxim Krupin by himself? No one's that good."

Rapp looked out the window as they started across the Potomac. She was right. At this point, all Azarov could do was create a mess or get himself killed. Neither outcome was in the best interests of the United States. At least not yet.

"Russia's a big place, Claudia."

"I know. We're working on it. Grisha's operating in a way he never has before. He's angry, he's alone, and by now Krupin will know he survived and assume he's coming. That means he can't use any of his normal methods or contacts. Basically, we're in a race against the Russians to find him."

Rapp rolled his head left and watched the city lights wash across her face. "That's fine. As long as we win."

They fell silent for almost a minute before Claudia spoke again. "Are we done with business?"

"Yeah."

She leaned over and kissed him, keeping one eye on the road. "I'm glad you didn't get shot or squeezed by a python."

He grinned. "You didn't tell me about the pythons."

"Or the scorpions with giant fangs. I didn't want to scare you."

"Where's Anna?"

"I left her with the Nashes. We can just walk over and get her in the morning."

Mike and Maggie Nash had recently finished building a home in Rapp's subdivision. The security benefits of being surrounded by loyal shooters turned out to be significantly overshadowed by the benefits of built-in childcare. The Nashes had a brood large and chaotic enough that it could take them two days to even notice Anna had moved in with them.

"We can swing by on the way home if you want," Rapp said.

She shook her head. "What I need tonight is a bottle of good wine and some adult time."

CHAPTER 15

ANDREI Sokolov opened the safe that had been delivered two days before, taking comfort in the substantial weight of the door. As one of the men responsible for the early subversion of digital communications, he had a strong preference for paper and steel.

The file in his hands was more than a centimeter thick and contained everything known about Maxim Krupin's medical condition. Despite having spent the last twenty-four hours poring over both it and a mountain of supplemental material, he found himself staring uselessly down at it.

The news was worse than even his most pessimistic expectation. Ironically, Krupin had been betrayed by the strength and toughness that had allowed him to rise to power. He'd ignored the worsening symptoms, allowing the tumor to wind its tendrils through his brain. At this stage, surgery would be dangerous and potentially debilitating, while the standard radiation and drug therapies would be of questionable efficacy.

He replaced the file, selecting three others before locking the safe again.

The world was becoming unmoored. America was retreating while China pressed its advantage. Western Europe was teetering between implosion and a new-found sense of interdependence. North Korea was creating instability that could lead to a war that would be certain to turn both nuclear and biological. New technologies were driving the world away from fossil fuels and toward a future of safe, cheap renewables.

It was a time of historic danger, but also one of opportunity that Maxim Krupin should have been able to exploit. But now the best-case scenario was a significant reduction in his ability to lead his country through the obstacles ahead. The worst-case was that his treatments would fail and he would leave behind a power vacuum that would tear Russia apart.

Sokolov sat behind his desk and poured himself a shot of vodka, downing it in one swallow. The unfamiliar burn flared in his throat for the first time in more than twenty years. If not today, when?

In some ways, the logistics necessary for Krupin's illness were even more complicated than the administration of war. While the external threats to him were significant, it was the internal threats that were most dire. Any hint of weakness would be identified and capitalized upon. He was a public figure in constant contact with the public, world leaders, and staff. Even with full control of the media, the symptoms of his illness would have to be carefully hidden, his absences during treatment would have to be explained, and any side effects would have to be anticipated. It was vital that Krupin continue to exude the strength, confidence, and brilliance that made him so feared and admired.

Given the opportunity, Krupin's traitorous political opposition would bring down everything he'd accomplished. They'd turn the country inward, slashing military and intelligence budgets, bribing Russia's youth with consumer goods and freedom. Russia would fade into irrelevance—a sparsely populated landmass with a languishing military capability and inconsequential economy. No longer would the Europeans tremble and the American presidents genuflect. No longer would countries in crisis seek their patronage. No longer would they be included at the table of the world's great powers. The last vestiges of the glory of the Soviet Union would disappear forever.

Sokolov opened a file in front of him and was faced with a young Grisha Azarov in a Spetsnaz uniform. He shuffled through the hastily prepared background information but found it too incomplete to be useful. Not particularly surprising of a man who had lived his life as a ghost in the president's employ.

The spotty intelligence was of little importance. Sokolov was intimately familiar with the man and his gifts. Much more interesting was Krupin's relationship with him. Why had he attacked this man? Why was he more frightened by a retired assassin than he was by Prime Minister Utkin? And what of the imprisoned Roman Pasternak and the nationwide demonstrations in support of him?

Was this an example of the periodic confusion that he'd described? The venting of pointless rage at a man who had abandoned and defied him? Subconscious jealousy of his youth and vitality? How had a puppet

master like Maxim Krupin concluded that there was
profit in moving against—and ultimately failing to
kill—Grisha Azarov?

Sokolov shuffled to the back of the file in order to
scan the most recent update. The photo he found had
been taken by Russian intelligence only a few days before. It depicted two still officially unidentified men
standing in the courtyard of a hospital in Costa Rica.
The one in shadow wore his hair long enough to hang
across his bearded face. The other, a blond man with a
military style haircut, was in full view.

He didn't need Russia's intelligence service to tell
him that the latter was Scott Coleman. And if that was
Coleman, it was likely that the man in shadow was
none other than Mitch Rapp.

He ran a hand over the photo, trying to imagine a
scenario that would have brought the CIA man there.
The details of his relationship with Azarov were hazy
but it was clear that a relationship existed. If he was
there with a combat team, it seemed certain that the
Agency had discovered Russia's involvement in sabo-
taging Costa Rica's power grid, as well as the fact that
it had been done in support of the effort to eliminate
Azarov.

And with this trivial operation, Krupin had created a number of non-trivial problems. The first was
obvious. Grisha Azarov, one of the most effective killers in the world, would be seeking revenge. Second, it
was feasible that Mitch Rapp, undoubtedly *the* most
effective killer in the world, would help him. And, finally, Krupin had added needlessly to the impression
that his behavior had become erratic—something that
would not be lost on the formidable Irene Kennedy.

There was a knock on his door and he closed the file. "Yes."

An impeccable young colonel recommended by Krupin entered with yet another file in his hand.

"We have some initial information on the medical matters you were interested in, General. Would you like to see them as they're received or—"

"As they're received," Sokolov said, tapping an empty spot on his desk. "And bring my car around. We'll be leaving for Moscow within the hour."

"Of course," he said, sliding the folders into position. "Is that all, sir?"

Sokolov nodded and waited for the man to disappear before shuffling through the recently gathered intelligence. He stopped at a printout of a cranial MRI, holding it up to examine a tumor growing in the brain of a woman being treated in Voronezh. It was similar in size and position to Krupin's, so he made a note on the file that action should be taken. The second folder contained information that was more theoretical—a collection of articles on various experimental and unconventional cancer therapies being carried out in other parts of the world. It was too much to go through before he left, but he would have enough time to digest it before his arrival in Moscow.

Sokolov walked to a mirror that he'd hung that morning. After smoothing a few imaginary wrinkles from his uniform, he turned his attention to the insignia designating him Marshal of the Russian Federation. As the second man in history to hold such a rank, he was keenly aware of its weight and of the challenges ahead.

He finally exited the office, starting down the hallway to the unfamiliar click of dress shoes against tile. His housekeeper appeared from the dining room, her weathered face registering shock at seeing him in a military uniform.

"Are you . . . Are you leaving?"

Her confusion was understandable. She had spent the better part of a decade caring for the needs of a man she'd come to know as a reclusive scholar. There had been no excursions into the outside world, no visitors, no communiqués. And now that reality had been turned upside down.

"I am."

"When will you return?"

"Soon."

"And President Krupin? Will he be coming again?"

Sokolov smiled. "Why don't you make me some tea for my drive?"

He watched her turn and limp toward the kitchen. Oskana was almost eighty years old and completely alone. Her only son had been killed in Afghanistan and her husband had been gone for almost as long.

She'd served him well, but she'd seen Krupin and there was no telling what she had overheard or surmised since then.

He opened the polished flap on his holster and pulled the pistol from it. The round hit her in the back of the head and she collapsed, having felt nothing. She would be missed by no one but him.

Sokolov was gratified to see his new assistant rush in with his own weapon drawn. He'd been chosen for his efficiency and intellectual capacity but it appeared that he had a backbone as well.

Sokolov started toward the door as the young colonel stared down at the fallen woman.

"Take care of this," he said as he passed.

"Of course, General. Don't think anything more about it."

cal theater. Inside a number of masked and gowned medical personnel were huddled around an operating table. On it was a middle-aged woman whose extremities were strapped down and whose head was secured in a metal frame. She shifted her eyes desperately from one side to the other, but couldn't otherwise move.

She was one of a number of people throughout Russia who had been identified as having health issues similar to Krupin's. They'd been offered inclusion in fictitious medical trials sold as having a high probability of saving their lives. The reality was somewhat different. While they were indeed involved in critical medical studies, the goal was to subject them to experimental drugs and procedures too dangerous to test on Krupin. This particular participant had a brain tumor similar in size and position to the president's.

One of the nurses spotted Sokolov through the glass and pointed him out to the man standing next to her. He was one of the top brain surgeons in the country, an arrogant little man of questionable politics and loyalties. At this point, he knew nothing of Krupin's situation or presence at the facility. His only task was to attempt to remove as much of the tumor from this meaningless woman's brain as possible. Potential dangers and benefits needed to be assessed and her recovery process had to be recorded in case it should become necessary for Krupin to submit to a similar procedure.

Judging by his gait as he rushed toward the glass doors leading from the theater, it wasn't a role he was happy about.

CHAPTER 16

ANDREI Sokolov stepped over the cable powering temporary overhead lighting and continued down a freshly painted hallway. The steel and concrete warehouse was no longer open in layout nor filled with refuse. On the contrary, it had been transformed into a state-of-the-art medical facility and temporary command center befitting Russia's leader.

He passed beneath a laborer securing gilt molding along the ceiling and then turned down a corridor still in the drywall phase. Based on his most recent briefing, there were only three workmen left—all cleared for top secret projects and all toiling outside the building's nerve center. They knew nothing of the structure's connection to Krupin or even where they were in Russia. And after being paid, they would have no reason to care.

The corridor evolved into something that felt more like a hospital than he would have liked, but the demands of hygiene had to be met. At its end, the plastic tent was gone, replaced with an elaborate glass surgi-

"Are you in charge?" he said, coming to a stop less than a meter away and examining Sokolov's uniform with open contempt.

"I am."

"What is all this? I was taken from my house in the middle of the night and told there was an emergency. Then I was put on a plane and brought here. I've not been allowed to communicate with my family and I have patients in St. Petersburg who—"

"Then complete your assignment here," Sokolov said, making an effort to ignore the lack of respect. The members of Russia's intellectual class were becoming unbearably arrogant, believing with increasing certainty that the state existed to serve them and not the other way around.

"Complete my assignment here?" he said, pointing at the terrified subject on the other side of the glass. "You mean operate on that woman?"

"I do."

"Then obviously you know nothing about brain tumors or surgery."

"On the contrary. I understand that she has a malignant tumor that will be extremely difficult to remove surgically."

"The chances of surgery significantly improving her prognosis are extremely low," he said in an exasperated, pedantic tone. "The dangers of a surgical intervention by far outweigh any—"

"And yet, surgery is exactly what you're going to do," Sokolov said, cutting him off.

The surgeon just stared at him, looking a bit dazed. "I will not."

Sokolov nodded, keeping his voice even. "Either

you operate or I'll tape your eyes open and make you watch me dismember your children."

The man took a hesitant step back, trying to process what he'd just heard. And in that brief lull, Sokolov decided he'd had enough. He slapped the man across the face hard enough to leave him on all fours, staring down at the blood draining from his nose.

"I want to be very clear, Doctor. What I just said to you isn't shorthand for some as yet undefined punishment. I will handcuff you to a chair in that operating theater, tape your eyes open, and make you watch while I use your instruments to cut your family apart. Am I understood?"

The physician didn't answer, instead reached up to try to stop the flow of blood. Sokolov used a meticulously polished boot to shove him onto his back before stepping down on his throat. "That wasn't a rhetorical question, Doctor."

"Yes!" he choked out. "Yes, I understand."

Sokolov started back down the corridor. "Then I look forward to reading your report on the procedure."

Sokolov picked up his pace, noting that he was running almost two minutes behind schedule. While undoubtedly productive, his meeting with the brain surgeon had taken longer than anticipated.

He approached a split in the corridor and struggled to recall which led to Krupin's private rooms. But then he saw the president standing in the middle of the hallway on the right.

"Sir! What are you doing out here? The area's not secure yet."

Krupin didn't react, instead continuing to stare silently through the glass wall in front of him. On the other side was an infirmary filled with people secured to beds. Most were sedated but a few were undergoing experiments that precluded it. Those few stared back at them through the window, a mix of rage, confusion, and fear playing across their faces. Slightly more concerning was the obvious recognition, but in the end it mattered little. None would leave that place alive.

"Who are they?" Krupin said finally.

"Patients suffering from ailments similar to yours and a few healthy prisoners who'll assist us with more general medical inquiries," Sokolov responded. "The man in the back with the tattoos, for instance, is undergoing an aggressive experimental chemotherapy that may have the ability to attack your tumor. He's about your age and like you quite powerful—still one of the most feared men in the Black Dolphin Prison. We'll use him to help understand the side effects should it be deemed safe and effective enough to administer to you. We'll use the information to adjust your schedule and duties."

Again, Krupin didn't respond, squinting into the glare coming off the glass. He seemed to be struggling to focus and, more concerning, to process what he'd just heard. Whether his confusion was physical or emotional was difficult to know. What *was* evident, though, was that the agelessness he'd always exuded was gone. He looked drained. Small.

"I'm sorry I wasn't there to meet you when you arrived, sir. It—"

"I didn't bring you back to be my welcoming committee."

Sokolov put a hand on his old friend's back and guided him down the hall. "Did everything go well? I imagine it was a taxing day."

Krupin had spent the last twenty-four hours moving from one wilderness camp to another by helicopter. Attended by a film crew and makeup people, he'd been documented hunting, white water rafting, and using an open fire to cook the game he'd ostensibly killed. The photos and video would be parceled out to state media as his treatments were carried out—providing an excuse for his absence from the Kremlin and depicting him at his most robust.

The white walls and linoleum floors gave way to the red carpet and rich paneling that had been inadvisable in the medical area. Lighting was now provided by chandeliers, and paintings of pivotal moments in Russian history adorned the walls.

"You've accomplished a great deal in the days you've been back," Krupin observed absently.

"I doubt you'll be here long, but I wanted you to be comfortable," Sokolov said, opening a door at the end of the corridor. The room it led to was just over ten meters square, consisting of a bedroom and living area furnished with Russian antiques.

The president's personal doctor, Eduard Fedkin, was waiting by an immense leather chair with an IV cart set up at its side. The custom cocktail of poisons it contained would be the first phase in Krupin's treatment.

"Are you ready, sir?" Fedkin said. "If so, please take off your suit jacket and we can get started."

Krupin laid it carefully across a table and sat, finally meeting Sokolov's eye as Fedkin tied a rubber band around his biceps. "What news of Azarov?"

It was improbable that this issue was at the forefront of Krupin's mind at that moment. More likely he needed to be distracted from what was happening to him.

"Our people believe he's currently in Maryland," Sokolov said. In truth, this was no more than speculation based on the location of Cara Hansen. There was no reliable information at all as to Azarov's whereabouts.

"And the people who helped him?"

The intelligence report identifying Scott Coleman hadn't yet been signed off on, so once again Sokolov demurred. "Likely mercenaries he had on retainer. The loss of electricity would have made him suspicious. You trained him to be paranoid and he learned his lesson well."

"Tarben Chkalov?"

The aging oligarch was debatably the second most powerful man in all of Russia. His personal fortune was in excess of ten billion U.S. dollars and his largely legitimate business empire stretched across the globe. He was equally well respected by his contemporaries, Russian government officials, criminal organizations, and foreign governments. Most dangerous, though was Chkalov's uncanny gift for feeling the winds of change before others did. If anyone could ferret out what was happening and take advantage, it was this decrepit old man.

"He's at his home outside of St. Petersburg, sir. Major Pushkin is completing plans for dealing with the situation. He seems quite anxious to prove himself after what happened in Costa Rica."

Krupin winced as the IV catheter entered his arm. "Azarov isn't in Maryland."

"Sir?"

"I know him, Andrei. I made him. And I can tell you, he's coming for me."

"I'll look into the progress of the investigation personally, but remember that he's just one man. A talented killer? Absolutely. But there's no way he can find you here and it would take an army to penetrate the security at the Kremlin. Certainly, Azarov would be aware of this."

Krupin fixed his eyes on a blank section of wall as the chemicals began to flow into him. "You're dismissed, Andrei. Get out."

CHAPTER 17

GRISHA Azarov was forced to slow his vehicle to a crawl when it finally started to rain. The Soviet era Škoda had been provided by Finnish smugglers he'd kept on retainer for the better part of a decade. It was comfortingly nondescript but otherwise not particularly confidence inspiring. The windshield wipers did little more than smear the glass, dispersing the glow from headlights that barely projected past the front bumper. Somewhere out there, though, past that dim halo, was Maxim Krupin.

Azarov had spent years in the man's employ, but it had taken only the first six months to discover that Krupin was a backstabbing monster whose life was ruled by fear and who believed that loyalty was a one-way street. In light of that realization, Azarov had funneled hundreds of thousands of euros to criminal organizations that kept multiple escape routes open to him. And while he'd cut those ties some time ago, the leader of one of those organizations had agreed to help him. The choice Azarov had presented him—earn a generous fee or die along with his family, friends, and everyone he'd ever met—turned out to be an easy one.

The clouds to the north parted for a moment, allowing the moonlight to illuminate a lake to his left and the empty expanse in every other direction. He accelerated again, trying to use the winding road to fend off the emotions threatening to overwhelm him. Was she dead? Alive? Had she woken to find him gone? To discover that she was alone again like she had been for so long?

He rolled down the window and let the cold, wet air fill the car. There was no way for him to answer those questions. He was a hunted man—not only by Krupin, but now undoubtedly by the Americans. Rapp could be trusted to make sure Cara was cared for, but his debt of honor ended there. Irene Kennedy was a cautious woman who would not want a wild card running loose in Russia. In the end, Rapp's loyalty was to her and to his country.

The darkness closed in again and he glanced at the GPS he'd been provided. Sixteen hours to Moscow.

And then what?

He'd never felt this way—or to some extent *any* way—before. Even in childhood, he had a strange sensation of detachment from the world. More an observer than a participant. He stood in the background, weighing alternatives, gathering data, and making carefully vetted assumptions. Only when satisfied that he understood all variables did he act on even the most trivial matters.

Now, though, he'd escaped Costa Rica with the very much non-trivial purpose of assassinating a man many had deemed the most powerful in the world.

No data gathered, no alternatives weighed, and no assumptions made. Overall, less thought than he'd put into the surfboard he'd had shaped for Cara's birthday.

Sixteen hours from now, what was he going to do? Storm the Kremlin with a pistol? No. He had to put the girl out of his mind and become the person he'd once been. But was that even possible anymore? It was surprising how distant that man felt. Surprising to find himself wondering what Grisha Azarov would do in this situation.

A cinder block and clapboard gas station emerged from the darkness, prompting him to pull in. He tried one of the pumps, idly musing about exotic poisons and how far an electrical current would travel along the puddles in Red Square. Things that the old Grisha Azarov would have already examined from every angle. The new Azarov, though, was more concerned with how unaccustomed to the cold he'd become and how far he felt from home.

The pump didn't work. Undoubtedly, he needed to pay first but no one seemed willing to brave the rain to take his money. He started for the dimly lit building, pondering Krupin's estranged family and the men close to him. Could they be the key to access? Their loyalty was based more on fear and patronage than any real kinship with the president or his rule. Unfortunately, the amount of fear and patronage Krupin could bring to bear was considerable.

The window was open to the left of the door and Azarov made note of it, glancing instinctively behind him. On a night like this, it was unusual but not outrageously so. The scent of mold was noticeable flowing from the building and it was likely that the cashier didn't want to be closed up inside. Still, Azarov's hand moved a bit closer to his weapon.

Shelves were plentiful and filled with staples needed by the few people who called this rural area home. Hearing the tinny audio of a Russian game show, he headed for it, finally spotting two booted feet propped next to a cash register.

"Could you turn on the pump?" he said over the sound of the television sitting on the counter.

"No gas. But the canned tuna's on sale."

Azarov ripped the pistol from his waistband at the American voice, holding it in front of him as he slowly drifted right.

Mitch Rapp was leaned back in an old office chair, seemingly intent on the television screen. His left hand was out of sight in his lap and was almost certainly holding the Glock 19 he favored. Worse, the open window behind Azarov offered a clean shot for a sniper outside. Almost certainly Charlie Wicker—one of the best in the business.

Despite his dire situation Azarov found it impossible to focus on his survival. "Is she alive?"

"Last I heard."

The gun wavered for a moment at the impact of those words.

"How did you find me?"

"Claudia's husband used those same smugglers to get into Russia when he killed Nestor Mushket."

"That was Louis Gould? I don't think our intelligence service ever determined who carried out that hit."

Rapp's hand began to rise and the Russian tensed, but he was only holding Russia's version of a Twinkie.

"So what's the plan," Rapp said, unwrapping it. "Just walk into the Kremlin and shoot the president?"

"I don't know."

The CIA man dropped his feet to the floor and turned in the chair to face him. "What did you do to Krupin to make him send that team?"

"Nothing. I swear to you," Azarov said, shoving his gun back in his pants. "What could possibly motivate me to anger the man? And if I did, why would I be completely unprepared when he retaliated?"

Rapp's expression softened a bit. "I have to admit that I was a little surprised they caught you standing in the window."

"I know Krupin, Mitch. He wasn't happy when I left him, but that's not enough to make him take action—particularly one this overt. I was the instrument he used in these kinds of situations and I can tell you that he used me sparingly. Only when an objective threat needed to be removed or a message needed to be sent. My death serves neither purpose."

Rapp didn't respond, instead biting the end off the Twinkie and chewing thoughtfully.

"So are you here to help me or kill me, Mitch?"

"Help you charge the Kremlin? I think I'll pass."

"With both of us and the CIA's resources, we might have a chance at killing him."

"Do you have people you trust in Russia?"

"No. Krupin made sure of that. He gave me every-thing and built my reputation into something that bordered on the supernatural. Anyone who knows who I am either hates me or fears me."

"Then this is starting to look like kind of a one-sided deal, isn't it? I gather the intel, provide backup, and run the risk of massive blowback on me and the Agency while you . . . What? Take the shot?"

"What are you asking me to do, Mitch? Walk away? You did that once. You showed mercy to the man who killed your wife. And, as I recall, that decision ended in the death of your mentor."

Rapp stood and leaned over the counter. His left hand was now behind a stack of cigarette cartons. Was that where the Glock was hidden? Azarov suddenly regretted speaking so plainly. He was in a box, and even if he wasn't, he wouldn't be able to draw his pistol before Rapp could reach his own.

Instead of making a move, though, Rapp took a step back. "What I'm asking you to do is help me figure out what's caused Krupin to go off the rails. If it's not a problem for the United States, I go home and you have whatever we've learned to help you with your vendetta. You kill Krupin or more likely he kills you and none of it makes any difference to me or the Agency."

"And if his issues *are* a problem for America?"

"Then you'll have me and Irene behind you, which I think you'll agree improves your chances of getting back to Cara in one piece." He paused for a moment. "If that's what you really want."

"What do you mean if it's what I want?"

"You lied to her about who you are and if you survive you're going to have to come clean on that. My wife knew who I was from the beginning. She was free to choose. Cara wasn't."

Azarov tensed, but Rapp didn't acknowledge it, instead coming out from behind the counter and heading for the door. Once again, he'd been wrong about the Glock. It hadn't been behind the cigarettes.

The Russian didn't immediately follow, instead thinking about what Rapp had said and finding more truth in it than he would have liked. When he finally walked back out into the rain, Rapp was gassing up the Škoda.

"What's our first move, Grisha?"

"Tarben Chkalov, I think."

"The fast food restaurant guy? He's still alive?"

"Old for certain, but by far still the most powerful oligarch in the country. He despises disruption and has sources everywhere. If anyone can explain Krupin's recent behavior, it will be him."

"Then let's go," Rapp said, replacing the pump and slipping into the vehicle's cramped passenger seat.

Azarov scanned the dark tree line. "What about your men?"

"What do you mean?" Rapp said, reaching for the broken door handle. "What men?"

CHAPTER 18

ANDREI Sokolov hesitated in the doorway of the opulent bathroom, hovering silently. Laid out on the marble floor was Maxim Krupin. His bespoke slacks had been replaced by a pair of sweatpants and his thick torso was bare and pale. He was asleep, or perhaps unconscious, with his head propped against the base of the toilet. A streak of vomit had dried across his cheek beneath sunken eyes.

Sokolov had hoped that the president would be one of the lucky patients whose chemotherapy reaction would be mild. In the end, though, it wasn't a matter of strength or will. It was just the luck of genetics and how a person's unique body chemistry reacted to the powerful toxins.

It was difficult for him to see the president like this and impossible to allow anyone else similar access. Maxim Krupin didn't just represent Russia. In many ways, he *was* Russia. Is this how the proud country of their fathers was to end? Weakened and rotting from within?

Sokolov began to worry about the man's stillness and crouched beside him. It took a few moments but Krupin's eyes finally fluttered opened.

"I'm dying, Andrei."

Sokolov lifted him to his feet and helped him to the bed in the adjoining room. "You're not dying, Maxim. It's just the side effects of the therapy."

Another half-truth. When pressed, Fedkin had put Krupin's chance of lasting a year at less than forty percent. And based on Sokolov's own assessment, even that number might be optimistic. Fedkin was thinking only about the cancer. There were many other threats that were just as grave.

"Can the brain tumor be removed, Andrei?"

He considered lying, but dismissed the thought after only a few seconds. While some things were better kept from Krupin, others had to be presented at face value. The president had to know what was coming in order to participate in planning.

"Removing all of it is impossible, but removing the bulk of it may not be. Having said that, the subject we operated on who had a similar tumor suffered complications."

Krupin raised himself on his pillows, squinting in Sokolov's direction. "What kind of complications?"

"Localized paralysis and some reduction in mental function."

"Where is she? I want to see her."

In fact, she was still in the infirmary under examination, but would be euthanized later that day. The condition she'd been left in wasn't relevant because Krupin would never find himself in that state. Sokolov would personally put a bullet in his head and the country would be told he died in a hunting accident. Perhaps attacked by the bear he was stalking. A glorious battle before succumbing to the only symbol of Russia more potent than him.

"I'm sorry, sir. She was of no further use, so she's gone."

Krupin sank back in the pillows, his eyes going out of focus. Sokolov was going to lower the lights to allow him to sleep but then thought better of it. He didn't need sleep. He needed a reminder of who he was.

"The video team has finished editing your outdoor footage," he said, picking up a remote and aiming it at a television hanging on the wall.

Images of Krupin sitting in camp by a lake, on horseback, shirtless and armed with a hunting rifle, began revolving across the screen. They seemed to have the desired effect, prompting him to sit up a little straighter against the headboard.

"When you're feeling strong enough, sir, we have matters we need to discuss."

"Now," Krupin said.

"It isn't necessary to—"

"If action needs to be taken, I'll take it. As I always have."

"Of course," Sokolov said, relieved to see the reemergence of the man he'd known for so long. "The first order of business is your treatment. Your reaction to the chemotherapy notwithstanding, we still need to start radiation and other complementary therapies immediately. It could exacerbate your discomfort, but it'd be unwise to wait. In the meantime, we'll be exploring unconventional therapies and techniques to make a possible future surgery as advantageous as possible."

"Surgery and unconventional therapies," Krupin repeated in a voice that had lost the force it once had. "I wonder if your scheming has the power to change anything, Andrei. If I don't submit to these treatments, I die. If I allow them to be performed I'll be weakened to the point that my enemies will fall on me like a pack of rabid dogs."

It was a realistic analysis. Loyalty at the Kremlin was directly correlated to power and constantly realigning with every perceived shift in it.

Absent the trappings of democracy or royal blood to legitimize succession, Russia's next ruler might be ordained in a violent and lengthy power struggle. Anyone with designs on Krupin's crown would have begun quietly laying the groundwork some time ago. They would not only be looking for opportunity, they would be in a position to seize it.

"It will be a difficult time," Sokolov admitted.

Krupin met his gaze for a moment before turning away. Normally, he'd be calculating every move, every consequence. Prioritizing actions, identifying threats, and formulating strategies. None of those things read in his eyes, though. The only thing visible was exhaustion combined with something Sokolov had never seen in the man before. Fear.

"I assume you have a recommendation?" Krupin asked finally.

"I do, sir."

"Let's hear it then."

"Your violent reaction to the chemotherapy and the potential for surgery in the future is going to degrade your ability to personally interact with the people, media, and government officials. In light of that, we need a distraction. Something that will pull the country together and make you look strong, among other things."

"You're speaking of Ukraine."

Sokolov shook his head. "A few days ago, I would have been. But your treatment is going to be much longer and more debilitating than we'd anticipated. I fear that a move in Ukraine wouldn't be sufficient to keep your enemies at bay."

He used the remote to replace the images of Krupin in the wilderness with a map of their country's western border. Current Russian troop concentrations were shown on the borders of Latvia, Estonia, and Lithuania where extensive exercises were taking place. Russia's military presence in southern Ukraine and Crimea was also depicted, including updates on their increasing concentration at the northern edge of the territory they controlled.

Krupin pointed with a shaking finger. "We've continued to move troops to Ukraine in a way that's obvious to the West. We've also stepped up the propaganda campaign aimed at convincing the ethnic Russian community that they're the subject of organized violence and discrimination. The hope is that if we move to take control of the rest of the country they'll join us. More important, though, it would give us a pretense for the invasion like in Crimea. We could say to the international community that military action was forced on us to protect our Russian brothers."

"I've familiarized myself with your preparations and

I think victory is all but assured," Sokolov said. "Your hackers have excellent penetration into Ukraine's systems and would be able to shut down a significant portion of their communications and power grid. Resistance would likely be light and the West has only a token contingent of advisors there right now."

"And yet you sound unimpressed," Krupin said.

"Certainly if the alternative is Ukraine joining NATO, then this would be a reasonable course of action. Even a membership vote would be a huge humiliation. I fear that your enemies would use it against you and that in your current condition they could inflict damage."

"Then we should attack now, yes? Move north, secure the country and set up Iskander missile batteries. Make it clear that we consider Ukraine Russian territory and that any move to take it back will be met with nuclear retaliation against Western Europe."

Sokolov examined the map, examining every detail in the ensuing silence. Finally, he turned back to the ailing politician. "My fear is that it would only be a glancing blow, sir. This isn't a defeat of NATO— Ukraine isn't a member. What it may accomplish, though, is to pull Western Europe together against a shared threat. Worse, it could cause America to renew its wavering commitment to the alliance. Finally, it seems a foregone conclusion that the West would increase their economic sanctions, further harming our economy and further turning away Russia's youth."

Krupin seemed a bit confused, having counted on Sokolov above all people to support military action. He swung his feet off the bed and walked unsteadily across the room, putting on a bathrobe and lowering himself into a chair along the far wall.

"You've become timid, Andrei. Perhaps I should have expected it. So many years in that dacha, away from Moscow and your military post. Have I made a mistake in choosing you for this position?"

"You misunderstand me, Mr. President."

"Do I?"

Sokolov widened the map view to include Poland and parts of Western Europe. "As I said, prior to knowing the full ramifications of your illness, the Ukraine gambit might have been a workable strategy. Now, though, I think we need to consider something more bold."

"More bold?" Krupin said, clearly relieved to find that the head of his military wasn't recommending retreat before the battle had even begun. "Explain."

"I believe that we find ourselves in a very rare position, Maxim. We're in the right place at the right time in history with the right tools at hand."

"To do what?"

"To annihilate NATO."

Krupin didn't respond, so he continued. "We've already spoken of this. The French are focused on internal terrorism, but they'll turn outward again when they get it under control. The British are off balance now because of Brexit, but it's inevitable that the divisions will heal and they'll remain aligned closely with Europe. Germany continues to be reluctant to project power but their fear of their own history is fading with the new generation and there are indications that they're becoming more amenable to the expansion of their military. Turkey, NATO's second largest army, is distracted by Syria and the Kurds, as well as its on-going transformation into a dictatorship. And, finally, the United States has turned inward and is consumed with fighting over political divisions we helped create but that won't last."

The Russian president just stared at him. The sound of the antique clock in the corner seemed impossibly loud as the seconds ticked by. Sokolov hadn't mentioned the other factor in their favor—Krupin's cancer. While he'd been a bold and aggressive leader who had strained against international norms, his instinct for self-preservation had demanded that he stay within them. Was that still the case? Sokolov had just described an environment that could lead either to a quick and decisive victory over the West or to World War III. Krupin would be well within his purview to have him dragged outside and shot.

He didn't, though. Instead, his eyes moved to the map on the wall. "I'm still listening."

Sokolov forced himself to remain calm as the weight of the moment became unbearable. "I propose that we use the troop buildup in Ukraine as a feint and attack NATO in the Baltic states."

"You're suggesting a simultaneous attack on Latvia, Lithuania, and Estonia?"

"We have a substantial number of well-drilled troops doing exercises on their borders. With some quiet reinforcement, we'd have a sufficient force to overrun all three countries before NATO could react."

"We'd be at war with America and the whole of Europe," Krupin said, sounding a bit awed at the prospect of it.

"Another benefit of the scale of this operation—

beyond its ability to create a nationalist wave inside of Russia—is its ability to isolate you. We could use the pretense of assassins and potential American drone attacks to move you to an undisclosed location."

Krupin's mind had been slowed by his treatment but not so much that he couldn't grasp the potential of his general's plan. "It's hard to see how the Western alliance wouldn't be torn completely apart. The Europeans wouldn't risk retaliation against their major cities to retake the Baltics and the Americans are in no mood to expend blood and treasure on countries their citizens have never heard of."

"That's my analysis, too, sir. NATO would have no choice but to pull back to Poland and set up a defensive position. But what would it mean at that point? Having failed to prevent an attack on three of its members and having no ability to retake the territory, NATO would be exposed as the paper tiger it is. Why would Ukraine or Georgia risk angering you to join a meaningless military alliance? Why would its existing members—particularly America, which doesn't need Europe to help defend it—maintain their membership? It's possible that we won't just be looking at the dissolution of NATO, but also the shattering of the European Union."

Krupin actually managed a weak smile, the dried vomit still clinging to his cheek. "Can you imagine the humiliation, Andrei? Even if NATO didn't dissolve they would have to revoke the membership of the Baltic states or agree to give us a vote in their council."

Sokolov actually laughed out loud at that, and at the expression on Krupin's face. His agreement was a foregone conclusion at this point. Krupin understood that the geopolitical complexities he'd faced his entire life were meaningless in light of his illness. He had nothing to lose by this war and everything to gain. Even if he eventually succumbed to cancer, Sokolov would make sure he was remembered as the man who dared to return Russia to greatness.

CHAPTER 19

RAPP opened his eyes, shading them against the sunlight in order to see the dashboard clock. It was one of the few things in the Škoda that still worked. "Shouldn't we be there by now?"

"We are," Azarov responded. "In fact, we've been on Chkalov's land for almost a half an hour."

The area was wooded and undulating, encompassing thousands of acres starting about a hundred miles outside of St. Petersburg. According to the CIA's dossier, Tarben Chkalov had built a modest house on the land just a few years after the fall of the Soviet Union. Since then it had been added to many times over, growing into something hovering in the fifty-thousand-square-foot range.

Reliable floor plans were hard to come by because of the haphazard construction method and because the Agency had never been all that concerned about the man. His net worth was in the eight-billion-dollar range, barely getting him into the top fifteen wealthiest men in Russia. His holdings were unusually international for an oligarch and diversified more along his lines of interest than a quest to maximize profits. He appeared to maintain the organized crime connections that had given him his start under the Soviets, but only peripherally.

"How old is this guy, Grisha? We don't have anything solid."

"I don't think anyone knows exactly. Over ninety, I would imagine."

"You've met him?"

"On two occasions."

"Is he still all there?"

"Mentally you mean? Very much so."

"What else?"

"Well, while he's not the wealthiest oligarch, he's unquestionably the most powerful."

"Why?"

"First, his businesses have largely moved outside of Russia."

"So he's not competing against the others."

The Russian nodded. "He's also a very reasonable and courageous man. Most important, though, he's extremely likable. It's a combination that makes him uniformly revered by the others."

In the distance, a gate came into view. It looked more like a border crossing than an entrance to an estate, though. Two guard shacks flanked a hand-actuated barrier. Dense, strategically placed trees stretched out on either side, taking on the role of a fence.

Rapp hadn't seen any reason to get fancy. Calling ahead hadn't been viable because of Krupin's control over communications, and slipping in under the cover of darkness would have been unnecessarily risky. Better to just do away with the melodrama and drop by.

"So security is five guards total?" Rapp confirmed as they approached.

"Unless something's changed. All former top operators from various countries and all very loyal. Also he has a lot of dogs."

"What do you mean by a lot?"

"Twenty? Maybe more. I'm not sure they're actually trained as attack animals, though. He may just enjoy their company."

One man appeared from each guardhouse to watch the Škoda's approach. Both had assault rifles across their chests and both had their hands on them. They didn't seem to be gripping them very tightly, though.

Azarov made a move for his gun but Rapp grabbed his hand and put it back on the wheel. "If we've been on his land for a half hour, they know we're coming and they know who we are. Relax."

Not surprisingly, Azarov was struggling to take that advice. He was one of the best killers in the world, but his ops had always been laid out for him in nauseating detail. The man despised improvisation and unknowns.

They eased to a stop at the gate and a man who looked to be from India leaned down toward the open driver's window. "Good afternoon, Colonel Azarov. Mr. Chkalov is expecting you. This road will take you straight to the front entrance."

The other man lifted the gate and Azarov pulled through, keeping an eye on the rearview mirror. "I don't mean to state the obvious, but that was too easy."

"Seems like."

"They didn't even look for weapons."

"Nope."

He pointed to the house beginning to blot out the horizon. It was an odd combination of French chateau, the Kremlin, and the Taj Mahal. Azarov was most interested in the erratic roofline. "They could fire down from there. An easy shot with a rocket launcher."

"They could. But it'd make a hell of a mess of Chkalov's lawn."

There was still no sign of contrails when they stepped out beneath a broad portico.

A British man in his early sixties met them on the steps. "Please come in. Can I take your jackets?"

Both refused, not wanting to make their shoulder holsters any more obvious than they already were.

"Coffee? Tea?" the man said, leading them up a grand staircase that led from the entryway.

"We're fine," Rapp said.

Azarov was scanning the space below them while still trying to keep one eye on the man in front. There was no question that Chkalov could be leading them into an ambush, but Rapp doubted it. If the old man wanted to make a move, he wasn't going to do it in a house filled with enough original artwork to make Claudia faint.

Their guide stopped at a nondescript doorway and motioned them inside. Azarov went through first, leaving Rapp to guard his flank.

"Colonel!" the man waiting for them said in accented English. "I'm so sorry to hear about what happened to Cara. I trust you don't think I'd have anything to do with something so sordid."

Chkalov was mostly bald, with a few wisps of gray

hair floating around gnarled ears. The unnatural curve in his back threw his head forward and down, but it didn't seem to slow him down. The most remarkable thing about him was his eyes—an intense blue, still full of curiosity and youthful enthusiasm.

"No," Azarov said. "I know who's to blame."

With that out of the way, Chkalov turned his attention to his other guest. "Mitch Rapp. You'll excuse me, but I have to admit to being a bit of a fan. Colonel Azarov is a very competent soldier, but in a cold, boring way. You, though. You're different."

He stopped a couple of feet from Rapp, examining him as though he was one of the paintings in his entry hall. "Do you have your weapon?"

Rapp nodded. "You should probably talk to your security people about that."

He dismissed the thought with a wave of an arthritic hand. "If it had been just the Colonel, I'd have defended myself. But both of you? Why sacrifice men who've been loyal to me when the outcome is inevitable?"

Azarov was right. The guy was impossible not to like.

Chkalov pointed to the slight bulge in Rapp's jacket. "May I?"

Rapp pulled the weapon from its holster and handed it to the man.

"Is this the one you've always had? I mean, since you switched from the Beretta?"

Chkalov wasn't kidding. He really was a fan. "No. A few have gotten away from me over the years."

"I'm surprised it's stock. I was expecting something more exotic—like the one the Colonel carries."

Rapp just shrugged.

"Of *course* it's stock," Chkalov said after a few seconds. "Why wouldn't it be? It's not the gun. It's the man behind the gun!"

He aimed at a marble bust near the wall and sighted along it, smiling broadly. "Did you know that I once met your mentor, Stan Hurley? Is it true that before he died, he used his teeth to rip out Louis Gould's throat?"

"Yeah. It's true."

Chkalov returned the Glock and limped back to his desk to sit. "A fitting death for a warrior. But you didn't come to talk about that. You came to talk about Maxim."

"He's run off the rails," Rapp said. "Why?"

"I have no idea."

"I didn't come here to play games, Tarben."

"I think it's clear that I know who you are and what you're capable of. I haven't lived this long by misunderstanding the situations I find myself in."

"Then tell me what I want to know and we'll walk out of here."

The man's brow furrowed and he fixed his blue eyes on Rapp. "Maxim Krupin is a destructive sociopath. But I and the others tolerate him because he shares our passion for political stability. But now that stability has disappeared. Why? Clearly he feels threatened— by NATO's overtures to Ukraine, by younger politicians, by the performance of the Russian economy. Even by Grisha here."

"But how's that any different than his situation a month ago?"

"Exactly! I don't know. All these situations are controllable. I see no evidence that he's losing his grip on power."

"So there's nothing you can tell me that I can use."

"I didn't say that. Something you probably don't know is that Maxim recently tapped Andrei Sokolov to lead the military."

"The war criminal?"

Chkalov nodded. "Andrei is a dangerous man prone to fevered visions of Russia's past glory. He's the only man Maxim trusts, though I've often wondered if that trust is well placed."

"What about you? Would he see you as a threat?"

The dull thud of chopper blades became audible, still distant enough to be more a vibration in Rapp's chest than a sound. Chkalov's hearing aids apparently picked it up, too. "That may be your answer, Mitch."

Rapp moved to the window as Azarov took a position next to the partially open door.

The view was onto the expansive back lawn which dead ended into trees after about two hundred yards. The sky had turned a deep blue but appeared to be empty. "I don't see anything. It must be coming in from another direction."

"The hall's clear," Azarov said.

"Is this common?" Rapp asked turning back to the old man.

"Uninvited helicopters flying over my property? No."

Chkalov pulled a cigar from his desk drawer and lit it. "I've been saving this for a long time. Cuban. I was told that they're rolled between the thighs of young girls. A lie, of course, but it conjures a wonderful image. Sun, sand—"

His voice was drowned out by an explosion that

rocked the entire house. Rapp and Azarov crouched when the automatic fire started, but Chkalov just kept puffing.

"If the two of you would be so kind as to kill Maxim Krupin and that son of a whore Andrei Sokolov, I'd be forever grateful."

Rapp grabbed the man by the shirt and dragged him out from behind the desk. "Time to go."

"I'm not as fast as I once was. I think I'll just stay here."

Rapp shook his head. "You might not know much about what's happening but you know more than we do. Irene Kennedy's going to want to talk to you."

The name of the CIA director seemed to pique his interest. "I've always wanted to meet her."

"Here's your chance," Rapp said, pulling him toward the door. Azarov was already moving down the hallway, disappearing into the thickening smoke. The sprinkler system went off a few seconds later, drenching them as they approached the stairs.

It turned out to be a bad call. Both staircases leading to the entry had men coming up them, two on the right and one on the left. None were clad in the heavy armor their colleagues in Costa Rica had worn, which was a positive since Rapp's magazine was full of standard ammo. On the downside, the lack of weight was allowing them to move with impressive speed.

Azarov spotted them and retreated, going for the thicker smoke behind him. Rapp took a corridor that split off the main hallway, keeping Chkalov in front of him.

"I saw three. Are there any more?" Rapp asked.

"Not that I could make out," he responded as they

backed along the corridor, getting out of the worst of the smoke. Not great for their cover, but it had been getting hard to breathe and Rapp's eyes were starting to water. Chkalov was still puffing on the cigar, unperturbed. He seemed to think he was just a spectator in all this.

"That's a hell of a lot of guns shooting outside," Rapp said. "More than I can differentiate. What kind of team would Krupin send?"

"Nikita Pushkin with at least fifteen," Azarov calculated. "Particularly after what happened in Costa Rica."

Rapp pointed to a bulky chest of drawers behind them and then at Chkalov. "Get behind that."

"Are you sure? I'd be happy to help."

"Go!"

The old man looked a little disappointed as he wandered toward it. Rapp spotted a disturbance in the smoke and both he and Azarov froze. A moment later that disturbance had become the outline of a man wearing goggles and a gas mask. His assault rifle was sweeping smoothly back and forth but he hadn't yet picked up his targets.

Rapp took careful aim and put a single round through one of the lenses covering his eyes. He hadn't had time to screw on his suppressor and the noise would be sure to bring the dead man's comrades running.

Before he could even turn, they appeared, guns on full automatic. The muzzle flashes reflected off the falling water and haze, creating enough visual chaos to make it impossible to aim.

Rapp spun and sprinted in the opposite direction,

diving to the soggy carpet near the chest of drawers where Chkalov had taken refuge. When he finally managed to get behind the piece of furniture, he saw that Chkalov was down. The bullet had been enough to kill him but not enough to dislodge the cigar or smile.

The piece of furniture was holding up surprisingly well to the fire it was taking, but it wouldn't last. He suspected that not much of the other side was still intact and that he was being saved by whatever had been packed into the drawers.

For a moment, he thought Azarov had abandoned him, but then he saw a muzzle flash from the far end of the hallway. One of the automatics firing at the chest of drawers went silent while the stream of bullets from the other arced toward the Russian's position. Rapp rolled from cover and fired a shot that hit the remaining man in the throat, putting him down.

Instead of retreating, Rapp ran forward, stripping two of the bodies of their AKS-74U carbines and spare magazines. The man he'd hit in the throat wasn't dead yet, but he was definitely on his way out. Rapp pulled a grenade off his vest as he choked on what had once been his Adam's apple.

Approaching shouts were audible coming from the stairs and Rapp ran back to Chkalov's body. He rolled the old man onto his face and then pulled the pin from the grenade before slipping it carefully beneath his body. After a life that long, Chkalov deserved one last fuck-you.

The voices behind were getting louder and he took off again, turning left into the hallway Azarov had taken.

"This place is a fucking maze, Grisha. Find us a way out. I'll slow these guys down."

The Russian took off with a brief nod, disappearing through a set of double doors on the right.

Rapp stayed low, exposing just enough of his head to keep one eye on the men appearing through the sprinkler mist. The smoke was starting to dissipate, but what remained, combined with the water falling from the ceiling, was enough to keep him hidden if he stayed dead still.

The question was how motivated these pricks would be after they discovered their target was dead. Why stick around and risk getting taken out fighting with Chkalov's hired guns? It's not like anyone was ever going to investigate the oligarch's death.

He identified three tangos moving cautiously in the confined space. Two knelt with assault rifles while one moved, leapfrogging each other. Well-trained for sure. But how smart?

His question was answered a moment later when the lead man reached Chkalov's body and reached for it.

"Nyet!"

The shout came from someone too far down the hallway to be seen, but it was a split second too late. With wet goggles, the man hovering over Chkalov didn't see the grenade until it was too late—and his two companions were even more in the dark. He tried to run, but the blast hit him before he could make it ten feet.

Rapp was forced to pull back to avoid the shrapnel, but then immediately peered around the wall again. The fact that all three men were down was expected. Less so was the fact that what was left of the chest of drawers had started burning with an intensity that was taking hold on the wet carpet and walls. He had no idea what Chkalov had stored in that thing, but in retrospect, using it for cover probably hadn't been a great idea.

Rapp watched as a silhouette on the other side of the growing fire approached. Whoever he was, he stayed back far enough to prevent him from becoming a target, but also far enough to make it impossible to get off an accurate shot through the flames and steam.

The way he moved, though, was familiar even through the distortion. Apparently, the RPG in Costa Rica had missed.

Rapp stepped out and the two men faced each other for a moment before he turned to follow Azarov.

"Another time, Nikita."

CHAPTER 20

"MORNING, Irene. Sorry I'm late. Things in my world are literally blowing up."

Kennedy came from around her desk and indicated a conversation area in the corner of her office. Anton McCormick, the head of the Agency's Russia operations, stalked toward a sofa, looking even more harried than normal.

He was one of Kennedy's most gifted people, having spent his first fifteen years of life in the Soviet Union before his mother's defection. About a decade ago, the Agency had hired him away from a St. Petersburg–based consulting firm that helped Western interests navigate the complexities of operating in Russia.

Of course, much of what he'd done in his prior job had been illegal—bribing government officials, providing women and drugs to the right people, and handling in a very direct manner the problems posed by Russia's organized crime network. Kennedy had been happy to overlook any past transgressions, as well as a few more recent ones, in exchange for his unusual ability to win on Maxim Krupin's distorted playing field.

"Coffee?" she asked as she took a seat across from him.

He shook his head. "Too much already."

"I take it things aren't going well?"

"You could say that. Tarben Chkalov's house is gone. And I mean *gone*, Irene. Burned to the ground. We think he's dead." McCormick's normally undetectable Russian accent started to emerge with the stress he was under.

"Mitch was there," Kennedy said.

"What? In Russia?"

"At the house."

"Are you telling me he did this? You moved against—"

"No," Kennedy said, holding up a hand in a call for calm. "He went to talk to Chkalov about what's happening in Russia. The fact that he was there during the attack is just another example of the bad luck that seems to be following him lately."

"I assume he got out okay?"

She nodded. "But I'm afraid you're right about Chkalov. He didn't."

"Fuck! I loved that old guy. It had to have been Krupin. None of the oligarchs have any reason to move against Tarben."

"There was an attack helicopter and what appeared to be a Spetsnaz team."

"Son of a bitch . . . Did Mitch get to talk to him before he died?"

"He did, but Chkalov didn't seem to have any ideas

about Krupin's recent behavior. He did have one inter-esting piece of information, though."

"What?"

"That Andrei Sokolov's been installed as the head of the armed forces."

McCormick wiped nervously at his mouth, but didn't otherwise respond.

"I assume you're familiar with him, Anton? I only know him from the war crimes in Georgia."

"Yeah," he said, leaning back into the cushions in a way that suggested he'd lost the strength to sit up with-out them. "Sokolov is a nut. A brilliant psycho blinded by visions of Russian tanks rolling over every country in the world. He sees the West as fundamentally weak and Russia's failure to thrive as being caused entirely by its restraint. He believes we'll split at the seams at the first sign of Russian aggression. And even if we don't, he doesn't think we have the balls to do what it would take to win anymore."

"Is he loyal to Krupin?"

McCormick let out a long breath. "That's a compli-cated question. The short answer is yes, but Sokolov sees Russia as more of an idea than a political entity or landmass. There's no question that he admires Kru-pin and thinks he's doing a great job of representing that idea. He might even have some genuine affection for that prick. But in the end, it's his vision that he's loyal to."

"So, I should be worried?"

"We prayed that he'd just get old in exile and choke on a chicken bone or something. Reactivated—and I'm not exaggerating here—he's the most dangerous man in the world."

She considered what she'd heard for a moment before changing the subject. "Putting aside General Sokolov for the moment, what more have you learned about Krupin?"

"Not much. Honestly, I'm embarrassed sitting here this empty-handed."

"I was in the same situation in my last meeting with the president. It wasn't a comfortable place to be. He wants answers. And so do I."

"We're pulling out all the stops, Irene. I have every informant on this and we're examining every news report right down to local papers in fishing villages. So far, nothing. That doesn't mean there *isn't* anything, though. We may just be getting another lesson on how much control Krupin has over information in Russia."

"Ukraine?"

"That's a problem," McCormick admitted. "He's moving more and more troops in there and ramping up the propaganda campaign aimed at the local Russian population. Have you seen it? Russian children being attacked, anti-Russian graffiti, reports of gang rapes by Ukrainian men. Just a heavier-handed version of the bullshit he sells all over the world."

"Do you think he'll try to take over the rest of Ukraine if it's admitted to NATO?"

"I think he'll do it even if it just comes to a vote. I know Krupin makes a lot of noise about the military dangers of being encircled by NATO, but he doesn't really believe it. NATO doesn't acquire territory and if we did, we'd pick something better than Russia. What he's afraid of—what keeps him up at night—is the idea of regime change. Losing Ukraine to NATO would make him look weak and that's something he can't afford. Particularly at his age. All I have to say is that if NATO wants to bring Ukraine's membership to a vote, we better be ready to fight. And with Sokolov back in power we better be ready to fight hard. He'd push into Poland and Germany if it was up to him."

"What you're telling me is that Russia's in exactly the same mess as it was a year ago," Kennedy said. "Or five years ago. Or ten."

"In a nutshell, yes. Russia's stable. But for reasons we can't figure out, suddenly *Krupin's* not."

"He certainly doesn't *look* like a man who's concerned about his situation."

"You mean all the hunting videos? Yeah, but you've got to read the subtext. All that shirtless bear stalking and vodka drinking is designed to make him look like a badass to his supporters. They also serve to create a contrast with the prime minister who's going around the world wearing five thousand dollar suits and getting blindsided by questions he can't answer. Strong versus weak. And the Russians hate weak like the stink of death."

"I said this earlier but I'm going to repeat it, Anton. I need answers. If I have to go back to the White House and tell the president that we *still* have no idea what's happening in Russia, I'm taking you to deliver the message personally."

"I know, Irene. Just give me a few more days. If there's something to find, I swear we'll find it."

CHAPTER 21

"THERE," Azarov said, pointing at a set of doors. "It's that one."

They'd been on the ground for only an hour and the Russian looked about half-dead from the events of the last few days. His face lost what remained of its color when Rapp let the Dodge Charger drift to a stop in front of the hospital building.

Their escape from Chkalov's property had been hairy but nothing that would have an impact on someone like him. They'd climbed through an east-facing window and used the dense smoke to cover their sprint to the woods. Chkalov's three surviving guards had followed a similar course and, after a few tense moments of everyone pointing guns at each other, Rapp had managed to organize them into a cohesive force.

Not surprisingly, Chkalov had chosen solid former soldiers—two were from Poland's GROM and one

from Shayetet. They'd formed up and beat an orderly
retreat through difficult terrain that severely reduced
the effectiveness of an already uninspired chase.
Spetsnaz's target had been Chkalov, not a bunch of extremely dangerous hired guns who just wanted to get
the hell out of Russia and find new jobs.

"Are you planning on getting out?" Rapp said. "Or
are we just going to sit here?"

Azarov's face had gone from gaunt to visibly scared.
His eyes flicked from the door to the road and back
again as though he was a wounded animal looking to
escape a predator.

"I wasn't here, Mitch. She woke up alone."

Rapp had pretty much passed out the minute they'd
gotten on the Agency's G550, but Azarov had spent
the entire flight wide-awake and obsessing about this
moment. Cara had regained consciousness almost
twenty-four hours ago and was now coherent enough
to wonder what the hell was going on.

"All right, Grisha. Pay attention. Here's the situation. Claudia's been in to see her a few times but hasn't
told her anything other than that you're all right.
Cara's aware of her condition—that the surgeries went
well, but that her liver's sho—"

"Does she remember what happened?"

"Unfortunately, every bit," Rapp sighed. "And my
understanding is that she's getting pretty pissed about
all her questions being evaded."

Azarov bit his lower lip, speaking in a low, nervous
tone. "It's hard to push her too far. But when you do,
she . . ."

It was the second time Cara had seen him
attacked—the first time was when Rapp had put a gun

to his head and marched him into the jungle. With a little fancy footwork, the first round could usually be explained away. Things got tough when it became a habit, though.

Rapp leaned over Azarov and threw open the passenger door "Take it from me. She's just lying there getting madder."

The Russian climbed out but then poked his head back through the open window. "What am I authorized to say?"

"Good try," Rapp said, starting to pull away from the curb. "But you're not getting me involved in this. Say whatever you want."

Azarov stepped back onto the sidewalk and watched the car recede before turning his attention to a young family leaving the building. He examined their stunned faces and listened to the quiet sobs of the youngest as her mother tried to comfort her. He'd seen similar expressions in the past—sometimes worn by the relatives of the men he'd killed. Why did he feel such horror now when before he would have felt nothing? Why, when Chkalov's mansion was attacked, had the battle elicited fear instead of the calm clarity it always had in the past?

Krupin would say it was weakness. Others might say it was humanity. Whatever it was, it was tearing him apart.

Maybe he should return to Russia. Not to kill Krupin, but to help him. To retreat into the money, power, and women that had been heaped on him in his home country. To wrap himself in the numbness that had protected him for so long.

Rapp had been through something similar years

ago. Had he felt the same crushing weight? The longing for the simplicity of killing and waiting for the day that it came to an abrupt end at the hands of someone just a little younger and faster?

No. He had Claudia now. Her daughter, Anna. A home. He'd sought to replace what he'd lost. Not to turn away from it.

Azarov forced himself to enter the building and follow the directions he'd been given. There were a number of armed men who didn't fit into the medical setting, but none made a move to stop him. Likely, security provided by Irene Kennedy.

The door to Cara's room was closed and he peered through the strip of glass in it. Her eyes were closed and her face uninjured. If he blocked out the oxygen line in her nose and the arm full of needles, she could have been sleeping in the hammock by their pool. It was almost possible to tell himself that they would soon be going home to a house that was still standing and a life that still existed.

Maybe it would be better to come back later. As he began to back away, though, her eyes opened and fixed directly on him. He thought the glare of the sun would make it impossible for her to see through the glass but her expression suggested otherwise.

Azarov slipped silently into the room and let the door swing closed behind him. "I'm sorry I wasn't here when you woke up."

"Who wasn't here? Grisha Azarov? Who is that exactly?"

Her voice was just a whisper, forcing him to move closer.

"I don't know what to say to you, Cara. I've been

thinking about it for days . . ." His voice faltered. "I'm so sorry. There's no explanation for what happened. If I'd have thought for a moment—"

"No explanation?" she said, the pain in her eyes deepening. She thought he was lying to her. Again.

"No. I didn't mean it that way. When I say—"

"Stop. Just stop talking."

She looked at a cup next to her bed and he picked it up, holding it for her as she sipped through the straw.

"My real name is Grisha Filipov. But I haven't used it for many years—not since I was in the Russian Special Forces."

She finished drinking but didn't speak. He took her silence as permission to continue.

"I was recruited by Maxim Krupin to work as . . . an assistant of sorts."

"An assistant," she repeated and he cursed himself silently. Honesty was something that had been beaten out of him over the years.

"I killed people he considered a threat."

She nodded weakly. "Tell me more. I'm curious about the man I've been sleeping with."

"I spent my early years on a farm in rural Russia. No siblings. I was taken from my family at a young age to train at a Soviet Olympic camp for biathlon. The doctors eventually found a small defect in my heart and I was ejected from the program. There was nothing for me to go home to, so I joined the military."

"You were good at it," she prompted.

"Yes. Good enough to attract the attention of Krupin, who had just risen to power and needed someone to help him keep it. I was taken from the special forces and put through a much more rigorous training program—not only combat but languages, culture, psychology. I was given more money than I knew existed in the world. Prestige, respect . . . women."

"Olga," she said, referring to the woman he'd lived with before her. "Where is she?"

"I buried her on the hill above the house."

"Did you kill her?"

His breath caught in his chest. If anything had ever hurt him as much as those four words, he couldn't remember it.

"No. Krupin did. As a punishment for one of my failures."

A single tear rolled down her face and onto the pillow.

"It's why I never paid any attention to you, Cara. Because if he ever found out how I felt, he could use you against me. It wasn't until I left him and Russia that I invited you to dinner. I swear to you that Krupin had no reason to send those men for me. I have nothing to do with his world anymore."

Her eyes closed and he watched her for a long time. Thinking she'd fallen asleep, he started to back away.

"I have more questions," she said, stopping him in his tracks.

"All right."

"Your friend, Mitch. He was there, wasn't he?"

"He saved us."

"Who is he?"

"Like me. But for the American president."

"Another murderer."

"He would argue against that characterization, but yes."

She fell silent again, but this time it was clear that

she wasn't asleep. Eventually, the stillness in the room became unbearable and Azarov felt compelled to fill it.

"I assume you want to leave me and I understand. Obviously you'll never need to worry about money or—"

"They tell me I need a new liver, Grisha. But they don't know when they'll have one. It could be . . ." Her voice cracked and he held the cup out for her again.

"It could be a long time. No more hikes through the mountains. No surfing. No exploring. Just this room. This bed. And the tubes running in and out of me."

"Mitch is a powerful man with powerful friends. He can—"

"No," she said firmly. "There's a waiting list and my name's going on it where it belongs. I won't cheat someone out of their chance to live because my boyfriend knows people everybody's afraid of."

"I asked if I could give you part of mine but our blood types aren't compatible."

He was surprised when a nearly imperceptible smile appeared at the edges of her mouth. "I heard. Doesn't matter. They say you should never accept a liver from a Russian."

He reached out hesitantly and took her hand. To his great relief she squeezed it.

"I figure I won't live long enough for the liver to be a problem anyway. Don't they call Maxim Krupin the most powerful man in the world? You weren't very smart about who you picked for an enemy."

Azarov laid her hand back on the bed. "Neither was he."

CHAPTER 22

NIKITA Pushkin entered through the double doors and walked across the expansive office with a soldier's precision. Krupin didn't rise or even look up from the report he was reading. Instead, he left the young man standing at attention on the other side of the desk while he pretended to finish digesting the document. The side effects from his initial treatment had faded, leaving him gaunt and weak but capable of returning to Moscow. Subtle makeup done by a woman who was now a permanent resident of the Kremlin helped his appearance, as did the beginnings of a beard. His frailty and the shaking of his hands, though, weren't so easily camouflaged.

Krupin finally leaned back and examined the young man through glasses tinted to hide bloodshot eyes. "I'm running out of men for you to lead, Nikita. First the casualties in Costa Rica and now this. How many people does it take to kill one old man?"

"Resistance was more significant than we anticipated. The intelligence I had stated five well-trained mercenaries who would retreat in the face of a government action. Instead, we found seven men with significant motivation."

"Tarben has had the same five guards for years and our intelligence is that nothing had changed as recently as last week," Krupin said, concentrating to ensure that his voice carried the same weight as it had so effortlessly in the past. "Who were the other two?"

"I only saw one of them personally."

"And?"

"I'm ninety percent sure that it was Mitch Rapp." Krupin's stomach clenched, causing a wave of nausea that he struggled to hide.

"If Rapp was there," he managed to say through clenched teeth. "Then I think we can be certain who his companion was."

"Grisha Azarov."

"And you let him escape a second time!" Krupin's accusation was intended to come out as a shout but fell short. Pushkin's brow furrowed slightly, providing critical information that was the subtext for this meeting. The boy was blinded by his new status and the privilege that went with it. He saw Krupin as father, benefactor, and vengeful spirit. Despite that, he'd managed to get a glimpse of something behind the façade. If he was able to penetrate it even slightly, more cunning men would be able to stare right through.

"I had no authorization to kill America's top operative and Azarov couldn't be taken without going through him first."

Krupin's anger continued to build, but he now knew that he wasn't capable of displaying it with the force that had terrified so many over the years. The chemicals and radiation were still affecting him, and when his body finally rebounded, Fedkin would poison him again. For the time being, his normal fire would have to be replaced by ice.

"You're not a simple soldier anymore, Nikita. You're expected to think. Why was Azarov so useful to me? Because of his speed? His accuracy? No. Because he could *think*! The missions in the world you now inhabit aren't straightforward and they aren't static. Why are you unable to understand what he grasped so easily?"

Pushkin stood completely still, fixing on the flag behind Krupin's desk to avoid meeting the man's eye. Grisha's legend had been an extremely effective tool in the younger man's training. Azarov had been elevated to godlike status—a shining example of perfection in all things. As intended, living up to that impossible standard had become an obsession for Pushkin.

"Sir, it was—"

"I don't want to hear your excuses, Nikita. I want you to find Azarov and to kill him like you should have done in Costa Rica. If Mitch Rapp tries to interfere, deal with him, too."

Pushkin straightened with a jerky nod.

"Now get out of my sight."

He turned on his heels and strode toward the door, but stopped when Krupin spoke again. His rage wasn't the only thing that motivated this boy.

"Rapp and Azarov were young once, too. If I didn't think you had the potential to rival them, I wouldn't have brought you to Moscow."

When Pushkin started forward again, his stride

had taken on a purposefulness that it had lacked a moment before.

The door closed and Krupin sagged in his chair. The exchange—his first of any consequence since returning to Moscow—had left him more exhausted than he expected. He had needed to familiarize himself with his capabilities and a meeting with a moderately intelligent child who worshipped him had been a relatively safe experiment.

First, the positive. His appearance seemed fine. At normal levels, his voice was steady and reliable. His vision and his mind were both clear, though that could change without warning.

On the other hand, raising his voice made him sound weak. He was also surprised at how quickly his strength faded. The meeting had lasted barely five minutes and he felt utterly spent.

Krupin rose and started for a nondescript door behind him. His hunched posture was reflected by a large mirror in the corner, and he forced himself to straighten as he reached for the knob.

The private room beyond was smaller and simpler than the intentionally overwhelming office where he received visitors. Bringing in a bed was out of the question, but a sofa had been installed. He lay down on it, glancing at his watch. One hour till a meeting that could prove to be not only his defining moment, but a defining moment for the modern world order.

Not finding the president in his office, Sokolov knocked on the door at the back. When there was no answer he cautiously opened it. Krupin was lying on the sofa, utterly motionless. A television across from him was playing a shaky, chaotic cell phone video. It went dark and immediately looped back to the beginning, allowing Sokolov to identify the subject matter: the brutal death of Muammar Gaddafi at the hands of his own people.

"Mr. President?"

Krupin's eyes fluttered open, but he seemed confused as he struggled into a sitting position. Sokolov made no offer to help, instead examining the awkwardness of his movements and the blank expression on his face. Would he be capable of doing what had to be done? One hour was all that was needed. After that, the die would be cast.

"Are you all right, sir?"

"It was Rapp," Krupin said by way of an answer. "He was at Chkalov's house. With Azarov."

"It may be true, but what of it? Semieducated assassins, sir. I hardly—"

"Don't underestimate them, Andrei. And don't forget that Rapp rarely moves without the knowledge of Irene Kennedy."

"They're two men armed with pistols, Maxim. And Kennedy is constrained by America's useless politicians. While they flail in the darkness, you'll be using your army to reshape the world."

Krupin managed to get to his feet without assistance and smoothed his suit in a way that was familiar to everyone who spent time with him. His eyes were partially obscured behind new glasses and his face was a bit drawn beneath uncharacteristic stubble, but otherwise he looked much like he always did.

The hallway had been cleared of personnel and they passed through it in silence. At the end, Sokolov opened the door to an ornate conference room and allowed the president to enter. The military leadership sitting around the table stood out of respect for Krupin but their attention was focused on Sokolov.

They had been informed of his new leadership position but none had actually seen him since his appointment—particularly not with the insignia of the Marshal of the Russian Federation. Sokolov knew all of them to some extent from the time before his forced retirement. Krupin had chosen them carefully and all were reported to be competent commanders.

"Be seated," Krupin said, taking a position at the head of the table. "I believe all of you know General Sokolov?"

There were murmured greetings and respectful nods, but little more. None of these men knew why they'd been called there and all knew of the war crimes accusations that had led to Sokolov's removal. They would remain guarded and analyze their new operating environment. At least for now.

"I've developed a plan for dealing with the challenges presented by NATO and Andrei's been instrumental in developing a strategy for carrying out that plan. In acknowledgment of that, I'm going to allow him to give the initial briefing."

Krupin punctuated his words with a regal nod and Sokolov responded with a calculatedly subservient one. It was uncommon for the president to cede leadership, but their history together and the military nature of the meeting would provide cover.

Sokolov stood next to a map of the region and met the eye of each of the officers now under his command. "As you all know, Russia is being encircled by its enemies. The Baltics are gone and Finland's military is increasingly coordinating with NATO forces. If Ukraine falls, then it's likely Georgia won't be far behind. Belarus will be all that remains of what was once a significant protective buffer. This is something that we can't tolerate. The last time we showed weakness to the West, Hitler murdered millions of our people and hung their bodies from trees to protect his soldiers from the wind."

There were a few nods and a murmur of assent, though not from everyone.

"President Krupin has determined that now is the time to act, and he intends to do so decisively." Sokolov turned his attention to the commander of the Russian ground forces. "What is our state of readiness?"

The old soldier seemed confused by the question. "Disastrous, General. My best troops have been reassigned from Ukraine to join the exercises on the borders of the Baltics. Our equipment is also being diverted. And while replacements have been coming in—flooding in, really—all are reservists or men recalled from retirement. Some haven't trained in decades and are as old as fifty. As far as the replacement equipment . . ." His voice faded for a moment. "Much of it isn't in working order and some is so old that finding the correct ammunition will be virtually impossible. It's my understanding that all of this was done at your order."

"It was," Sokolov said simply.

The man shrugged. "If we achieve air superiority quickly we can still take Ukraine, but the fight will be more difficult and longer than we anticipated."

Sokolov once again scanned the faces of the men at the table. Their confusion was expected. They still believed that Ukraine was the objective. He'd purposely left them in the dark, interested in seeing their reaction when they learned the truth.

"The plan devised by the president is a simple one. We will continue to ratchet up our pro-Russia propaganda campaign in Ukraine and we'll continue flooding the country with the men and equipment you find so inadequate. The West will become focused on the situation and the precariousness of it will exacerbate the rifts between the Americans, Ukrainians, and Europeans."

He tapped a finger against the map near eastern Poland. "NATO's current exercises will be coming to a close before long and the foreign forces will be returning home. Their men will be spent both physically and mentally, and their equipment will be in need of servicing."

The generals were beginning to lean forward, gazing intently at the map, unclear where he was going with this.

"After the NATO forces disperse—but before most have returned to their bases—we'll use the troops we have massed on our western border to simultaneously attack Lithuania, Latvia, and Estonia. If we act decisively, we can gain control over all three countries before NATO forces can respond. Once secured, we'll set up tactical nuclear missile batteries in those countries and make it clear that we consider them Russian territory. That any counterattack will be treated as an incursion into Russia itself."

The men's attention turned to Krupin, who managed a smile behind his artificial tan. The illusion was an impressive one. The great man, undiminished.

"With all due respect . . ."

The man speaking was the youngest in the room. Oleg Gorsky had been chosen as the commander of Russia's aerospace forces because of his admittedly impressive grasp on technology. More and more that kind of expertise was becoming a requirement for anyone directing a modern air defense system.

"Yes?" Sokolov said.

"While I think what you're suggesting is logistically possible, the ramifications seem incredibly far reaching. The economic sanctions against Russia will be tightened—"

"You don't think President Krupin has thought of this?" Sokolov asked, letting the anger creep into his voice. "Those sanctions will be offset by the increase in commodity prices that always follows instability."

"That's not all, though, sir. The Americans—"

Krupin finally spoke up. "The American president is in no mood to send his men into a bloodbath to liberate three countries his constituents have never heard of. And the Europeans will be paralyzed by the thought of a nuclear weapon being used against Stockholm or Berlin."

Krupin's voice was quieter than it would normally have been, but the force of it was still sufficient to cause the young general to retreat.

"I want to be clear, sir. I'm in favor of moving against Ukraine if they insist on bringing NATO membership to a vote. But what you're describing is very different. A miscalculation by any one of myriad players could cause an escalation that no one can control."

"NATO is utterly unprepared for a move like this and doesn't have the men or matériel in place to stop us," Sokolov said. "In the aftermath of this humiliating defeat, the alliance will fail. Why would any nation be interested in membership in an organization that is incapable of carrying out its mission? Why would—"

"I agree with your tactical assessment," Gorsky said, daring to cut him off. "We're in a position to take the Baltics. But what then? Perhaps NATO will implode, but just as likely it will wake from its stupor and retool itself to resist an active threat. I agree that the West won't risk nuclear retaliation with an attack en masse, but that's not their only option. What if they just encroach slowly from Poland—pushing their border out? Or quietly insert special forces via the endless Baltic coastline? What if they simply supply an endless insurgency like they did decades ago when we moved into Afghanistan?"

Sokolov glared at the man, but didn't immediately say anything. He had no issue with his junior officers speaking their minds and this particular one voiced valid concerns. The problem was that none of these men understood the situation in its entirety. Nor could they be permitted to.

This wasn't just about the external threat posed by the West. It was about preventing Russia from falling into the hands of some weak-kneed political hack. Now, more than ever, they needed war. They needed a level of chaos that Krupin could disappear into. But even more, they needed glorious victories that reminded the Russian people who they were and what they could again become.

It was Krupin himself who broke the silence stretching out in the room. "If you don't feel you can do your duty, General Gorsky, I would be happy to remove you."

The man stiffened. "I made an oath to give my life in service of Mother Russia. I intend to keep that oath."

"Then General Sokolov will follow up with you individually to clarify what's expected of you in the coming days and weeks." He rose from behind the table with a movement that was a little too careful, but not so much so that anyone would notice. "We're adjourned."

CHAPTER 23

RAPP accelerated through his isolated sub-division, scanning its dark edges even more thoroughly than he normally did. There were a few completed houses with lights on and two more under construction, but most of the lots were empty. One day, they'd all be occupied by shooters he trusted and connected by a linked security system.

Not that it would matter in the shit show he now found himself in. All his plans were built around the idea of turning back a bunch of terrorist pricks or, at worst, a private contractor he'd crossed. Maxim Krupin was a very different kind of threat.

Rockets, drones, gas. Hell, bio. What good was concrete and bulletproof glass against that? And what about the water supply? They were on a combined well that would be a bitch to compromise by ISIS, but a walk in the park for the Russians.

He passed Scott Coleman's nearly finished home and heard the sound of a circular saw running. The

former SEAL liked tinkering after work even though
he was paying a contractor an unconscionable amount
of money. He said he found it relaxing. Distracting
was more accurate. A Spetsnaz team could roll by in
a tank completely unnoticed with the racket that saw
made.

A barn emerged on the left and in the road next to
it, a tiny figure was walking north. He pulled alongside and leaned out the window, looking down at
Claudia's seven-year-old daughter.

"What are you doing out here at night, Anna?"

"You're back!" she said, not breaking her stride.
"Did you have a fun trip?"

"I asked you a question."

"I was working on the horse stall. Scott said he'd
help me paint it. It's gonna look cool. Maybe tomorrow. And it's not really night. It just got dark early
'cause of the clouds."

She'd been wearing him down on this horse crap
since she moved in. Of course, she'd promised to take
complete responsibility for her new half-ton pet, but
he knew what that was worth. He and his brother had
said the same thing about the dog they'd conned their
parents into buying.

"Get in the car."

"I can just walk," she said, picking up on his mood.
"I'm okay."

"I said get in the car. Now."

He stopped and Anna jogged around the front,
yanking the door open and slipping in. She focused
silently on the dashboard as they accelerated up the
street and passed through the gate that protected his
house.

"I want you to stay inside the walls after dark from now on. Do you understand? And if you leave during the day, you need to tell me or your mother where you're going."

"Why?" she whined.

He was about to say "because I said so" but then remembered how much he'd hated those words when they'd come from his mother.

"Because it's not safe."

"But there's no one up here, Mitch! Just a bunch of your friends."

He pulled to a stop near the front door and turned off the engine. "Don't argue with me, Anna. Just do what I tell you."

"Fine!" she said, displaying a flash of the rage that had gotten her father in so much trouble. She tried to slam the door but the Kevlar made it too heavy for her to get the desired effect. Rapp swore quietly under his breath as he watched her run into the house. At what he wasn't sure. Probably the fact that he was playing around at the edges of fatherhood and he sucked at it.

Finally stepping out into the warm evening, he walked through the open front door and tossed his keys in a bowl that probably wasn't meant to do anything but radiate artistic significance. The house was built around a central courtyard and he slipped through the slightly overgrown landscaping to get to a glass door leading to the kitchen.

Claudia was lying on her back in the cabinet beneath the sink, leaving only her long legs and grimy work jeans visible.

"What are you doing?" he said, stopping near her feet.

She writhed sideways, nearly knocking over the trash can in an effort to look up at him.

"Welcome home!" she said in French. "The garbage disposal died. Can you believe it? Almost brand-new. I'm replacing it."

"Ever heard of a plumber?"

"I couldn't get any to return my calls."

"There are at least two working on houses in the neighborhood."

"Hard to get their attention for such a small job."

"Are any going to be working tomorrow? I'll get their fucking attention."

She put down her wrench and stood, looking into his face with her head slightly cocked. "The company sent me a new one and the instructions are easy. I don't think we need to shoot any plumbers in the knees."

He didn't respond, instead walking to the refrigerator and digging around for something to eat.

"I understand that Russia didn't go exactly as planned," she prompted.

He closed the fridge empty-handed and turned back toward her. "No."

"But Irene tells me you're all right."

"Fine."

"And Grisha's at the hospital?"

"Yeah."

"Why the one-word answers?"

"I'm just tired."

"No, you're not. You sleep like a baby on planes. What's wrong with you, Mitch?"

He leaned back against the counter and folded his arms across his chest. "If Krupin doesn't know that was me at Chkalov's house yet, he probably will by to-morrow."

"And?"

"Look what he did to Cara. That could be you lying in the hospital wondering when your new liver's going to show up. Or Anna. I can't protect you from him. Maybe I can't protect you from anyone. Most of the time I'm not even here."

"Anna and I would already be dead if it weren't for you."

"But you're not. You're alive. Maybe you should start thinking about how you're going to stay that way."

"I have enemies, too, Mitch. The new identity you gave me is good, but no lie is perfect. Can you protect me from Maxim Krupin? Probably not. But I'm much more likely to be targeted by someone from *my* past than yours. And in light of that, living with a vindictive professional assassin isn't bad for me."

"Tell that to the people who scraped my wife off the sidewalk."

She let out a long breath. "Are you sure this is about me and Anna? Or is it about you? If you drive us away, you can have your nice neat life back. Just you and Scott's supermen. When one of them dies you all get drunk together and talk about honor and duty and all that other male nonsense. Then you forget them. You tell yourself that their time was up or that they made a mistake you wouldn't have. And when it's finally your turn, they'll do the same for you. Drink and tell stories and forget." She shook her head. "Life's messier than that, Mitch."

CHAPTER 24

RAPP crammed the Egg McMuffin in his mouth and chased it with what was left of his Coke. A garbage can had recently appeared in the corner of Irene Kennedy's private elevator, likely because she'd gotten tired of finding his fast food wrappers on the floor. He took advantage of it and watched the numbers above the door climb.

Rapp normally steered clear of Langley, but a text he'd received at 1 a.m. suggested this meeting would be worth an exception. Apparently, the Agency's Russia analysts had finally come up with something more useful than shrugs and bullshit speculation.

Kennedy's assistants weren't in yet and he strode through the reception area, leaving his empty cup on one of their desks. Azarov had beat him there and was standing in the middle of Kennedy's office, looking a little lost. She was oblivious to them both, sitting at her desk, talking quietly into her phone.

"How is Cara?"

"Her spirits are improving. But there's more to think about. To talk about."

Rapp remembered waking up in the hospital to the news that his wife was dead. It had been the worst moment of his life, but at least it had been over quickly. Seeing Cara full of tubes and knowing that she was going to stay that way for the foreseeable future was something completely different. Azarov had to face her every day with the knowledge that he was the cause of her suffering. It was better than the alternative, but Rapp wasn't sure by how much.

"He's ready for us," Kennedy said, hanging up the phone. "We're going to meet in the conference room down the hall. The AV equipment is better."

They followed her to a room where Anton McCormick was connecting his laptop to a projector. He nodded a casual greeting as they entered but froze when Azarov appeared. As the head of the Agency's Russia team he would be familiar with Azarov's history, but knew nothing about his relationship with Rapp. That was on a purely need-to-know basis and the names of the people who needed to know could fit on the back of a postage stamp.

"Grisha, I'd like you to meet Anton," Kennedy said. They exchanged a brief greeting in Russian and then McCormick switched back to English to get started.

"Thanks for coming out so early. My people have been working 'round the clock and we just struck on this a few hours ago. For now, details are sketchy, but we'll be filling them in as fast as we can."

He clicked to a slide of a shirtless Maxim Krupin drinking vodka by a lake. "Despite everything going on in Russia, Ukraine, and NATO, Krupin's been unusually quiet. One interview and no personal appearances have been logged in weeks. And more than that, he has the state run media focusing very much on the growing corruption scandal surrounding his prime minister."

"So he decided to go camping?" Rapp said. "Maxim Krupin handed his country over to a bunch of flunkies so he could go get promo shots of him fighting grizzlies with a pocketknife? I don't think so."

"I'm not sure our bears are technically grizzlies," Azarov corrected.

"Point's valid, though."

"Agreed."

"Are you two finished?" Kennedy said. "Anton, please continue."

"Thank you. The Russians eat up this kind of testosterone-fueled propaganda. But Mitch is right. The timing and sheer amount of footage is something we haven't seen before."

"Like you say, though, it plays well with his base," Kennedy said. "So unusual, but not shocking."

"There's more. We have detailed maps of Russia and we've tracked down all the locations where those videos were made. All were done within a twenty-four hour period inside an area that spans about a hundred miles. He basically spent an entire day being ferried around for photo ops."

"Again, this doesn't seem that unusual," Kennedy said, playing the role of devil's advocate. "He wanted to get all the propaganda out of the way so he could spend the rest of the time hunting in peace."

"No," Azarov said. "Maxim doesn't actually like the outdoors. He does it entirely for the cameras. He wouldn't spend valuable time away from the Kremlin if there was no filming being done."

"Exactly," McCormick agreed. "And that leaves a lot of time unaccounted for. If Krupin wasn't wandering around in the woods with a film crew in tow, where was he?"

"Mistress?" Rapp said.

"No," Azarov said. "He has many, but it's an open secret. And they all live in or around Moscow as far as I know. Krupin doesn't like leaving the city. Security arrangements are complicated and he's afraid of people plotting against him while he's away."

McCormick advanced to a video of Krupin on a Russian news program. "This is from a year ago. The audio isn't important—it's just another kiss-ass state media interview. What's interesting, though, is comparing it to the one he did just yesterday." McCormick clicked forward again. "Notice anything different?"

"He's wearing tinted glasses," Azarov said immediately.

"The interview's being done outside and it's sunny," Kennedy pointed out.

"One of Krupin's greatest weapons is his stare," Azarov countered. "I know this as well as anyone. The idea that he would choose to wear glasses like that in an interview is hard to imagine."

"In fact, we have over a hundred examples of Krupin speaking outdoors and he's not wearing sunglasses in a single one," McCormick confirmed. "Do you notice anything else?"

"He's pretty tan for a guy who you say was just outside for a day," Rapp said.

"Bingo. You've touched on another superlative, Mitch. This is the darkest we've ever seen him."

"I admire what you must have gone through to get a quantitative analysis of his tan," Kennedy said, "but are we perhaps getting into the weeds here?"

"I wish I had a smoking gun for you, Irene, but what I'm working with is more of an accumulation of circumstantial evidence."

"Leading somewhere, I hope."

"Bear with me just a little longer and look how many cuts there are during this interview," McCormick said, fast-forwarding through it. "This is a five minute piece and there are three. Normally, Krupin would do that in one push. And then there's the sun again. If you look at the angle, this interview took a half an hour to shoot."

"I agree with Anton that this is unusual to the point of being suspicious," Azarov said. "Maxim is very jealous with his time and has a powerful disdain for the press. Even his own."

The Russian stood and approached the frozen image, examining the beginnings of a beard on Krupin's chin and then his obscured eyes. "He's ill."

McCormick didn't bother to hide his surprise. "That's exactly the conclusion we came to. It fits everything we've seen: the absence, the marginalizing and imprisoning of his political opponents, killing Tarben Chkalov who had an uncanny way of figuring out what was happening in Russia. And most of all, risking bringing back Andrei Sokolov, the man he trusts more than anyone else in the world."

"When you say ill," Rapp said. "What are we talking about?"

"Still working on that."

"He must have a personal physician," Kennedy offered.

"Eduard Fedkin. A man who's normally pretty easy to find—he has a family and a well established practice. Interestingly, he dropped off the radar recently."

"Can you locate him?" Rapp said.

"If Krupin's behind it? Probably not. He's pretty much all powerful inside the borders of Russia and he knows how to keep secrets. Particularly ones like this. So we're casting a wider net. If he really is ill, he's going to need a medical team specializing in whatever his problem is. And he's going to go for top people."

Rapp looked around him. Azarov's face was blank—either reveling in imagining Krupin dying a slow, painful death, or trying to figure out how to get to him before Mother Nature robbed him of the kill. Kennedy, on the other hand, looked shaken. Few people would have noticed, but Rapp had known her for too long.

"Thank you, Anton," she said finally. They watched in silence as McCormick packed up and headed out the door, closing it behind him.

"Thoughts?" Rapp asked.

Kennedy was the first to speak. "We recognized the potential for this a long time ago. The hope's always been that he would die of a sudden heart attack or, frankly, be quietly murdered by a rival who was in a position to take over. A prolonged illness is a worst-case scenario for us."

"Agreed," Azarov said. "Krupin's always been wary, but watching the fall of dictators like Saddam Hussein and Muammar Gaddafi has made him paranoid. He pictures his bleeding body being dragged through the streets and then hung from a Moscow bridge. I can tell you that there is nothing—*nothing*—that he won't do to prevent that from happening."

"Then there's only one question we need to be asking," Rapp said. "Where does he go when he's not in Moscow? If he's sick and his doctor's disappeared, it doesn't take a genius to figure out that he's got a hidden treatment facility somewhere. And if secrecy is at the forefront of his mind, he's going to be away from population centers with limited security coverage."

"There's more to this than finding him and killing him," Kennedy said.

"Really? What do you think, Grisha?"

"I'm very much in favor of finding him and killing him."

"Thank you both. That's very helpful."

Rapp leaned forward in his chair. "Come on, Irene. I know you. I can see those wheels spinning around in your head. You're thinking about making a deal to help him to keep Russia stable and move Sokolov out. You want to force the Euros to kiss his ass enough that he's comfortable putting one of his rivals in his chair. It's not going to work. What you've got out there is a wounded animal with a nuclear arsenal."

"All the more reason not to run in with guns blazing, don't you think?"

"Running in with guns blazing is pretty much my job description. And if I remember right, it's made a lot of your problems go away over the years."

She leaned back and examined him for a moment. "This is still speculation. We don't know for certain he's sick and if he is we don't know how serious it is.

My main concern now is Ukraine. NATO's in a staring contest with a man who may not have anything to lose. Up until now we've explained away the troops flowing into Crimea and Southern Ukraine as an intimidation tactic. But now I wonder if the opposite is true. Maybe he *needs* this fight."

"So what's our move?" Rapp asked.

She turned to Azarov. "Do you have contacts in Ukraine?"

"None at all, Director Kennedy. If I arrived in that country, it was for only one reason."

"What about you, Mitch? You used to know the head of their Foreign Intelligence Service, didn't you?"

"We did an op together once. Probably almost fifteen years ago. I wouldn't say we were close."

"I seem to remember that you saved his life."

Rapp shrugged. "I'm not sure he'd remember it that way. Scott has solid relationships in the region that are a hell of a lot more recent."

"In that case, I'd like you and Scott on the ground there. I need a clear picture of what's happening with the Russian troop movements in the south. The international observers can't get access anymore and I'm working mostly with reports approved by Ukraine's political machine. If I'm going to make recommendations to President Alexander, I'm going to need a lot more than speculation about Krupin's health and the word of Ukrainian politicians."

CHAPTER 25

MAKE another pass to the east," Sokolov said.
The green carpet of southeastern Ukraine
stretched out in every direction beneath the helicopter. After the annexation of Crimea, Russia had helped
separatists in this region gain autonomous status.
Control was in a constant state of diplomatic dispute,
but it was all for the cameras. Everyone knew that
Moscow held sway.

He regretted having been forced out of the military for many reasons, but this was one of most poignant. There had been an opportunity to push farther
west, which would have made it easier to link up with
troops stationed in Crimea. An opportunity lost, but
in retrospect an unimportant one. In the chess game
between Russia and the West, Ukraine had been demoted from queen to pawn.

His pilot came in low, allowing Sokolov to examine a series of half-constructed barracks and a heavy
machinery maintenance facility that was somewhat
further along.

Satellite photos of the structures were undoubtedly being examined in great detail by Western intelligence agencies and he was committed to ensuring that all those details were perfect. In reality, the buildings were just hollow shells designed to divert NATO's attention from the growing military presence on the borders of the Baltic states.

This visit was designed to serve a similar purpose. He was arriving in civilian clothing and by way of a civilian helicopter, but the details of his arrival had been purposely leaked. Spies would be everywhere, documenting as much about his time there as possible, further stoking fears of an impending attack into the heart of Ukraine.

The chopper touched down and Sokolov ran crouched toward a man waiting twenty meters away. General Ruslin Nikitin had been a well thought of junior officer when Sokolov was removed. By all reports, he was competent, efficient, and patriotic—a man whose loyalty to Krupin had thus far proved unshakable. He was also somewhat notorious for speaking his mind.

"Welcome, General," Nikitin said, offering a hand in place of a salute. Unaware of the true purpose of this inspection, he wouldn't do anything that might reveal Sokolov's identity. "I trust your journey was a pleasant one?"

Sokolov shook the man's hand and nodded before starting toward a pre-fab building to the north.

It wasn't until they passed through its doors that Nikitin offered a crisp salute. "It's a pleasure to host you, sir, but I haven't been provided an agenda. It would have been helpful to prepare for your needs."

"I wanted to come personally and get your opinion of your readiness."

The man looked concerned. "We're escalating the propaganda campaign aimed at ethnic Russians, but informal polling suggests we're not making much headway. They want autonomy from Ukraine and close ties to Russia but not necessarily Russian rule. And the hope that we can count on them during a push north is optimistic in the extreme. More likely, many would see it as overreach and turn against us."

"Then they'll have to be dealt with," Sokolov said.

"Yes, sir, but that would be easier said than done and could turn the local Russian population against us."

"So you're saying we'll have to rely entirely on Russian troops."

The man's gaze shifted downward.

"Is there a problem?"

"Yes, sir. But one you're already fully aware of."

He motioned in the direction of the buildings that were being erected. "I've been given the resources to enclose those structures but haven't been told when the beds, electrical, and other equipment will be delivered."

"It's not our job to provide for the comfort of soldiers, Ruslin."

He didn't immediately answer, instead working up his infamous resolve. "Soldiers? I'm not sure the men I'm being sent qualify. I'm trying to drill them but if I push too hard, I'm concerned they'll literally start dropping dead."

"Wars are lost with poor leadership, not with poor soldiers," Sokolov countered. "Never in human history has a general gone to war with an army he thought was adequate."

"I understand your point, sir, but this is going to turn into a bloody battle fought in difficult terrain by men incapable of running up a hill."

It was hard to be too angry with the man. Sokolov would have lodged the same complaint if he'd been in Nikitin's position.

"Your concerns are noted. Now, I'd like a tour of your new facilities."

"There's nothing to see, sir. With all due respect, our limited time together could be better spent here."

"How so?" Sokolov asked, though he knew full well.

"I'd like to discuss the likelihood that an attack order will be given."

"That depends entirely on whether NATO decides to bring the subject of Ukraine's membership to a vote."

"And if they do?"

"We'll push back."

"Then give me the tools to fight, General! You've already backed me into a corner and now your presence here exacerbates the problem. There are eyes everywhere. Your visit will be reported on and the West will bolster the Ukrainian troops." He paused for a moment. "While the president spends his day hunting and reassigning my resources to pointless exercises."

"I'm aware of your reputation as a straight talker, Ruslin. But I'd caution you to think before you speak."

"I'm going to be the one here fighting and in all likelihood dying if I'm ordered to push north with the men and matériel I've been provided."

"Has it never occurred to you that a move in

Ukraine could precipitate a NATO counterattack on us from the Baltics? That we need reinforcements there as a deterrent to an invasion of Russian soil?"

"They wouldn't dare," Nikitin said.

"I wonder how many empires have fallen with those words as their banner? Now are you capable of carrying out my orders or not?"

The man spoke only after taking the time to carefully consider the challenges facing him. "I can turn these men into functional fighters and I can find a way to work with the equipment I've been provided. But I need time."

"We all need time, Ruslin. In matters of war, though, it's a luxury."

"Then I'd request an opportunity to speak directly with the president. To explain my situation and to impress on him the importance of delaying any action as long as possible."

Sokolov glanced at his watch instead of responding to the man's request. If everything was on schedule, Krupin arrived at his treatment facility five hours ago and should have already begun his latest round of therapy. It was unlikely that he would be disposed to discuss with Nikitin an invasion that would never happen.

More concerning than his disposition, though, was his ability.

A number of prisoners similar to Krupin in age and condition were simultaneously undergoing the same treatments. In addition, they were being subjected to various stimulant cocktails designed to allow Krupin to appear publicly without displaying weakness or confusion. One of the test subjects had been pushed too far and died from heart failure but Dr. Fedkin seemed to be closing in on a mixture that would allow the president to approximate the man he'd once been for the better part of an hour.

"I'll pass along your request for an audience, General. But, as you can imagine, the president is quite busy."

"Sir, I—"

"Enough!" Sokolov said, allowing the volume of his voice to rise. He'd already allowed this conversation to go on too long. While it was desirable to have Nikitin motivated, the purpose of the trip was for the supreme commander of Russia's military to be seen in Ukraine. "I have to be back in the air in twenty minutes, General. And I intend to inspect the progress of your construction projects before I leave."

CHAPTER 26

M ITCH!"

The Ukrainian intelligence chief had the same molasses-thick accent and bull-in-a-china-shop demeanor that he'd had more than a decade ago. He strode across his office and enveloped Rapp in a bear hug that nearly lifted him from the ground.

"It fills my heart to see you again," he said, pulling back. "The years have been hard on you."

"Thanks, Danya. I appreciate your honesty."

"You know that, to this very day, my wife lights a candle in your honor every Christmas. For saving my life."

"I don't remember you being all that grateful at the time."

He waved a hand dismissively. "I was young and proud. We all were."

"I don't think you know Scott," Rapp said, pointing to Coleman who was hanging back by the door. "Scott, Danya Bondar."

"Only by reputation," he said, shaking the former

SEAL's hand vigorously. "My counterparts in the Baltics speak highly of you."

The CIA had paid Coleman's company millions to help Latvia, Lithuania, and Estonia create asymmetric strategies to counter a Russian invasion. While all three of the Baltic states were members of NATO, it was quietly acknowledged that the West couldn't move quickly enough to repel an attack. They would have to fend for themselves until a response could be organized.

"Now what is it I can do for you?" Bondar said indicating two chairs in front of his desk.

"Irene wants to know what's going on with the Russians."

"Don't we all."

"I mean in southern Ukraine specifically."

"Our government has been providing regular reports."

"We don't trust them."

"You still don't mince words, do you Mitch?"

"Irene thinks your president may be spinning the intel for political reasons."

"And do you agree with her?"

"No. I think he's a useless piece of shit who's outright fabricating it."

Bondar froze for a moment and then walked across the office to make sure the door was fully closed. "The truth is somewhere between your two analyses. Our president is very concerned with the continuation of his own power and doesn't know from where that power will flow in the coming years. The West? Perhaps, but Europe is showing cracks and America is turning inward. Standing against Maxim Krupin is becoming an increasingly lonely position."

"Do we really have to sit here and bullshit each other, Danya? Your president has designs on being a dictator and Krupin will be a hell of a lot more helpful in getting him there than the United States or Germany. If Russian tanks start rolling north, the only thing he's going to do is call the Kremlin and sell you down the river."

Bondar lowered himself into his chair. "I find myself in general agreement with you, Mitch. But, at least for now, I live in a democracy. The fact that the people of Ukraine were unwise enough to elect him doesn't change my duty."

"No, but it also doesn't prevent you from telling me off the record what's happening down south."

The man didn't immediately respond, calculating how far he wanted to go.

"Our intelligence gathering capabilities in the Russian-dominated areas of Ukraine are surprisingly poor."

"I'd think your government would want you to have a heavy presence there," Coleman said.

"The president is concerned that if any of our people were caught, they could be held up as spies in Russia's propaganda machine."

"And he doesn't want Krupin to see him down there stirring up trouble," Rapp added.

"I imagine that this was part of his calculation."

"So to summarize, you're telling me you don't know shit."

"I think that's an overstatement. We are tracking troop movement, propaganda campaigns, known—"

"We've got all that at Langley, Danya."

"I don't know what you want from me, Mitch."

"If you can't tell me anything, then give me a few men so Scott and I can go look for ourselves. They don't even have to be shooters. Just familiar with the territory."

"I don't think that would be in my best interest, Mitch."

"Yeah, but it might be in the best interest of your fucking country."

Bondar slapped his hands down on his blotter and leaned forward. "The things you've done have made you a hard man, Mitch."

"And that desk has made you a soft one. But I knew you before you had a chauffeur and got invited to all the right parties. Now what are you going to do, Danya?"

"Screw you, Mitch."

"Does that mean you're going to get off your fat ass and give me something?"

"No. It means I'm going to have you thrown out of my office and physically dragged across the Polish border."

"Before you do, I forgot to mention that Andrei Sokolov was seen yesterday outside of Donetsk. How do you think that's going to work out for you?"

Bondar's face went blank long enough that Rapp started to wonder if he'd had a minor stroke. Finally, he spoke. "Is this the truth or one of Irene's games?"

"We have some nice color eight-by-tens." Rapp glanced over at Coleman. "He looked great, didn't he?"

"I think he's been working out," the former SEAL agreed.

"Swear you're not playing me, Mitch."

"Not my department. You have my word."

Bondar let out a long breath and glanced past Rapp, checking the door again. "I have an informal network in the Russian dominated areas. Locals who've lived there for generations. A few are relatives of mine. They're not operatives but they know the terrain and have been informally tracking Russian movements and construction projects. I could put you in touch with them. But after that it would be up to you."

CHAPTER 27

IRENE Kennedy leaned over her assistant's shoulder, examining his computer screen.

"There's just no way you're going to make your lunch with Senator Barnes," he said, pointing to the calendar. "There's not even enough time to chopper you in."

"Is Mike back in town?"

"He's on a plane now. Touches down at Dulles in an hour."

Kennedy smiled. Mike Nash was a good-looking former Marine and bona fide national hero. Madeline Barnes—and most everyone on Capitol Hill—fell all over themselves for a photo op with the man.

"Tell him to go straight to the restaurant from Dulles and let Madeline know he's going to sit in for me."

Her assistant winced. "Mike's going to read me the riot act after the ten-hour flight he's been on."

"Tell him I'll pay for lunch," she said, straightening when Grisha Azarov entered the office suite.

He had the same effortless gait as Rapp, but everything else was different. The dead eyes and expressionless face, the close shave, the tailored slacks and jacket.

She'd given him a key to her private elevator and forbidden her security people from asking him if he was armed. Not that she trusted the man—there were only a handful of people who she could say that about. But it was unlikely that he was an immediate danger to her or her people. Unless he was provoked.

The question was what would the man register as a provocation? The cool demeanor he'd been born with had been turned to ice by the events of his life. Being taken from his parents and put into the Soviet athletics mill. His unceremonious ejection from that program and time in Russia's Special Forces. His life as an executioner trapped in the orbit of Maxim Krupin.

Now all that carefully cultivated structure had disappeared. Now, he was completely adrift—trying not only to build a life for himself but to understand what that even meant. Cara Hansen wasn't just the woman he loved. She was the life raft he clung to.

So somewhere behind the mask, the second most dangerous killer in the world was collapsing. The potential ramifications of that were beyond even her ability to predict. What she did know, though, was that she needed to find a way to get him through it. If he lost control, there would be little choice but to eliminate him—an action that would be extremely unfortunate and incredibly difficult. Mitch was the only man in the world who could reliably perform the task and he would push back hard. Azarov had demonstrated loyalty to him and that wasn't something he took lightly.

"Thank you for coming, Grisha. We're in the conference room again."

He nodded respectfully and walked beside her to the hallway. She considered asking about Cara's condition, but there was no real point. He'd know that the Agency was being provided regular reports.

"You remember Anton," she said as they entered the conference room. The two men shook hands before joining her at the table.

"Anton's people have refined their analysis and I wanted you to be here for the briefing. Having so much personal history with Maxim Krupin, our hope is that you can provide some insight."

"I'll do what I can."

She nodded toward McCormick and he began.

"After we decided that Krupin was probably sick, the question became *how* sick. It could be anything from a relatively minor illness that would tarnish his image as a Russian superman to something terminal. A secondary question was what kind of treatment would be necessary—he could need a one-time procedure like heart surgery or a longer term treatment regimen like you'd see for cancer. Each scenario has its own complexities."

"And?" Kennedy said.

"Bad things, Irene. We still can't find his personal doctor and believe me it isn't for lack of trying. All his office will say is that he's on sabbatical and we haven't been able to get to his wife. What we're even more worried about is that one of Russia's top brain surgeons was called away on an unknown emergency. No one seems to be sure where."

"He hasn't reappeared?"

"Actually, he has. He was killed in a car accident on the way home."

She nodded thoughtfully. "It's compelling but still circumstantial. I was expecting more."

"Be careful what you wish for, Irene. Because I've got more. A lot more." He opened the file in front of him. "One of our analysts had the bright idea of looking at Russian chat rooms—specifically support groups for people with different serious illnesses."

"I think it's unlikely that Maxim Krupin would be looking for emotional support on the Internet," Azarov interjected.

"Agreed. That's not what we were looking for. We were interested in finding a way to corroborate the disappearance of physicians. Sick people are very attached to their doctors and would probably complain about any disappearances on a forum. As you can imagine, there are a lot of these kinds of groups— some general and some very specific as to illness. People discuss treatments, alternative therapies, their experiences . . . Whatever."

"Based on the disappearance of that brain surgeon, can I assume that you prioritized forums dealing with those kinds of ailments?" Kennedy asked.

"You can. And we found a flurry of recent activity on a chat room relating to brain tumors. But not about missing docs. About the fact that a number of people with very serious diagnoses had been offered places in an experimental treatment study. As you can imagine, most agreed."

"What information do we have on these studies?"

"There's nothing *to* know about them. As far as the scientific community is concerned they don't exist.

And it gets worse. None of the treatments are being done at local hospitals. The patients have been transported to an unknown location, supposedly for sterility issues and radiation danger."

"They must have contact with their families, though. I agree that sick people are attached to their doctors but they're even more attached to spouses, children, and parents."

"No physical contact and no phone contact. Only email."

"Do we have those emails?"

"Some. Personal accounts with minimal security."

"Did you find anything of interest?"

McCormick nodded. "The correspondence coming from the patients is fairly nonspecific with regard to family history. Also, when you run it through the computers, it's pretty clear that the writing styles have changed when compared to older emails."

"That doesn't seem surprising," Azarov said. "Certainly a severe illness—particularly relating to the brain—could explain that."

"If the writing got worse, yes. But one guy jumped *up* three grade levels based on our software."

"So someone else is writing their correspondence," Kennedy said.

"We're one hundred percent sure of that."

"It's possible that they're so sick from the therapy that they're having someone else type. Or even using voice recognition that could produce stylistic changes."

"Sure, but all of them? From day one? And finally, one of the patients has been returned to her family dead. Her body was accompanied by a nice letter that the docs had done everything they could and no one seemed inclined to ask questions beyond that."

"I appreciate what you've done here," Kennedy said. "But where does it lead?"

"We're working on that. The connections are kind of tenuous and we—"

"You Americans are so blinded by your sense of morality," Azarov said, causing McCormick to fall silent. "Your passion for individual rights, your democracy. Even here at the Central Intelligence Agency, there are dark places you can't see into."

"But as a Russian you can?" Kennedy asked.

"There are many therapies for terminal patients, some well supported, some untested or experimental, and some completely rejected by mainstream science. Each has its own risks and each can leave a patient incapacitated for different lengths of time and to different degrees."

"He's experimenting on them," Kennedy said.

"Of course. It would be completely natural for him. And even more so for Sokolov. They're men who leave nothing to chance and are completely devoid of any sense of compassion. Women, children. It wouldn't matter to them. They'd want to test the effectiveness and side effects of every possible therapy."

Kennedy leaned back in her chair and turned her attention back to McCormick. "What was the condition of the woman who died and was sent back to her family?"

"A more or less inoperable brain tumor."

"And now not only is she gone, but so is one of Russia's top brain surgeons. This suggests to me that Krupin has a similar tumor and that the surgeon attempted to remove it. Perhaps using some technique that's still experimental. When he failed, he became nothing more than a security risk."

"If that's true, then we've just rearranged the European chessboard in a big way," McCormick said. "We've been working under the assumption that Krupin's just saber rattling in Ukraine. But if he's facing serious health issues with long-term ramifications, he's going to need a diversion. If I were him, I'd order my army to invade tomorrow."

"I strongly agree," Azarov said. "Krupin won't care about the human toll or the long-term cost to Russia. His only concern will be creating a nationalist wave through the country and ensuring that everyone is too distracted to notice his decline."

Kennedy turned her attention to a blank section of wall near the door, trying to sort through what she'd just heard.

"So war," she said finally.

"And not just war," McCormick said. "Victory. The Ukrainian military isn't going to be able to stand against Russian forces and NATO isn't going to get involved to protect a nonmember country."

"Then I'm afraid we're back to the question Mitch asked in our last meeting. Can we find him?"

"Unlikely," Azarov said. "Krupin is very much the master of Russia. If he wants to hide, I doubt either you or his enemies in the Kremlin will ever find him."

"Anton?" Kennedy said.

"I hate to admit it, but Grisha's right. Krupin doesn't just know how to operate the Russian machine, he designed and built it."

"Then we'll shift our focus. Anton, you said that

only *most* of the people contacted about taking part in Krupin's fake medical trials agreed. Right?"

"Yeah. Some are terminal and have had it with treatments. Some are responding to other therapies. Others don't want to leave their homes and families. What are you thinking?"

"We need to set up surveillance on them. If Krupin's already killed one of his guinea pigs, he's likely to kill more. Eventually he may need to replenish his supply."

"I like it," McCormick said, rubbing the stubble on his chin. "If we can't track Krupin, we track the people he's victimizing. It plays right into his psychology. They're meaningless. Why would he be as thorough obscuring their movements as he is his own?"

"There's no guarantee they're experimenting on these people in the same place as they're treating Krupin," Azarov said.

"No guarantee, but a good bet," Kennedy countered. "The simpler a situation is, the easier it is to control. There'd be no reason to spread facilities and medical personnel across the country. All right. We have a plan. Keep me apprised of your progress."

Understanding he'd been dismissed, McCormick rose. "We'll be able to prioritize the patients within a few hours. Getting physical surveillance on them will be a lot harder. I'll let you know where we're at before you leave tonight."

They watched him go and Azarov spoke just as the door clicked shut.

"He has to die, Dr. Kennedy."

"I understand your position, but—"

"This isn't just about what he did to Cara. The level

of destruction he'll be willing to unleash in order to maintain his power has no limit. I know him as well as anyone, and I can tell you that he won't think twice about firing nuclear missiles at Europe or even the United States if he believes that it could help him maintain power for one more day."

Kennedy examined the man, but there was nothing to see that she didn't already know. In the context of his home country, he was the best operator in the world. Was that enough to risk directly involving him?

"Would you be willing to go to Russia for me, Grisha?"

His tone was guarded. "To do what?"

"I don't know," she said honestly. "The goal of the United States is to act in a way that minimizes chaos around the world. That may mean taking extreme action or it may mean taking none at all."

"It occurs to me that if you decide Krupin has to die, I would be a convenient instrument. A Russian with no real connection to America and a clear reason to want him dead."

She smiled. "I'd be lying if I said that hadn't crossed my mind. But something else that's crossed my mind is the possibility that with Krupin gone Sokolov could take over. And that wouldn't serve my purposes. So my second question is can I trust you to wait for a green light that may never come?"

"Yes."

The chance that he was telling the truth was probably less than fifty percent, but with Rapp in Ukraine, Azarov was the best weapon she had.

CHAPTER 28

R APP felt something nudge him in the ass and he swung a hand back, smacking his horse on the nose. It finally wandered off in search of something to graze on.

His guide, Nazar, was lying next to him in the trees ten feet from the edge of an empty road. His expression suggested he might cut and run at any second, but so far he was staying put. The man wasn't former military or even Ukrainian intelligence. He was just a slightly puffy farmer who had grown up in the region and had the bad luck of being Danya Bondar's cousin.

While ops weren't his thing, there was no denying his informal skills on the intel gathering front. He'd built an impressive network out of like-minded rural neighbors, tracking Russian movements, taking surreptitious photographs, and keeping logs of men and equipment. Not pros, but motivated as hell not to have the Russians roll over them and their families.

"It's been three hours," Nazar said in passable English. "Our information must be bad. We should go."

So far all they'd seen were a couple of deer and the

shortening of the shadows thrown by the trees. The intel that had been passed to them from the locals suggested that a contingent of Russian troops had split off from a larger force just after crossing the border. Even at a crawl, they should have been there an hour and a half ago. But Rapp wasn't ready to give up yet. This was a perfect location—remote, with dense foliage that made it easy to get close to the road and would cover their retreat if things got out of hand.

He glanced over at the Ukrainian, examining his weathered face, wool coat and cap, and passed down hunting rifle. He likely owned better gear but wanted to reinforce his image as a simple farmer—a station in life that he'd mentioned on at least ten occasions already.

"Could they have turned off, Nazar? Taken another route?"

"No," the man admitted. "There's nowhere to do this. Maybe they went back?"

Rapp doubted it. Military commanders tended not to change their minds on simple matters like moving troops in noncombat environments. A more likely explanation was that one of the local informants had ratted them out and the Russians were now creeping up on them from every direction. No reason to tell Nazar that, though. He already seemed stretched to his limit.

Another ten minutes passed before Rapp's satphone began to vibrate.

"Yeah," he said quietly into it.

"I've got eyes on them."

Coleman was in a similar position across the road and about a hundred yards to the south.

"How many?"

"One Ural-4320 transport truck riding high on its suspension. I'd swear it's empty. Fourteen men walking behind it."

The situation in Ukraine seemed to get more bizarre every minute. If the Russians were in the process of supplying an invasion, why send an empty truck up a shitty mountain road to nowhere? And why soldiers on foot? They'd all fit in the back of the Ural. Was it part of a plan to capture the locals recording their movements? Maybe. But using resources to run down a bunch of farmers playing spy didn't seem all that rational.

The sound of a rough-running motor started to separate itself from the quiet scraping of Nazar scooting back toward the horses. Rapp grabbed him by the jacket.

"The human eye picks up movement. If you're still, they'll go right by."

Predictably, the man froze. He wasn't a coward— just a family man well outside the world he normally inhabited.

"All armed with AKs," Coleman said quietly over Rapp's earpiece. "But some look like they're surplus from the Taliban."

The truck came into view and Rapp studied it, examining the hazy image of the lone man in the truck's cab and then turning his attention to the soldiers shuffling along behind. Most of them were overweight— some significantly so—and a few actually had gray hair. There was no formation, just men trying to find the easiest path along the dirt road and struggling to maintain what looked to be barely a two-mile-an-hour pace.

One thing was made clear by their appearance: this wasn't a spec ops group in search of insurgents. As near as Rapp could tell, it was a group of long-retired reservists in desperate need of basic physical training.

The truck crept past, allowing Rapp to pick out more detail. They weren't just ragtag, they were ragtag to the point of not making sense. A symphony of exhaustion, ill-fitting uniforms, and round shoulders slung with poorly maintained rifles. Beyond that, they had no gear beyond small hydration packs. Clearly their commander was smart enough to know that they'd collapse under anything heavier.

"Are you seeing this?" Coleman said over Rapp's earpiece. "What the fuck? Are these the assholes we've been worried about all these years?"

The soldiers were too close for him to respond verbally, so he tapped in a text.

Something wrong. Need closer look.

"What the hell does that mean?" came Coleman's immediate reply.

Rapp waited for the last of the stragglers to go by before speaking. "I'll come in from the front while you flank them."

The relief on Nazar's face at the Russians having passed faded. "Danya said you can only watch! If you try to do anything else he said I should—"

"Shut up. Scott can you do it?"

"Well, my knee's bothering me and my calf's stiffened up pretty bad. But since we're going up against fifteen armed Russian soldiers I don't think that's going to make much of a difference."

"So you're good?"

"What could possibly go wrong?"

"On my signal, then."

Nazar started scooting back and again Rapp stopped him. "Your part's easy. When Scott and I have control, I want you to come out, look in the trees on both sides of the road, and shout at all your imaginary men to hold their fire. Can you handle that?"

"What if you don't get control?"

"Then get on your horse and ride it like you stole it."

Rapp grabbed the AK next to him and ran crouched through the trees. When he was about five yards in front of the lumbering truck, he leapt into the road and fired at the windshield, aiming at the empty passenger side but still causing the driver to dive beneath the steering wheel. Two more controlled bursts sounded from the back of the truck, followed by Coleman shouting in Russian. He didn't really speak the language, but his profession demanded mastery of a few useful phrases in dozens of languages. It was hard to get by for long without "Drop your weapons," "If you move, I'll cut your balls off," and "Where's the closest bar?"

By the time Rapp made it to the back of the truck, half the soldiers had dropped their guns and the other half were trying but had gotten tangled in the slings.

Surprisingly, Nazar hadn't bolted. He appeared from the trees with his rifle held in front of him, shouting in Ukrainian to their non-existent comrades in the woods.

Behind Rapp, the vehicle's door opened and a man nearly fell out. He looked to be in his late twenties—decades younger than his men—and wore a better fitting uniform identifying him as a low-ranking officer. He didn't even bother to glance back, instead bolting immediately for the trees.

Rapp indicated for Nazar to gather the weapons lying on the ground and then took off after the young officer. After a two-minute chase, Rapp rammed him from behind and sent him sprawling across the rocky ground. He tried to roll to his feet, but Rapp shoved a boot down on his throat. For a moment, it looked like the Russian was going to try to fight back, but the barrel of Rapp's AK pressed to his chest changed his mind.

He was even younger than he'd appeared when he'd jumped from the truck, with a pale, unlined face and stylishly cut hair. A recent university graduate spending a little time in the military to kick start his rise through Russian society. Perfect.

"I assume you speak English?"

"Yes," he managed to get out. "I . . . I studied it."

"Who are you?"

"My name is Grigory Eristov. I—"

Rapp smacked him in the forehead with the barrel of the gun. "I don't give a shit about your name. Who *are* you? Regular Russian army?"

"Yes! Yes. I joined six months ago. I was in the top of my officer training cla—"

"What about your men? Where'd you dig them up?"

"Reservists," he said, confirming Rapp's suspicions. "Some haven't served in years. They were recalled to protect Russian interests in the region."

"What are you doing up here in the mountains? Why didn't you just take them straight to one of your bases?"

"I don't know. I was told to use this route and to make them march."

He probably really didn't know. Combat readiness was just a concept in a book to the kid. This was just a brief stop on his way to a cushy job in the extraction industry, bureaucracy, or politics. In Krupin's Russia, contacts and demonstrations of patriotism were everything.

"What are you transporting?"

"Almost nothing. Just their equipment."

"Kind of a big truck for a few duffels."

Eristov's expression suddenly became guarded. His initial panic had subsided and he'd figured out that he was being interrogated.

"Who are *you*?" he said, finding his backbone. "Not Ukrainian. American?"

Killing or significantly delaying these men was going to cause more trouble than it was worth. Unfortunately, so was leaving visible marks on them. So Rapp pulled his boot from the man's neck and drove it down between his legs.

Eristov immediately curled up into the fetal position, covering his wounded testicles with his hands and letting out a choking moan. Rapp grabbed him by his impeccable hair and dragged him through the dirt, finally slamming him into a sitting position against a tree.

"Listen to me, you pampered little cocksucker. I'm not going to touch your men because they just look like a bunch of assholes who were in the wrong place at the wrong time. But you're a professional soldier. I'll take you to a cave and spend the next month doing shit to you that no one's thought about for five hundred years."

The Russian was still focused on his suffering, but not so much so that he didn't register the threat.

"The truck . . ." He struggled to get words out. "Picking up soldiers . . ."

"You're dropping these men off and picking up others?"

He nodded.

"Where are you taking them?"

"Back to Russia. To join the exercises."

"Exercises? You mean on the borders of the Baltics?"

He nodded weakly. "Estonia."

"Have you done this before?"

"Three times."

"Always the same?"

He shook his head. "The first time, I brought in an empty truck. No men."

"What did you take out?"

The pain had subsided enough to be replaced by courage. Instead of responding, he just glared.

Rapp shouldered his weapon and pulled out a combat knife. "Don't be stupid, kid. You don't want to get carved up over Ukraine. You want to do your time in the army and then get rich."

Eristov looked at the dull black blade for a moment and then seemed to see the wisdom of Rapp's words. "Antiaircraft weapons. I took out antiaircraft weapons."

"To the border of Estonia?"

"Lithuania."

"And the second time?"

"I brought men in and took other men out to the Estonian border."

"Same kind of men?"

He seemed confused by the question.

"Fat old guys in, fat old guys out?"

He shook his head. "Men like these in, but younger, better-trained men out."

"Shit . . ." Rapp said under his breath. Then he sheathed the knife and began dragging Eristov to his feet.

When they came out of the trees, all the Russians were disarmed and on their knees under Coleman's watchful eye. Rapp shoved the young officer to the ground and went over to Nazar, who was in the back of the truck, emptying duffels of their contents.

"What did you find?" Rapp said, speaking quietly enough that none of the others could hear his English.

"Nothing unusual."

"Okay, grab an empty bag and fill it with anything valuable. Then shake down the men. Cash, jewelry, phones. Anything worth stealing."

Rapp walked over to Eristov and crouched, speaking quietly into his ear. "Do you understand what I'm doing for you here? No one has to know about our conversation or that any of this ever happened. All you have to do is remind your men that if Andrei Sokolov ever hears that they were mugged on their way to base, he'll slit their throats and hang them from the rafters."

CHAPTER 29

WHEN Irene Kennedy's SUV pulled up to Air Force One, the president was already striding across the tarmac. He stopped when he saw her chasing after him, waiting at the base of the stairs to let her go first. Always the southern gentleman.

"Sorry to drag you around the country, Irene. My schedule's down to the second this week."

Alexander led her into his surprisingly spacious office, waving off staff seeking a moment of his attention. Taking a seat at his desk, he indicated a leather chair on the other side.

"No tea or pleasantries today," he said as she settled in. "I'm speaking to a rally in Ohio in two hours and I haven't even had time to look at my speech."

Kennedy understood his responsibilities, but they seemed almost comically trivial. More and more, the presidency was about cameras, television, and social media. Alexander's job was to project the America his constituents wanted to see without giving his opponents an opening. The political parties were no longer organizations concerned with administering the country's affairs. They were election-winning machines.

Fortunately Alexander still saw himself as a problem solver. While he'd become more amenable to political spin and assigning blame to his opponents, it was still a secondary concern. She doubted the CIA would be so lucky with his successor.

"I understand, sir. How much time can you give me?"

"Twelve minutes."

He punctuated his words by actually setting a timer on his phone—something he'd never done in the entire time they'd known each other.

"I think we've uncovered the reason for Maxim Krupin's erratic behavior."

"About time. The Europeans are melting down about the troop buildup in Ukraine. What is it?"

"We believe that he's extremely ill. Possibly terminal."

Alexander's expression froze and she couldn't help feeling a little sorry for him. He'd been a good president—smart, open-minded, and decisive. He was also less risk-averse than most politicians, sometimes to the point of being hotheaded. Unfortunately, he was also far enough into his second term that his ability to focus was fading. He'd accomplished what he was going to and was looking to run out the clock.

"With what?" he said finally.

"Cancer. We strongly suspect brain, though we can't be certain."

"Evidence?" he said, seeming to lose his ability to string words together.

"It's complicated and not something we should spend our twelve minutes on."

"But you feel confident that it's true."

"I do."

The plane started to taxi and he looked out the window, considering his Russian counterpart's position. Alexander would understand better than anyone the challenges Krupin faced in trying to maintain power. As important as optics were in the United States, they were even more so in Russia. Krupin's survival depended entirely on his unshakable aura of strength and indomitable will.

"And we have confirmation that Sokolov is his right hand man?"

"Yes."

Alexander finally turned back to face her. "This changes everything."

"That's our analysis, too, sir."

"I've gone hoarse telling the Europeans that Krupin's buildup in Ukraine is just theater. As long as NATO doesn't hold a membership vote, he's not going to do shit. Now, though . . ." He fell silent.

"He needs a nationalist wave—something to get his constituents behind. And he needs a diversion," Kennedy said. "His treatment is going to be difficult and time consuming. Beyond chemotherapy and radiation, he could be looking at brain surgery. We think it may be too much to cover up with action in Ukraine."

His expression turned guarded. "What are you saying, Irene?"

"Mitch is on the ground and he believes that Krupin's forces there are a smoke screen."

"I don't understand."

"It appears that the Russians are moving in empty transport trucks and men unfit for duty. Then they're using the trucks to remove crack troops and cutting edge weaponry."

"Why? Where are they taking it?"

"To reinforce the troops on the borders of Lithuania, Estonia, and Latvia."

The timer on his phone chimed and he silenced it with a jab of his finger. "You're telling me that you think the Russians are going to simultaneously invade three NATO countries?"

"Yes, sir. Our best guess is that they'll initiate the attack at the most opportune time during the breakup of the exercises in Poland. When Western forces are in disarray and on their way home."

"What the hell are you talking about, Irene? Those exercises are winding down *now*!"

"Yes, sir," she said calmly. "Our people expect the Russian army to start their push into the Baltics in approximately three days."

Air Force One started to accelerate down the runway and the president stood, steadying himself against his desk. "Are you seriously sitting there telling me that World War III is scheduled for later this week?"

"I'm sorry, sir. I wish I could have given you more notice, but this just wasn't a scenario we were gaming. Krupin only does things that strengthen his position at home and an invasion of the Baltics never qualified."

"Until now," he said numbly.

"Until now," she agreed. "This will disrupt every aspect of Russian politics and everyday life. Normally, that's the kind of instability that he works to counter. But now it's the goal. Everyone will be just as off-balance as he is. And, in the long run, if it turns into a disaster—"

"He doesn't care," Alexander said, finishing her thought. "He's thinking in terms of weeks, maybe months. There probably is no long run for him."

"Exactly."

He sank back into his seat, looking uncharacteristically out of his depth. "I . . ." His voice faltered again. "Recommendation?"

"Our first order of business should be to announce an extension of the NATO exercises. That could cause the Russians to delay their invasion."

"It's primarily a European operation," Alexander said. "We're not running it. Just participating."

"That would have to change. We need to announce that we're joining them in a significant way and massively expanding the scope of the exercises."

He considered that for a few moments. "If we move a bunch of ships in there and put thousands of boots on the ground in the Baltics, the Russians will call it a provocation. Krupin will see his window closing and he'll use our increased presence as political cover. At that point, his invasion won't look crazy, it'll look decisive—a strike against the West before they march on Moscow."

"I don't disagree, sir. But you asked for recommendations and that's the best we've been able to come up with."

He shook his head slowly, trying to process the information he'd been given. "If you're right, there is no way to stop it. He isn't going for economic gain or geographic expansion or to put down a threat to his country. His goal is chaos. How do you deter that?"

It seemed to be a rhetorical question but she answered anyway. "I'm not convinced that we can. And I don't think we can get sufficient troops and equipment in place to repel it. I also don't think that we can win those countries back by conventional means once they're gone. Krupin will declare them Russian territory and threaten a nuclear response to any counterattack."

"So you're telling me that seventy-two hours from now, three NATO countries are just going to disappear? What good is a military alliance that can't protect its members from the exact threat it was designed to fight off?"

"I don't know, sir. Playing a game against someone who isn't in it to win is . . . problematic."

He locked his eyes on hers. "You always choose your words so carefully, Irene. Why did you say *problematic* instead of *impossible*?"

"Let me answer your question with another question, sir. When you were a quarterback in college, what would you have done against a team whose only goal was to injure as many of your players as they could?"

He thought about it for a moment. "Taken my guys off the field."

"Exactly. Years ago, we helped the Baltics create a contingency plan for a Russian invasion. The goal was to bog the Russians down long enough for NATO to respond. Unfortunately, the plan is so destructive to their infrastructure and economy that no one's ever even dreamed of using it as a preemptive strategy.

But what if we could convince them to trigger it *prior* to the invasion? Krupin needs a worthy opponent to make him look powerful. He needs spectacular battles, glorious victories, even heart-rending defeats. For him, this is about drama and nationalism and disruption. What if it was possible to deny him all that?"

CHAPTER 30

THEY say I can't even have one glass of wine. I'll bet if I were Russian it wouldn't be problem."

Azarov gripped his phone tighter, knuckles whitening and the plastic flexing noticeably. Cara's voice barely carried over the marginal connection. The energy and joy that had once propelled it was gone. Taken by him.

"You didn't laugh," she said. "My delivery isn't as good as it used to be, I guess."

"I'm sorry."

His apology sounded laughably hollow. Sorry for what exactly? Dragging her into his world? Letting her sacrifice herself for his sins? Leaving her to fend for herself, full of tubes and trapped in a hospital bed? The list seemed to have no end.

"What are you doing?" she said, trying to pry more than two words out of him. While she was undoubtedly improving, conversations in which he took the lead were easier for her.

"I'm at CIA headquarters. Helping them understand what's happening in Russia."

Another lie that would eventually lead to another apology. In fact, he was sitting in a dilapidated apartment in northwestern Russia, staring through a dirty window at the rain. Across the street, a gray house listed slightly to the right behind an unmaintained wooden fence. It was the home of a former soldier who shared it with his wife and two school-aged daughters. He'd left the army almost a decade ago to take a series of mining jobs throughout the country. This would be the last of them, though. It was here that his brain tumor had been discovered and deemed inoperable.

He'd been offered an opportunity to participate in Krupin's sham medical trial but refused. His situation was hopeless and he wanted to go quickly surrounded by his family and in possession of all his faculties. A brave man looking to spare his family the pain and burden of a lingering death.

"Are you getting anywhere?" Cara said. "I've been watching the news about Russia. Isn't that funny? I don't think I've ever watched the news in my life. But now I feel like I'm part of it . . ." Her voice withered and he could picture her taking a labored sip from the cup next to her. "Imagine, Grisha. Me. Mixed up with Maxim Krupin and the CIA. Maybe they could make a TV show about us. It'd be like that movie with Brad Pitt and Angelina Jolie."

"*Mr. and Mrs. Smith.*"

"How do you know that? You sleep through every movie I put on."

"You taught me to surf. Maybe it's time I teach you to fight."

"I don't think it'd suit me. Maybe I could just play your adoring secretary. Like the one James Bond had. What was her name? Moneypenny. That's it."

A woman appeared on the sidewalk below, and Azarov watched the wind attack her umbrella. It seemed like Krupin would send a somewhat more formidable operative to drag off the dying soldier, but it wasn't certain. Force was his preferred method, but in this case perhaps he felt that secrecy was more important.

Azarov felt a distinct wave of disappointment when she passed by without giving the house a second look. As she disappeared into the mist, Maxim Krupin disappeared with her.

"Moneypenny was M's secretary," he said. "Not Bond's."

"Know-it-all."

He leaned into the window, scanning up and down the street. Once again it was devoid of life.

"I understand Claudia visited you yesterday."

"With her daughter," Cara confirmed. "Have you met them? So sweet. Anna's—"

An unexpected knock on the door caused him to lose focus on what she was saying.

"Dr. Kennedy just came in," he lied. Again. "Can I call you back?"

"Sure. But you need to be more interesting next time. I'm pretty sure the boredom of lying in this bed is going to kill me before the liver does."

"I'll work on it. If you promise to get some rest."

He disconnected the call as a second knock

sounded, this time insistent enough to cause dust to float from the old wood. Azarov looked around the room, taking in its details again. The entire space was perhaps four meters square with a small table in the center and a rudimentary kitchen along the north wall. A pullout sofa partially blocked the door to a minuscule bathroom. The only window was the one he was sitting at.

If Krupin had found him, there would be no escape. Rapp wasn't going to come to the rescue again and Nikita Pushkin wouldn't repeat the mistakes of Costa Rica. He'd have no fewer than thirty men, multiple attack helicopters, and satellite coverage.

In light of all that, there seemed to be no reason not to answer.

Azarov crossed the room and opened the door, not bothering to even put a hand near his weapon. Instead of Pushkin and a Spetsnaz team, though, he found a lone man in his late twenties. He wore sunglasses despite the gloom and his damp shirt strained to contain a physique sculpted more for appearance than athletic prowess. He was prettier than most, but still identifiable as a member of one of the gangs that infested this part of Russia.

"Can I help you?" Azarov asked, already knowing the answer. He was new in town and had used a significant amount of cash to rent a room that was barely better than sleeping outside. This young thug would assume he was on the run—from the police, from people to whom he owed money, from the military. A man on the run was easy prey.

"The landlord made a mistake," he said, entering without an invitation. "The rent is actually double the amount he told you. And it would be best if you paid me my half in cash on the first of every month."

He squared off with Azarov, tensing slightly to make his muscles ripple under the cloth constraining them. "The first installment is due now. My mother needs a new heater for her apartment."

His eyes were blue and clear, his hair full, and his skin smooth. Azarov's gaze fell to the tattoos snaking around his thick forearms. High-quality artwork from a shop that would follow professional hygiene standards.

"Do you talk or are you some kind of idiot?" the young man said as Azarov fixed on the pack of cigarettes in his breast pocket. Disappointing, but not catastrophic.

"Hey! I'm fucking talking to you!"

A powerful hand shot out and grabbed the front of Azarov's shirt, breaking him from his trance. He raised his gaze from the man's chest to his face, examining the furious expression without really seeing it. "You wouldn't happen to know your blood type, would you?"

He released his shirt. "Are you on drugs or something?"

Azarov didn't answer, instead reached out and closed the door.

Azarov pulled a broken cigarette from the pack and held a lighter to it. The blood-soaked tobacco resisted the flame at first, but finally it caught and allowed him to draw the smoke into his lungs.

He remembered being poor before being taken by the Soviet athletics machine. People helped each other then. There had been a sense of community built around lives mired in despair and hopelessness. So much had changed since then. And so much had stayed the same.

The blood beginning to penetrate the cracks between the floorboards needed to be addressed. People tended to mind their own business in this part of the country, but if a crimson rain started in the apartment below, the police would be called. There were towels in the bathroom and a few threadbare blankets on the sofa. They'd be enough.

He picked up his phone and dialed Joe Maslick, who was on the outskirts of Novosibirsk, surveilling a woman afflicted with leukemia. She was an intentionally low-priority target, leaving him with the time to act as the CIA's coordinator for this operation.

"Go ahead," the American said, picking up the call.

"I need a courier to take an item to Dr. Kennedy. Time is of the essence."

"You got something?"

Azarov looked at the dead man lying at his feet and at the large hole in the right side of his back. A sloppy job, but considering it had been done with a folding knife and a few YouTube videos, a respectable one.

"Yes, but nothing related to the task at hand."

"How big and heavy?"

Azarov put his cigarette out on the linoleum tabletop and walked to a small refrigerator. The liver, with a significant amount of flesh still clinging, was lying next to a carton of eggs. "Let's say a thirty centimeter cube weighing perhaps three kilos."

"Understood."

"It will need to be transported in a cooler with ice."

"Could you repeat that?"

"A cooler. With ice."

Maslick didn't respond immediately, but when he did he didn't ask questions. A good soldier through and through.

"It'll be at least three hours before I can get anyone there. Then onto a private jet from the local airport. Call it another twelve hours to Langley."

"That'll be acceptable. But no longer."

CHAPTER 31

LEFT up ahead."

Coleman turned onto a traffic-choked street as Rapp scanned the sidewalk through his open window. The scene seemed almost surreal. The day before he'd been mugging a group of Russian soldiers and then escaping into the woods on horseback. Now he was looking out on cafes packed with people talking, laughing, and gesturing with wineglasses.

No one in Riga seemed the least bit worried about the troops building on their eastern border. Latvia was a NATO nation that had prospered since its break with Russia, working toward a free, modern, and westward-leaning future. For many, their Soviet past was just ink in history books and rambling stories from their elders.

"Hard to believe, isn't it?" Coleman said.

"What?"

"That all this could be gone in a few days. And for what? A sick old man trying to cling to power for another few months."

They'd made the long drive partially to stay out of airports that were easily monitored by the Russians, but also to give the Agency and military intelligence time to reexamine their data through the filter of Krupin's illness. What they'd come up with wasn't encouraging.

Coleman let out a long breath that spoke volumes. The threats posed by the terrorist groups across the Middle East were massive and ever evolving, but completely different in scope than those posed by Russia. It was a country with a sophisticated military machine made up of more than a million professional soldiers armed with cutting-edge equipment. And that was leaving aside the nuclear arsenal capable of wiping out the majority of life on the planet.

They continued in silence through the city to an office park in the suburbs. It was intentionally nondescript, a place designed to house bookkeepers and host meetings about marketing laundry detergent. The only hint of its real purpose was the two guards monitoring the entrance to the underground parking garage. The uniforms were the expected ill-fitting polyester, but everything else about them screamed spec ops.

Coleman handed their passports through the window and after a careful examination the gate went up. Inside, a man armed with an MP5 waved them into a parking space and then waited for them to get out. He motioned for them to raise their hands to be searched but Rapp shook his head.

He seemed unsure what to do, finally calling someone on his radio. After a brief conversation in Latvian, he indicated for them to follow and led them into a sea of gray carpet, green walls, and drop ceilings.

The need for anonymity became clear when Rapp and Coleman entered a large conference room filled with people milling around nervously. As expected, Kennedy's counterparts from Latvia, Lithuania, and Estonia were there, as were a number of generals. The surprise was the presence of those countries' top politicians. Obviously President Alexander had made some personal calls.

Coleman knew a number of them from his consulting days and waded in, shaking hands and exchanging greetings. The former SEAL was received warmly but all eyes were on Rapp as he leaned back against a wall. The president of Latvia finally called the meeting to order and everyone settled into seats.

"I don't know if any of you have met Mitch Rapp personally," he said. "But I think we all know him by reputation. Also, I assume it's been impressed on you that in the context of this discussion, he speaks for the American government."

Rapp pushed himself off the wall and the focus on him intensified.

"How much have you been told about Russia's military moves over the past weeks?"

"We know about the increasing threat to Ukraine," Latvia's president responded. "We assume that this meeting is about our potential involvement should that country be invaded. And while we're sympathetic to their plight, we're in a difficult situation with regard—"

"It's not about that," Rapp said.

The man fell silent with an expression that suggested he wasn't accustomed to being interrupted.

"The Russians aren't going to try to take the rest of Ukraine. That's the good news. The bad news is that in about forty-eight hours, we expect them to mount a simultaneous invasion of your three countries."

Not surprisingly, everyone started talking at once. Rapp held up a hand and they fell silent. "The Russians have been moving viable men and equipment from Ukraine to the forces on your borders. In the last twenty-four hours we've also seen a significant increase in Russian submarine activity in the Gulf of Finland."

"I don't understand," the president of Estonia said. "This makes no sense. We're NATO countries. I understand that Maxim Krupin has been behaving erratically recently but this would be insane. How could it possibly benefit him?"

A great deal of thought had been put into whether to tell them about Krupin's illness and the decision had been to keep it quiet. It would almost certainly leak, which could generate a destabilization of Russia as Krupin and Sokolov faced off against their internal opponents. Kennedy and Alexander had decided that an invasion of the Baltics would be easier to handle than a full-scale meltdown at the Kremlin.

"We don't know."

"What are America and NATO going to do about this?" one of the generals demanded. "Our militaries are no match for Russian forces and we have only token foreign troops stationed here."

"I'm not going to stand here and blow smoke up your ass," Rapp responded. "NATO isn't going to do anything. Krupin's been smart. The fake troop buildup in Ukraine blinded us and the wind down of exercises in Poland has us off-balance. We—"

"Do you have proof of any of this?" the president of Estonia interrupted.

"That's the problem with these kinds of things. The attacking force tends not to take out ads on TV. It's unlikely that even their field commanders know yet. All this is being done under the cover of readiness exercises."

"Then you're just speculating."

"This isn't politics," Rapp said. "Sticking your head in the sand and making fancy speeches isn't going to do you any good when Russian tanks are rolling across your borders. Even if you don't care about your countries, think about yourselves. Because Andrei Sokolov is going to line everyone in this room up against a wall and use you for target practice."

"How long have you really known about this?" the Estonian president shouted. "Did you wait until the last minute to tell us so that you'd have an excuse not to live up to your agreement to protect us? America doesn't want to involve itself in a fight in Europe. You want to fight amongst yourselves fueled by the Russian propaganda machine!"

"Calm down," someone Rapp didn't recognize said. "The Americans' motivations are of little importance at this point. If what we're being told is true, then we need to make plans."

"Plans?" came the panicked response. "For NATO turning its back on us while the Russians invade? What—"

"You have a strategy that you developed in conjunction with the Agency and Scott's company," Rapp said, talking over the man. "We're recommending that you implement it. The hope is that it'll take away Krupin's incentive to attack."

A stunned silence descended over the room and all

eyes slowly moved to a man sitting on the right side of the table. He was in his early sixties, wearing an army uniform that had been modified to accommodate the arm he'd lost years ago in battle. Rapp had dealt with him a few times in the past—a tough, smart military man with little patience for politics. His purpose in life was to defend his country and, like Rapp, he considered all other subjects too trivial to worry about.

"General Strazds?" the Latvian president prompted. "What do you think of all this?"

The man looked around the table and then at Rapp, collecting his thoughts before speaking.

"I have concerns. First let me say that I don't think the Americans have been duplicitous in this and I think Mitch believes what he's saying. However, what he's asking us to do would largely destroy not just our political and military institutions, but our economies and much of our infrastructure. We created this contingency plan to face an *imminent* threat from the Russian—something we're not seeing. The troops on our borders have become something of a permanent fixture and the movements from Ukraine can be explained any number of ways. I agree that Krupin has been unusually erratic lately, but a war with NATO? With all due respect to Mitch and Dr. Kennedy, this seems unlikely. Certainly too unlikely to purposely implode the Baltics. We'd be doing Krupin's job for him, wouldn't we? No need for him to spend a dime or lose a single man. We'd bring *ourselves* to our knees."

"Obviously the NATO countries understand the sacrifice you'd be making," Rapp said. "And we're willing to commit to seeing the damage done to your countries put right. No matter how much it costs, it'd be cheaper than war."

"I appreciate that, Mitch, but the damage you're asking us to do won't be so easily fixed and the other NATO countries have their own problems to deal with. I'm concerned about their actions matching their words."

Rapp watched as the Baltic leadership nodded and whispered among themselves, knowing that he'd lost them. General Strazds was well respected for a reason and his analysis was dead on given the intel he was working with.

"I have a piece of information that I'm not authorized to tell you," Rapp said, silencing the group again. Coleman's face fell and he used his finger to make a subtle slashing motion across his throat.

"Before I share it, I want to make something very clear. It's not to leave this room. If it leaks, I'll use all the Agency's resources to track down which one of you was responsible and I'll kill you."

"Are you threatening us?" the Estonian president asked, his earlier panic turning to indignation.

"If any of your English skills aren't up to understanding what I'm saying, you should get someone to translate because you don't want to miss this. If you screw me, one day you'll wake up in the middle of the night to find me standing over you with a silencer pressed to your head. President Alexander won't be told anything about it and Irene Kennedy'll figure out how to blame it on the Russians."

Before the Estonian could speak again, General Strazds interjected. "Based on Mitch's history, I think we should take him at his word. If anyone here isn't confident in his or her ability to stay silent, now would be a good time to leave."

No one made a move for the door so Rapp continued.

"Maxim Krupin has brain cancer. At best it's extremely serious, at worst it's terminal."

Another uproar prompted General Strazds to take charge of the Baltic side of the discussion. About time. With this many politicians in the room, getting them to shut the fuck up was half the battle.

"This would explain a great deal. How good is your intelligence on this, Mitch?"

"Ninety-nine percent."

"Then I retract what I said earlier. An attack on the Baltics would be *very much* in Krupin's best interest. I agree with Mitch's recommendation that we move forward with the nuclear option."

In fact, the Baltics had no nukes—it was just what they'd come to call their last resort strategy for dealing with a Russian invasion. They'd empty their cities and destroy critical bridges, runways, and communications. They'd dismantle their military and disperse small, self-contained guerilla units throughout the territory. The prosperous, modern country he and Coleman had driven through would cease to exist. Healthcare, schools, food distribution, and commerce would implode. In many ways, they would be sending themselves back to the nineteenth century.

The theory was that when Krupin saw this happening, he'd have no choice but to scrap his invasion plans. In order to hide his illness and shore up his power base, he needed to put on a show. He wanted to have Russia's citizens glued to state-run media, watching images of their soldiers protecting the motherland from a Baltic threat. Instead Krupin's army would roll across an empty landscape before finding itself mired in a grinding guerrilla war that would make Russia's fight with the Mujahideen seem like a schoolyard brawl.

"We could also simply surrender," the Estonian president offered hopefully. "Agree to become part of Russia and pull out of a NATO that is freely admitting it's incapable of living up to its obligations. There would be no bloodshed and no destruction of our infrastructure."

"And no freedom," General Strazds said. "In order for us to avoid Sokolov's firing squads, everyone in this room would have to become one of his pets."

"Either way, the time for running your mouths is over," Rapp said. "You can fight or you can get on your knees. Which is it going to be?"

CHAPTER 32

R EPEAT that, Doctor. You cut out."

Andrei Sokolov was seated in the back of an armored truck modified to transport VIPs in and out of military bases without attracting attention. The plush leather seats and wood trim seemed overly opulent even for general staff, though he approved of the soundproof glass separating him from his assistant.

"Subject nine has died. The stimulant cocktail given to him was too strong. His heart failed."

Sokolov gazed out onto the muddy field they were traveling across. The rain was forecasted to stop around midnight, bringing partly cloudy skies and low wind speeds that would persist for the better part of a week. The breakup of NATO's exercises was continuing and would soon reach its zenith. Based on the latest intelligence, Western forces were approaching the moment that they would be in maximal disarray. Everything was coming together for the invasion and every variable had been quantified save one: Maxim Krupin.

Even with a modification of his treatment schedule, he would be a shadow of his former self on the day of the incursion. Of course, his weight loss could be hidden with clothing. Custom contact lenses were being fabricated to replace the tinted glasses obscuring his eyes. The expected hair loss hadn't materialized, thank God, and his growing beard had minimized the amount of pale skin in need of makeup.

On the other hand, his voice was weak and wavered noticeably. Worse, his mind had lost its laser-like focus, now tending to wander. It was critical that he give the attack order personally and that he be physically present in Moscow to announce the invasion. In his current condition that would be impossible.

And that's where Dr. Fedkin came in. He was working to create a cocktail of antinausea medication, stimulants, and other drugs that could temporarily reinvigorate Krupin. It was a difficult balancing act, though. The medicine had to be potent enough for him to project the strength that made him so admired and feared, but not so much so as to kill him.

"Then the obvious course would be to reduce the dosage, Doctor."

"It's not that simple. Small reductions in dose have significant reductions in efficacy."

Even in the situation he'd been put in, Fedkin thought only of the well-being of his patient. Understandable, but laughably small-minded. The geopolitical currents buffeting the region were far more powerful—far greater—than any one man. Alliances were crumbling. Borders were being redrawn. The world order, in place since the fall of Nazi Germany, was struggling for breath.

"Continue refining your formula, Doctor. You have sixteen hours. Safety is a major consideration but the priority is effectiveness."

There would be little point to Krupin surviving the stimulants if his enemies noted weakness and set upon him. His death from Fedkin's cocktail could be explained away as an assassination and Sokolov could cast suspicion on Krupin's inner circle in order to secure power. An outcome to be avoided, for sure, but one that Mother Russia could survive.

"I want to be perfectly clear, General. I strongly recommend against using stimulants on the president. I'll accept no blame if they injure or kill him."

"And I want to be perfectly clear that I'll blame you for whatever I choose."

Through his window, Sokolov spotted a formation of tanks bursting from the trees. A barely perceptible smile played at his lips as he watched them speed across the open plain. "Another subject will be delivered to replace the one who died, Doctor. Just make sure your stimulant mixture is ready to be administered."

He disconnected the call and used the vehicle's intercom to speak to the driver. "Stop here."

"Here, sir? We're still—"

"I said stop here."

The truck's tires hunted for traction when he applied the brakes, but finally they slid to a halt. Sokolov stepped out into the rain, opening an umbrella above him as he walked through the deep mud. He would have preferred to feel the rain on his face, but this inspection was quite different than the one in Ukraine. He was dressed in civilian clothes and had arrived on a commercial airliner emptied of passengers. The umbrella was perhaps an abundance of caution with the thick cloud layer, but it was impossible to keep up with the West's technological advances.

The tanks passed and Sokolov watched them recede, reveling in the roar of their motors and the scent of diesel. No human endeavor could ever compare in grandeur to that of war. Nothing else existed that could generate such focus, ambition, and industriousness. Displays of courage and cowardice, brutality and mercy, loyalty and treachery all gained an intensity that didn't exist in any other arena.

Every scenario they'd run—even the worst-case ones—suggested that NATO would be powerless to stop an invasion of the Baltics. Initial victory would be secured within a few days, with approximately two more months to destroy any remaining organized resistance. After that, it would just be a matter of controlling the borders and dealing with the occasional isolated insurgents.

More important than putting down insurgents, though, would be the propaganda surge designed to convince the world that NATO wasn't just ineffective but also a provocation that sabotaged any hope of peace. The American people were particularly susceptible to this message. Secure in their distant land, they saw the organization as nothing but a financial drain and creeping threat to their sovereignty.

Out of the corner of his eye, Sokolov saw a jeep speeding toward him. It skidded to a stop some ten meters away and a man in the uniform of a colonel leapt out. He rushed forward, nearly falling in his zeal.

"Please refrain from saluting me, Colonel."

"Or course, sir," he said, coming alongside. "Did your vehicle bog down in the mud? Why didn't you call? I was just—"

"Colonel. Be silent."

He did as he was told, scanning the empty field in an attempt to discover what had so captivated Russia's supreme commander.

"Are the exercises going well?" Sokolov asked finally.

"Yes, sir. We've received significant resources from Ukraine and have integrated the men and equipment into our forces."

"Then they're combat ready?"

The colonel jerked a bit straighter at the question. "Absolutely, ready. If you're anticipating a confrontation in Ukraine, sir, there are no better men in the Russian army."

"I'm not expecting a confrontation in Ukraine." Sokolov glanced over at the man and was pleased to see a hint of disappointment. "No. Instead, you will lead a full-scale invasion of Latvia."

The expression of disappointment turned to one of shock. "Sir?"

"Your counterparts will be carrying out similar attacks on Estonia and Lithuania."

The man looked nervously toward the Latvian border, hidden by distance and mist. "May I ask our end goal, sir?"

It was a reasonable question from a man who had

grown up in a time where militaries were used more for gaining political advantage than seizing territory.

"Nothing less than the permanent reintegration of the Baltics into Mother Russia and the destruction of the Western alliance."

CHAPTER 33

A YOUNG man with a ponytail appeared at the end of the hallway, sprinting in their direction. Rapp stepped aside to let him pass and then watched him disappear into the gloom. "They look a little panicked."

He and Coleman were walking down a stone passageway that ran across the back of an ancient building in central Riga. Many years ago, it had housed the country's main phone exchange, but more recently it had been taken over by popular shops and restaurants. The modernized parts of the structure were closed for the night but the forgotten sections behind and below had been transformed into one of the many autonomous command centers springing up throughout the country.

"It's a little hectic right now, but not as bad as it looks. The Baltic countries have been worried about a Russian invasion since the day they gained their independence. I think you're going to be pleasantly surprised at how well prepared they are."

Footsteps became audible from behind and again Rapp moved aside. This time they were passed by a woman who, despite carrying what looked like a computer from the eighties, wasn't much slower than her colleague.

"Really? Because it looks like a clusterfuck to me."

"Always the cynic," Coleman said. "You see panic, I see hustle."

Coleman's good cheer was understandable, but a little irritating given the circumstances. His body was working again and he was about to see a battle plan his company had spent years developing go into action. But most of all, he was about to—as he was fond of putting it—go toe to toe with the Russkies. Not everyone's idea of a good time, but for a former SEAL and military history buff, it was a dream come true.

"It's pretty incredible what's been accomplished here, Mitch. They've spent hundreds of millions of dollars and managed to keep it all off Krupin's radar. They've also uncovered a lot of Russian malware on their military and civilian systems—particularly the power grid and communications. Instead of diplomatic protests, though, they've kept it under their hat and written code that can wipe it out at the touch of a button. It's made the Russians lazy. If they think they've got good penetration, they don't bother upgrading."

"Wars aren't won with computers, Scott."

"That's just the tip of the iceberg. The government's done a good job of convincing people to keep emergency stores of food, water, and fuel. Also, the way this country's modernized, most urban dwellers still have close relatives living in rural areas. Riga's the largest city in the Baltics, but it only has about half million residents. They can empty the city in less than twenty-four hours, which will cut down on civilian casualties and throw a wrench in Krupin's propaganda machine. Saying that Latvia's a threat that has to be dealt with and then driving your tanks into an empty city won't play well on TV. Even Russian TV."

"Weapons?"

"Caches all over the country in addition to what the military will take with them when they scatter. And we took a lesson from the Afghans during their fight with the Russians. Do you remember the Muja-hideen's favorite saying?"

"We're not afraid of Russians. We're afraid of Russian helicopters."

"Exactly. The Baltics have spent a huge amount of money on bleeding-edge mobile surface-to-air missile systems and spread them out all over the country. This stuff's a long way from the handheld crap the Afghans used. It's an autonomous, artificially intelligent system that can identify and take out even stealth-equipped aircraft. Best part? iPhone compatible. Seriously."

"Yeah, but every fight eventually gets bloody. How are things going to go when they've got to look the Russian army in the eye?"

"They're good fighters and their knowledge of the terrain is going to give them a serious advantage. So will their motivation. Small raids by small teams. In and out. Sustainable for the long haul. It won't take long for the average Russian soldier to wonder why the hell he's in Latvia waiting to get picked off by a sniper or blown apart by a mine."

Rapp nodded. The strategy Coleman had helped the Baltics design was typically smart and streamlined. But in the face of war, even the most perfect plans tended to go to hell. When the Russians would threaten Europe with nukes and the locals would fall apart when Sokolov started executing, starving, and freezing the civilian population. The truth was that the era of wars between modern powers was over. No matter how they were carried out, everyone lost. Everyone but Maxim Krupin.

They turned the corner and found themselves at a dead end.

"Are you impressed yet?" Coleman said as the stone wall in front of them began to slide to the side. "I love this shit. *The Addams Family* meets *Get Smart*."

Inside they found a rusted spiral staircase leading to an expansive concrete bunker that looked like it dated back to at least the Soviet era. Power cables snaked in every direction and stacks of generators and batteries obscured one wall. Chairs and desks had a thrift store look, though the computers and the twentysomethings manning them all looked state-of-the-art.

General Markuss Strazds was barely recognizable in his civilian clothing. The stoic expression that Rapp associated with him had been replaced by one of stunned resignation. Not surprising. Rapp had thwarted more terrorist attacks that he could count, but he'd never been faced with the sudden end of America. Organizations like al Qaeda could do a hell of a lot of damage, but they weren't likely to sail up and annex the East Coast.

"You were right," Strazds said. "It's begun."

He was referring to the cyberattack that everyone assumed would be Russia's first wave.

"What's that say?" Rapp asked, pointing to a set of computer screens mounted to the wall. Each one had gone dark with the exception of a few lines of illegible script at the center.

"It's a ransomware message. Hackers demanding the equivalent of a million U.S. dollars in bitcoin to unfreeze our system. In this case the grid that powers the northeastern portion of the country."

"It's what I'd do," Rapp said. "If the attacks were traceable to the Kremlin it'd telegraph their intentions. Krupin knows you want to believe it's not them and they're giving you a reason to."

"If it weren't for your warning that's exactly what our politicians would be doing. Burying their heads in the sand, delaying action until Russian tanks were traveling our streets."

Despite the fact that they were underground, the dull wail of an air raid siren suddenly became audible.

"We're beginning the evacuation of the cities," Strazds explained. "Cellular and the Internet are down, but we've managed to keep cable television and most of the radio stations running. Within twelve hours, our major population centers should be all but abandoned."

"Power?" Coleman asked.

"About twenty percent of the population is currently without electricity, but we'll have that down to ten percent in the next hour. I imagine that piece of shit Maxim Krupin will be pissing himself. Based on the malware we've found, he would have been expecting most of the country to be dark."

"How long until you can get Internet back online?" Rapp asked.

"We're not sure. The newer and more sophisticated equipment is the most vulnerable."

"Cell service?" Rapp said.

"We're not anticipating getting cellular back. By the time we get the servers rebooted, we assume that the Russians will be actively jamming signals. It won't cripple us as badly as they think, though. Come, let me show you."

As he led them toward the back of the bunker, everything went dark. Noisy swearing rose up from the kids behind the computers, quieting again when the generators kicked on.

Strazds continued through the dim emergency lighting, ushering them through an archway that looked like it had been built by the Romans. What they found on the other side wasn't that much more modern. Women in headphones, many who seemed to have been snatched from nursing homes, were seated at an enormous board tangled with cables. All were talking into headsets and making physical telephone line connections. Along the opposite wall was a man sorting through hundreds of deteriorating wires that occasionally showered his greasy overalls with sparks.

"Ludvigs!" the general shouted. "Why do I have no power?"

The man pivoted on a bad leg. "I've been doing this since before you were born, Markuss! You should show me respect!"

"I can't show you anything because you're half-blind and there isn't enough light!"

The man shook a fist in their direction before going back to work.

"Latvia didn't modernize as quickly as the West," Strazds explained. "Some of this equipment was in use as recently as twenty-five years ago and many of the people who operated it are still alive. There was never any real reason to go through the trouble of getting rid of it, and when we began planning for a potential Russian invasion we were grateful we hadn't."

"This stuff's completely impervious to cyberattacks," Coleman said, picking up on the general's thought. "The whole country is full of wire and physical switches that have been refurbished. It may not be fast and it may not be sexy, but the only way the Russians can take it out is to blow it up. And that assumes they can find it. Most of the schematics for this stuff were never digitized. It was all just rotting away in basements of old government buildings."

"How are Estonia and Lithuania doing?" Rapp asked.

"As well as can be expected," Strazds said. "The Estonian president was still skeptical and they were reluctant to fully commit. But now I'm told they're doing everything they can to make up for lost time."

The old man trying to get the power back on grabbed hold of a switch that belonged in a '50s horror film. A quick yank got the lights going again but left him patting flames on his sleeve.

"If you want out of Latvia, now's the time," Strazds said. "I have a plane that can evacuate you to Sweden."

Rapp looked over at Coleman's hopeful expression and shook his head. "If I made Scott leave now, he'd never forgive me."

CHAPTER 34

DESPITE his wool coat and hat, Azarov could feel the cold beginning to penetrate him. The blood on the floor had been simple to sop up but there was no practical way to get rid of the body. It was still lying in the middle of the floor where it had fallen. The problem had become delaying decay as long as possible. While the apartment building already smelled of mold, cigarettes, and urine, it was nowhere near strong enough to mask the stench of a rotting corpse.

Azarov reached for the pack of cigarettes on the table but remembered he'd smoked the last one hours ago. It was 3 a.m. and there was nothing to keep him company but the wet breeze flowing through the open window and the dead man staring at his back. He shaded his phone with a hand, holding it low so it didn't illuminate him when he checked the screen. Still nothing from Kennedy saying that she'd received the package he'd sent for Cara. The only communication he'd received in the last twenty-four hours was a brief text from Joe Maslick saying that cyberattacks had begun. But not on Ukraine. On the Baltics.

A direct confrontation with NATO was an action so extreme that even Azarov found himself stunned. In retrospect, though, he probably shouldn't have been. The combination of Krupin's weakness and Andrei Sokolov's involvement should have made this move obvious. Perhaps even inevitable.

He leaned back in his chair, examining the silent outline of the house across the street. The interesting question was whether Krupin's Baltic gambit would be remembered as madness or as one of the most brilliant strategic moves in history. The West had become lost—struggling to remember what it was and losing sight of what it aspired to be. Did it still have the cohesiveness and sense of purpose necessary to enter a fight of this magnitude?

The sound of a motor became audible over the wind and Azarov slid the chair back, ensuring that he would be invisible from the street.

When he saw that it was an ambulance with its emergency lights dark, his heart rate rose—something that rarely happened to him unless Krupin or Cara was involved. He remained motionless as it glided to a stop and four men in paramedic uniforms stepped out.

They went to the back and pulled out a gurney, moving with a noticeable lack of urgency. For a moment, Azarov thought that the man inside might have succumbed to his illness but dismissed the idea almost immediately. All four men seemed to have an inordinate interest in the empty neighborhood around them, constantly scanning the street and the silent houses that lined it. One, a wiry dark-haired man with a confident gait, turned his attention to Azarov's second-floor window. The light flowing from the back of the ambulance illuminated his features enough to make them recognizable.

Nikita Pushkin's eyes lingered, staring into what from his position would be impenetrable shadow. The fact that the window was open in this weather would register as unusual, though explanations abounded— the apartment might be abandoned, the latch could be broken, the resident might be unaccustomed to the stink of the old building.

In the end, youth and arrogance overpowered caution. Pushkin turned to follow his men toward the house, undoubtedly anxious to complete the task Krupin had charged him with.

Yuri Lebedev opened one eye, staring into the darkness as his wife snored softly next to him. For a moment, he thought the noise had been part of a dream, but then it came again. Someone was knocking.

He rolled on his side, suspecting he knew the person responsible and deciding to ignore it. He'd barely gotten the blanket back over him when it came again, this time insistent enough to have the potential to wake his wife.

Swearing under his breath, Lebedev rolled out of bed and snatched his robe from a hook on the wall. If it was his daughter's on and off boyfriend, drunk and weepy with remorse again, there would be hell to pay.

The tumor in his brain was unquestionably killing him—he could feel its effects every moment of every day—but he wasn't dead yet. Even with the weight loss, he still tipped the scales at a solid eighty-four kilos. Not that it was his intention to injure the boy—he wasn't really a bad kid. But his daughter was driven and beautiful and near the top of her class at her school. Russia was hardly the land of opportunity, but there were places at the top for a girl like her. All she had to do was get away from this town and the people in it.

Lebedev padded across the living room, turning on an overhead light before yanking open the front door. Instead of a lovesick teen, though, he found three men in the uniforms of an ambulance crew.

"Who are you?"

The man in the center smiled, but there seemed to be a vague cruelty to it—not what you'd expect of someone in his profession. In fact, none of them were. They looked more like the special forces men he'd known during his military days than the paunchy, bleary eyed locals who held jobs like this.

"We were notified of a medical emergency," the man said through his frozen smile.

"You have the wrong house." Lebedev started to close the door.

"A young woman made the call. Her name was Tatyana."

His brow knitted. "That's my youngest daughter's name."

"Are you certain she's all right?"

He didn't know why she wouldn't be. Tatyana was a healthy and reasonably sensible girl. On the other hand, she'd just turned thirteen. The age when women went insane.

"Come in," Lebedev said, starting toward the room his two girls shared.

The men brought in their gurney and he heard the front door close right before the barrel of a gun was pressed against the back of his head.

His jaw tightened in anger as he raised his hands. What the hell was happening to his country?

"We don't have anything of value. Certainly, nothing that would pay the rent on your fancy uniforms and fake ambulance."

"Not true," the man behind him said as his companions moved toward the back of the house. "I've been told that you're the most valuable man in all of Russia."

Lebedev heard struggling and a brief scream. The reason for that brevity became clear when his wife was dragged into the living room with a garrote around her neck. A few moments later, the second man appeared with Lebedev's daughters, each with a similar wire subduing them.

He moved forward instinctively, but the man behind grabbed him by the throat and increased the pressure of the gun barrel against his skull.

"What a beautiful family, you have, Yuri. You're a lucky man. Except for the tumor eating your brain. They tell me you're going to lose your mind and control of your body. That you're going to die slowly and horribly. Why would you want to put them through that? It's the act of a coward."

"You're the one who needs a gun to protect him from a dying man and three women. If you're going to run your mouth, why don't you use it to tell me what you want?"

His wife's eyes were starting to bulge and the wire was disappearing into the flesh around her neck. His daughters were both frozen in their nightgowns, tears flowing silently down their cheeks.

"I want you, Yuri. I want you to accept the generous offer of treatment for your disease."

Lebedev nodded slowly and the pressure around his throat eased slightly. He'd turned it down because his doctor—one of his closest friends since grade school—had advised him to. People had been offered similar opportunities, but there were no details about the study itself or the outcomes of the subjects who had agreed to take part. The lack of information went beyond unusual, crossing the line into suspicious.

As it had been so many times before, his friend's advice seemed to have been sound.

"My family won't be harmed?"

"Of course not. I need them here to tell people you had a seizure that convinced you to join our study. Or something like that. I don't really care about the details as long as it's convincing. If it's not, I'll come back here and visit them again. Do you understand?"

CHAPTER 35

THE pain behind Maxim Krupin's eyes was considerable, but different in both quality and magnitude than he'd become accustomed to in recent months. It wasn't the result of his tumor or an indication of an upcoming attack, but instead the result of the stimulants he'd injected.

The benefits of Dr. Fedkin's potion had exceeded even his wildest hopes. The details of the corridor he was walking along had sharpened. The red of the carpet, green of the military uniforms, and gold of the ornate molding glowed with newfound intensity. Intoxicating, but also an undiluted glimpse into how much he'd weakened. Until now, the decline had been too slow to fully grasp.

His short-term memory had been restored, as had his unparalleled ability to sort and prioritize information. The sensation of being in control again—of bending the world to his will instead of being overwhelmed by it—was intoxicating.

The guards at the end of the hallway snapped to attention and opened doors leading to a cavernous room that had been converted into a military command center. When he entered, though, the expected machinations of modern war were nowhere to be found. The junior staff appeared to have been dismissed and his generals were arguing over a tabletop map of the Baltics.

Sokolov snapped to attention while the others fell silent and offered somewhat less enthusiastic acknowledgments of their president's arrival.

"What is this?" Krupin said, waving a hand around the empty room. "My understanding is that the cyberattacks have begun and we're fully operational."

"That's correct," Sokolov said. "Unfortunately, the initial phase of the invasion hasn't been as effective as we'd anticipated."

Krupin turned to Oleg Gorsky, the young air force general who oversaw their cyber warfare unit. "Explain."

"I can't. We had excellent penetration into all the Baltic systems. We're trying to evaluate—"

"They knew," Sokolov interrupted. "Their security forces have been searching for our malware and then doing nothing to eradicate it. They lulled this fool into complacency while creating patches that they implemented minutes after our attack."

"The disruption is still significant," Gorsky was quick to add. "Electrical interruptions, the collapse of Internet traffic and the cellular netw—"

"Most of the electrical interruptions were only temporary," Sokolov interrupted. "We're estimating that the enemy controls power in more than three-quarters of our operating theater. There's also evidence of a telephone landline system that we weren't aware of. Emergency radio is operating as are a number of cable stations. They're using those capabilities to organize a reaction that's surprisingly far-reaching."

"How so?" Krupin said.

"Residents are evacuating to rural areas in an extremely orderly fashion. It appears that our troops will arrive to find their major objectives abandoned."

"I was told that the cyberattacks were veiled as ransomware," Krupin said, struggling to understand what he was being told, even with his stimulant-enhanced mind. "Millions of people are abandoning their homes over hacking that you just said wasn't even particularly effective?"

"There's more," Gorsky said. "It's not just the cities that are emptying. It's the military bases. Soldiers are abandoning their uniforms and disappearing into the countryside with their equipment and crews. Perhaps worse, virtually every warplane in the Baltics is in the air and on course to bases across the Polish border."

"Have we moved into Baltic territory without my orders?"

"No, sir," his ground force commander said. "We've made no threatening moves that could telegraph our intentions."

"What's the status of NATO?"

"The forces withdrawing from the exercises in Poland are turning around and supply lines are being reestablished," Sokolov said. "Again unexpected, but too little too late."

"We're also seeing an increase in naval activity," Admiral Vladimir Zhabin said. "Two American carrier groups are moving in the direction of the Baltic while another two are on their way to the Barents Sea. We've also logged an unusual amount of submarine activity near our territorial waters and an additional British destroyer entering the Black Sea. Concentrations of European warships in the Mediterranean are—"

"Another meaningless display of hardware," Sokolov said disparagingly. "We aren't fighting a naval battle."

His words ignited another argument between the commanders that Krupin only half listened to. Instead, he struggled to analyze the facts he'd just been provided. Had he been betrayed? Had one of the few officers who knew of the Baltic gambit leaked his intentions to the Americans? Far more dangerous, was it possible that the Americans suspected that he was ill? Had Irene Kennedy discovered a clue he had carelessly left behind?

"Enough!" Krupin said finally, silencing the men. "What does all this mean for our tactical situation?"

Gorsky spoke immediately, clearly trying to wrest control from Sokolov. "It leaves our plans in tatters, Mr. President. We're facing a protracted guerrilla war against formidable opponents operating in their own territory. Further, it's likely that the Baltic air forces will mount nightly raids and then retreat back across the Polish border. Their bases and runways will be out of our reach unless we're willing to push into Poland, a move that would catastrophically overextend our resources."

Admiral Zhabin was the next to speak, seeming to have derived some courage from his more forthright colleague. "If the Americans decide to take the Baltic

Sea, they'd be in position to supply a significant insurgency. We can resist to the last man, but the outcome is preordained. Their naval budget is significantly higher than our entire annual spending on defense."

"We could use ground-based weapons systems to target their ships—" Sokolov started, but Gorsky dared to cut him off.

"Our supply of those kinds of weapons in the Baltics will be extremely limited at the outset and launching missiles from Russian territory would invite direct retaliation. At that point, all pretense would be lost. Russia would be at war with the West."

"They wouldn't dare!" Sokolov shouted. "We have tactical nuclear weapons that could wipe out every major city in Europe over the course of a few minutes."

"Are we now talking about a nuclear war?" Gorsky said, matching the volume of Sokolov's voice. "Over the annexation of three countries that pose no immediate threat to us? Have you gone insane?"

"You're relieved," Krupin said.

The impact was somewhat less than expected. Gorsky simply gave a jerky nod of acknowledgment instead of respect and then walked out. His gait suggested more relief than humiliation.

"Recommendations?" Krupin said, turning his attention to the map built into the table in front of him.

"Abort and reassess," the leader of his ground forces said. "We can blame the cyberattack on independent hackers and our forces have done nothing provocative. In fact, we can protest the unannounced extension of NATO's Poland exercises and the sudden increase in American naval activity. More examples of unprovoked aggression against the motherland."

Krupin considered the man's words for a moment and then just shook his head. "Get out. All of you."

His remaining commanders filed through the door and he waited for it to close before he spoke again.

"What are the Americans playing at, Andrei?"

Sokolov folded his arms across his chest and looked around the empty room. "The governments of the Baltic states were more clever than we gave them credit for. What we saw as corruption and waste in their military spending now appears to have been the diversion of funds into creating an asymmetric capability."

"Did it work?"

"Given another set of circumstances, perhaps. But the immediate threat to you isn't from the Americans or the Europeans. It's from the men who just left this room and their allies. It's from Prime Minister Utkin, who is out of the country but still very much in contact with his supporters inside our borders. It's from Roman Pasternak, whose followers are demonstrating for his release from prison."

"I agree that we need to keep my internal enemies off-balance, but does an endless insurgency fought across three separate countries accomplish that?"

"These insurgents would be nothing more than terrorists killing our troops in cowardly ambushes. We'd crush them and use the Russian media to show them for what they are."

Krupin looked into the eyes of his most loyal disciple and saw the nationalistic fervor burning in them. He was in many ways unique. A man of great personal strength but not great personal ambition. A man who lived only to serve the glory of Russia and to see its power extend throughout the world.

These traits made him extraordinarily useful, but also twisted his perceptions. He believed that with a sufficient show of military resolve, the world would suddenly awaken to the reality of Russia's inherent superiority. Krupin, on the other hand, had no such delusions.

A bloody, protracted war would siphon their resources and national will. The Americans would keep their actions just below the threshold that would justify a large scale response. They would smuggle supplies, advisors, and special operations teams. They would engineer ever more crushing economic sanctions. And they would pull Europe together and rebuild their military capability. The Russian people would find their lives adversely impacted and would look for someone to blame. Even with the skillful use of the media, it was impossible to imagine that he wouldn't become the target of their rage.

"We need a quick, decisive victory, Andrei. Not a slow-moving disaster."

"The situation has changed," Sokolov admitted. "We'll win, but the fight will be more difficult than we anticipated. In the end, that's the nature of war."

"Unacceptable."

"Sir, there is no—"

"We'll abort our invasions of Lithuania and Estonia. The freed-up troops will be used to reinforce our attack on Latvia. We'll bring such an overwhelming force to this war that the insurgency will never have a chance to take hold. It'll be clear to the Latvians that resistance can produce nothing but the destruction of their country and the loss of their lives."

"Sir, we have meticulously laid plans to take all

three countries. I'd advise against changing them at this late date."

Krupin's instinct was to make it clear that his orders were not to be questioned, but forced a softer response. The stimulants would soon wear off and Krupin's next treatment was already scheduled. For the time being, the general had to be kept happy.

"Field commanders are always clamoring for more men and equipment, Andrei. Now we can give it to them. We'll split the Baltics and still deliver a humiliating—perhaps even fatal—blow to the Western alliance. Lithuania and Estonia will still fall to us. But not today."

Krupin strode down the hallway clutching a portfolio in one hand and keeping the other in his pocket. His vigor and ability to concentrate had been waning, forcing him to inject another vial of Fedkin's stimulants. They'd done their job, but at the cost of a dangerously racing heart and a shaking in his extremities that had to be obscured.

The gilt doors looming ahead began to open and he heard the familiar rumble of people rising from their seats. The sound system announced his arrival and he picked up his pace as he entered the auditorium. The full membership of the Federal Assembly filled his peripheral vision but he ignored them, focusing on taking the steps to the podium at his customary half jog. The hand in his pocket felt unnatural enough that he removed it, letting it swing loosely by his side before slipping it behind a lectern placed center stage.

It was a substantial, ornate piece of furniture that hid most of his body and had a small desktop where he could still his trembling hands. The quilted velvet upholstery on the back was a new addition, but everything else in the room was familiar—the vaulted ceiling high overhead, the gold chandeliers, and, most of all, the faces of the politicians staring up at him.

"Please be seated."

They did as he asked, the sound of their movements once again echoing through the hall.

"I'll keep my remarks brief. As you know, Russia has been the target of increasing aggressions from the West. Their overtures in Ukraine and growing interest in Georgia. Their provocative ongoing exercises in Poland, the treatment of ethnic Russians in former Soviet republics . . ."

He paused and looked out over the nervous faces of his audience. All were aware of the cyberattacks targeting the Baltics and would be worried about being called into this emergency session. Cowards.

"More recently, our intelligence community has uncovered a plan by NATO to place men and equipment on our border with Latvia, less than six hundred kilometers from our capital."

A lie, of course, but one that caused concerned murmurs to fill the hall.

"We can no longer tolerate this slow campaign of encroachment. Our country is being carved up and encircled. Marginalized and isolated. I had hoped that our diplomatic efforts and deep commitment to peace would halt the aggression, but it's only served to embolden our enemies."

The sweat broke across his forehead but he resisted the urge to wipe it away.

"Ten minutes ago, and with great regret, I found

myself with no other option than to move our military into Latvia."

There was an expected stunned silence and then a cacophony that quickly turned deafening. A number of his bolder political opponents actually dared to stand and shout directly at him.

"Be seated!" he said, bringing his mouth closer to the microphones lined up in front of him. "We had—"

The force of the explosion slammed him into the lectern, toppling it and sending him sliding across the floor. The heat was next, penetrating his suit and scalding the back of his neck as smoke billowed over him.

Other than that he was uninjured. The carefully calibrated direction of the blast and the heavy upholstery on the lectern had done exactly what Sokolov said they would.

Krupin managed to stand, squinting through the haze at the members of the Federal Assembly visible in the first few rows. Most were panicking, running over the top of one another in a desperate effort to escape. A few were unconscious and at least two appeared dead, the victims of a flagpole that had become a projectile.

Krupin began barking orders, pointed to an injured woman struggling to remain upright as her colleagues rushed past her. He made a show of trying to fight off his security detail as they began dragging him offstage, but it was just for the cameras. His breath was becoming labored and his heart felt oddly hollow in his chest.

He'd accomplished what was necessary and now it was time to rest.

CHAPTER 36

GRISHA Azarov slipped on his coat and buried the bottom of his chin in a coarse wool scarf. A threadbare fedora pulled low on his forehead completed the disguise. Not the most extravagant he'd ever worn, but in the rain and darkness it would suffice.

He descended the apartment building's stairs, crossing the poorly lit entry and opening the front door a few centimeters. There was a single man standing behind the ambulance, his eyes sweeping up and down the empty street. Pushkin and the two remaining men had gone inside Yuri Lebedev's home with a gurney.

Azarov finally stepped through the door, slapping his arms around his torso against the cold as he crossed the street.

"Is Yuri all right?" he asked the man posing as a paramedic.

"Just fine. You should go back inside."

"He's a friend of mine," Azarov said, ignoring the advice. "I know he's been ill."

"Just a little trouble breathing. We're taking him to the hospital for an evaluation. Now why don't you go back to bed? It's late."

The front door of the house opened and Pushkin came out, leading his two men and a rolling gurney. Strapped firmly to it was an unconscious Yuri Lebedev. His wife appeared in the doorway a moment later, looking terrified and periodically turning to speak to someone behind her. Undoubtedly a feeble attempt to reassure her two daughters.

Azarov stepped back, keeping the vehicle between him and Pushkin. When they started loading Lebedev inside, he pulled a GPS tracker from his pocket and used the magnet to secure it to the chassis.

He retreated farther into the darkness as two men climbed in the back with their patient. By the time the vehicle pulled away, Azarov had slipped into a muddy gap between his apartment building and the one next to it. The CIA tracking application on his phone took a few moments to locate the hidden GPS, but finally a blue dot appeared on the map.

He dialed as he walked toward the car he'd parked two blocks north. Joe Maslick picked up on the second ring.

"Please tell me you don't need another cooler."

"Nikita Pushkin just picked up Lebedev. The tracker is five by five. I'll be able to follow them at a comfortable distance."

There was a brief pause over the line. "Roger that. I've got it up on my screen. Target heading east. I'll call Dr. Kennedy and see if we have any satellite coverage but your weather doesn't look like it's cooperating. I'm a few hours out on getting you backup."

"Understood. Keep me updated on your progress."

Azarov disconnected the call, struggling to keep his pace from accelerating unnaturally. Would that ambulance lead him to Krupin? Could it be that easy? Kennedy had made him promise that he wouldn't make a move without her approval, but she would be fully aware that he was lying. Krupin's death at his hands would leave her with Sokolov to deal with, but that wasn't an insurmountable problem. He was a clever and ruthless man, but also one with many powerful enemies.

The car's motor cut out, leaving Azarov coasting down the empty road. He'd erred on the side of anonymity when he'd bought a car not much better than the Škoda he'd been forced to abandon at Tarben Chkalov's house. Now he was paying the price. Would Maxim Krupin survive because of a clogged fuel filter? Would it be a corroded spark plug wire that precipitated a nuclear exchange and allowed Krupin to escape retribution for what he'd done to Cara?

When the engine kicked in again, it sounded a bit stronger. He pressed the accelerator and the vehicle actually managed to accelerate to sixty kilometers per hour. His phone was still receiving a strong GPS signal, displaying the position of the ambulance as it entered a local airport that would be closed at this time of morning. Azarov switched to a satellite image and watched the ambulance pass by the terminal in favor of a runway along the southern edge.

The map showed a service road that circled the airport and he turned onto it, feeling the quality of the asphalt deteriorate. That, combined with the fact that he was forced to turn off the car's headlights and navigate by the dim glow of the terminal, caused his progress to slow significantly.

The chain-link fence encircling the airport appeared on his right, providing him a point of reference as he curved around to the back of the facility. The ambulance's headlights finally appeared in the distance, pulling to a stop next to a military transport plane.

The wind picked up with the arrival of dawn, covering the sound of his approach to a degree, but not so much that he was comfortable getting close. The motor cut out again and he released the accelerator, allowing the vehicle to glide to a stop about two hundred meters north of the plane.

Azarov got out and climbed the dripping wire fence, running crouched through the overgrown marshland on the other side. At fifty meters, he started to enter the glow thrown by the ambulance lights and illuminated cockpit, forcing him to drop to his stomach and crawl through the brush and mud.

His wool coat kept his torso dry but his pants were soaked through immediately, conducting the cold from the ground. He could hear voices but was unable to make out individual words as two men rolled Yuri Lebedev toward the plane's open cargo bay. Nikita Pushkin and one other man remained near their vehicle, scanning the landscape with AN-94 assault rifles slung across their chests.

Azarov rolled to cake the back of his clothing with mud and then scooped up a handful to spread over his face and hair. It would be enough to allow him to creep forward another twenty-five meters before the risk of being seen was too great. Pushkin's gaze swept toward him and Azarov squinted to reduce the reflection off his eyes.

Unable to close in further, he could do little more than watch as the two men reappeared on the already rising cargo ramp. They jumped off and jogged back to the ambulance while the propellers started to turn. Pushkin's attention was split as he shouted orders over the whine of the plane, and Azarov used the opportunity to gain another four meters.

To what end, he wasn't certain. Krupin wasn't there. At best, he was waiting for the plane somewhere else in Russia. But even that was far from guaranteed.

When the aircraft started to taxi, Pushkin and his men climbed back into the ambulance. Yuri Lebedev had been kidnapped, his family terrorized, and now he'd been handed off to the Russian air force. For good reason, Pushkin considered his job done.

The vehicle pulled away as the plane lumbered onto the runway in front of Azarov. A blast of wind and the illumination washed over him for a moment and then left him in dark stillness again.

He was about to call Joe Maslick to give him a sitrep and see if there was any way to track the plane, but instead rose to his feet and chased it. His fitness was far less than it had once been, but the image of Cara lying in the hospital propelled him at a speed that would have impressed even his disapproving former trainer.

He reached the tarmac, using the hard surface to accelerate to a full sprint. The plane was still positioning itself for takeoff, traveling at a speed that allowed Azarov to close in on it. He aimed for the landing gear on the right side, fighting the gale generated by the propellers and managing to grab hold of the vertical pillar supporting the wheels. The roar in his ears was deafening as he leapt onto a steel bar protruding from the back of the assembly.

He'd used the only GPS tracker he had on the ambulance, leaving him with one option. He pulled his coat off as the plane began to accelerate, taking care not to allow it to get caught in the spinning tires.

His first attempt to tangle the heavy wool in the landing gear mechanism failed and the coat was almost blown from his hand. On his second try, he managed to snag it on something sharp.

The act of getting the coat secured while standing on the precarious, rain-soaked foothold had taken so much concentration that he hadn't tracked the plane's speed. His perspective was badly distorted by the water lashing his face, leaving him no recourse but to simply let go. He curled into a ball and tried to protect his head as he half slid, half rolled across the tarmac. When he finally came to a stop sprawled in a shallow puddle, he didn't immediately move, instead watching the plane lift into the air. Eventually, he began moving his limbs in a methodical search for broken bones or paralysis. Once he'd confirmed that everything was more or less functional, he laid back and let the rainwater run down his face.

The secure satphone had been given to him by the CIA and he assumed they were using it to keep tabs on him. If it managed to stay on the plane and the signal was powerful enough, they could track it. Would it lead directly to Krupin? Probably not. He was too cautious for that. But it would get them one step closer.

CHAPTER 37

ONCE again, the world around them had turned deceptively normal. Rapp and Coleman were riding in an SUV driven by a young Latvian army officer wearing civilian clothing. They were west of the Riga airport, cruising along the A5 with the windows open and the lights on. The only thing that hinted of something amiss was the unusually heavy 3 a.m. traffic. Residents fleeing the city.

Rapp spotted a formation of lights in the sky, following them with his eyes for a moment before registering what they were. Not Russians. Latvian air force choppers headed for the safety of Poland.

"From a base to the southwest," their driver Jarus explained. "They're late. It should have been completely abandoned by now."

"The Russians will target that, too," Rapp said. "How far will they be from where we're headed?"

"Perhaps two kilometers?"

"So, they could be on top of us too fast for us to react."

"Yes, but it's not likely. The base has been heavily booby-trapped and mined. They'll have their hands full."

He took an exit and headed east on a two-lane road cut through the trees. Unlike the highway, it was completely empty.

"Kind of eerie, isn't it?" Coleman said from the backseat. "The calm before the storm."

Another turn put them on a dirt track that penetrated into the forest. It was narrow enough that Rapp had to close his window to keep tree branches from hitting him in the face.

"Do your people know we're coming?" Rapp asked.

"Most likely. But communications aren't terribly reliable."

Coleman and the Latvians had created an interesting experiment in unconventional warfare. The theory was solid, as was the country's preparation, but it all relied on the destruction of the chain of command. Would it work in practice? Isolation and chaos were operating environments that Rapp had become accustomed to over the years, but soldiers tended to like more structure.

"Take it easy, then. I don't want to die from friendly fire before the war even starts."

Jarus took his advice and slowed. The headlights barely managed to penetrate the foliage and Rapp leaned forward, squinting through the windshield. Finally, he grabbed the young man's arm. "Stop."

Jarus released the accelerator and let the vehicle roll to a halt, but didn't seem sure why. "I was told—"

He fell silent when five men armed with assault rifles appeared from the trees.

"Turn off your lights and roll your windows back down," Rapp ordered.

The men approached through the darkness, one putting the barrel of his weapon against Rapp's temple. A flashlight snapped on and just as quickly snapped off.

"Jarus. You're overdue," the man said in English. "The Russians have crossed our border."

"What? When?"

"Only a few minutes ago. It's begun."

Rapp pushed the gun away from his head and stepped out of the vehicle, savoring the silence that wouldn't last for much longer. The chances of averting this war had always been around zero, but somewhere in the back of his mind he'd held out a little hope. Now it was gone.

They abandoned the vehicle and hiked through the woods to a canvas-covered cart that had bogged down in the soft ground. It had been designed to be pulled by a horse, but for some reason that critical component was missing.

"Weapons?" Rapp asked.

"Worse. Batteries. The weight estimates we were given were low by half."

The CIA man glanced behind him, confirming that there was no way in hell they were going to get the SUV in there. "How far?"

"We need to make it to the edge of the tree line. Perhaps five hundred meters."

"All right. Then we're doing it the old fashioned way. Scott, take the left wheel. I'll get the right. Jarus, you get on the front. Everyone else is in back."

The thick wooden spokes provided reasonable handholds, and after a few tries, the cart was rolling again.

They were right about the weight. Every time the grade turned up, it put the cart in danger of rolling back and crushing half the team. Once they got their technique down, though, they managed to make progress.

The light slowly improved as they moved forward, and after a little less than an hour, Rapp spotted a human silhouette ahead. Or, more precisely, half of one. The man's lower body was hidden in the hole he was digging. When he saw the cart, he jumped out and ran to help.

"Pull it to the side of the hole and turn it," Jarus said, just loudly enough for Rapp and Coleman to hear. "We need access to the back."

They got it into position and the men collapsed to the ground in exhaustion. Finally, Latvia's main commercial airport was visible through the trees. Its buildings and runway were partially illuminated less than a mile to the east.

The power was still on, creating an easy target for the paratroopers who were undoubtedly on their way. Securing the airport and repurposing it as a Russian base would be one of Sokolov's first priorities.

Coleman came up alongside Rapp and studied the airfield in the distance. "I feel like I'm going to wake up any minute and find out it was all a dream. This isn't some hairy op that's going to get stamped Top Secret and shoved in a filing cabinet in the Agency's basement. Russia's invaded NATO. We're standing right in the middle of a historical crossroad that could set the world order for the next hundred years."

"Try it again," Rapp said.

A series of dull flashes worked their way through the cracks in the cart they'd overturned.

"It works!" came the muffled reply from the man beneath it. He was standing in the hole they'd dug, slicing through a half-inch steel plate at the bottom. The battery-powered plasma cutter hadn't wanted to cooperate at first, but now they were under way.

A secured hatch would have been a hell of a lot more convenient, but Rapp could see why the Latvian command had decided against it. Beneath the plate was a control system that had to be physically attached to a one-of-a-kind remote. Installing nearly a metric ton of live explosives beneath a commercial airport wasn't something you did without creating a very long list of fail-safes.

Rapp turned and walked back to the edge of the trees, where Coleman was still looking down on the empty terminal building. The anticipation seemed to be getting to him.

"How much longer, Mitch?"

"Not long."

Less than a minute later, the drone of approaching planes became audible, causing the activity behind them to grow in urgency. Rapp aimed a night scope at the sky, finally spotting a Russian transport. It was only the first of many, and soon the sound of them drowned out everything else. Canopies began opening and filling the sky, strangely beautiful in the green glow of the lens.

It was impossible to keep his mind from drifting to the World Wars fought on this land so many decades before. The sheer magnitude of them. Economies completely commandeered. Battles that went on for months or even years. Millions dead from combat and millions more succumbing to cold, disease, and starvation. If humanity couldn't learn from those mistakes, maybe the whole species was hopeless.

The men behind him finally shoved the cart off the hole and connected a cable to the circuit board they'd exposed. Jarus approached with a large controller that he held out to Coleman. "General Strazds says it's your honor. In thanks for everything you've done to help protect our country and our freedom."

Coleman stared down at the innocuous little box. "Really? He said that?"

The Latvian nodded and dropped it into his hands before rejoining the men solemnly watching their country being invaded.

Rapp peered through the spotting scope at the landing paratroopers, scrutinizing every detail as they freed themselves from their chutes and went for position. He had to admit to being impressed. They spread through the complex like a virus. Gear that had been dropped was snatched up almost before it hit the ground. Machine gun placements appeared in maximally strategic positions, disciplined teams fanned out in the terminal that only a few days ago had been clogged with vacationers and business travelers.

"They're pretty good," Coleman commented as Rapp turned his scope back to the sky. A few minutes passed in silence before the sound of a second wave became audible. The runways were secure and now they could expect an endless line of planes landing and being emptied of equipment and men.

"You've got a Russian transport inbound," Rapp said.

"I hear it," Coleman said. "Do you think anyone else is shooting yet?"

Rapp glanced over at him, having to examine his expression for a moment before he understood the purpose of the question.

"I doubt it. There's no plan to resist the invasion at the border, right? And if it were me, the Riga airport would be first on my hit list."

"So it could be me," Coleman said, toggling the master switch on his remote control. "I could be the guy who fires the first shot in World War III."

"I don't think you want a statue for that."

"You sure? 'Cause I look good in marble." He twisted a dial and the power died throughout the entire airport complex. The meticulously prepared Russians immediately began firing up generators. By the time the first aircraft's wheels touched down, the tower lights were already back on.

Not that it mattered. Another button caused pillars of flame to erupt from the runway. A geyser of shattered asphalt caught the plane beneath one of its wings, turning it on its side and spinning it into a grassy field where it caught fire.

"Ever see one of those shows where they demolish buildings with explosives?" Coleman asked.

"Yeah."

"Check this out."

A series of small charges exploded near the base of the tower, kicking up a cloud of dust and causing the structure to topple into the building next to it. After that, Coleman just ran a finger along the switches, detonating charges hidden all over the complex.

The result could only be described as carnage—both human and structural. The runway was dotted with deep craters and most of the complex's buildings were beginning to burn. The Russian troops that had been so impressive a few moments ago lost all cohesion. Rapp watched through his scope as they sprinted in any direction that would put distance between them and the airport buildings. In truth, though, most were fucked—either torn apart by the initial explosions or trapped in the ensuing inferno.

Coleman dropped the controller and raised two middle fingers in the air. "That's Coleman with a *C*, motherfuckers!"

Rapp swore under his breath and grabbed the man by the collar, dragging him back toward their vehicle.

CHAPTER 38

EVERYONE stood when President Alexander walked into the conference room. Irene Kennedy looked around her at the ashen faces of generals, politicians, and advisors as they waited for America's leader to speak. Instead, he just motioned for them to sit and pointed at his UN ambassador.

She nodded respectfully before speaking. "Everyone agrees that Latvia has been unambiguously invaded by Russia. Article V, the collective defense clause, will be voted on and approved later today."

"So later today we'll be at war with Russia."

"Yes, sir."

"Where's Jim Templeton?" he said, referring to the chairman of the Joint Chiefs.

"Poland," Kennedy responded. "He's helping to wind back up the military presence there and integrate more of our troops."

Alexander turned to his ranking army general. "What's the latest information we have?"

"Latvia, Estonia, and Lithuania scattered their militaries, evacuated their cities, and have started preparations for protracted insurgencies. Our analysis is their actions spooked the Russians. Based on the position of their troops and equipment, it appears that they originally planned a simultaneous invasion of all three countries. Instead, they attacked only Latvia and are now in the process of reconfiguring their resources to support the incursion force."

"So Estonia and Lithuania are still more or less intact?" Alexander said.

"More or less. They're still dealing with the aftermath of the Russian hacking effort, but they still have a significant portion of their infrastructure intact. The cities have been mostly evacuated and will probably stay shut down until the situation stabilizes a bit and they feel confident the Russians aren't going to move against them."

"Latvia?"

"That's a different story. The Riga airport is a ruin, with significant Russian casualties. Other airstrips, bridges, and anything else the Russians would find useful are either destroyed or in the process of being destroyed. Mines are being placed, buildings are being booby-trapped, and surface to air defenses are being set up."

"But our role is basically nonexistent."

"We have approximately twelve hundred NATO troops in the fight there, led by the Canadians. We're also doing what we can to transfer supplies from our ships in the Baltic to shore, but it's a very limited operation. We simply weren't prepared for this."

"But we can ramp it up?" Alexander said, turning to the chief of naval operations.

"In theory, yes, sir. We have a significant presence in the area, as do the Europeans. But there's a lot of Russian naval activity in the Baltic and they're going to want to cut off those supply lines. The question is, how far are you willing to go?"

Alexander fell silent for a moment, pinching his lower lip between his index finger and thumb. "I assume that everyone here has been briefed on the CIA's evaluation of Maxim Krupin's health?"

Nods around the table.

"Do you still stand by that, Irene? He didn't look weak speaking to the Federal Assembly yesterday."

"I do, sir."

"And the attack on him?"

"Overly convenient. The Russian media has announced that he's been moved to an undisclosed location where he can lead the war effort safe from assassins. They're also implying that the attempt on his life was the work of my organization."

"So you're saying it was a publicity stunt. That he did it to himself."

"Almost certainly. It's a typically brilliant move on his part. It doesn't matter anymore how sick he gets or how difficult his treatment is. No one expects him to appear in public anymore."

The president considered his words carefully before speaking again. "What nobody in this room knows is that Krupin finally returned my calls this morning. He said his forces have complete control of Latvia and that he considers it to be back in the Russian fold. Their military has set up tactical nuclear weapons throughout the country and has them aimed at Europe's major cities. He made it crystal clear that any attempt to take back the country will trigger a nuclear response."

The solemn nods around the table suggested that no one was surprised. This kind of a move had been studied by military experts for years. In the end, though, it had never been considered a credible threat. The assumption was that Krupin would calculate too much risk for not enough reward. Until now.

"In light of his health, we have to take his threat seriously. This isn't about long-term strategy, expanding Russian territory, or buffering NATO. This is about him looking strong enough to hold on to power while he figures out if he's going to live or die. Irene? Are we on the same page?"

"Yes, sir. The key to this situation is understanding that it's entirely about optics. Latvia denied Krupin impressive battle victories by not actively resisting, and video of the disaster at the Riga airport is already making its way through the media. The Latvians are tough and know their territory. Russia is about to find itself in the middle of a very bloody insurgency that isn't going to play well on TV."

Alexander's national security advisor spoke up. "But with Russian troops being diverted from the borders of Lithuania and Estonia, Krupin's going to have an overwhelming force. That insurgency may not last."

"It will with our help," Alexander said. "This isn't just about Krupin being sick. The Russians have been pushing harder and harder every year. They can't get their own shit together so they have to try to bring everyone else down to their level. They're becoming the wrench in the machinery of the world."

"But if we really believe that Krupin will retaliate with tactical nukes—and I agree we should—it limits our ability to act," his national security advisor said.

"We just have to stay below the threshold of an act that would bring about that kind of response," Alexander said. "We can provide supplies, advisors, and spec ops teams, right? We can move in heavy to Lithuania and Estonia, surrounding the Russians. And we can give the Latvian air force a virtually unlimited number of planes and pilots—all based safely across heavily fortified NATO borders."

"We can do all that," the air force chief of staff agreed. "But we've got to start before the Russians can get their surface-to-air capability fully up and running. And it's still going to be an ugly fight. The Russian air force isn't going to just turn tail."

Alexander turned to the chief of naval operations. "Can we get control of the Baltic Sea?"

"With the combined navies of the United States and Europe? Definitely. But our ships—and to a somewhat lesser extent our subs—will be vulnerable to attacks from land-based systems."

"But we wouldn't be as vulnerable to those kinds of attacks farther out to sea, correct?"

"I don't understand the question, sir."

"What would it take to sink every deployed vessel in the Russian navy worldwide?"

The man's eyes widened noticeably. "It would take a lot."

"But it's doable."

"NATO's combined naval strength dwarfs Russia's. The question would be finding them and getting into position. Also, I assume that when they figure out what we're doing, they'll hit back hard and make a run for the safety of Russian waters."

"But if we anticipate that, couldn't we cut off that retreat?"

"To a large extent, yes."

"What about it, Irene? If we start sinking Russian ships everywhere we can find them, what would Krupin do?"

"I don't know," she admitted. "It's risky, but not a direct assault on Russian territory. Certainly it would counter the image of strength and control he's trying to project."

"Are we going too far here?" Alexander's national security advisor said. "What about just releasing the information we have on his illness? Show the Russian people that all this is a political stunt by a dying man."

"It's a strategy we're exploring, but we want to make sure it doesn't blow back on us," Kennedy said. "That's a direct attack on Krupin and we're concerned about the retaliation. Any way you look at it, he's not going to go quietly."

There were nods around the table and Alexander leaned forward in his chair. "Let's take a break. I've got a call with the U.K.'s prime minister in a few minutes, and I imagine everyone needs to touch base with their offices for updates. We'll reconvene in thirty minutes."

Everyone rose and started filing for the door except Kennedy and Alexander.

"What did you want to talk to me about?" the president asked. "I've got two minutes before I have to take that call."

"We believe that we have a good chance of locating Krupin and Sokolov."

"Are you talking about an assassination attempt?"

"I think it's unlikely that opportunity will present itself, but if it does, it's something we should consider. Krupin is out of control and Sokolov is a psychopath. Normally, we worry about succession, but it's hard to see how it could be worse."

"You don't have to sell me, Irene. I'll wait for the navy's assessment, but my intention is to completely wipe out Russia's naval capability. A lot of good men are going to end up dead for no reason. If you can take him out and give the United States even barely plausible deniability, I'm on board. We can figure out how to deal with the fallout later."

CHAPTER 39

RAPP reached over and pulled the phone out of Jarus's pocket, then shoved it into his hand. The young Latvian army officer suffered a moment of confusion but then fumbled with the screen to start filming.

He was a smart, solid kid, but not exactly battle hardened. Watching the Riga airport blow apart from a mile away had been the first action he'd seen. Now he was getting a close-up look at the face of war that Rapp had become numb to so long ago. He assumed that he'd once worn the same horrified expression as his new comrade, but honestly couldn't remember anymore.

The farmhouse visible through the trees wasn't much different than any of the others in the area—a compact structure built from local wood grayed by the years. A steep, shingled roof created a silhouette against the dawn breaking on the horizon.

Angled sunlight made the grass glow a deep green that contrasted with the blood splattered across it. The source of that stain was a man lying facedown in the yard. A woman who appeared to be his wife was kneeling beside him, wailing and pulling back and forth on his shirt as though he could be awakened. Hovering over her was a Russian army officer, shouting unintelligible questions.

Rapp turned his attention to the barn when three terrified children around Anna's age emerged. They were being forced to drag a heavy wooden crate by two equally menacing soldiers. One grabbed a crowbar and pried the top off, dumping the medical supplies, ammunition, and food Rapp was there to collect.

Caches like these were distributed throughout the country and the small team he and Coleman were tagging along with had been assigned this one. Their orders were to set up a base of operations in the forest east of there and coordinate with similar teams hidden throughout the region.

Unfortunately, Russians had beat them to it. If they hadn't been delayed by a bridge blown up ahead of schedule, they'd have collected the supplies and been gone hours ago. The soldiers would have found nothing but livestock and farming equipment.

Coleman's voice became audible over his earpiece, but it was hard to make out his words. The radio was intentionally feeble, producing a signal too weak to bring Russians choppers down on them.

"Say again."

"I've made it into the north field. No contacts."

He and Jarus's men had surrounded the house to the degree they could, with Coleman managing to cross some dangerously open ground behind the barn. His report suggested that the Russians had no backup. So an officer, two soldiers, and however many others might be inside the structures. It was that last unknown that caused Rapp to hesitate.

"Stay put, Scott. They might let this go."

The farmer was dead and his family consisted of women and children. This wasn't ISIS. It was a professional army. Most likely they'd kick up a little more dust and move on.

The man in command grabbed the woman by the hair and dragged her to the truck his team had arrived in. He threw back the canopy, revealing the body of a Russian soldier with half his head missing—a victim of one of the many snipers the Latvians had posted along the country's roads. His shouts rose to the level of screams as he threw her to the ground and pulled his sidearm. The kids near the barn started wailing but were held back by the men guarding them.

Rapp swore under his breath. It was just this kind of unprofessional bullshit he figured he wouldn't have to deal with when fighting the Russians. Apparently, he'd given them too much credit.

"This isn't going to go easy," he said into his throat mike.

"Roger that," came Coleman's response

Rapp fired a single round from his silenced Glock and the Russian officer crumpled. The two men standing over the kids looked on, frozen by a moment of confusion.

It should have provided enough time for Rapp to quietly put a round between each of their eyes, but the officer's pistol went off when he hit the ground. The sound broke them from their trance and they began spraying the trees with their assault rifles.

Jarus covered his head with his hands, but Rapp just

stayed on target. Dirt, leaves, and bark rained down, but the chances of hitting someone while sweeping with a machine gun was pretty low. Stan Hurley had actually put a number to it and Rapp found himself hoping the old bastard hadn't just made it up.

He squeezed the trigger and the soldier running to the right went down. The other was smarter. He'd grabbed one of the kids and was using her as a shield while he backed toward the barn. Rapp dropped one of his hands to the dirt and used the ground to steady his aim. Another careful squeeze of the trigger shattered the man's right eye socket, leaving the girl standing in the yard, panicked and shrieking uncontrollably.

"Move in on the barn, Scott. We're taking the house."

"On it," came the reply as he grabbed Jarus and sprinted toward the front porch.

He took the stairs in one leap and kicked open the front door, knowing that speed would have to take priority over precision. It wasn't going to be long before the Russians noticed the shooting and sent an airship in support.

He entered with his pistol held out in front of him, finding a single open room with an arched entrance to a kitchen at the back. He pointed Jarus toward it and let his momentum carry him toward a set of steps to the left. They were dangerously tight and straight, but there was no other option for clearing the top floor.

As fast as Rapp was, he wasn't quite fast enough. The barrel of an assault rifle appeared at the top of the stairs and the deafening roar of blind automatic fire followed. He threw himself against the railing, discovering that it wasn't as solid as it looked when it gave way. The uncontrolled drop back to the ground floor seemed unavoidable for a moment, but then he remembered the ancient beams above. The old wood was rough enough for him to get a good grip with only one hand and he arced out over the room below. After hitting the apex of his swing, he started inevitably back toward the stream of bullets pummeling the steps. Rapp emptied half his Glock's magazine in the direction of the shooter, but didn't really have much hope of hitting anything. He was about to drop to the floor when the shooting stopped and was replaced by unsteady footsteps on the floorboards above.

Rapp landed back on the stairs and started up them again, this time at a more cautious pace. He reached the landing and swiveled smoothly onto the second floor, leading with his weapon. It consisted of a single open space with steeply angled walls that tracked the roofline. The soldier was kneeling next to a twin bed, begging in Russian and bleeding badly from a wound in his stomach.

Rapp fired a single round into his forehead. The man's comrades had made it clear that no quarter would be given in this fight. Not to civilians. Not to women. And not to children. Rules of engagement that Rapp was extremely familiar with.

"You all right?" he said as he came back down the stairs.

Jarus was on the floor, trying to get a connection on a telephone that looked like it had been around since the 1950s. "Yes. There was no one down here."

Rapp activated his throat mike. "Scott. You copy? Give me a sitrep."

"There was one tango in the barn. He's down and we're loading supplies on the horses. I can feel those Russian choppers bearing down on us, though."

"Me too. If I'm not out there when you're loaded, take off. We'll catch up."

"Roger that."

Jarus's expression suddenly transformed from one of concentration to one of genuine surprise. "I'm through! I have a connection!"

Rapp leaned in, listening to a woman who sounded even older than the phone speak Latvian.

"Do you have the number you wanted to call, Mitch? I don't know how long this is going to last."

Jarus relayed Irene Kennedy's private number to the woman and then started pulling the bottom off the phone while Rapp waited to be connected. There was a USB port hidden in the simple electronics and the young Latvian connected his cell to it as the line started ringing.

"Hello?"

"Irene! Can you hear me?"

"Barely. Where are you?"

"Still Latvia. Roughly in the middle," he said, not wanting to give his exact location over the line. "What's going on out there?"

"The good news is that our plan partially worked. The Russians aren't moving against Estonia and Lithuania."

"Let me guess the bad news. They're reassigning all those troops here."

"I'm afraid so. And I need you out of there. Now."

Rapp glanced at Jarus. The Russians were about to swarm his country like some kind of biblical plague, and unless he missed his guess, NATO wasn't going to be able to do much about it. Abandoning him and his team felt wrong.

"I think I'm in this for the long haul, Irene."

"We have a high-priority target for you in a different country," she said, obviously also concerned about the line. The implication was clear, though. She'd located Krupin.

"By the time I get to a border, it's going to be locked down. Let my Russian friend handle it."

There was a pause over the line that was long enough to make him wonder if he'd lost the connection.

"I don't think we can trust him to do it alone."

"Why the hell not? I guarantee you that you're not going to find anyone more motivated."

"That's true. But I recently received a package from him." Another pause. "I think he may have lost his mind."

Rapp yanked the horse's reins and skirted a log that had become lost in shadow. They'd been working only with a map and compass, necessary because of the Russians' ability to zero in on electronic signals. It was a strange sensation to be on the other side of the technological equation—to be forced to use all the low-tech tricks that al Qaeda and the Taliban had used against him.

"How much farther?" Jarus asked, pulling alongside him when the trees thinned out enough to allow it. Rapp saw movement ahead and motioned with his head. "We're here."

A man holding a Heckler & Koch G36 appeared from the foliage, but immediately lowered it when he recognized Rapp's companion. He led them on a circuitous route north, undoubtedly to avoid the mines and trip wires set up on the perimeter.

The camp consisted mostly of military tents beneath structures built of tree limbs and leaves, making everything invisible from above. The majority of people hiding out there were young men, but Rapp spotted one of the kids from the farm being comforted by a woman in civilian clothes.

A blond head appeared from a cave to his left and a moment later Coleman was jogging up to him. "Did you stop for lunch?"

"Phone call."

"Anything interesting?"

"I've got to go. Irene's going to try to get me onto a submarine from a beach near Lilaste."

"The Russian navy's got to be all over those waters."

"We'll see."

"All right. Let me grab a horse and some supplies."

Rapp shook his head. "I'll make my own way. You can stay."

"Not a chance," he replied, grinning broadly. "With your map reading skills, you'll end up looking for that sub in a swimming pool outside of Barcelona."

CHAPTER 40

MAXIM Krupin stood motionless, staring through the glass at the test subjects on the other side. As his treatment dragged on, he found himself in that sterile hallway more and more.

All were strapped to beds and, increasingly, all seemed to represent a part of what he'd become. Some stared back with defiance and rage. Others fear or pain. A few had minds damaged by experimental drugs or untested procedures. At the back was a woman with unblinking eyes fixed on the ceiling. He couldn't remember what protocol she'd been subjected to, only that it had failed. Like the others, her body would be returned to her family with the story that her illness had been too advanced to reverse.

He finally found the strength to focus on his own reflection—the wheeled IV stand in his hand, the tracksuit that hung loose on once powerful shoulders. The bandage covering a burn on the back of his neck that his body could no longer heal. And, finally, the hollowed out eyes that stared back at him.

He heard a shout at the other end of the hallway and turned, squinting into the semidarkness. This sector of the facility was off-limits to everyone but medical personnel and a few trusted guards.

Three men emerged from the gloom, one wearing handcuffs and chains on his ankles. He was flanked by the commander of Krupin's security detail on one side and, on the other, Nikita Pushkin.

Krupin examined the prisoner, mesmerized by the strength with which he fought against his bonds and the two men holding him. He appeared to be in his early fifties, with the same bearlike build that Krupin himself had enjoyed before his illness. Yuri Lebedev, he remembered. A retired soldier from Salekhard.

The man stopped struggling when he saw Krupin, locking eyes with his president as he stumbled forward. When he saw the room behind the glass, though, he dropped to the floor, thrashing wildly as he was dragged inside.

Krupin watched as they strapped him to a bed. His screamed obscenities echoed through the hall for a moment, finally going silent when the soundproof door swung closed. Pushkin started back toward the hall, leaving the security chief to secure Lebedev's remaining free leg.

"Sir," Pushkin said, saluting crisply, but failing miserably to keep the surprise and concern from playing across his face. There had been no reason to tell him anything about this and he still wouldn't know if Krupin had remained hidden in his living quarters. It mattered little, though. He wouldn't be leaving.

"I need you here now, Nikita. I need to be surrounded by people I can trust."

"Of course, sir."

The thought of having Pushkin close provided a certain amount of reassurance. Outside of the prison Krupin had confined himself to, his enemies were multiplying and becoming stronger. Even Sokolov's eyes were beginning to become glassy with visions of glorious battles and subjugated enemies. His strength and brilliance were beyond question, but his loyalties were complex. The general romanticized Russia like a Soviet schoolboy. He would give his life and anyone else's to see it rise again.

Pushkin lacked such grandiose aspirations—or any aspirations at all, really. That, as much as his physical prowess, had been critical in qualifying him to replace Grisha Azarov. While not as smart or mentally tough as his predecessor, his simple nature and tendency toward hero worship were benefits that outweighed any drawbacks.

"You've become very much a son to me, Nikita. I'm pleased to have you at my side during these times."

As always, Pushkin stood a little straighter at the affection denied to him by his own father. There was no question that, unlike Azarov, this boy would carry out his duty until he drew his last breath.

"I've arranged quarters for you. You're dismissed."

Andrei Sokolov slowed and finally came to a stop in the dim overhead light. Twenty meters ahead, Krupin was once again standing with one hand around a wheeled IV pole and the other pressed against the glass looking in on the test subjects.

It was disorienting to see a force of nature like Maxim Krupin stand so still. To watch him waste his hours obsessing over people who were of no importance.

Sokolov started forward again unnoticed. Without Fedkin's stimulant cocktail, the president had lost his awareness of what was happening around him, falling further and further into himself. Now that it loomed so near, he shared the same pointless fear of death that lesser men did.

It was something that had always baffled Sokolov. Even the longest-lived creatures existed for only a blink of an eye. What mattered was building something that was *greater*. Bending that uncaring universe to your will and finding immortality through those efforts. Caesar died in his fifties, but what he built—his reshaping of civilization—would live on until the last human turned to dust.

"I don't understand your fascination with these lab rats, Maxim."

Krupin was slow to respond. "What are you going to do to him? To Lebedev?"

Sokolov followed the president's gaze to a man fighting futilely to free himself from the straps securing him. "We're exploring the possibility of using the Zika virus to attack cancer cells without damaging the healthy brain tissue around them. Promising, but experimental. More important, how is the burn on your neck? Please let me apologize again for that. The force of the explosion was controllable, but the heat from it less so. The threat to you had to look . . ." He paused for a moment. "Dramatic."

"And?"

It was concerning that Krupin spent his time here instead of monitoring the media—something he'd done to great effect before his illness.

"You appeared quite heroic and powerful. The state-run news programs are blaming Latvian terrorists and suggesting that they had American support. Perhaps even more important, a number of your most strident detractors in the Federal Assembly were badly injured."

"But not Prime Minister Utkin."

"He's of no importance. Sending him around the world exchanging gifts with leaders no one has ever heard of has made him look weak. Now, after the invasion, he's being assaulted daily with questions he can't answer. He doesn't just look weak, he looks like a fool."

"You underestimate him, Andrei. He has supporters in Russia. Not just in the population, but in the military and the government. If my position weakens, it's he who most benefits."

"Your position hasn't weakened, my friend. Latvia is fully under our control in less than half the time we anticipated and with far fewer casualties."

"Not a victory," Krupin said. "There's little support to be gained from our tanks rolling into empty cities and our men being massacred at the Riga airport."

"It's simply a matter of spin," Sokolov countered. "Instead of hard-won, courageous victories, we've pivoted to saying that the lack of resistance was proof that Latvia wanted to return to the Russian fold. That they've come to understand that NATO is a useless ally."

"That lack of resistance won't last, Andrei. NATO has declared Article V and the Latvians have laid the groundwork for an effective insurgency. Arrange a call with the other generals. I want an update on our situation."

"I'd strongly recommend against that," Sokolov said, searching for a reason to explain his objection. "A video call would be expected and that's impossible in your present condition. I'm concerned that even your voice could invite questions. You don't sound like yourself."

When Krupin glanced in his direction, there was a hint of something in his eyes that couldn't be easily identified. Suspicion?

"So all my information is to come from you then, eh, Andrei?"

"For a short time, Mr. President. Until the effects of your therapy have diminished enough for you to use Dr. Fedkin's stimulants again."

"Then let's hear it. Where do we stand?"

"In very good position," Sokolov exaggerated. "The troops you ordered in from Lithuania and Estonia are already crossing the border and we'll soon have an overwhelming force in place. The damage to Latvia's infrastructure from sabotage was more extensive than we anticipated, but we have enough engineers and men in place to repair it. NATO troops are moving into Lithuania and Estonia as we anticipated, but they're still in disarray from the dismantling of their exercises. To date, they've made no particularly aggressive gestures. It appears that your conversation with the American president was productive."

"Air?"

"We have complete superiority."

"So you're telling me that we've met no resistance?"

"Not at all. In fact, we've had higher than expected casualties due to a more extensive SAM capability than we anticipated. Also, the Latvians are flying cross-border sorties from Estonia and Lithuania, which has slowed our ability to set up our own defenses. We'll get them in place over the next week, though."

"But no NATO aircraft, Andrei? Just Latvian planes?"

Sokolov considered lying, but it was difficult to tell just how engaged Krupin was. Not the man he had once been, but likely still the most formidable political leader in the world.

"We're seeing more sorties than we would have expected the Latvians to be capable of. That suggests that NATO is reflagging planes and using them to supplement the Latvian force. We don't have any hard evidence of that yet, though. If we can shoot one down and capture a foreign pilot—"

"It's just the beginning," Krupin said. "Their navy will move into the Baltic. They . . ." He fell silent for a moment. "You have to finish this, Andrei. Quickly. We can't get bogged down in another Afghanistan."

"Sir, this isn't Afghanist—"

"It's worse!" he shouted, and then descended into a brief coughing fit. "These aren't Middle Eastern animals. They're people many of our troops can trace their roots to. They're citizens of a peaceful, prosperous country! NATO can afford to bleed us forever. Before, Westerners were concerned only with money and privilege and bickering among themselves. Now they feel threatened."

Sokolov didn't immediately respond. His affection and respect for Krupin only went so far. Had the man weakened to the point that he was now controlled by fear? It took a great deal to win a war but very little to lose one—a severed supply line, an unanticipated move by the enemy, a momentary lack of commitment from leadership. Throughout history, if anything had differentiated victors from the defeated, it was execution without hesitation. Now was not the time to pursue moderation or compromise.

Perhaps it was time to convince Krupin to have surgery. He was losing his ability to see clearly. It was understandable with the physical and emotional stress he was under, but still unacceptable. Allowing the president's temporary weakness to destroy Russia would be a dereliction of Sokolov's sworn duty to protect both.

"You need rest, Maxim. Standing in this corridor is a waste of the strength your country desperately needs from you. I'm meeting with your generals this evening and I'll fly back as soon as possible to report what they said. By then we should have a clearer picture of our strategic position and detailed recommendations for our next steps."

Krupin examined him for a moment and then lowered his gaze to the medals adorning his uniform. Then he just turned and shuffled off.

CHAPTER 41

PRIME Minister Boris Utkin found himself beset on all sides, unable to see the lobby of the Waldorf Astoria for the crush of security men guiding him through it. Not Russians, though. Krupin had sent only a bare-bones detail, the head of which was conspicuously absent at this moment. No, his life was now in the far less than capable hands of the Panama police.

While his line of sight was obscured, he could still hear the shouts of the press. Questions in English, Russian, and Spanish mingled with the chants of the protesters who had forced him to cut short his press conference with the Panamanian president.

Utkin tried to pick up his pace, pushing against the guard in front as cameras sparked around them. Even if he wanted to speak, he'd have nothing to say. Krupin hadn't informed him of his insane plan for an invasion of Latvia and had returned none of his calls since it had occurred. Of course, Utkin had quietly made contact with his supporters in the military and the

Federal Assembly—some of whom had been injured in the highly suspicious attempt on the president's life. But they'd been able to tell him little.

From the Western news agencies he knew that Russian forces had faced little resistance and that despite Article V being declared, NATO was proceeding cautiously. In all likelihood, they would continue to do so. Any overt attempt to retake Latvia would at best be a bloodbath and at worst prompt a nuclear response. No, NATO would take the long view—reinforcing their presence in vulnerable member nations, further isolating Russia economically, and perhaps even attempting to expand into Ukraine and Georgia while Russian troops were bogged down in the Baltics.

He finally reached the open elevator and retreated to the back as two of his borrowed security detail slipped in with him. The doors closed, bringing a welcome change from chaos to stillness. Perhaps it was preferable that he was here, he thought as the elevator began to rise. Certainly better than being impaled by a shattered flagpole at Krupin's recent speech.

"Stay out here," Utkin said to the men with him.

They posted in the hallway as he entered his suite and slammed the door behind him. The room was certainly less than he was used to, but adequate considering where he was—the marble floor was spotless, the furniture was modern and, most important, there was a well-stocked bar at the far end.

"Leonid. Make me a drink."

No answer.

His assistant hadn't picked up his call on the way back from the presidential palace, nor had he answered various texts. Had Krupin called him back to Moscow? Was that to be the latest humiliation? Would he now have to make his own travel arrangements? Perhaps carry his own luggage and write his own speeches? The latter would be interesting. He certainly had a great deal to say about Russia and its leader.

"Leonid!" he shouted, feeling his anger rise along with his growing sense of impotence.

"He's not here."

Utkin spun at the sound of the woman's voice and found himself face-to-face with Irene Kennedy.

She approached and held out a hand, smiling in a way that was intended to be disarming but was very much not. How had she gained access to his room? Was she here to kill him? No, that was idiotic. If she wanted him dead, she wouldn't come personally. She'd send her attack dog Mitch Rapp.

"Where . . . where is he?" Utkin stammered. An irrelevant question designed to give him time to assess his situation.

"Leonid? On his way to Washington. I hope you won't be upset when I tell you that he's been on our payroll for years." She indicated a seating area in the middle of the room and he followed her to it. The upper hand was obviously lost. Best to let her lead for the time being.

"Part of the game," he said calmly. "My compliments."

Another mollifying smile as she sat. "President Alexander wanted to have a personal conversation with you about what's happening in Russia. Unfortunately, it's difficult for him to travel without attracting attention."

"So he sent you? It seems that a State Department representative would be more appropriate."

"No. I don't think it would be."

He nodded knowingly. "You think I'm a traitor. That I'm an ambitious man who can be convinced to betray my president in hopes of American backing when it comes time for succession."

"Something like that."

"Then you've gravely misjudged me, Dr. Kennedy."

She remained the epitome of outward civility but seemed to look right through him. "I know you're a busy man, sir, so I'll get straight to the point. Maxim Krupin has brain cancer that is likely terminal. He's not in a bunker hiding from assassins, he's in a secret medical facility outside of Zhigansk getting medical treatments."

Utkin tried to keep his expression passive while he struggled to absorb what he'd just heard. The only reasonable conclusion was that it was true. Everything that had happened—the crackdown on protesters and opposition, the fool's errand he'd been sent on, the endless hunting trips. Sokolov and the war. It all made perfect sense now. Chaos had turned to order again. Krupin, the consummate strategist, was doing exactly what a man in his position needed to do in order to cling to power.

"You're lying," he said, unwilling to put himself in a position to be blackmailed by this woman. "Maxim has shown America and NATO for what they are and now you're willing to go to any length to undermine him. Desperation doesn't flatter you, Dr. Kennedy."

She seemed to understand his position. "I'm not recording this conversation, Mr. Prime Minister. It wouldn't be in the best interest of either one of us."

He wasn't sure whether to believe her but his curiosity was overwhelming his sense of caution. "If you want to talk, talk. I'm sure Maxim will be quite interested when I tell him of our conversation."

She nodded politely. "He's betrayed your country, Mr. Prime Minister. His actions are calculated entirely to keep himself in power with no regard to Russia's prosperity or even survival. Your country simply doesn't have the resources for a prolonged confrontation with the West. But he doesn't care. Russia isn't his concern."

Utkin remained silent. He'd always been a careful politician—building alliances from the shadows, generating and collecting debts, waiting for an opportunity. Was this it? Was this his moment? The moment to leverage all that groundwork and act boldly?

"If what you're saying is true, Dr. Kennedy, I don't know what you want me to do about it. I can assure you that my return to Russia without the president's consent would not be a triumphant one."

She seemed to consider her next words carefully. "What would you say, Mr. Prime Minister, if I told you that there's a small chance I can neutralize Krupin?"

His eyebrows rose involuntarily. "Are you speaking of assassinating the leader of Russia?"

"I'm talking about precipitating the already inevitable death of a man who seems intent on bringing your country and the world down with him."

The sensation Utkin had of hovering over the point of no return became overwhelming. Was he being set up? Could this woman see something he was blind to?

"You believe that you can put me in power and have a grateful puppet in the Kremlin. I think you'd be disappointed, Dr. Kennedy. I despise America. Its arrogance, its hypocrisy and lack of stability. If you want Krupin out, there's nothing I can do about it from my exile in Panama. But should I succeed him, I'd feel no debt at all to you or your country."

She fixed her gaze on the wall behind him, seeming to use the blank slate to help form her thoughts. "Over the years, I've come to believe that we need enemies. They're how we define ourselves and fighting them gives us purpose. In the absence of a viable external threat, we begin turning on ourselves. I don't want Russia as an ally. I just want to keep the cold war between us from becoming hot."

He stared silently back at her.

"You're surprised?"

"It's a clearer view of the natural order of things than I would expect from an American."

"People in my position don't have the luxury of illusions, Mr. Prime Minister."

"Nor mine. Perhaps one day when we're old and senile, we can have a drink and contrive stories about the nobility of our species."

This time her smile seemed a bit less dangerous. "I'll look forward to it, Mr. Prime Minister."

CHAPTER 42

THE trees closed in again as the southeastern wind turned salty. Rapp and Coleman had hobbled their horses a mile back and were moving silently through the intermittent glow of a half moon.

"Should be just ahead," Coleman whispered as Rapp passed by him and scanned the landscape through a night sight mounted to his borrowed HK G36.

Latvia had a lot of coastline and this section was one of the most remote—undoubtedly the reason it had been chosen for his escape from the country. On the downside, the Russians would be heavily focused on these out-of-the-way beaches as obvious paths for supplies, equipment, and men.

Rapp started forward again, staying low. Another three minutes brought them close enough to the sea to hear the lapping of waves. When they were about twenty yards from the edge of the sand, Rapp stopped and held a hand out. Coleman froze for a moment and then took cover behind a tree.

There had definitely been a flash of movement

ahead, but it took almost a minute to pick it up again. A lone man standing behind something mounted on a tripod. Even with light amplification, though, it was impossible to confirm what that thing was.

He motioned Coleman forward.

"You see him?" Rapp said, pointing.

"I don't see shit."

The man had gone still again, blending perfectly into the terrain.

"Likely machine gun placement. Pointed out to sea. One operator."

"We could go around," Coleman suggested.

"Where there's one, there's bound to be more. My guess is that they've got assholes like this set up at intervals."

"Yeah, but the fact that he's alone is a good sign. It means they're still in the process of securing the beaches with limited manpower."

"If we can quietly take this guy out and the intervals to the next placements are wide, we'll have a straight shot to the water."

The former SEAL nodded. "Those are big ifs, but I'm willing to gamble. We're right where we need to be and I want to keep this swim as short as possible. We don't know what the currents are like and that water's gonna be barely sixty degrees."

Rapp laid his assault rifle on the ground and motioned for Coleman to stay put, moving forward with just his tactical knife. The brittle foliage beneath his feet slowed his pace considerably, forcing him to consider every footfall. It took more than ten minutes to close to within twenty feet of the Russian and he stopped there, pressed against a tree to obscure his outline.

The man had his back to the forest, looking out over the empty beach in front of him. The weapon was indeed a tripod-mounted machine gun—some kind of PK with a long belt inserted. A number of other ammunition boxes were stacked along with food and other gear. They were digging in for a long fight.

This close to the water, the wind was gusting intermittently and Rapp synchronized his approach with the rustling of the trees. It allowed him to get to within ten feet but then he was compelled to stop again. Whether it was natural or planned, the machine gun placement was surrounded by a carpet of dried leaves. Silent and easy wasn't going to be doable.

Rapp examined the man's broad back and the white glow of his hands resting on the gun. If you couldn't be quiet, a good substitute was quick.

He sprinted as hard as he could across the leaves but as fast as he was, sound traveled faster. The man began to spin, swinging an arm out as Rapp slammed into him at a full run. They both went down, rolling across the ground until the trunk of a tree stopped them. The Russian was a bull of a man—easily Joe Maslick's size and suddenly flooded with adrenaline.

Normally not a problem, but Rapp's priority was less killing him than keeping him quiet. There was no way in hell he was the only Russian out there but it was impossible to know how near his comrades were. Certainly within shouting distance, but maybe even closer than that.

Rapp managed to snake an arm around the Russian's neck, cutting off enough of his breath to stop a cry for help. As he was focusing on that, though, powerful fingers dug in around his knife hand. The man rolled and slammed him into the tree again, but Rapp ignored the impact, keeping the pressure on his throat.

Unfortunately, his assessment of the man being as powerful as Maslick was spot-on. The Russian leapt to his feet as though Rapp's one hundred and eighty pounds didn't exist. The pressure of his grip increased to the point that the bones in Rapp's wrist felt like they were on the verge of shattering. The chances of him keeping hold of the knife for much longer were falling fast.

He was dangling from the man's neck, unable to let go and finish the job out of fear that he'd have time to shout a warning before he died. The third impact with the tree was expected, but also significantly harder than the first two. They bounced off and the Russian prepared to drive back into the trunk again, but Rapp tangled a foot in his legs and caused him to stumble.

They landed in a pile of brush and Rapp ended up on the bottom. The Russian's movements were noticeably less violent than before, though. The lack of air was starting to weaken him. Not enough that he didn't start driving his elbow repeatedly into Rapp's ribs, though. The CIA man wrapped his legs around him from behind, interfering with the momentum of his arm and trying to keep the sound of snapping branches to a minimum.

Rapp had resigned himself to taking a serious beating while slowly choking the life out of the man when the Russian suddenly stiffened. A moment later, the grip on Rapp's wrist relaxed and fell away. Tilting his head to the side, he saw the hilt of a knife protruding from the Russian's chest. Beyond was the blond head of Scott Coleman.

"What took you so long?" Rapp murmured, sliding out from beneath the weight of the body.

"It looked like you had him."

Rapp was extracting a broken branch from his side when a Russian voice became audible only a few feet away. They spun in its direction but the tinny quality immediately identified it as a radio. Both waited in silence for a response, but none came. Instead, the same voice crackled to life, this time more insistent.

They were calling for the dead man.

Rapp snatched up the radio and exhausted a good portion of his Russian vocabulary by saying the word "copy" into it.

"Time to get out of Dodge before his buddies figure out what happened," Coleman whispered.

Rapp glanced behind him at the black expanse of the Baltic Sea. Whitecaps glowed in the moonlight, breaking lazily against the beach. None looked much higher than a couple of feet—easy to swim out past but not offering much visual cover.

Worse was the beach itself. There were a good fifty yards of flat sand between them and the water. And even if they made it that far, there would likely be another ten of running through increasingly deep water before they could completely submerge. Unfortunately, better options weren't on offer.

Rapp started to follow Coleman, who was running toward the beach, but then his mind registered something he'd glimpsed a few moments before. He dove forward, grabbing one of Coleman's ankles and taking the man down before he broke out of the trees.

The SEAL reacted just as he'd been trained, roll-

ing to cover and sighting over his rifle at the beach.
"What?"

Rapp pulled him back to the machine gun placement and pointed to a saucer-shaped device partially
obscured by leaves.

"You've got to be kidding me," Coleman groaned
as Rapp pushed the lids off one crate after another,
finding all of them empty. "We're already ten minutes
behind schedule and now we've got a mined beach?"

When a Russian voice erupted from the walkie-
talkie again, Coleman crouched and thumbed back at
the body behind him. "Oh, yeah. And that guy's buddies are about to come down on us like the wrath of
God. I vote that we get the fuck out of here and live to
fight another day."

It was the smart move, but not among their choices.
Maxim Krupin needed to be dealt with before this
thing escalated out of control and Kennedy had lost
confidence in Azarov.

"There's an American sub out there waiting for us
and we're going to be on it."

"Bullshit, Mitch. Sometimes you're just beat and this
is one of those times. Whatever Irene's got going on in
Russia, someone else is going to have to handle it."

The voice on the walkie-talkie came on again,
and the tone of it was easily deciphered. People were
on their way. Rapp looked around him at the empty
crates, the dead man's sleeping bag, and finally at the
machine gun. Time to get creative.

He walked up to the weapon and grabbed the hearing protection hanging next to the stock. The last thing
he heard before everything went silent was Coleman's
quiet voice.

"Please don't do that, Mitch."

The gun bucked in his hand, spewing a line of tracers out onto the beach. He directed fire at the sand in front of him, churning up a section about two feet wide as he walked his aim toward the water. The barrel of the gun was already beginning to glow red when a mine finally exploded about ten yards away. He closed his eyes as the sand blasted his face, but kept his finger on the trigger.

When he opened his eyes again, he saw sand erupting about fifteen yards to the right of where his rounds were hitting. Another Russian machine gun placement had opened fire. Not certain what the target was, they were taking their cues from him.

When his ammo belt ran out, he ripped off his hearing protection and ran for the sand he'd churned up. The Russians were still firing, but their rounds were impacting well to his right, kicking up a cloud of dust that helped obscure him. There was no guarantee that he'd managed to clear all the mines and the tension of knowing he could step on one at any moment was tempting him to push too hard on the unpredictable surface.

When he was about ten yards from shore, the sound of the Russian gun changed subtly but there was no way he could look back to find out why. He hit the water at full speed, lifting his feet high to try to maintain speed. When it got knee deep, he dove into the frigid sea, scraping across the bottom on his way to deeper water.

No rounds were penetrating around him, so he surfaced, letting his head penetrate the surface just enough to see. The Russian gunner had spotted Coleman when he was in the middle of the beach and the former SEAL had been forced to turn back.

Rapp tensed as he watched his friend going for cover in the trees with the Russians doing everything they could to stop him. It turned out that when being chased by a few hundred rounds per minute, Coleman could still haul ass. He disappeared into the darkness and Rapp dove again, staying beneath the surface as he put distance between him and the shore.

Coleman would be fine. While it was true that he still wasn't a hundred percent, it wouldn't matter. Even at three quarters speed, he'd cut a path through the Russians that they wouldn't soon forget.

CHAPTER 43

THE KREMLIN
RUSSIA

ANDREI Sokolov, noting that he was running almost a minute ahead of schedule, slowed his pace. The normally empty corridor was bustling with young officers, all of whom squeezed to its edges as he passed.

He was barely aware of their presence as his mind continued to focus on the ongoing situation with Maxim Krupin. Dr. Fedkin had offered no resistance at all, immediately agreeing to try to convince the Russian president to undergo a dangerous surgery that had little chance of improving his prognosis. It was something that initially had pleased Sokolov, but that now worried him. Fedkin was focused entirely on his own survival and had come to believe that Krupin was irrelevant to it. While he remained outwardly positive and proactive, it was clear that he no longer believed his patient would survive.

Two guards opened a set of double doors and Sokolov passed through, entering the cavernous hall that had been repurposed to coordinate the war. Massive screens had replaced the paper maps once used to track troop movements. Computer terminals had sprouted in place of typewriters and calculating machines, and encrypted satellite communications had taken the place of telephones and couriers. None of that mattered, though. The men, the vague scent of sweat, and unparalleled focus had been unchanged for thousands of years.

When his presence was noted, his military commanders gathered around the table centered in the room. Their faces were uniformly drawn, with eyes reddened from lack of sleep and stubbled chins. Their acknowledgment of his approach was muted, no more than brief nods and murmured greetings.

"Report," he said to the commander of Russia's ground troops.

"Reinforcements continue to arrive from Lithuania and Estonia, but having had no plan for their integration, we're still struggling to make effective use of them. Cities, military bases, and strategic crossroads have been secured but aren't proving as useful as we'd hoped. Electricity and water to them has been selectively cut off in ways that will be hard to repair, and that's interrupting supply lines that are already overwhelmed by the increased troop numbers. Critical roads, bridges, and runways have been destroyed, slowing our men's movements and making them easy targets for the insurgency. Also, the entire country has been booby-trapped. Everything from sophisticated laser triggered mines to simple sawed-through floorboards."

"How long until you've dealt with all those traps?"

"Years," the man admitted. "We don't have enough

men with that kind of training, and even if we did, it's incredibly time consuming work. Probably half the population has fled their homes and many have left traps behind. Add to that the fact that it's impossible to differentiate civilians from soldiers an—"

"I didn't come here to listen to excuses!" Sokolov shouted. "If there's a question as to whether someone is a noncombatant or a member of the insurgency, you will treat them as the latter. If the Latvians are booby-trapping their homes, then we'll burn them to the ground. Am I clear?"

His generals all looked at one another before his new air force commander dared to speak. "I know you've been traveling, sir, so can I assume you haven't seen the international news in the last hour?"

Sokolov shook his head and the man tapped a few commands on a keyboard. The computerized map that made up the tabletop morphed into a video that looked like it had been taken with a mobile phone. It depicted a woman sobbing over the body of her husband as her children were forced to carry a crate from their barn. A Russian officer suddenly grabbed her by the hair and dragged her to a transport truck. He pointed to a dead soldier in the back and then threw her to the ground, drawing his sidearm as the video faded to black.

"Will President Krupin be joining us?" the director of Russia's intelligence operations said. "Perhaps by phone?"

"He had other matters to attend to."

"Other matters . . ." The man's voice faded for a moment, but then came back stronger. "This video is only the first of many, General. Virtually the entire world opposes our invasion. That opposition will only grow in intensity."

"This is war. Expecting the approval of our enemies seems a bit naïve for a man in your position.

He bristled at the insult. "It's not just our enemies, General. It's our allies. This video is circulating through the Latvian population, turning the ethnic Russian population against us. And while we can keep it off the state controlled media, we can't keep it off social media. Our population—and our troops—are already uncertain why we're in Latvia and they fear the West's retaliation."

Sokolov felt his jaw tighten at the entirely accurate assessment of Russia's troops. He hated the weakness of the new generation of soldiers. During World War II, Germany taught the world what could be accomplished with unwavering focus, efficiency, and ruthlessness. It was unimaginable what he could accomplish with the troops and leadership Hitler had enjoyed.

There was a sudden commotion in the far end of the room, and a navy captain ran toward them, pulling his commander aside and whispering urgently into his ear. Admiral Zhabin nodded calmly, finally giving a brief response that sent the man running back to his station.

"What is it?" Sokolov said.

It took a few seconds for him to find his voice. "NATO vessels have carried out a number of attacks on our navy. We've lost contact with three of our submarines and the *Kuznetsov*, our only aircraft carrier, is on its way to the bottom of the sea. Our destroyer the *Ushakov*—"

"The *Kuznetsov*?" Sokolov interrupted. "What are you talking about? It's nowhere near the Baltic."

"I didn't say that our vessels in the Baltic were under attack," the man countered. "I said our *navy* was under attack. We're also seeing movements of American vessels toward our shores. I can only assume to cut off our retreat to Russian ports."

Sokolov was momentarily stunned by the news. Why would the American president risk so much for a country that his constituency cared nothing about?

"You sound as though you've surrendered, Adm—"

"I have surrendered nothing!" the man shouted back. "My sailors have sunk at least one U.S. submarine and the HMS *Diamond* is burning. The battle continues and we'll inflict heavy damage on the West, but we're fighting a simultaneous war against four of the world's most powerful navies. I can turn the Baltic into a graveyard but, by tomorrow, NATO will control it. As for the rest of our ships throughout the—"

"Do we have coastal batteries in place to support the navy?" Sokolov asked the commander of his ground forces.

"No. We've prioritized setting up defenses against NATO landing small teams and supplies. The—"

"What about Russian-based weapons?"

The man paused before answering. "We have significant capability, obviously. But we would have to carefully consider the rules of engagement when NATO inevitably retaliates against Russian soil."

"The Europeans have heavy population concentrations within easy reach of our tactical nuclear weapons," Sokolov said. "They won't violate the sanctity of our border."

"Enough of this," Admiral Zhabin said, insinuating himself back into the conversation. "You say that President Krupin has other things to attend to. What? Hunting? Sunning himself by some mountain lake while you talk about starting a nuclear war with Europe? You don't have the authority. Get Krupin on the phone. Now."

The other generals did nothing to defend the chain of command, instead attempting to stare him down. Had this been planned? A mutiny? Unlikely, but his situation was still dire. Without Krupin's direct involvement, this military campaign was in jeopardy. With it, though, the situation might be even worse. The president's resolve was waning with his strength.

Sokolov motioned to three military policemen he'd brought in for just such an eventuality. One of them grabbed the admiral's arm, but the old sailor shoved him back and marched straight-backed toward the door. Rebuked, the MPs followed meekly behind.

CHAPTER 44

"THIS thing just went pear-shaped," the British submarine captain said, putting a hand on Rapp's dripping back and guiding him down a narrow corridor. "We're now engaged in a full-scale naval war."

"Come again?" Rapp responded through chattering teeth. He'd won a number of triathlons in water around that temperature, but the fact that his wetsuit was hanging on a peg in his garage wasn't ideal.

"NATO's commander just ordered an attack on every targetable Russian navy vessel worldwide. The good news is that we caught them flatfooted and did some damage. The bad news is that they're coming back at us hard."

"Are you going to be able to get me where I'm going?"

"I've been ordered to do that or go to the bottom trying," he said, stopping and slapping a door to his left. "Shower. Your gear's inside."

They shook hands and the captain started back along the corridor, calling over his shoulder as he went. "If you Agency boys have a plan to get us out of this, sooner would be better than later."

Rapp entered the cramped shower room and pulled off his wet clothes. The salt was rinsed off in a few seconds, but he stayed beneath the hot stream of water until he stopped shaking.

Reluctantly, he finally stepped out and toweled off, wondering if at that moment they were being targeted by the Russians. No point in dwelling on things beyond his control, he reminded himself as he unzipped the duffel that had been left for him. Sea battles were the navy's problem.

The bag was meticulously packed with a pair of clippers and a razor on top. There was a sticky note with the word *beard* inside a circle with a line through it. Claudia's handwriting.

He left his facial hair on the floor and sink, then went back to the duffel. The next layer contained black jeans, a cotton shirt, and a pair of light hiking boots— all from his closet. The banged-up eyeglasses with clear lenses, though, were new to him. As was the brushed nickel ponytail holder in the shape of a peace sign.

Under other circumstances, he'd have actually gotten a laugh out of that.

Rapp put the glasses on and then went to toss the ponytail holder in the garbage. When he did, he saw that Claudia had scrawled something on the back.

Don't throw this away.

Ignoring the advice, he returned to the duffel but didn't find the weapon he was looking for. An unusual lack of thoroughness on her part. The Glock he'd brought with him to Latvia was now residing on the sea floor.

Rapp left the clothes from his swim on the floor and opened the door to the shower room. Two men passed and pressed their backs against the bulkhead in order to get around a woman wearing the uniform of a French naval officer. They struggled not to stare at her but Rapp didn't bother to make the effort.

"What the hell are you doing here?" he said in French.

"My job," Claudia responded. "What did you do with Scott? Is he—"

"Safer than us. Your job is logistics. Not operations."

"I'm here to brief you," she said, starting down the corridor. "That falls under logistics."

"In the middle of the largest fucking naval engagement since World War II?"

"It's not something I wanted someone else to do," she said. "And, besides. There was no way to anticipate this."

He opened his mouth to argue, but then just gave up. Winning arguments with her was virtually impossible, and in this case she was right. The fact that the president had approved this kind of an escalation came as a surprise even to him. He—and the Russians—had expected the Baltic to be a chess match with both sides primarily concerned with not allowing the situation to spiral out of control.

"Is Grisha here?"

"Yes."

"And where's his head at?"

"I haven't spent enough time with him to give you a useful assessment. But Cara's surgery went well."

"What about my gun?"

"You'll find one waiting for you on a bank of the Olenyok River. Or at least that's what I'm told. Irene's office is handling that end of the operation."

She led him into a cramped conference room where Azarov was waiting.

"How was your swim, Mitch?"

"Cold."

Rapp made himself a cup of coffee while Claudia started her briefing.

"The man Grisha was watching was picked up by Nikita Pushkin. We were able to track him to Zhigansk, a small town in rural Russia and then to a decommissioned military installation to the north-west. We've analyzed the satellite images from the last few months and there's been a significant uptick in activity. We suspect that Krupin's getting his treatments there."

She spread a map out on the table and tapped a red circle on it.

"Remote," Rapp commented.

"If it isn't the middle of nowhere, it's only a few kilometers away."

"Do you think he's there now?"

"We're giving it a seventy-five percent chance."

"Can you get us there?"

"It isn't going to be easy. Not only is it remote, there's only one road going in and out. There's no reason for anyone to be up there, and that road's going to be under heavy surveillance."

"Can I assume that you've worked something out?" Rapp asked.

She nodded, though a bit reluctantly. "I got to thinking about your last operation in Russia—the one where you went in with a nature outfitter. It worked once, so we thought it might work again. Maybe a hunting guide, which would give you an excuse to be armed."

"Your tone suggests you weren't able to find one," Azarov said.

"I'm afraid not. No one's operating any kind of tour in that area right now. That's the bad news. The good news is that we did find an inhabited camp." She tapped another circle on the map. "Here."

"That doesn't look very close to our target," Rapp said.

"About seventy miles as the crow flies."

"Of some of the most rugged terrain on the planet," Azarov commented.

"Virtually impassable," she agreed.

The submarine dove suddenly enough that Rapp had to reach out and steady her. She fell silent for a few seconds but when no torpedoes or depth charges exploded, she ran a finger along a thin blue line on the map. "You can cover most of it using the Olenyok River. The rest, you'd have to do on foot."

"You say 'inhabited camp,'" Azarov said. "What kind of camp?"

"Scientists. Mostly botany and wildlife. And this is where we got lucky. There are two American academics on their way there now."

"You want to make a switch?" Rapp said. "Substitute us for them?"

Another uncertain nod.

"What do they study?" Azarov asked.

"Wolves."

"I don't know anything about wolves. And I suspect that Mitch doesn't, either."

She held up two thumb drives. "Everything you ever wanted to know about Canis lupus as well as your cover stories."

"You don't seem convinced," Rapp said.

"I don't think you should do it."

"It's your plan."

"So you should listen to me when I tell you how horrible it is. Irene ordered me and her team to come up with the best strategy we could and this is it. It's unworkable, Mitch. Your cover story is incredibly weak. You're not a scientist and you have almost no time to prepare. The terrain is—"

"You said we could use the river."

"That makes moving easier but leaves you exposed to possible overhead surveillance. If you're caught, there are going to be questions, and you don't even speak the language."

Rapp nodded and scanned the map for a few seconds. "No one in that camp's going to quiz us on basic wolf biology. As long as we know what we're there to do and limit our contact, we should be okay. Can we travel on the river at night, then sleep in the woods during the day?"

She shook her head. "Too far north. The sun doesn't set this time of year."

"It just keeps getting worse, doesn't it?"

"It's what I keep telling you."

"How much traffic is there on that part of the Olenyok?"

"Virtually none," Claudia admitted. "But that's no guarantee."

"Wrong business for guarantees. Let's assume we can sell ourselves as scientists, and that we reach our objective without drowning, getting shot, or being eaten by a bear. What are we going to find?"

"Basically an ammunition and equipment dump with eight warehouse-type buildings," Claudia said. "The number of guards is a question mark. If there are any outside, they're doing a good job of staying out of sight. How many are inside would just be speculation. Pick a number between zero and a hundred."

"That's helpful."

"I'm sorry."

"Okay," Rapp said. "Let's be optimistic and say we get in there. What then?"

"We kill him," Azarov responded in a tone that suggested he wasn't entertaining other options.

Claudia nodded. "The president and Irene are fine with that, but they'd prefer something . . . Subtle."

Rapp actually laughed. "So we make it through seventy miles of no man's land, get through whatever guards there are outside, gain access, get through the guards inside, and then make it look like natural causes?"

"That's my point," Claudia said. "This isn't a plan, it's desperation. In all likelihood, you'll get killed or captured. And after that it won't take them long to identify you. That would make a disastrous situation even worse."

Rapp took a chair and gulped down some of his coffee, feeling it burn down his chest. "Can I count on you to back me up, Grisha?"

The Russian's gaze lowered to the tabletop. "If I'm honest? I don't know."

"Explain."

"My fitness is worse than it's been since I was a

child, and I'm having a hard time focusing. Two issues I've never had to deal with during an operation."

"My understanding is that Cara's doing fine."

"Yes. But did Dr. Kennedy tell you why?"

"The liver? Yeah. You managed to surprise her. That's not easy."

"She seems to think I've become mentally unbalanced. That I'm emotionally incapable of handling my new life. She's a wise woman and I'm concerned that she's right. While I very much want to be the man who kills Maxim Krupin, I have to consider the possibility that my involvement could cause the mission to fail. Maybe you'd be better off relying on the team you normally work with."

Rapp leaned back in his chair, examining the man. He was probably right, but Coleman was stuck and his men were all engaged in other operations. Not to mention the fact that none of them spoke Russian. "Give me specifics. Could you still run a marathon?"

"Of course."

"How fast?"

Azarov's eyes narrowed as he calculated the number based on extensive training history. "Two hours fifty-five on a flat asphalt."

"Good enough to float down a river and do a little bushwhacking."

"But there's still the mental side. I—"

"What the fuck are we talking about?" Rapp said, finally losing patience. "The liver? Cara needed one and you found a donor. But that's not going to mean shit if Krupin survives. He can't leave you breathing and she's going to end up getting dragged in again. The only way you and Cara have a future is if Maxim Krupin doesn't."

Azarov turned to Claudia, apparently not convinced that Rapp was a reliable arbiter of sanity. "And you? What do you think about what I did?"

Her eyes actually misted up. "I think it's the most romantic thing I've ever heard."

CHAPTER 45

RAPP leaned forward to examine the landscape below the chopper. A whole lot of nothing. Marshy plains, tree-covered mountains, and a distant river that he assumed was the one Claudia had told him about. Irene Kennedy was trying to get a raft and other gear onto its banks, but when they'd boarded the helicopter in Zhigansk, it still hadn't been done.

The sub had gotten them to Sweden, only to find the airspace so full of warplanes and the occasional missile that the CIA's G550 had been turned back. They'd been forced to divert to Denmark, putting them well behind schedule. The original plan had been to meet with the scientists they were replacing. Instead, the two men had been stopped by MI6 in London and then transported to a forgotten corner of Africa where they'd stay until this thing was over.

Rapp and Azarov had taken their seats on the last plane going to Moscow before travel between Europe and Russia was shut down. The pilot arced south of the chaos in the Baltic, but fighter formations and smoke rising from burning ships had been visible against the clear sky. The passengers had spent much of the six hours searching their windows for military activity, speaking in agitated whispers, and consuming the galley's entire supply of vodka.

When the helicopter finally touched down, the Spetsnaz team Rapp half expected didn't materialize. Instead, a man with dreadlocks and cargo pants ran toward them in a practiced crouch. He removed some of their gear and jogged away with what he could carry as the chopper took to the air again. When the noise faded, he introduced himself.

"Chase Mason. Glad you guys could still make it with all the shit that's going down."

"We are, too," Rapp said, shaking his hand. "I'm Mitch. This is Greg."

"Nice to meet you both. Let me show you to your tent. I'm afraid you're going to have to share, but it's pretty spacious. We don't have all the creature comforts, but on a sunny day like today, it's not so bad. At least the bugs are down. Be thankful you weren't here last month."

Rapp worked up a friendly grin, only half listening as he studied the camp. Not much more than an outdoor cooking area, two latrines, and six yurts skinned with dirty white canvas. The largest of them was flanked by a freestanding satellite dish and its stovepipe was the only one producing smoke. It looked newer than the others, with a beat-up lawn chair out front and a generator humming just out of sight.

Their quarters were more basic, but still better than what Rapp was used to in the field. A single circular space with a rusty woodstove for heat and a battery powered lightbulb for after sunset. A wood slat floor kept them off the soggy ground, and two cots were piled with enough blankets to hold back the cold nights.

"They probably told you," Mason continued, "but we've got signal on a couple of collared wolves. You'll be happy to hear that they're only a few miles east of here and there's a pretty good game trail that'll take you most of the way."

"Sounds great," Azarov said, in an impressively neutral American accent.

"Go ahead and get settled in for a few minutes," Mason said. "But don't take too long. Sergei wants to talk to you."

"Sergei?" Rapp said. Claudia had given him a dossier on everyone at the camp and there was no mention of a Sergei.

"Yeah. He showed up a month or so ago. Some kind of government representative. Harmless, but a pain in the ass. He's basically a red tape machine who wants to hear about everything that's going on but doesn't really understand any of it." Mason lowered his voice. "We figure he's some politician's dumber brother and he needed a job."

Rapp tested his easy grin again but this time it was even more strained. The good news was that the sudden appearance of a political officer in the middle of nowhere suggested they were on the right track. The bad news was that Russian bureaucrats despised unexpected changes. Whoever this Sergei was, he'd be suspicious about the last-minute substitution of Rapp and Azarov for the team he expected.

"Yeah, no problem," Rapp said. "Where is he?"

"Big tent with the dish. You can't miss it."

Rapp banged on the plank door and was immediately rewarded with an answer from within.

"Come in!"

He did, rounding his shoulders and regretting tossing Claudia's peace sign ponytail holder. Fooling a bunch of young researchers whom he could largely avoid had never worried him much. A Russian intelligence officer was a different story.

"Welcome," Sergei said, examining him and Azarov from behind an oddly ornate desk. The floors were covered with thick rugs and there was a well-stocked liquor cabinet behind him.

"Thanks. We're happy to be here. It was touch and go there for a while."

The Russian clearly wasn't worried about reinforcing stereotypes in his tracksuit, garish rings, and comb-over. An ample belly strained at the scarlet polyester and deep-set eyes tracked with more intelligence than Chase Mason had given him credit for.

"I'm sorry the others couldn't make it," he said in solid English. "How fortunate that you were both available at the last moment."

Rapp just nodded while Azarov followed his lead and remained silent. The less said the better.

"I understand that they were called away on an emergency in . . ." Sergei glanced down at a piece of paper on his desk. "Senegal. I have to say that I wasn't aware that there was such a thing as a wolf research emergency. Or wolves in Africa, frankly."

This time an answer was clearly required. "Canis anthus," Rapp said. "They may be infected with a strain of rabies that no one's ever seen before. Probably not, but the WHO guys were worried enough to want to bring in a couple experts."

"Your paperwork only got to me a few hours ago," the Russian complained.

Rapp gave the expected disinterested shrug.

"You look a little old to be a PhD candidate."

This wasn't going to go as easily as he'd hoped. Fortunately, Claudia and the Agency had seeded their legends all over the Internet—Facebook, university sites, expedition blogs. All complete with doctored pictures of them tagging animals, working in labs, and teaching classes.

"I was working for an outdoor equipment retailer in the States but this had always been my dream. I guess I got a late start."

"I enjoyed your blog about the trip you did to Europe to try to find a sheep."

"It was an ibex, actually. They—"

The man held up a hand and turned his attention to Azarov. "Have you two known each other for long?"

"We met on a project in China years ago and stayed in touch." His American accent was holding. Bland Middle America with a few West Coast overtones. Calculated to be something no one would remember or be able to place within a thousand miles.

"Why?"

"No reason, really. We hit it off and both of us specialize in wolves. I'm not a full-time academic, though. I work for Wyoming Game and Fish. Mitch called me when this opportunity came up and I jumped. Beautiful country you have here. It kind of reminds me of home."

Sergei nodded, but continued to contemplate them. "I'd love to hear more, but I have other matters to attend to. Perhaps I'll go out with you tomorrow. The weather service is calling for another cloudless day."

It was clear from his physique, pale complexion, and comfortable surroundings that going out with them was the last thing he wanted to do. Krupin's people had undoubtedly sent him there with orders to look for anything suspicious. Now he'd found it and he was going to make sure nothing got by him that could bring down his president's wrath.

"That'd be great," Rapp said, knowing he had no other option. "It'll be nice to have someone familiar with the terrain."

True to Sergei's promise, a high-pressure system had settled in over the region, bringing with it clear skies and unusually cool temperatures. It was supposed to last for another five days, which would be more than Rapp could afford to take. The way the war was heating up, Western Europe could be an uninhabitable wasteland by the middle of next week.

"We've got oatmeal or granola with soy milk," a young woman said, stirring a large pot hung over a fire. The sun still hadn't broken over distant peaks, and so far she and Rapp were the only two people who had ventured outdoors.

"Oatmeal."

The woman—Ingrid from the University of Oslo based on a brief introduction at dinner the night before—filled the two bowls on Rapp's tray and then poured in a little milk.

"Have you seen the news yet this morning?"

"Nope," Rapp responded, trying to avoid unnecessary conversation without seeming overly unfriendly. While he'd become reasonably knowledgeable about wolf biology, his newfound expertise wouldn't survive the scrutiny of the real scientists in the camp. Fortunately, all anyone wanted to talk about was the war.

"NATO says it has control of the Baltic Sea. That every Russian ship has been destroyed but that there may be a few hidden submarines. They say that at least a thousand sailors have died. Do you think that's possible? So many people?"

"I dunno."

In truth, the estimate was likely low. NATO was wreaking havoc on Krupin's navy while trying not to cross the line into anything that could be construed as an attack on the homeland. But where was that line exactly? With Krupin's brain rotting away and Sokolov controlling the war effort, the situation got blurrier every day.

"Men are crazy," she concluded.

"You have no idea."

"Are you going out this morning?"

"Yeah. We're meeting Sergei in twenty minutes."

She rolled her eyes. "He's going with you?"

"Yeah."

"Plan for a long day. His cigarette breaks alone will take over an hour."

"We're going to be crossing some pretty rugged terrain. Maybe he'll change his mind."

Her blond ponytail flopped across her back as she

shook her head. "He's suspicious of everyone. I think he believes we're all a bunch of CIA assassins."

Rapp smiled and grabbed a few rolls left over from the previous night. "Thanks for the oatmeal."

"How are we looking?" Rapp asked, entering the yurt and kicking the door shut behind him. Azarov was hunched over a laptop, tracking the movement of the collared wolves they were ostensibly there to study.

"They've moved toward the river," he said accepting a bowl of oatmeal. "That puts a mountain between us and them."

Rapp examined the satellite image on screen. The fact that the pack appeared to be on its way to the river that was their objective was good news. And the mountain wouldn't play well with Sergei. It looked steep as hell and then they'd have to cover a good half a mile of craggy ridgeline before coming to a viable descent.

"Long, hard day," Rapp said, assuming that there were listening devices hidden in the yurt. "Probably twenty hours with a lot of elevation gain. We should take headlamps for the way back."

Hopefully, that would be enough to discourage Sergei from coming. They hadn't known the man was going to be in camp and still didn't know what they were going to do with him if he still insisted on tagging along. The fact that Krupin had chosen him for this detail suggested that he was smarter and more determined than he looked. Best to bring along a shovel just in case.

"How many wolves were transported here from the Chernobyl Exclusion Zone?"

The terrain had turned uphill, but the dense trees made it impossible to pick up the pace enough to discourage Sergei's thinly veiled interrogation.

"Four," Rapp said. "But one died almost immediately and never got a chance to breed with the local pack."

His unusually detailed memory had saved his ass too many times to count and this was quickly becoming another example.

"I understand you were a lacrosse player, Mitch."

Their legends included lacrosse for him and biathlon for Azarov. Always best to stay as close to the truth as possible.

"Yeah. Back in school."

"Intriguing sport. I was watching a match recently on television."

Rapp calculated the chances of that at around zero.

"Maybe you could clear something up for me. What does FOGO stand for?"

"Face off get off," he said, using a machete to hack through a bush that opened up to a rock-strewn slope.

Finally, it was possible to accelerate enough to get Sergei huffing instead of running his mouth. The route to the top of the mountain was in full sun with virtually no air movement. Rapp would keep the Russian near his limit—not hard enough to make him demand a break, but hard enough to make him suffer. With a little luck, his heart would give out.

Rapp took the path of most resistance, glancing back at Sergei's glistening face and Azarov bringing up the rear.

The ground underfoot was dangerously loose, creating minor slides that left dust trails leading back toward the trees. Rapp aimed for a comfortable-looking boulder but then turned before reaching it, finding an even steeper line to the distant summit. As expected, Sergei didn't follow, opting instead to take a seat on the boulder. His tracksuit was soaked through, as were the nylon straps holding the Makarov PM pistol beneath his left arm. He'd undoubtedly worn the holster for the purpose of intimidation, but was now likely regretting the extra weight.

"How much longer?" he panted.

Rapp squinted at the ridge looming above. "Maybe two hours?"

"And how long have we been climbing?"

"About ten minutes," Azarov said.

"At least it's not hot yet," Rapp said. "The way back's going to be brutal."

"And I hear that there's been a lot of bear activity in the area later in the day," Azarov added.

The possibility of an animal attack was the last straw.

"I have a conference call with the Kremlin early this evening," Sergei said.

"I don't think we're going to make that," Rapp responded, shooting for a tone of sincere regret, but going a bit wide of the mark.

The Russian nodded gravely as his breathing finally began to slow. "I'm afraid I can't miss it."

"No problem," Rapp said. "We'll just head on up and see you back at camp tonight."

The political officer looked at them, going from one face to the other, finally settling on Azarov. "You've not said much on our journey. Why don't you tell me a bit about what you hope to accomplish with your research?"

"We're studying the persistence of radiation-induced genetic mutations passed down through generations of wolves."

"That sounds like something you read in a book."

"What do you mean?" Rapp said, coming to Azarov's rescue. "We're biologists. *Everything* we talk about came from a book."

Sergei returned his attention to Rapp. "You're very convincing, Mitch. But your friend here . . . I don't trust him."

"What do you mean?" Rapp said. "What's to trust? We're going to go over this mountain, dart a few wolves, get a few blood samples, and go home. I mean, I know about all the stuff that's going on in Latvia, but what's that got to do with us? Wars start, wars end, nothing's accomplished. Science goes on, man."

Sergei lit a cigarette, drawing on it and letting the smoke roll from his mouth as he spoke. "Your presence online is impressive, but there's a flaw."

"Flaw?" Rapp said as Azarov looked on with an increasingly dead expression. "What are you talking about?"

"There isn't a single clear picture of either of your faces. Always just a bit out of focus, a bit distant, or bit shaded. What do you think the chances of that are?"

Pretty fucking low, actually. Those photos had been processed in a way that would make them impossible to identify by Russian intelligence.

"Are you kidding? With phones, people take a million pictures a minute and all of them suck. You want to see what we look like? You're staring right at us."

Sergei stood. "We'll go back to camp and talk more. Perhaps take some clearer photos and send them to Moscow. If all goes well, you can come back out later this week."

Rapp let out a long, slow breath. "No way I can change your mind?"

Something in his voice or expression alerted the Russian and he dropped his cigarette, jerking his hand toward the gun holstered beneath his arm.

Rapp slammed a palm into his nose, hard enough to disorient him, but not hard enough to drop him. The gun came out but the Russian's grip was no longer strong enough to keep Rapp from plucking it from his hand.

"What . . . what are you doing?" he said, stumbling back against the boulder while his nose poured blood down the front of his tracksuit.

Rapp ignored the question, dropping his backpack and pulling out a rope. It took just a moment for him to fashion a noose and slip it around Sergei's neck. The Russian panicked and tried to get it off, but Azarov pinned his arms behind his back. Rapp attached the other end of the rope to the back of his pack and started up the side of the mountain again. Sergei stumbled along behind, grabbing at the rope but unable to generate enough slack to escape.

"You fucked with the wrong people," Rapp said over the man's gagging. "We Americans take our research seriously."

They made it to the ridge in just under the two hours Rapp had predicted. Sergei had probably fallen to his knees fifteen times over the last three hundred yards but credit where credit was due. The fat fuck was still alive.

They stripped off their packs and looked down the back side of the mountain at the river and the endless wilderness beyond. Sergei was on all fours, clawing the noose off and gasping for breath. He finally tried to get to his feet, but Azarov slammed a foot into his ribs and left him writhing on his back.

"Steep and narrow here," Rapp said. "Lots of loose rock. An accident waiting to happen."

Azarov grabbed Sergei's ankles and Rapp took his wrists. They carried the struggling man to the edge of the slope and after a few vigorous swings, let go. He screamed as he arced out over the steep terrain, going silent again when he hit ground thirty feet below and began cartwheeling down the slope. His broken body finally came to rest against a boulder a good three hundred yards from the summit.

"He didn't start a slide," Rapp said, disappointed.

"Perhaps he was too light."

Rapp emptied most of the contents of their backpacks and threw the items to create a trail that made it look like they'd gone down the same way.

The next task was more difficult: trundling boulders off an outcropping until one finally started the chain reaction they were looking for. They ended up with an obvious slide that buried most of their gear but left Sergei's body partially visible.

"How much time do you think we have?" Azarov said.

"They won't start to worry until we're at least a couple hours overdue. A few more hours to put together a search party and then four more to get up here. Maybe another couple days before they're sure our bodies aren't in that slide."

"Not much time," Azarov said.

Rapp just jumped off the ledge in front of him and started down the slope.

CHAPTER 46

ENTER!"

The voice barely carried through the door and Andrei Sokolov didn't immediately comply, instead taking a moment to collect himself. These personal visits to Krupin's medical facility were long and complex—something the general had neither the time nor energy for. There was nothing that could be done, though. The secrecy surrounding Krupin's illness and the handling of the man's growing weakness became more critical every day.

Sokolov finally entered Krupin's opulent living quarters, but instead of finding the Russian president wallowing in bed, he was sitting behind a modest desk, clear-eyed and wearing a business suit. The slight shaking of his hand was an indication that he was once again under the influence of Dr. Fedkin's stimulants.

Even more concerning was the presence of Nikita Pushkin standing silently in the far corner of the room. Sokolov saw no reason to acknowledge him. He was nothing. A weapon was only as dangerous as the man wielding it.

Krupin's attention lingered on his general for a moment and then returned to a television hanging on the wall. The screen depicted a high-altitude flyover of the Baltic Sea and the smoke plumes that represented the fate of the Russian fleet there.

"Where to from here, Andrei?"

Sokolov had been prepared for a number of specific recriminations, but not for a question so open-ended. He found himself in the rare position of fumbling for a response.

"We fight on, sir."

Krupin laughed. "That's the strategy you've devised for me? We fight on?"

"NATO has been a more aggressive opponent than we expected. But at their foundation, they're weak. They—"

"Weak!" Krupin shouted, leaping to his feet with the power the stimulants had temporarily given him. "Half my navy is at the bottom of the ocean and the other half is either being hunted or trapped in port. And you did nothing."

"Our ability to attack naval targets from Latvian soil hasn't come online as quickly as we hoped. We've prioritized those systems and within forty-eight hours we'll be in a position to retaliate against NATO vessels."

"What NATO vessels, Andrei? My understanding is that they're abandoning the Baltic."

Sokolov didn't immediately answer. While true, he wasn't certain where Krupin acquired the information. Had the international media started reporting

on the pullout while he'd been traveling incommuni-
cado from Moscow? Or had the president reinitiated
direct communication with Russia's other military
commanders?

"They're one step ahead of you, Andrei. They attacked with everything they had knowing that you
weren't ready. And now they're moving their vulnerable surface ships out and leaving their submarines to
supply the insurgency. I don't look strong. I look like
an idiot."

"I'm aware that we've lost control of the media nar-
rative but we'll regain it. Latvian terrorists have carried
out a number of brutal attacks on our troops. We'll be
able to regain the sympathy of the Russian peop—"

"You think Russia is run by being the object of
pity?" Krupin shouted. "Our disinformation efforts
are dead! You've provided the West the external
enemy they needed to end their squabbling and pull
together. And what of the glory the Russian people
crave so deeply? What have they been provided? The
defeat of our navy, mounting economic sanctions, and
the capture of cities inhabited only by people too old
or infirm to leave."

"These Latvian terrorists will—"

"They aren't Afghan animals," Krupin yelled, the
red of his face turning vaguely unnatural around
bulging eyes. "The international press is portraying
them as courageous patriots trying to repel invasion.
The success of this operation turned on a quick and
decisive victory lauded by Latvia's ethnic Russian
population. A demonstration that the country would
be stronger backed by the stability of Russia rather
than the constant upheaval of democracy."

His strength faltered and he lost his balance. Pushkin was immediately in motion, helping the man back into his chair.

"Sir, you're not well," Sokolov said. "Dr. Fedkin—"

"Fedkin is of no consequence," Krupin said, lowering his voice to a sustainable level. "There will be no more procedures and no more treatments until I've gained control of this situation."

Sokolov nodded respectfully, but felt his anxiety deepen. Krupin didn't have the stamina to lead this war effort and he was increasingly hampered by his inability to differentiate between himself and Russia. The quick, easy victory he needed was no longer possible. Sacrificing focus on the larger battle to concentrate on his political survival would create a slow moving disaster that the country might never recover from. This war was now about Russia's future while Krupin was becoming part of its past.

"Contact your counterparts in the West, Andrei. Reiterate that we've moved nuclear weapons into Latvia and make sure they understand that they'll be used at the first *hint* that the Latvian insurgency is being assisted from the outside."

It was precisely the wrong strategy, devised with a man who was thinking in terms of days and weeks instead of years and decades. NATO had indeed surprised them, but it was too early to determine if it would matter to the final outcome of the war. Certainly, a tactical nuclear strike might eventually become necessary, but the timing, target, and retaliation would have to be carefully considered.

"Yes, sir."

"This isn't an idle threat, Andrei. It can't be. What's

the least populous major city within easy reach of our weapons?"

"Sir, I think we—"

"Answer me! I have no more time for your failures. Every minute that passes without a victory strengthens my enemies in Moscow. They're plotting against me. I can feel it. I've always been able to feel it."

"Copenhagen," Sokolov said, finally. "Approximately three quarters of a million people."

"Then make the threat specific—choosing the major city with a low population will convince them. We'll see just how much the West is willing to bleed to try to take back a country that's rightfully ours."

"I understand," Sokolov responded, not sure what else there was to say.

"I want you to set up a video conference between us and the rest of my military commanders, Andrei. Fifteen minutes from now."

"Then you'll have to excuse me so I can make preparations."

He turned on his heels and heading for the door.

The breakup of the Western alliance and the resurgence of Russia was within reach, but it would be a long and difficult path. Their fist would have to be slowly closed around Latvia, proving to the surrounding nations that NATO was powerless to protect them. Internet disinformation campaigns would have to be expanded and modernized, turning countries and citizens against one another. The election of autocratic leaders sympathetic to Russia would have to be supported. Chaos would have to be fomented in Syria and North Africa in an effort to create a refugee crisis that would overwhelm Europe.

Krupin had started this process, but it was increasingly obvious that he was no longer capable of finishing it. It was time for Sokolov to begin laying the groundwork for taking control of Russia. Krupin would have to be isolated in such a way that he could still be used as a power base but would have no involvement in generating strategies or setting policy. His strength and intelligence would be missed, but it was the only way that Russia could live on in his image.

CHAPTER 47

THEY'D been slower than even Rapp's worst-case scenario. The back of the mountain they'd come down had been more treacherous than expected, and they'd nearly been taken out by two separate rock falls. Worse, Azarov hadn't been kidding when he'd said his fitness had slipped. The superhuman he'd been when he trained six hours a day and pumped himself full of PEDs was just a memory now.

It wasn't all bad, though. The Russian was still one of the top five operators in the world and the wolf pack had been content to just watch the two men intruding on their territory instead of tearing them apart.

Even better, the gear they'd been promised was right where it was supposed to be. Bushwhacking across seventy miles of some of the world's most rugged terrain with no food or water and then attacking a fortified ammo dump with sticks and rocks wasn't something that was going to turn out well.

Rapp dragged a waterproof duffel from where it had been buried and emptied the contents onto the ground. Their tents, sleeping bags, and a raft were already lined

up in the dirt—all brands commercially available in
Russia. The dry bag contained more technical equipment, including night-vision gear, a GPS, and solar
powered chargers. Weapons were limited to a couple
of hunting rifles and two Serdyukov SPS pistols. The
Agency got high marks for putting together all this
weathered Russian crap, but he doubted it would be
enough for anyone to buy them as a couple of buddies
on a fishing trip. Particularly with Sergei's body rotting
on the side of that mountain and theirs missing. Survival now turned on moving fast and not being spotted.

He finally found their communications equipment
packed with a bunch of freeze-dried Russian provi-
sions. Borscht and beef Stroganoff? He'd have to get
Azarov to read the labels.

He turned on a portable satellite radio receiver he
found, using the included Bluetooth earpiece. It was
tuned to an English language station out of Moscow,
and despite the government spin, he was able to get an
idea what was happening.

All the talk about NATO's "ambush" of peaceful
Russian navy ships and subsequent "cowardly retreat"
suggested that Western forces were continuing to kick
ass on the water. The price would be high, though. It
was hard not to wonder how many men and women
he'd served with over the years were now on the bottom of the Baltic Sea. Just as bad, it appeared that Krupin had threatened Copenhagen with a nuclear strike.
At the behest of the "treacherous American government" the "cowardly Danes" were abandoning their
capital city. Based on the chances Rapp gave himself
of pulling off his mission, he hoped they were running, not walking.

Beyond that, information was hard to come by. There was no thumb drive with an encrypted briefing or additional reports on the war effort. Not even an update on the whereabouts of Krupin or Sokolov. No big surprise. They'd been cut loose at this point. If they got caught, the Agency would say that he'd never been officially reinstated to the CIA after his actions in Saudi Arabia and feign ignorance of his actions. If pressed, Kennedy, would cite his personal debt to Azarov and point out something that Krupin understood better than anyone: if you hit Grisha Azarov, he was going to hit back.

So, from now on, his life would be ruled by the unknown. How heavily was Krupin's treatment facility guarded? How could they gain access to the building? Hell, was he even there or would they be charging a bunch of medical personnel and a couple of bemused janitors?

Their campsite finally descended into shadow, forcing Rapp to slip on a down jacket as he inflated their raft. A little help preparing would have been useful, but Azarov was dozing in a pile of leaves near the shore. Better to have him rested than screwing with foot pumps and weapons checks.

"I'm sorry," Azarov said, appearing from the trees. "I didn't think I'd sleep that long."

"The good life can be destructive," Rapp said pointing to a few cold sausage links and something that resembled a Russian Pop-Tart.

"And I'm its most willing victim," he said, walking over to the food. "Is there anything I can do?"

"No. We're pretty much packed up."

The Russian sat on a log and took a bite of sausage, studying the wide, slow moving river. "It's funny. More and more when I try to look back on my life, I wonder what happened. You chose this. I stumbled into it."

"One last mission."

He nodded. "I never cared about any of the others. Or anything, really. I joined the Soviet athletics program because I had no choice and my parents saw it as a way to get me out of poverty. I joined the military because I needed work and because I was good at it. When Krupin recruited me, I agreed because it paid better than Spetsnaz and because he's not a man you say no to. It's interesting how we came from opposite directions to end up in the same place."

"Yeah?" Rapp said absently, shoving a few critical items into a waterproof bag with some rocks. He'd dangle it off the side of the raft and if they were discovered, subtly cut it loose.

Azarov picked up another sausage and gnawed thoughtfully on one end. "Your life has been driven entirely by passion. The death of your young love prompted you to join the CIA. Then your love of country and rage at the people attacking it kept you there."

Rapp slid a rifle between a cooler and the side of the raft, but didn't respond. It made sense that Azarov would know a great deal about him—the SVR undoubtedly had everything from his college transcript to his shoe size. It made for an odd conversation with the man who had tried to kill him multiple times.

"I have a lot of explaining to do to Cara," Azarov continued. "It's forced me to take stock of who I am."

"And?"

"I can't even remember the names and faces of many of the men I've killed. Do you think that's evil? Or is it something worse?"

Rapp sat on the edge of the boat and examined the Russian for a moment. Now was not the time for introspection. Maybe he'd made a mistake. Maybe he shouldn't have left Coleman screwing around with the Latvian insurgency.

"Krupin will be different."

"Revenge," Azarov said. "An opportunity to look into his eyes and see them go blank for what he did to Cara. Would you believe it if I told you that he's the first person I've ever hated? It's a strangely uncomfortable feeling."

"Yeah," Rapp said, standing and starting to drag the boat toward the river. "It is."

CHAPTER 48

RAPP stayed in the shadows, circling to the east and keeping his eye on the dilapidated buildings and military refuse piled up around them. They'd spent two days on the river and then another eight hours bushwhacking through dense woods and wet marshes to get there. Now, though, he was starting to wonder if all that effort had been wasted.

Skies were clear and the afternoon sun left little hidden. Even in the unrelenting glare, there was nothing to suggest that this facility was anything more than what it looked like—a graveyard for damaged and obsolete military equipment. The fact that his satphone signal seemed to be getting jammed was the only thing giving him hope that the Agency eggheads hadn't completely whiffed this one. Irene had surrounded herself with quite a brain trust but sometimes they had a tendency to get lost in their data and assumptions. Great in a warm, dry office in Langley, but often not worth shit in the real world.

He finally picked up movement in his peripheral

vision and crouched lower as a man became visible weaving through the debris. He was wearing the dirty, ragged clothing of a workman, strolling past a partially collapsed warehouse with a complete lack of urgency. It made sense that there would be someone posted to the area—a coordinator of shipments, cataloger of inventory, and deterrent to anyone looking to scavenge weapons.

Rapp used a set of compact binoculars to examine him in more detail. He didn't have the Asian features of the people who inhabited the area, but that didn't mean much. He had a wiry build in place of the bulk normally associated with someone working in this environment but, again, what did that prove? That he wasn't a big eater? He seemed a little more interested in the tree line than expected. Again, though, so what? Maybe he was a fucking bird watcher.

A twig snapped to Rapp's right and he eased back deeper into the trees, going for a knife instead of the unsuppressed Russian weapon the Agency had provided. In all likelihood, it wouldn't be necessary. Azarov had been circling the facility in the other direction and probably made the sound intentionally to warn of his approach. Rapp picked up a small stick and broke it audibly. A moment later, the Russian was crawling up alongside.

"If this really is a high tech medical facility, then Krupin's done a hell of a job camouflaging it. Are we wasting our time?"

Azarov shook his head. "I passed a building north of here that has a man standing by the entrance."

"A guy passed me a few minutes ago, too. Could just work here."

"Except I know this man. Badden Voronin. One of Krupin's elite guard."

Rapp surveyed the cinder block and steel of the buildings, the debris that offered a thousand places for a security force to hide, and the weapons that looked inoperable but might be locked and loaded. Irene's eggheads scored again. The question was what could he do about it?

The rust-streaked door was clearly heavier and newer than anything on the buildings surrounding it. Voronin was seated beneath an overhang constructed of multiple layers of corrugated metal that had been left shiny on the underside. Rapp scanned the scene, lingering for a moment on a pile of tangled steel and debris just past the edge of the improvised roof. "Look right," he whispered. "See the horizontal line in that pile of junk?"

Azarov nodded. "I'd guess that's actually two walls joined together at that line. The top part can be pushed over."

"If they went to the trouble of building a barrier like that, you can bet they put something heavy behind it."

"Agreed."

"Now that you've seen the place, how many people do you think we're up against?"

In his previous life, Azarov would have been involved in setting up these kinds of security measures. Still, he took some time to think about it.

"Outside, I'd guess five or less. Krupin has a passion for secrecy, and if he's sick that passion will have become an obsession. Having said that, there would be no reason for him to reveal the purpose of this place to the exterior guards."

Rapp nodded. "If it were me, I'd just play it off as some kind of beyond-secret military research facility. But inside, it'd be hard to hide what's really happening."

"Correct. Inside, I'd expect to find the head of his personal guard and Nikita Pushkin. Perhaps a handful of other men who have demonstrated blind loyalty in the past."

"Okay then. We have a building with one visible ingress point, about forty meters square. Heavy door that I think we can assume is locked. Unknown interior layout. One guard visible, probably another with a fixed machine gun placement just out of sight. At least one more guard roaming who's going to come up behind us if we start shooting. Probably more. Maybe a lot more. Did I miss anything?"

"You didn't say anything about the men we speculate are inside."

"Hard to imagine we'll make it that far."

"Again, I agree. Even if we kill Voronin and his exterior team, how do we breach the door?"

Rapp had taken a careful mental inventory of the mothballed military equipment at the facility, with just that question in mind. His preference would be to find something capable of blowing the entire building into the stratosphere and getting the hell out of there. Krupin wasn't that stupid, though. Either there had never been that kind of matériel stored there or he'd had it removed.

"Could the CIA get heavy explosives to us?" Azarov asked, obviously thinking along the same lines.

"They barely got that raft onto the river bank."

"Then as much as I want to see Krupin dead—as

much as I *need* to see him dead—I don't see a path forward."

"Unacceptable."

"We could wait for him to come out," Azarov suggested.

"That could be days or even months from now. By then Europe's major cities could be gone and NATO could be shelling Moscow and St. Petersburg."

"Guard changes? Men coming out and others going in?"

Rapp shook his head. "Like you said, the guys inside know he's sick and the ones outside probably don't. My guess is that the men he has with him went in before his first treatment and won't leave again until he's cured or dead."

"Then we're back to having no path forward."

The wind gusted, rattling the discarded metal and whistling through the buildings. Badden Voronin glanced up as the roof over him strained against the bolts securing it, then went back to scanning the area.

"Krupin made you into a ghost story that his enemies told to each other," Rapp said finally. "The whole point was that you were a boogeyman hiding in the shadows. How much would someone like Voronin know about you?"

"Very little," Azarov said. "We've met, but Krupin provides information only on a need to know basis— sometimes going so far as to intentionally create confusion, even in his allies. He considers the people closest to him the greatest threats and is quite effective at keeping them off-balance."

It was exactly what Rapp wanted to hear. "Would Voronin know you quit?"

Azarov seemed to realize what he was being asked and considered his answer carefully. "My leaving would have been a humiliation for Krupin. And the fact that he didn't immediately punish my betrayal could have made him seem weak."

"And even if he did say something to Voronin, it could have just been disinformation. He's not a man who goes around telling his security people his long game."

"It's possible. But it's just as possible that Voronin is under orders to kill me on sight. In fact, after what happened to Cara, I'd say it's likely."

Rapp had read Azarov's psych evaluation and one thing stood out—the man's passion for order and predictability. He'd been too valuable for Krupin to risk in any operation that wasn't completely nailed down. Winging it just wasn't part of his world.

"Likely is different than certain."

"Mitch, I—"

"Listen to me. These assholes are afraid of you. And they have no way of being a hundred percent sure what your real relationship with Krupin is."

"I think you're being overly optimistic."

It was probably true, but there was no point in acknowledging it. "This'll work, Grisha. All you have to do is go out there and sell it."

CHAPTER 49

WHEN they emerged from the trees, Badden Voronin immediately slammed his assault rifle to his shoulder. Azarov's stomach clenched but he made sure it wasn't outwardly visible. To his left, Rapp seemed utterly unconcerned about their situation. The CIA man had spent his life fighting unpredictable enemies motivated by religion and visions of glorious martyrdom. A far cry from the calculating, wealth- and power-obsessed men whom Azarov had targeted.

Voronin remained nearly motionless, tracking them with minuscule adjustments of his weapon. He was an extremely gifted former Spetsnaz officer whose loyalty to Krupin was utterly unshakable. It would take only a slight twitch of his finger to succeed in doing something so many men had died trying to achieve.

But his finger didn't twitch. And the wall next to him didn't drop to reveal the machine gun placement that was inevitably behind it. He just stood there, wide-eyed, reeling through what he'd been told and trying to calculate how it fit with what he now saw with his own eyes. He was desperately asking—as Azarov himself had done so many times—what did Krupin expect of him?

"Badden," Azarov said.

The calm greeting seemed to pull the man from his trance. "Colonel Azarov. What are you doing here?"

The hint of fear in his voice bolstered Azarov's confidence. He wasn't a man to be afraid of a fight. No, his concern was that he might fail his president and country. That he had missed some subtlety to Krupin's orders that would allow him to act decisively.

"We had information that the CIA may have found this site," Azarov said. "That they sent a team to try to assassinate the president. Another cowardly attack like the one they carried out in Moscow."

The man's eyes widened and flicked to Rapp before looking past them into the woods.

"I think it's nonsense," Azarov continued. "But the president wouldn't be the president if he didn't send me out into the wilderness for days to search for nothing."

Normally, he wouldn't have been so talkative, but under the circumstances, it seemed appropriate. And it worked. Krupin was a man prone to asking the impossible of his people, often for no fathomable reason. Voronin, who may have been living for months beneath that corrugated overhang, would understand this better than most.

He lowered his rifle and a moment later, a young man appeared from cover to Azarov's right. They had been correct about the weapons placement.

"Colonel," he said respectfully.

Azarov recognized him but couldn't put a name

to the face. He ignored the greeting and instead just pointed toward the door. It was what Cara called the moment of truth—usually in reference to a new recipe that would turn out inedible or to a wave that would throw him from his board and suck him under.

Voronin hesitated for a moment and then turned to punch a code into the keypad.

"Stop!"

The desperate shout came from a man Azarov had known since he was quite young. One of Krupin's most trusted guards, but one who had aged to the point of losing his edge in combat situations.

"Pavel!" Azarov called, turning to see the man sprinting toward them with speed he wouldn't have thought him capable of. "The president has you out here in the—"

"Kill him! Kill Grisha now!"

The door was already sliding open and Voronin, true to his nature, made no effort to defend his own life. Instead, he slammed his fist into a panic button that started to close it again. Azarov lunged forward, grabbing the man from behind and twisting his head one hundred and eighty degrees as bullets began sparking off the metal next to him.

He shoved Voronin's body across the threshold and dropped to the ground, rolling right as the door closed on the man's limp shoulders. He could hear the electric motor straining as he passed over the body of the other man, killed by Rapp in some way that was neither immediately evident nor important.

He saw Pavel go down, but not from the impact of the shot that Rapp had just taken at him. The old man was still impressive, sliding behind cover as Rapp

struggled to achieve his normal accuracy with the unfamiliar Russian pistol.

A shot from an unknown source hit only a foot
away from Azarov, sending shards of metal into his
arm as he crawled over Voronin and slipped inside the
building. He lay on his side, firing over the corpse in an
effort to provide Rapp cover. The CIA man was staying just ahead of the rounds of a still invisible sniper
and he went high, diving through the narrow gap as
the door continued to pulse, trying to break through
the blockage and fully close.

A moment later Rapp had rolled to his feet and was
kicking at Voronin's torso as Azarov continued to fire
around him. His weapon ran out of ammunition and
he shouted at Rapp, who threw him his weapon and
continued trying to work the body out of the doorway.

He finally succeeded clearing Voronin's shoulders,
allowing the door to travel farther, stopping again on
his skull. One last kick and the barrier finally was able
to slam home.

Rapp picked up Azarov's empty weapon and inserted another magazine before firing two rounds into
a keypad attached to the wall. He was rewarded with a
cascade of sparks that would likely make entry impossible for the men outside. The fact that it would make
escape equally difficult was something they'd have to
worry about later.

The hallway was narrow and devoid of exits, forcing
them to trade caution for speed in search of room to
maneuver. Azarov was bringing up the rear, his footsteps inaudible through the ringing in Rapp's ears.

Despite their precarious tactical position, Rapp

slowed when the wall to his right turned to glass. On the other side was a large room full of patients, all meticulously secured to their beds. Some were unconscious, others were hooked up to IVs, and a few had machines breathing for them. The ones who didn't look like they were on death's door had their eyes on him, shouting silently and straining at their bonds.

He'd seen a lot in his time at the Agency, but nothing like this. Azarov had called it. Krupin was performing medical experiments on his own citizens in hopes of extending his life. Rapp locked gazes with a muscular, tattooed man in his early fifties, causing him to thrash even harder, rocking his bed back and forth on the tile floor. Whoever he was, he understood that the two filthy men on the other side of the glass represented a shift in the balance of power. And he wanted to be part of that shift.

Rapp started out again, leaving the window behind and approaching a gap in the hallway probably ten feet across. He scanned the ceiling and couldn't find any cameras. It was possible that they were just well hidden, of course. But why bother? More likely, Krupin's security people never expected a breach and so they hadn't prioritized electronic surveillance. Still, Rapp made certain that his subtle hand signal would be visible only to Azarov.

The Russian understood and immediately started sprinting toward the gap. Just before he broke into the open, Rapp slipped his gun around the edge of the wall.

The passage wasn't empty, as he'd hoped. There was a lone man standing about fifteen yards away, wearing an expensive suit and holding a custom pistol similar to the one Azarov had favored during his career. The precision and speed of his movements immediately identified him as Nikita Pushkin.

Azarov dropped to the floor and slid across the gap with impressive speed, but not as impressive as it would have been a few years ago. Pushkin ignored his predecessor, leaping to the right and adjusting his aim toward Rapp. They fired simultaneously, Pushkin in midair and Rapp trying to compensate for the unfamiliar Russian weapon while tracking Azarov in his peripheral vision.

Pushkin landed on one shoulder, rolling gracefully around a corner and out of sight. Rapp's shot was pulled off line when Pushkin's—fired from midair—caught the edge of his sleeve and jerked his hand off target. He was starting to get really fucking tired of these Russian supermen.

Azarov, safe on the other side of the gap, was scrambling back toward it when the barrels of two assault rifles came around the corner near where Pushkin disappeared. Rapp pulled back and waved Azarov off as a spray of rounds began pulverizing the wall to his right.

Rapp shook his head, indicating the obvious—that no one else was crossing that gap in anything less than a tank. Azarov turned and started to run in the other direction while Rapp took a moment to try to figure out how this wasn't going to turn into a complete clusterfuck. The hope that they could slip in and slip out without being identified had never been particularly realistic, but now it had completely disappeared into the rearview mirror. He hoped to hell that Kennedy and Alexander knew what they were doing.

The guns went silent, maybe reloading, but probably just waiting for him to show himself again. It was a stalemate he couldn't afford. If he was going to complete his mission and have even a snowball's chance in hell of getting out of there, he needed to tilt the playing field back in their direction. And to do that, he'd need some help.

Rapp ran back the way he'd come, passing by the glass wall he'd seen earlier and pushing through a door at the far end. "Does anyone here speak English?"

He got a few assents, with the one from the big, tattooed man at the back being the most intelligible. Rapp cut him free, speaking slowly so that he could simultaneously translate for the others. "I need to kill pretty much everyone in this building."

Based on the voices that rose up around him, everyone was on board.

Rapp handed the man the knife so he could finish freeing himself and went for a scalpel that was sufficient to sever the bonds of a thirtysomething woman who looked to be in pretty good shape.

With some haphazard teamwork, it took less than two minutes to free everyone capable of standing. Rapp surveyed his army, taking in the pale faces, questionable balance, and squeamish way they disconnected themselves from IVs and monitors. Most were over fifty, some had evidence of recent operations, and others seemed partially sedated. It wasn't the worst group of allies he'd ever had—none would shoot him if he turned his back on them—but it was close.

"What's your name?" Rapp said to the big man as he helped a teenage girl to her feet. She had eyes that were in danger of being swallowed by the dark hollows around them, but managed to stay upright when he let go of her.

"Yuri Lebedev."

"Army?"

The man nodded. "For twenty years. Before I got sick."

"Can anyone else here handle a weapon?"

Lebedev translated and the only affirmative response came from a formidable looking woman who was unquestionably north of seventy. Not exactly Scott Coleman, but she'd have to do.

"Does anyone know if Maxim Krupin is here?"

The name elicited angry murmurs from the group, but Lebedev managed to silence them. "He often stands at the window. The last time was a few hours ago. Are we to kill him, too?"

"Hell yes. The only man who's off-limits is about my height and just as filthy. Light brown hair. Understand?"

He translated and one woman protested.

"She wants to know about the doctors and nurses."

"You tell me."

"I think they're trapped here like we are."

"Then let's see if we can recruit them. Does anyone know the layout of this place?"

"Only some of it. The area between here and the place where they do medical procedures."

"Fine. Take me there."

The group was large enough to fill the hallway, creating an easy target for anyone with an automatic weapon. Rapp and Lebedev moved out front and the rest of the group started to spread out based on ability. His hearing had fully returned from the gunfight earlier but he was starting to wish it hadn't. The sound of shuffling feet and someone vomiting was less than confidence inspiring.

They were twenty yards from the gap Azarov had crossed when a man with an AK appeared from around it.

"Down!" Rapp shouted, dropping to his stomach as the deafening roar of machine gun fire erupted.

Lebedev turned and plowed through the people behind them, knocking the frozen ones to the floor. They were in a kill box and Krupin's man knew how to use it. He was wearing a ballistic vest, forcing Rapp to go for his head, which was partially hidden behind the assault rifle he was sighting along. His first attempt missed and he swore at the unfamiliar Russian pistol. A woman behind him screamed when she was hit but he ignored her, concentrating on the weapon's imprecise sights. His second shot struck the body of the man's rifle and the shrapnel from the shattered round hit him full in the face. He was still on his feet but now he was firing blind.

Rapp sprinted forward, weaving as the man swept his weapon back and forth. He hit him low, taking out his legs and twisting the rifle from his grip. A hard blow from the butt caved in his forehead and then Rapp pulled back, straining to hear anyone who might be coming to their comrade's aid. Nothing.

"Is everyone all right?" he asked, backing toward the group still lying on the floor. Their pale skin and gowns made for surprisingly effective camouflage against the tile and had probably saved a few lives. Unfortunately, the sterile white of the corridor also made blood stand out as though it had its own power source. A woman had been hit in the chest and was lying on her side, staring sightlessly at the wall. Behind her, a man who had barely been making it as it was, had taken a round to the thigh. He clearly wasn't getting up again but Rapp's two shooters—Lebedev and the old woman—looked unharmed.

Rapp tossed Lebedev the rifle and then turned his attention to the girl with the sunken eyes. "Help this man back to the medical area. See if you can stop the bleeding in his leg."

Lebedev translated and she nodded, looking a little shell-shocked. Whether she'd be able to pull it together and give the man the first aid he needed was probably no better than fifty-fifty. But Rapp couldn't make that his problem. Not until this was finished.

CHAPTER 50

AZAROV paused when he heard gunshots echoing through the building, but then decided to ignore them. Rapp would do what he always did. Kill everyone who got in his way and then somehow come out the other side alive.

The hallway widened as he continued down it, newly hung drywall still stinking of the white paint that covered it. He crept up on a doorway that had hinges installed but no door, rotating smoothly into it with his weapon held out in front of him.

The space was no more than three meters square, with exposed, rusted girders and decaying electrical wires dangling from the ceiling. Oddly appropriate. Like Krupin himself, the entire building was nothing more than a rotting husk beneath a hastily applied veneer.

Azarov slipped back out and continued moving cautiously down the corridor. The blank white of it helped him focus, but nothing could turn him into the man he once was. The indifference that had steadied his hand through so many operations was gone forever. He was driven now by the desire to make Krupin suffer. To look into his eyes as the life drained out of them. But even more overwhelming was the desire to take Cara home and spend the rest of his life making up for what he had done to her.

She'd never hidden the fact that she considered him a man who desperately needed to get in touch with his emotions, but now wasn't the time. While hate had been effective tools for Rapp and his mentor Stan Hurley, it was something he had no idea how to use.

"Azarov!"

The voice preceded the man, but only by a split second. Nikita Pushkin appeared from a door twenty meters away, wearing a bulletproof vest undoubtedly made by Azarov's former armorer. Worse was the custom pistol that would be light, perfectly balanced, and deadly accurate. Particularly in his hands.

Pushkin paced back and forth across the broad hallway, keeping his opponent in his peripheral vision. At that distance, to hit center of mass would be a simple matter, but the head shot necessary to end the confrontation would be extraordinarily difficult. Even at the height of Azarov's training and with his own weapon, the chance of a clean kill would have been less than fifty percent.

"You're nothing but a traitor, Grisha."

"To what? Maxim Krupin isn't Russia. He's a dying old man who's spent his life perpetuating his own power. Any promise our country had after the fall of the Soviet Union is gone now. He's stolen it."

"He gave you everything!" the young man shouted.

"Money. Women. The fear and deference of powerful men. All things that don't matter."

The boy was young, as Azarov had once been. Daz-

zled by everything he'd become and bowed beneath
the weight of the debt he believed he owed Krupin. But
it was more than that. Azarov had recognized Krupin for what he was from the beginning. His successor
seemed to lack that clarity.

"I served Maxim faithfully for years, Nikita. I killed
countless people, most of whom were guilty of nothing more than threatening his power and privilege.
But then it came time for me to pursue a life."

"With hundreds of millions of his euros in your
bank account. It wasn't your house in Costa Rica that
burned. It was his."

Azarov felt his anger flare, but he didn't allow it to
get a hold of him. "You attacked me and the woman I
love. But I understand your position and don't blame
you for it. I'm here for Krupin. Not you."

"The ice prince, Grisha Azarov. Did you ever even
care for him?"

Azarov inched forward as he considered the question. The greater the distance between them, the
greater Pushkin's advantage.

"No."

The walls on either side of the corridor seemed to
be the boundary of his operating environment, but
was that really true? Was it possible that this part of
the building was covered in the same flimsy drywall
shell he'd seen earlier? And if so, was there any way to
determine where the studs were?

"How many of his colleagues and former friends
has he asked you to kill or intimidate, Nikita? Do you
believe you're different? That he thinks of you as a son?
Of course you do. It's one of Maxim's greatest gifts.
He makes everyone around him feel as though they

have a special place in his inner circle and in his heart. You're just a tool like I was. Something he'll use up and discard."

"Liar!" Pushkin shouted. "You have no idea how he feels about me!"

"This is all meaningless now, Nikita. He's a fading old man. When he dies, your power base will die with him. You'll be hunted by the men who succeed him. They fear you."

"He's stronger than you ever gave him credit for, Grisha. He's going to survive. And imagine my reward when I drag your bleeding corpse to his rooms."

Azarov continued to inch forward. Pushkin didn't seem to notice, or perhaps was just too confident to care.

"You may well kill me, Nikita. But you won't survive a confrontation with the man I came here with. Believe me when I tell you this. Don't die here. Not for Krupin. Take the money you've been paid, find a woman, and have children. Die fat and old surrounded by them."

The head shot was doable now, but only vaguely. A miss would open him up to return fire that he'd be unlikely to survive. And that left him with no choice but to do something unexpected. His talent, experience, and training were no longer enough. He'd have to rely on luck.

Pushkin stopped pacing and faced him. The time had arrived but Azarov didn't feel the fear he'd expected to experience after so many years of numbness. Only regret. He didn't want to kill this boy. But even more, he didn't want to die. It wasn't time for that. Not yet.

"Step aside, Nikita. Let me do what I've come here to do."

Pushkin's speed was exactly what one would expect of a young man with his history and devotion. His hand came up in a blur, but Azarov was already lunging to the left. The inexplicable move caused Pushkin to hesitate. His indecision lasted only a split second, but it was enough for Azarov to get off a shot before colliding with the wall.

He struck full force and, as he had prayed, the thin drywall gave way. His unlikely plan worked, but the execution was less than perfect. A stud caught his left shoulder, spinning him into a steel barrier that likely made up the building's east wall.

The gap between metal and drywall was less than a meter wide, but extended into darkness in every direction. Options were limited. He could move into the gloom and wait for Pushkin to come after him, but it would leave him with no room to maneuver. Trying to squeeze through the narrow space in hopes of finding an escape was a possibility, but relying on blind luck twice in one day seemed unwise.

With no other choice, Azarov slung his gun hand around the edge of the hole he'd made and blindly fired two of his remaining rounds. The drywall provided little more than psychological protection, so there was no reason not to bring one eye around its edge and peer down the corridor.

Miraculously, Azarov's desperate shot had found its mark. Not a kill shot, but enough to put the younger man down and make his efforts to rise into a sitting position unsuccessful. The blood flow from Pushkin's scalp was heavy enough to suggest that his disorientation was real and not just a trick designed to draw in his opponent.

Azarov approached cautiously, crouching to pick up the weapon that the younger man had dropped. He aimed it between eyes burning with fear and hate. It was an expression he'd seen many times before and it always filled him with revulsion. Not because of what it said about his victims, but because of what it said about him.

He squeezed the trigger and felt the beautifully controlled recoil against his hand. The bullet struck just above the bridge of Pushkin's nose and he fell back, his head making a wet thud when it hit the tile floor.

Azarov shook his head imperceptibly.

Pointless.

CHAPTER 51

RAPP finally seemed to have crossed to the right side of the tracks. Whitewashed hospital walls and fluorescent lights had given way to rich wood paneling, gilt moldings, and chandeliers. The introduction of carpet silenced his footsteps and muffled various bursts of gunfire emanating from elsewhere in the building.

The undisciplined shooting was followed by somewhat more controlled—but clearly desperate—return fire. The ebb and flow of it suggested his ragtag gang of patients had managed to get the drop on at least two people. Hopefully one was Krupin. Not only a poetic end to that piece of shit, but also one that kept America's hands somewhat clean.

Of course, the actual chances of him being that lucky were around zero. But hope sprang eternal.

He eased up to a door on the right side of the hallway and looked down at the knob. The lack of a locking mechanism suggested he wasn't going to find Krupin there. More likely a storage room or something similar, but he couldn't take the chance of someone getting behind him.

He twisted the knob and threw the door open. The screaming started the moment his gun slipped around the jamb and then transformed into terrified whimpers when he penetrated into the opening. There were three women and two men inside, all dressed in medical garb. The room seemed to be their quarters—five cots bolted to the walls and two chests of drawers that probably contained nothing more than clean scrubs. A cart with some basic equipment—a blood pressure cuff, stethoscope, gloves—rounded out the room's contents. Everything they'd need to keep a round-the-clock eye on their only patient.

"Where's Krupin?" Rapp said.

Two of them pointed in the direction he'd been going.

There was no reason not to believe it. If the CIA's analysts were right—and he had to admit that they were on a winning streak—these people had been snatched just like the patients he'd found.

Rapp motioned them out and they took off in the direction he'd come from. The more people he had running around loose the better. His ignorance of the building's layout put him at a disadvantage, so whatever chaos he could create would work to reduce his opponents' advantage.

The hallway curved to the right finally dead ending into a heavy oak door designed more for its imposing appearance than any real concern over security. A door befitting the most powerful man in the world? There was only one way to find out.

Rapp dropped to one knee and fired two rounds into the jamb next to the knob. The door swung back a couple of inches and shouting immediately rose up on the other side. Rapp wouldn't bet much on his ability to identify Maxim Krupin's voice, but the tone was hard to mistake—a man accustomed to barking orders and having them followed. Another voice became audible—a little hesitant, but still firm. Whoever he was and whatever his argument, it was clear that he was going to lose.

It wasn't much to work with, but still Rapp could make some fairly solid assumptions. Krupin was cornered in that room with at least one guard, and he wanted the man to go out and neutralize whoever had just shot up his door. The guard, being a top operator and not a complete fucking idiot, wanted to stay under cover and wait for the reinforcements he hoped were still breathing.

More shouting preceded a boot flashing into view and kicking the door open a few more inches. Rapp backed along the curving corridor until he could just barely keep the edge of the doorframe in view. A gun appeared around it a moment later and the shooter emptied half his mag in a random pattern down the hall.

Rapp responded with three carefully placed shots, stitching them across the wall to the right of the frame. They penetrated and at least one hit its target. Not that it did any real damage, but the impact with the man's bulletproof vest was enough to cause him to stagger across the crack in the door. Starting to get used to his Russian weapon, Rapp managed to put his next shot into the guard's temple, dropping him onto the plush carpet.

Rapp rushed forward, kicking the door hard enough to push the body out of the way and then roll-

ing into the dimly lit room. A man in a white smock
was coming at him but Rapp recognized him from the
pre-op briefing Claudia had put together. Dr. Eduard
Fedkin—by all reports a decent human being who had
the bad luck of being Krupin's personal physician.

The reason for his charge became obvious a moment later. The Russian president was behind him,
crouching for cover and shoving him forward. Fedkin
slammed into Rapp, knocking him back as Krupin
went for the gun. His hand clamped down on Rapp's
wrist with shocking force as the three of them collided
simultaneously with the wall.

Krupin kept Rapp's gun hand pinned to the wall
while he rammed a fist into whatever target he could
find. Rapp deflected the frenzied blows to the degree
he could while trying to figure out what the fuck was
happening. This wasn't the dying old man the Agency
had sent him after. The son of a bitch was faster than
most twenty-year-olds, and he hit like a Mack Truck.

When Krupin lined up a roundhouse to the side
of Rapp's head, the CIA man finally reacted, duck-
ing and letting the man's momentum throw him
off-balance. A kick to the side of the knee created an
audible crunch as the bones gave way.

Krupin should have collapsed screaming in pain
but he didn't seem to even notice the injury. Rapp hit
it again, this time hard enough to fold the joint sideways. The Russian finally dropped, but instead of
staying down he crawled frantically for the far wall,
dragging his injured leg behind him.

Rapp was starting to wonder if he'd given Kennedy's brain trust too much credit. No medical
equipment was immediately evident. The room was

dominated by a four-poster bed, an overstuffed chair, and a bank of televisions silently feeding news from various international organizations. Finally, his eyes fell on the doctor who was partially visible behind a massive armoire.

"What the hell was that?"

Fortunately, Fedkin not only spoke English but understood the question.

"Stimulants," he said, pointing to a series of pens lined up on a writing desk. Upon closer examination they were syringes—two of which appeared to be empty. "They're extremely dangerous, but he forced me to administer them."

"Who are you?" Krupin said, trying to push himself to his feet but finding his shattered knee unable to support the maneuver. His bloodshot eyes bulged noticeably and his hands were shaking.

"You know who I am."

"Mitch Rapp," he said through clenched teeth. "What are you going to do? Kill me? And then what? Escape unharmed from this building and then make it across Russia to a friendly border without being captured?"

"Something like that."

Krupin laughed, through his visibly quivering jaw. "Your president and the Europeans are worried about *Latvia*? If it's discovered that I was assassinated by a CIA operative, Latvia will be nothing. You'll have started World War III."

"Are you sure?" Rapp said, aiming his gun between the man's eyes. "Who are all these people who are going to give a shit that you're dead? The generals you got into this clusterfuck? The nationalists who just watched you get half their navy sunk? Or all the backstabbing Russian politicians waiting to take your place?"

Some of the man's rage was replaced by uncertainty as his amphetamine-fueled mind began to grasp the precariousness of his situation. "I . . . I can give you Andrei Sokolov. He's in the building."

Rapp closed one eye, focusing on Krupin's increasingly pale face over the sight of his Serdyukov SPS. "What's Sokolov to me?"

"This is his doing. *He* wanted this war. Not me. I'll admit to being ill. We can say that he took advantage of my situation and I'll order a retreat."

Rapp just kept aiming. "I'm not State Department, Maxim. I don't work for the negotiating part of the U.S. government."

"Wait!" he shouted. "I'm willing to make concessions. Tell me what you want."

Even half-dead and high as a kite, Krupin wasn't a stupid man. Russia was an almost purely destructive force in the world—a country consumed not with improving itself but with bringing everyone else down to its level. And Krupin was behind all of that. An offer of major concessions from him wasn't something to just shrug off. On the other hand, what was that offer really worth? Even assuming he survived his illness and managed to maintain power, he'd walk away from any promises made while staring down the barrel of a gun.

Like the consummate politician he was, Krupin read his hesitation. "There's a communications room in the building. We can use it to call President Alexander. I'll talk to him personally. We can make a deal."

Rapp kept his gun on target but looked over at Dr. Fedkin. "What's his condition?"

"Serious," he responded hesitantly.

"I'd rather not shoot you, Doc. But I wouldn't lose any sleep over it."

"Likely terminal," the man quickly corrected. "He'll continue to decline and probably be dead in three months. It would be a miracle if he lasted six."

When Rapp turned back to Krupin, the man's face had gone blank. One of the by-products of being a brutal dictator was that people tended to softball everything they told you. The unvarnished truth spoken in such a matter-of-fact way didn't seem to be sitting well. Not that it mattered. Rapp hadn't come there to make deals. He squeezed the trigger.

Instead of the comforting buck of the weapon in his hand and scent of gunpowder, there was nothing. The piece-of-crap Russian pistol had jammed.

He swore quietly under his breath, trying to work the stuck slide as Krupin crawled desperately for the door. He'd made it over his dead guard and halfway into the hallway before Rapp grabbed him by the foot and dragged him back. The Russian leader thrashed wildly, but his broken leg prevented him from getting any real leverage. The syringes on the desk were within reach and Rapp picked one up, slamming it into Krupin's calf.

The reaction was immediate—his strength and desperation increased to the point that it was like trying to hold on to a wildcat. Rapp grabbed another syringe and dropped his weight onto the man, this time breaking the needle off in the man's collarbone. There was enough of a barb left, though, to get it into his neck and depress the plunger.

That was the one that pushed Krupin over the edge. His body went rigid and his breath caught in his chest. Rapp backed away, watching the Russian convulse for a few seconds before finally going still.

The shit had now officially hit the fan.

CHAPTER 52

AZAROV kept his back pressed against the polished wood behind him, sliding slowly along the curved wall. There was little doubt that he was on the right path. The passage had gone from simple hospital corridor to a level of opulence that would have been at home in the Kremlin.

A finely carved door came into view, confirming the description given by the medical personnel he'd intercepted a few minutes before. Even more telling was the dead man lying near the threshold and the bullet holes near the latch.

The door opened onto an opulent room furnished with a massive bed and various wall-mounted televisions. Rapp was gone but had left his handiwork behind. Krupin was on his back, staring at the ceiling with a grotesquely broken leg and syringes still hanging from his calf and neck. Not the CIA man's customary head shot, but no less effective.

Azarov knew that there was nothing for him there, but still he found himself unable to move from his position on the blood-soaked carpet. What would he have become without the man lying dead before him?

Without the training, money, and education? Without his upbringing by the state, first in the Soviet athletics program and then in the army?

A farmer like his parents and their parents before them? The possibility of that seemed almost laughable now. Those days came to him only in brief flashes now. Triggered by smells, sounds, or briefly glimpsed images, the memories dispersed like smoke the moment he tried to grab hold of them.

He aimed his weapon at Krupin but felt none of the expected rage or catharsis. There would be no pleasure to be derived from firing into his lifeless body. The few rounds he had left could be put to better use.

Azarov retraced his route through the corridor, allowing himself to move somewhat more quickly than he had earlier. Krupin's guards would have fallen back to defend him and the fact that there had only been one suggested that the threat inside the building was neutralized.

He crossed into the building's main medical facility and stumbled on a scene that reminded him of one of the low-budget horror films that Cara loved so much. They were usually poorly lit and atrociously acted, with improbable storylines that climaxed either in boiler rooms or abandoned hospitals.

Andrei Sokolov, in full dress uniform, had barricaded himself in an operating theater made entirely of glass. Outside those transparent walls was a group of people in hospital gowns, some with partially shaved heads, others bleeding from where IV catheters had been recently removed.

The glass had been damaged by gunfire but was holding, and Sokolov had taken refuge behind an

MRI machine. One of the patients, a big man with forearms covered in tattoos, discarded his empty AK and sprinted toward the door leading into the enclosure.

Azarov watched, transfixed, as the man's ghostly compatriots followed at speeds that ranged from a full run to an unsteady lurch. Sokolov fired his service pistol, missing the big man and instead hitting a woman behind him. It was one of those minor errors that could be so fatal in a combat situation. His aim had been wide by only a few centimeters but now the man was on him. A few more muffled shots sounded but it was impossible to know if they hit anything in the frenzy that ensued.

Azarov backed away as the patients dragged Sokolov toward an operating table that many of them had likely experienced firsthand. It would have been desirable to question the man, but it seemed unwise to try to get between those people and their tormentor. Nothing—not even Mitch Rapp—was going to stop them from tearing Sokolov apart.

"I lost her. Get her back. Now!"

Azarov recognized the voice coming from the room ahead and strode toward it, avoiding the oxygen cylinders strewn across the floor. It appeared that they'd fallen from a medical cart that had been repurposed as a battering ram. A hasty, but effective improvisation. The steel door it had been used against now hung twisted and dented from damaged hinges.

"I'm trying!" came a Russian-accented reply.

Azarov stuffed his weapon into his waistband and stepped slowly into the doorway with his hands open in front of him. As expected, he found himself staring down the barrel of Mitch Rapp's gun. The CIA man was sitting in front of a bank of communications equipment that was likely the facility's only connection to the outside world. He lowered his weapon as Azarov took a position that would allow him to see anyone approaching.

"There!" Eduard Fedkin said, typing frantically into a keyboard. "You should have her back."

"Irene!" Rapp said into the microphone in front of him. "Can you hear me?"

"Is it done?" came Kennedy's distorted voice.

"Yeah."

"Is there any chance it could be played as natural causes?"

"That'd be a stretch."

"Understood. What's your situation?"

"Not good. The doc knows the facility and he says there's no back way out."

Rapp indicated to Azarov, who just shrugged and shook his head.

"Yeah. We're fucked. The men Krupin has outside won't use any serious explosives because they'll think they might injure him but they'll get in here sooner or later."

"You being captured and identified isn't going to go well for relations between the United States and Russia."

"It's not going to go well for me, either, Irene."

There was a brief pause. "I have someone who may be in a position to help you, but it's going to take time. How long can you hold out?"

"Depends on—"

Everything went dark for a moment before the emergency lighting came on.

"Get her back!" Rapp yelled.

"How?" Fedkin said. "There's no power. I'm not an engineer, I—"

"Shut up," Rapp said, moving to the door. "Grisha. You got anything?"

Azarov shook his head.

"Then maybe this is going to go our way."

"How so?"

"They cut the power from outside. They're already seeing this as a hostage crisis and they'll use the power as a bargaining chip. We can play for time."

"I admire your optimism, Mitch. But I have to admit that I don't share it."

CHAPTER 53

RAPP continued sifting through the pile of weapons, picking up an AN-94 assault rifle and checking the magazine. Only a few rounds left. A 9A-91 was in a little better shape, with about half a mag remaining. The people watching him from behind makeshift barricades were all wearing the same expectant expressions and blood-splattered hospital gowns. According to Azarov, those stains were about all that was left of Andrei Sokolov.

Most had never experienced combat before that day, but all were handling it with the fatalism that Russians were famous for. They were no longer strapped to beds being experimented on and had managed to serve themselves up a heaping plateful of revenge. Overall, not a bad day for a group of people who figured they'd soon be dead one way or another. At least now they had an opportunity to go down swinging.

He finished his inventory and walked to where Azarov was watching a shower of sparks penetrate the wall. The steel there was flimsier than it was on the door, but still formidable. Whoever was outside had gotten their hands on some kind of cutting tool and was using it to inch his way through.

"How much longer?" Rapp said.

"I'd guess four hours. How much ammunition?"

"Enough to make some noise, but that's about it. Have you thought up a list of bullshit demands that'll tie up Krupin's men?"

Azarov was going to identify himself as a Chechen terrorist and offer up a time consuming list of demands in return for Krupin's release. As plans went, it was shit, but it'd buy some time. How much was impossible to know.

"I'm still working on it. But I'll be ready when they get through."

Rapp glanced back and motioned to Eduard Fedkin. Unlike the patients, he and his medical team looked scared. Until they'd been kidnapped and imprisoned there, all had been planning long, prosperous lives. Outside these walls, they had families, friends, and careers that they weren't done with yet.

"What do you have that we can use as a weapon, Doc?"

"Weapon? What do you mean?"

"Be creative. Could we pump anesthesia through that gash in the wall and knock the people on the other side out?"

The physician wiped at the sweat building on his forehead. "No. It doesn't work that way."

"Then what do you have that's poisonous? Or that'll blow up?"

"We have medications that given in the right doses would be deadly. You've already proved that. But blow up? I don't know. Medical equipment is designed *not* to blow up."

"There must be something."

"Our job is to save people. Not kill them."

Rapp dismissed him with a wave of the hand and started passing out the guns they'd collected. "Don't fire unless I give the order. Understand?"

Yuri Lebedev translated as he accepted an AS Val assault rifle with a nearly full magazine.

"What happened to Krupin?" he asked.

"Dead."

The former soldier smiled cruelly. "I wish I had been the one to pull the trigger."

"Me too," Rapp responded sincerely.

Unfortunately, Kennedy was right. He couldn't be captured here. Even if he managed to hold out in the interrogation, it wouldn't take Russian intelligence long to ID him. On the other hand, if they all died in that place, there was a solid chance America could get away with this. The Russians would likely assume he was just some mercenary that Azarov had hired and be anxious to bury him along with all the other evidence.

The collapse of Russia's government in the middle of a war with NATO would create enough chaos on its own without leaked stories about medical experiments and brain tumors. Krupin's death would be blamed on a heart attack or unnamed foreign agents or whatever it took to keep the country from blowing itself apart at the loss of their strong man.

The one thing that could change that was finding the CIA's top operative locked in a building with Krupin's corpse. The Russian hardliners would trot Rapp out as proof of everything they'd been telling their people about the West. Krupin would be portrayed as a selfless leader who had given his life to keep his country from being encircled by Western forces. Russia's citizens, wary of the war effort until now, would get fully behind it. Fighting would spread to the other Baltic states and Ukraine. Assuming the nukes were kept in their silos, there would be hundreds of thousands of casualties. If they flew, then that number would climb into the millions.

Checkmate. After two decades in the business, it looked like he may have finally run out of road.

The wall was nearly cut through, but it had taken more than double Azarov's four-hour estimate. One of the patients was a former construction worker and had come up with a credible theory for the delay—the angle grinder being used was battery powered and constantly in need of recharging.

With only a few minutes left, the wind was starting to push at the loose steel flap, creating a rhythmic clanging. Behind Rapp, the people who didn't have guns had gathered up anything they could find that could be used as a weapon. The medical personnel still looked hesitant, but everyone else seemed ready— maybe even anxious—to face the men who had helped imprison them there.

The sparks reached the ground and, a moment later, the section of wall fell inward. Everyone tensed, but to their credit, no one fired. Rapp made his way to the hole and peered out, scrutinizing the visual chaos of the munitions dump. No evidence at all of the force he assumed had surrounded them, though there was now a personnel transport vehicle parked about twenty-five yards away.

Azarov moved alongside and scanned the scene with similar intensity, but after a few seconds, just shrugged.

"Open a dialogue," Rapp said and Azarov shouted out a few of their bullshit demands in Russian. Hopefully, a few steaks and a case of beer.

No answer.

Rapp could understand Krupin's men wanting to play this cool, but after an hour of silence it was starting to feel a little *too* cool. After about thirty minutes Azarov had started making a series of increasingly graphic threats. At forty-five Rapp had thrown out one of Krupin's fingers, still wearing a ring with the insignia of the Russian Federation on it. Still no reaction.

Two hours in, he'd had enough.

"I'm going out. You want to hang back?"

Azarov shook his head. "Waiting for death makes me nervous."

They motioned for the others to stay and stepped through the door, Rapp holding an AN-94 and Azarov clutching the custom pistol he'd taken from Nikita Pushkin.

They moved slowly, sweeping their weapons smoothly as they searched for signs of Krupin's men. But there was nothing. Just the sound of the wind whistling through the debris around them.

"Grisha!" Rapp called out, finally.

"I don't see anyone," the Russian reported.

Rapp eased toward the transport vehicle, jumping onto the running board and looking through the window. Empty with the keys hanging in the ignition. Was it a trick? Only one way to find out. He waved Azarov off before opening the door and twisting the key. If the engine bay was packed with C4, his problem of being identified would definitely be solved.

Instead of the expected pillar of fire, the engine started and began idling smoothly. He slid out of the cab and motioned for Azarov to cover him as he yanked open the canvas flap covering the back.

It was dark, but he could see well enough to know there were no soldiers there. Climbing in, he rummaged around for a few seconds before dropping back to the ground.

"What is it?" Azarov said.

"Blankets, medical supplies, food, and water."

"I don't understand."

"Irene pulled another rabbit out of her hat."

Azarov looked a little disoriented at the news. He'd expected to die and was now having trouble adjusting to the idea that his life was stretching out in front of him again.

Rapp started jogging back toward the warehouse. "Let's move! We need to load these people up and get the hell out of here before someone in Moscow changes their mind."

EPILOGUE

YOU sure you got that?" Rapp said.

"Sure," came Anna's disembodied voice from the other side of the cardboard box. "It's super light. I'll bet it's full of pillows. Those ones that have all feathers inside."

He admired the bravado, but backed down the moving van's ramp at a careful crawl.

"You know what would make this way easier?" she said.

"A horse," he muttered.

"A horse. You know, before cars that's how they moved stuff. In carts that they pulled."

"I don't think Scott would like it much if you let a horse loose in his new house."

"I'd stop at the door!" she said, her tone suggesting he was a complete idiot. "But we wouldn't have to carry stuff so far."

Anna continued to extoll the virtues of pack animals as they passed through the flagstone entry and into a living room with a north-facing wall made entirely of ballistic glass. Security seemed a little lax in the design, but Coleman joked that his main strategy had been choosing a lot outside of the blast radius around Rapp's house.

Claudia was on a ladder above the fireplace hanging a painting that had been her outrageously expensive housewarming gift to Coleman. As near as Rapp could tell, it was a bison painted by a nine-year-old with access only to primary colors. Everyone else seemed enthusiastic about it, though.

"Where's it say this goes?" Rapp said.

Anna struggled a bit with the word scrawled on the side. "Lan . . . ding."

"That means right here," Rapp lied, and helped her put it on a coffee table. He'd carry it up the stairs when she inevitably fell asleep on the sofa.

Coleman appeared from the kitchen. "You get that truck emptied out?"

Despite his time living in a Latvian cave and some pretty ugly exchanges with the Russians, he didn't have a mark on him. The only thing out of the ordinary was the fact that his blond hair was even more closely cropped than normal. Apparently, he'd gotten a little too close to a missile strike and the flash had singed the right side of his head.

"Almost!" Anna said. "But Mitch isn't working very hard."

"He's not? Then why don't we give him a break. I'll bet you and I can finish up faster without him dragging us down."

She seemed to agree and charged off with the former SEAL right behind.

In the ensuing—and undoubtedly short-lived—calm, Rapp grabbed a beer and fell into a plastic-covered chair. The TV leaned against the wall seemed to be hooked up so he used the remote to turn it on.

It didn't take much searching to find a news channel covering Russia. Krupin's death had been blamed on his cancer and Andrei Sokolov was being set up as the villain. A trusted friend who had taken advantage of Krupin's illness to follow his own traitorous agenda. Yadda, yadda.

Prime Minister Utkin was consolidating his power faster than anyone expected. He had the full support of the Russian military brass, most of whom had opposed Krupin's Baltic adventure from the beginning. And, of course, a little under-the-table assistance from Irene Kennedy hadn't hurt. Another one of her many deals with devils throughout the world. Hard to complain, though. It was Utkin who had called off the dogs at the ammo dump and let Rapp transport Krupin's lab rats across the Finnish border.

He had to hand it to Russia's prime minister. The guy was a complete asshole, but he wasn't the second-rater he'd looked like when he was stuck in Krupin's shadow. Russian troops were already pulling out of Latvia and, despite the devastation left behind, he'd actually managed to make the move seem magnanimous. In fact, he was already calling the sinking of Russian naval vessels an illegal act and demanding restitution.

Rapp took a pull from his beer bottle. Fucking Russians.

He heard familiar footsteps come up behind him and then Claudia dropped into his lap.

"Did you get your painting straight?" he said in French.

"It looks fantastic! We should get something from that artist. We could hang it in your gym."

"I assume you're joking?"

"You'll never know, will you?" She wrapped her arms around him and settled against his chest. "Anna and I are happy to have you home. I wasn't sure this time."

"How's Cara?" he said, intentionally changing the subject. The op was over and he'd survived. No point in revisiting it.

She paused long enough to let him know that she was consciously letting him get away with diverting their conversation. "Good. We're going to use Irene's plane to transport her to Maui. I found them a beautiful house overlooking the ocean. Grisha thought she'd be happier there during her recovery."

Rapp nodded and turned his attention to a video depicting the annihilation of the Riga airport. Coleman's handiwork was even more impressive on TV than it had been in person. Claudia watched silently with him for a few seconds before speaking again.

"Some people are saying that this was a good thing. That NATO is already committing to better financing, better training, and better coordination."

He shook his head. "The politicians will get sidetracked. They'll start complaining about the money and in a few years no one will remember the invasion of Latvia any better than they do the invasion of Georgia," Rapp said. "The Russian situation has never been complicated. They can't be reasoned with or helped or turned into an ally. All you can do is contain them."

He pushed her off his lap and stood, draining the rest of his beer. "History's a broken record, Claudia. The best we can hope for is that next time it'll be someone else's problem."

Pocket Books proudly presents

LETHAL AGENT
Vince Flynn

Coming Soon

Turn the page for a sneak peek at the latest
Mitch Rapp thriller by Kyle Mills, *Lethal Agent* . . .

CHAPTER 1

MITCH Rapp started to move again, weaving through an expansive boulder field before dropping to his stomach at its edge. A quick scan of the terrain through his binoculars provided the same result it had every time before: reddish dirt covering a seemingly endless series of pronounced ridges. No water. No plant life. A clear sky stained yellow by dust and starting to turn orange in the west. If it were ninety-five below zero instead of ninety-five above, he could have been on Mars.

Rapp shifted his gaze to the right, concentrating for a good fifteen seconds before spotting a flash of movement that was either Scott Coleman or one of his men. All were wearing custom camo made from cloth specifically selected and dyed for this op by Charlie Wicker's girlfriend. She was a professional textile designer and a flat-out genius at matching colors and textures. If you gave her a few decent photos of your operating theater, she'd make you disappear.

A couple of contrails appeared above, and he followed them with his eyes—Saudi jets on their way to bomb urban targets to the west. This sparsely populated part of central Yemen had become the exclusive territory of ISIS and al Qaeda, but the Saudis largely ignored it. Viable targets were hard to engage from the air, and the Kingdom didn't have the stomach to get bloody on the ground. That job had once again landed in his lap.

Satisfied they weren't being watched, Rapp started forward in a crouch. Coleman and his team would follow, watching his back at perfect intervals like they had in Iraq. And Afghanistan. And Syria. And just about every other hellhole the planet had to offer.

The Yemeni civil war had broken out in 2015 between Houthi rebels and government forces. Predictably, other regional powers had been drawn in, most notably Iran, backing the rebels, and Saudi Arabia, getting behind the government. The involvement of those countries had intensified the conflict, creating a humanitarian disaster impressive even by Middle Eastern standards.

In many ways, it was a forgotten war. The world's dirty little secret. Even among US government officials and military commanders, it would be hard to find anyone aware that two-thirds of Yemen's population was surviving on foreign aid and another eight million were slowly starving. They also wouldn't be able to tell you that hunger and the loss of basic services were causing disease to run rampant through the country. Cholera, antibiotic-resistant bacteria, and even diphtheria were surging to levels unheard of in the modern era.

And anyplace that could be described using words

like "forgotten," "rampant," and "war" eventually became a magnet for terrorists. They were yet another disease that infected the weakened and wounded.

An unusually high ridge became visible to the northwest, and Rapp dropped to the ground again, studying it through his lenses. He could make out a gap just large enough for a human about three hundred yards away.

"Whatcha got?" Coleman said over his earpiece.

"The cave entrance. Right where they said it would be."

"Are we moving?"

"No, it's backlit. We'll let the sun drop over the horizon."

"Roger that. Everybody copy?"

Bruno McGraw, Joe Maslick, and Charlie Wicker all acknowledged. The four men with him made up about half the people in the world Rapp trusted. Probably a sad situation, but one that had kept him alive for a lot longer than anyone would have predicted.

He fine-tuned the focus on his binoculars, refining his view of the dark hole in the cliff face. It was hard to believe that Sayid Halabi was still alive. If Rapp had been any closer with that grenade, it would have gotten jammed in the ISIS leader's throat. But even if his aim had been way off, it shouldn't have mattered. The blast had brought down a significant portion of the cavern he'd been hiding out in.

The collapse had been extensive enough that Rapp himself had been caught in it. In fact, he'd have died slowly in the darkness if Joe Maslick wasn't a human wrecking ball who had spent much of his youth digging ditches on a landscaping crew. Oxygen had been getting pretty scarce when Mas had finally broken through and dragged him from the grave he'd made for himself.

Despite all that, the intel on Halabi seemed solid. A while back, someone at NSA had decrypted a scrambled Internet video showing the man standing in the background at an al Qaeda meeting. The initial take had been that it was archival footage dredged up to keep the troops motivated. That hope hadn't lasted long. Analysts quickly dated the images to six months *after* the night Rapp thought he'd finally ground his boot into that ISIS cockroach's throat.

The video had led to the capture of one of the people at that meeting, and his interrogation had led Rapp to this burned-out plain. Word was that Halabi had been severely injured by that grenade and had been hiding out here, convalescing. The sixty-four-thousand-dollar question was whether he was *still* there. The Agency knew he was healthy enough to be going to meetings and raiding al Qaeda for its best talent, starting the process of rebuilding ISIS after the beating it had taken in his absence.

The sun finally hit the horizon, causing an immediate drop in temperature and improvement in visibility. Waiting for full darkness was an option, but it seemed unnecessary. He hadn't seen any sign of exterior guards, and night versus day would have little meaning once he went inside.

"We're on," he said into his throat mike.

"Copy that," came Coleman's response.

Rapp angled left, moving silently across the rocky terrain until he reached a stone wall about twenty yards from the cave entrance. Staying low, he crept along the wall's base until he reached its edge. Still no sign of ISIS enforcers. Behind him, the terrain was similarly empty, but that was to be expected. It was impossible to anticipate the environment inside the cave, and he was concerned that it could get tight enough to make a force of more than one man counterproductive. Coleman and his team would remain invisible until they were needed.

When he finally slipped inside the cavern, the only evidence that it was inhabited was the churned dirt beneath his feet. He held his weapon in front of him as he eased along a passage about three feet wide and ten feet high. The familiar weight of his Glock had been replaced with that of an early model Mission crossbow. His weapons tech had modified it for stealth, pushing the decibel level below eighty-five. Even better, the pitch had been lowered to the point that it sounded nothing like a weapon. Even to Rapp's practiced ear, it came off more like a bag of sand dropping onto a sidewalk.

Crossbows weren't the fastest things to reload and there hadn't been much time to train with it, but he still figured it was the best tool for the job. The quietest pistol he owned—a Volquartsen .22 with a Gemtech suppressor—was strapped to his thigh, but it would be held in reserve. While it was an impressively stealthy weapon, the sharp crack it made was too loud and recognizable for this operating environment.

The darkness deepened the farther he penetrated, but he moved slowly enough for his eyes to keep pace. Based on what had happened last time he'd chased Sayid Halabi into a hole, it made sense to prioritize caution over speed. Mas might have forgotten his shovel.

A faint glow became visible at the end of the passage, and Rapp inched toward it, avoiding the rocks beneath his feet and staying to the soft earth. As he got closer, he could see that the corridor came to a T. The branch going right dead-ended after a few feet, but the one to the left continued. A series of tiny bulbs wired to a car battery was the source of the glow.

One of the downsides of LED technology was that it made hiding out in caves a lot easier. A single battery could provide light for days. But it also created a vulnerability. Power supplies tended not to be as widely distributed and redundant as they used to be.

Rapp reached down and flipped the cable off the battery, plunging the cavern into darkness.

Shouts became audible almost immediately, sounding more annoyed than alarmed. Rapp could tell that the voices belonged to two male Arabic speakers, but picking out exactly what they were saying was difficult with the cavern's acoustics. Basically a little name-calling and arguing about whose turn it was to fix the problem. When all your light came from a single improvised source, occasional outages were inevitable.

One of the men appeared a few seconds later, swinging a flashlight in his right hand but never lifting it high enough to give detail to his face. It didn't matter. From his youthful gait and posture, it was clear that it wasn't Halabi. Just one of his stooges.

Rapp aimed around the corner and gently squeezed the trigger. The sound profile of the crossbow and the projectile's impact were both outstanding. Unfortunately, the accuracy at this range was less so. The man was still standing, seemingly perplexed by the fletching protruding beneath his left collarbone.

Rapp let go of his weapon and sprinted forward, getting one arm around the Arab's neck and clamping a hand over his mouth and nose. The man fought as he was dragged back around the corner but the sound of their struggle was attenuated by soft ground. Finally, Rapp dropped and wrapped his legs around the man to limit his movement. There wasn't enough leverage to choke him out, but the hand over his face was doing a pretty good job of suffocating him. The process took longer than he would have liked, and he was gouged a few times by the protruding bolt, but the Arab finally lost consciousness. A knife to the base of the skull finished him.

Rapp slid from beneath the body and was recocking the crossbow when another shout echoed through the cavern.

"Farid! What are you doing, idiot? Turn the lights back on!"

Rapp yelled back that he couldn't get them working, counting on the acoustics to make it difficult to distinguish one Arabic speaking male from another. He ran to the battery and put the flashlight facedown in the dirt before crouching next to it. The illumination was low enough that anyone approaching wouldn't be able to see much more than a vague human outline.

A stream of half-baked electrical advice preceded the sound of footsteps, and then another young man appeared. He didn't seem at all concerned, once again proving the grand truth of all things human: people saw what they wanted and expected to see.

Rapp let the terrorist get to within fifteen feet before snatching up the crossbow. This time he compensated by aiming low and left, managing to put the projectile center of mass. No follow-up was necessary. The man crumpled and landed face-first in the dirt.

Certain that he wasn't getting up again, Rapp started reconnecting the battery. He was likely going to need the light. Things had gone well so far but, in his experience, good luck never came in threes.

Support for that hypothesis emerged when a man who was apparently distrustful of the sound of falling sandbags sprinted around the corner. Rapp's .22 was in an awkward position to draw, so instead he grabbed one of the bolts quivered on the crossbow.

The terrorist had been a little too enthusiastic in his approach and his momentum bounced him off one of the cave's walls. Rapp took advantage of his compromised balance and lunged, driving the bladed head into his throat.

Not pretty, but effective enough to drop the man. As he fell, though, a small pipe sprouting with wires rolled from his hand.

Not again.

Rapp used his boot to shove the IED beneath the man's body and then ran in the opposite direction, making it about twenty feet before diving into a shallow dip in the ground. The explosion sent hot gravel washing over him, and he heard a few disconcertingly loud cracks from above, but that was it. The rock had held. He rolled on his back, pulling his shirt over his mouth and nose to protect him from the dust. The smart money would be to turn tail and call in a few bunker busters, but he couldn't bring himself to do it. If Halabi was there, Rapp was going to see him dead. Even if they entered the afterlife together with their hands around each other's throats.

The sound of automatic fire started up outside but Rapp ignored it, pulling the Volquartsen and using a penlight to continue deeper into the cavern. Coleman and his boys could handle themselves.

The cave system turned out to be relatively simple—a lot of branches, but almost all petered out after a few feet. The first chamber of any size contained a cot and some rudimentary medical equipment—an IV cart, monitors, and a garbage can half full of bloody bandages. All of it had the look of having been there for a while.

The second chamber appeared to have been set up for surgical procedures but wasn't much more advanced than something from the First World War. A gas cylinder that looked like it came from a welder, a tray with a few instruments strewn across it, and a makeshift operating table streaked with dried blood.

And that was the end of the line. The cave system dead-ended just beyond.

"Shit!" Rapp shouted, his voice reverberating down the corridor and bouncing back to him.

The son of a bitch had been there. They'd brought him to treat the injuries he'd suffered in Iraq and to give him time to heal. A month ago, Rapp might have been able to look into his eyes, put a pistol between them, and pull the trigger. But now he was long gone. Sayid Halabi had slipped through his fingers again.

Novels by Vince Flynn

And by Kyle Mills